# CHANGE OF WILL

# CHANGE OF WILL

Where Hollywood, politics
and religion collide

## ALI AZAM

Whittles Publishing

Published by
**Whittles Publishing Ltd.,**
Dunbeath,
Caithness, KW6 6EG,
Scotland, UK

**www.whittlespublishing.com**

© 2012 Ali Azam

ISBN 978-1-84995-061-9

Printed and bound in Great Britain by
4edge ltd, Hockley. www.4edge.co.uk

# ACKNOWLEDGEMENTS

I would like to pay tribute to the late Gary Boulden, who helped me a great deal, and also the late Barrister Lakha who helped me in my research, may their souls rest in peace. The support received from Kausar Kazmi is much appreciated and thanks are due to Reza Kazemi, who has been an inspiration to me. Without Bob Whittington this book would not have been possible and I would also like to thank Keith Whittles, my publisher, for his kindness and having confidence in me and Kerrie Moncur at Whittles for having done such a wonderful job in cover design and layout. The support of Diana Soltmann at Flagship Consulting and the wise suggestions of her colleague Adrian King are very much appreciated. I would like to thank my father who had been so keen and anxious to see this book published. And most of all to my children and my wife for putting up with me - thank you so much.

# CHAPTER ONE

If he had not been reading his papers he might have noticed.

His son noticed but boys like fast motorbikes. It was a Kawasaki, probably a 110. Not a big bike and very old but this was Karachi not Hollywood. At least it was red – the best colour. The traffic had stopped. It always did at this roundabout in rush hour. However it allowed a closer inspection.

The engine was smoking a bit but it was the noise the boy liked. The revving engine. The men wore short tunics and billowing trousers but he would be in leathers. Never mind the blistering heat, he would be looking cool. He had seen the magazines and you had to wear leathers to look good on a bike. He would get his own when he was older, when his father couldn't object. It would definitely be red.

The 11 year old was over-excited. He was being allowed to go and watch his school's under 15s cricket team play their arch rivals at the opposite end of the city later that day. He longed to be selected to play himself but he knew he was a good few years away from such an honour. There was also his family's strict religious background. He often wondered if his father – son of an Imam – would approve of his passion. He began dreaming his recurring dream, picturing himself at the crease. Victory was in sight but the team needed just six more runs in the final over. It was up to him. He had batted all day while others had lost their wickets. Light was fading and the spinners were hard to play. Finally with one ball of the match left, now just three runs needed for a draw and four for a win, he stared down the pitch as the bowler approached. He'd been serving up leg breaks with his last five balls so this one was bound to be an off break, slightly wide of the stumps and looking for the nick and a catch in the slips.

Stepping away from his crease, there was nothing to lose; with every last ounce of energy he swept the ball away to the boundary. The innings and the match were saved for Pakistan. He would be a national hero. There could be nothing like it. A professional cricketer – idolised by the nation.

But sport was not what a true Muslim should be thinking about. It would take some persuading and he would need his mother's help. His father would come round to the idea in the end, just as his grandfather had accepted that his own son wanted to be an industrialist and not a cleric.

A smile lit up the boy's face as he remembered the extra spending money his mother had given him to take to the match. Maybe he would be able to save enough to buy a bike one day. He wanted to do it himself rather than take it as a gift. He would surprise his father by riding through the gates of their town house. His mother had winked at him as they drove away, still waving as they left for school. It was their little secret, which of course his father knew all about. He was growing up now. He would soon be 12 and he would have to have the conversation with his father before long. Grown man to grown man. His future was certain.

His younger brother in the back was not so happy. He had been told he was too young to go the match – and anyhow he thought it was his turn to sit in the front today.

'Father, those two men on the bike keep looking at us,' he said.

'They are probably wondering why you look so grumpy,' replied his father with a smile, barely glancing up from his work.

The car – a Mercedes C200 – inched forward and stopped again. The Clifton area of Karachi – home to the rich and famous since Independence – was not immune to snarl-ups. Too many cars mean traffic jams, regardless of status of the passenger or make and model of the car. The shoppers who flocked to the malls had not ventured out yet but it seemed the rest of the city was there in force and all driving. The car had inched its way down from the bridge and had almost reached the Tin Talwar Chowrangi roundabout, the three sword-like monuments towering over the chaos around them; symbols of discipline, faith and unity. The driver joined the chorus of blaring horns – discipline at least was forgotten at rush hour.

Nothing was moving today, which was perfect.

The boy in the front shifted in his seat to get a better look at the bike. The passenger had got off, no doubt to see what had caused the hold up and was blocking the boy's view. He sat forward to see if he could guess the model of the bike. This meant the first burst of bullets missed him as they smashed through the side window – but not the second. His body jerked back and he lay dead sprawled across the driver's lap.

The stripped-down Kalashnikov snarled again. Two more bursts finished off the driver. The gunman calmly walked round to the other side of the car, raised his weapon, aimed carefully and fired again at point blank range. The man in the back seat lay motionless in a pool of his own dark red blood. The files lay scattered on the floor. His son next to him seemed pinned to his seat with his face obliterated by the final burst of bullets.

'Be sure you fire enough rounds,' he had been urged. Nothing must be left to chance. They cannot survive. Not one of them.

The gunman paused to check his work. There could be no doubt; they had all been eliminated. Satisfied, he climbed onto the back of the red Kawasaki 110, registered in 1984, and they were gone.

Another Monday. Another traffic jam in Karachi. Another murder seen by dozens, witnessed by no one. Those nearby stared into the car, strangely silent, almost matter-of-fact as though they were assessing the quality of the shooting. They had plenty to compare it with over the years, although this type of random killing of prominent officials was increasingly rare. Perhaps they were getting to the end of the list. Everyone knew there was such a list: a collection of names of people who had been selected by some unseen mullah, picked just for believing what they did.

One thing was certain though – the work on the power station would now stop. The Chief Executive, Ali Haider, was dead.

Jabbar's arms clung tightly round Sharif's waist; his heart pounding, bursting with adrenalin and pride. The gun was now hidden beneath his billowing shirt. This was his first mission. A smile − almost a sneer − curled across his face. By tomorrow he would have travelled to the north; his own territory, out of reach of any police investigations. Besides, he knew his network was protected by high-ranking officials. They shared the same ideology and also used the same web of clandestine services that spirited people through the mountain passes of the Kashmir Pakistan border region. The thought that almost 15,000 trained men had been on similar missions was enough comfort.

'How many of those were all around him here in Karachi, watching and admiring his work,' he wondered?

Jabbar didn't know Ali Haider. He didn't really know what his job had been or why it mattered so much to someone that he should die. All that was relevant was he, Jabbar, had done his duty. Jabbar didn't even know about the list of names that someone had deemed to be legitimate targets. Teachers, clerics, businessmen, officials in mosques. All Jabbar knew was they were the enemy. Pakistani they may be, but they were also Shia. That was it. He had not been trained to question, just to act − and at that moment he reckoned he would be one of the best. He would never be caught and even if he were, what would he do? Beg for his life? Never. All he would ask is the chance to be allowed back on the streets and to do it all over again. Behind the helmet visor, his eyes were blazing with passion. It had been just as he was told. He was fulfilling his calling.

As Sharif gunned the throttle speeding through the congested streets to escape the scene, he was fighting hard to hold back tears.

It was not so long ago that he was the same age as the boys they had just killed. But why was he so shocked? This is what all the training had been all about. He knew that if Jabbar hadn't been called to deal with these targets it would have been him on the back seat taking the war to the Shia infidels, firing the shots. Would he have been as brave? If something had happened to Jabbar he would have had to complete the mission. He too carried a gun hidden beneath his *koti* waistcoat and shirt, the cold metal pressing against his skin as a reminder of his duty. How would he have reacted when faced with the innocent questioning eyes of the boys staring out of the car? Would he have been as calm and professional as Jabbar? He tried to blot out the faces as he pushed the bike harder.

'Slow down, Sharif. We are out of danger,' Jabbar yelled in his ear. Jabbar always knew what to do.

Despite the heat, Sharif started shivering uncontrollably.

'Was his faith weakening?' he asked himself yet again. 'Why these doubts?' Even though he knew he was fighting on the side of God, the recollection of the young boys' faces suddenly turning to panic as they realised what was happening was all that consumed his mind, all that he could focus on.

These were weak thoughts, shameful feelings. What would his compatriots think? They would never understand his motives, his doubts. There was only one morality. The true faith. There was no room for hesitation or questioning in their minds. They would consider him weak and unfit for the duties he was destined to perform. He would keep quiet just as he had done for the past seven years.

If he had been able to analyse his young life, Sharif would have wondered about the dumb acceptance with which his father handed him over to the visiting teachers from the madrassa school. They had appeared one morning in the village just as Sharif and his brother were returning from the fields. Tall and imposing with beards and turbans, Sharif instinctively realised they were talking about him. His life was about to change forever. They had promised to take care of him, feed him, teach him the faith and make his father proud of him.

As a poor shepherd struggling to put food in front of his family, it would have seemed a good offer. Sharif's father already had an older son who looked after the sheep and – God willing – his daughter would soon be married. He could not afford to have another mouth to feed. Other boys had gone from the village and their parents were proud – or said they were. What choice did he have? Prolonged hardship for the family or the promises of education and possible prosperity for his son? If he was worried, it didn't show but he did not see much joy in the other parents' eyes. Their children must have done well because they never returned to the village. No one asked: 'How is your son doing? Is he a teacher now or a doctor?'

The teachers had made good on their promises. They had fed Sharif and they had taught him the faith: he should always remember that he was following Sunnah, the only true path of Islam. The Shias were no better than Hindus, Jews or Christians. So many lessons, so much praying. And they had taught him other things and today they had put those lessons into practice. Would his father's heart be leaping for joy this day if he had known? His father who was so tender with animals – would he have raised a gun, pulled the trigger and been proud of his morning's work?

So that was it. That was how to take another life. They had been planning the mission for weeks. They had practised over and over again, following the same route from the target's house less than a mile away as he dropped his children off at school before work, even making passing manoeuvres, approaching close to the car at the precise spot where the shooting would take place.

They had followed the car from the moment it swept through the gates of the house. They had watched from the shadows of the trees as the mother waved her family off. She would never see them alive again. They could not wait to see the sheer horror in the eyes of the many who would witness the murder of two young kids at their father's side. This would create such a fear in the hearts of these bloody Shias.

They faced certain risks – even death – but resolute with conviction, they had little doubt in their ability and were totally focussed. The only difference today was they had carried loaded guns – even Sharif, but only as a backup. This was Jabbar's mission. The instructions had been hammered into them: 'You must get clean shots; get up close'.

'You have to be certain of the kill. There can be no chance of survival.' They called it precise killing at their training camps in the mountains near the border between Pakistan and Afghanistan. So far the method had been successful. Shoot then escape before anyone has a chance to react, taking any one of the roads leading away from the scene. No one will stop you, as they will be too shocked and scared. And even if you do get caught, you have done God's work so what is there to fear?

But they had done it. They were away. It all seemed so easy. Jabbar slapped Sharif on his back and shouted 'Allahu Akbar,' above the din of the engine as they sped out of the city. 'God is indeed great,' thought Sharif. They had succeeded but what was the price? There is always a price to pay.

The red carpet cut like a vivid scar through the crowds of photographers, TV crews and journalists shouting for the attention of the celebrities scurrying from their limousines to the shelter of the foyer. The rain lashed down from the Hollywood skies. The beautiful and the handsome paused and posed for the shots, their umbrellas tilted back momentarily. Some of the outfits would be ruined, but just think of the publicity. Hollywood in the film premiere season: it was a must, to be seen and photographed looking a million dollars regardless of the weather.

Only Jackson Clarke seemed to be in no hurry. The rain never bothered him – it reminded him of home in Scotland. How he longed to be back there away from all this nonsense. But duty called and he was one of the stars of this new blockbuster. All guns and explosions. He'd almost forgotten its name. Another thriller which required younger, fitter heroes like Paul Everitt who was milking the limelight for all it was worth on the other side of the carpet. A young vision of beauty was on his arm, hoping for some reflected glory and – who knows? – a chance to be in the next box-office winner that Paul no doubt had lined up. In reality she would probably be ditched for a newer, younger, prettier model in the coming months or weeks, even days.

'Jackson, this way!'
'What's your next movie?'

'Great outfit, Jackson!'

Jackson smiled his slow quizzical smile, which he had perfected over the years – on and off the screen. He looked more grizzled now with a smoky grey beard adding to the mysterious look. He paused and smoothed down the front of his high-buttoned, jet-black jacket – part tuxedo as they insisted on calling dinner jackets in America, part Asian formal wear. No tight dress-shirt required, no impossible bowtie to keep straight all evening.

'It was all I could hire,' teased Jackson, 'You guys had already taken the best suits.' Why it was necessary for the photographers to dress up in evening clothes just to stand in the rain, he would never understand. All part of the pizzazz that made up film premieres, he supposed.

'Don't knock it,' Jackson thought – it had kept him in fine food and fine homes on three different continents. He wondered for how much longer? They barely needed actors anymore. Computer graphics and other gizmos could generate images of actors from the past and make them perform. No hissy-fits from over-paid stars with egos bigger than their talent. Just put a techie in front of a computer for a few days and you could create anything. Good luck to them. Jackson had enjoyed the best times that the profession could to offer. It was all run by accountants now, like everything else. Balance the books, bugger the art. Nevertheless he still felt he had one more big role in him. Perhaps that was the mistake every fading actor made; there is just one more star turn in me, one more Oscar, a chance to become a legend and preferably in my own lifetime. Jackson scoffed at the very thought; he needed none of it. You are either content with your work, content with yourself or you are condemned to a lifetime of chasing impossible dreams. Balance was all that you should strive for, and on balance he had had enough of the weather and the flash photography for one evening.

'Can I get in out of the rain now?' he growled in mock irritation. 'You should go home yourselves.' He was popular with the media. He knew they had a job to do and what they did helped him so there was no point in being difficult. He never had trouble with the paparazzi as a result. Give them the shots they wanted and they would leave you in peace.

What would his next project be? There was really only one script that looked remotely interesting, but it was risky. Not because of the subject matter, but because of the location. Whatever his reservations he knew that this was the one he had to do. And it had nothing to do with winning an Oscar – there was no more room on the bathroom shelf for a start. No, they would not be giving Oscars for this one. It would be too provocative and Hollywood didn't like trouble.

The first trouble might be the director. He could turn a remake of *The Sound of Music* into a scandal. He had worked with Andy Lucas before – in fact Lucas had sent him the script. They had had words on-set in the past; they had had blazing rows but somehow it had always worked out. However, Jackson had a feeling that there would be little room for tantrums on this picture. They would be watched, and not just by the producer trying to keep costs down. They had worked together in Russia before the collapse of Communism, and that had had its interesting moments and no shortage of interpreters watching them rather than helping them. The Mafia had been overly helpful on a movie about drugs and gun running in Sicily, which Jackson said could (and probably should) have been shot in any location other than Palermo. He was convinced Lucas had insisted on the place as a bet. Somehow they had got away with it. Not even the Mafia it seemed was prepared to take on Lucas.

'Jacko! Man, have you read the script? Brilliant. It's made for you.' Andy Lucas heaved into sight across the foyer, scattering everyone in his path. Lucas didn't do courtesy. He didn't do low key. He was a big man in girth as well as volume. But there were no secrets in Hollywood, least of all where one of America's top directors was concerned. Everyone knew Andy Lucas was trying to put together a controversial movie and was hiring talent. After tonight, everyone knew he had Jackson Clarke in his sights as one of the stars.

'Hell, what did it matter'? Jackson thought. He was past caring about the film industry's tittle-tattle. He would either do the movie or he wouldn't. As usual it would be on his terms and no one else's. Lucas would not be able to apply pressure, just by bellowing across some cinema foyer – premiere or no premiere.

'Good evening, Andy. I was just thinking of you' said Jackson, attempting to introduce a little decorum into the proceedings. 'It's good to see you too.'

'The script, Jacko? What about the script? Have you read it, Goddamn you?'

'I've glanced through it,' lied Jackson, 'and I shall study it more closely on the flight home tomorrow. I promise to let you know by the end of the week.'

'Yeah sure. You've read it. You love it and you're going to do it. Fair enough: play the cool, calm Limey.'

'Actually I'm Scottish, but I am happy to be considered cool at my great age. Now what do you think of this new film of mine?'

'Yeah, yeah not bad, but ours will be in a different league. I'll be waiting for your call.' And with that Andy Lucas barged through the crowd once more making straight for another quarry. Jackson laughed as he sent canapés flying – most of them down his jacket – but Lucas didn't do tuxedos either.

# CHAPTER TWO

'*This is the Gatwick Victoria Express. Welcome aboard. I am pleased to say we have a buffet trolley serving hot and cold drinks. Please keep the aisles clear of luggage....*'

The interminable tannoy announcement droned on. Danyal didn't want a thing. He was still at 36,000 feet and his body-clock hours out of synch. His flight from Washington had been delayed. He was jet-lagged but at least he was nearly in London.

He tried to read a freesheet newspaper someone had discarded but even that was too much effort. Just gossip about footballers, film stars and B-list celebrities, and photo opportunities with near-naked models. Not the sort of material a good Muslim boy should be reading. He gave a little smirk at the thought, but he didn't have the energy even to admire them. He had been travelling – including sitting in an airport departure lounge – for the best part of day and all he wanted now was bed, if only he could stop his brain cells pounding for just a moment.

The train pulled out of the station and Danyal tried to get comfortable enough to catch up on his sleep. Insomnia and excitement battled incessantly. How would he follow up a year-long internship in the heart of the US government? His stint with the Foundation had culminated in the plum appointment in Washington. He would have to find another job, but it had to provide some real stimulation. It would probably be something in politics but he was hardly likely to be offered an easy constituency seat by any of the parties. Danyal Sarwar MP – that was a joke. Still, he had a decent 2:1 degree in sociology majoring in political science, which must count for something – and now he had the experience of Washington to add to his CV.

The trouble, Danyal had to admit, was that he was a bit of a mixed bag. Having spent most of his later childhood and adulthood in England, he was a Brit by experience but of course he was a Pakistani by birth.

'Join the club', he thought. 'There's plenty more like you struggling to find some firm foothold'. Twenty-eight next birthday – God, he was practically middle aged.

As he closed his eyes, his mind was still in America. He put working with the senator down to pure luck. With his background, he had always doubted that he would have been able to find a home in the heart of the British Government, let alone America. The interview might have gone so differently: 'Great qualifications, good degree, British parents – oh dear you're a Muslim and you're, well, not white; in fact your family is originally from Pakistan. Very sorry you're in the wrong queue, buddy, get into that one marked "potential terrorist".'

And yet somehow he had made it. Senator Vance Friedland said he valued Danyal's 'international perspective' – whatever that meant. The Foundation – Foundation for Global and Economic Understanding to give it its full title – had been equally surprised. When Danyal had first put his name forward to be considered for the secondment, the director had raised an eyebrow – actually she had raised both eyebrows: 'It's a bit of a long shot, Danyal, in the current climate,' she said. 'But you're as qualified as anyone. In fact I will only nominate you this year. As you know, we normally give them a short list of three, but you deserve it and you could bring a breath of fresh air.'

When the approval came through, to celebrate the director had even taken Danyal out for a meal at her club which had only recently got used to allowing women members, such was her astonishment and delight. She also wanted to give him a briefing.

'You're going to find this pretty tough, Danyal. America is jittery to say the least. Getting through immigration will be interesting enough, but you do have a work permit and all the necessary paperwork from the senator.' The director paused as though she was thinking hard about her next piece of information. It also allowed the waiter time to clear their plates, although Danyal was certain all the staff at the director's exclusive club had been pre-screened for their integrity. You could never be too sure though – everyone had their price.

'The senator has been in the spotlight recently, Danyal, as you know. He has made some strong speeches about the direction Pakistan is taking – not least its increasingly close ties with China. Be careful what you say and what you put in writing.'

Danyal looked across the table at his boss. She had taken him under her wing and perhaps given him a break he might not have expected. She was staring straight at him from behind her no-nonsense frameless glasses, probing for signs of hesitation or doubt. She had never married, but regarded all those who passed through her hands at the Foundation as her children.

'You are not trying to make me pull out now, are you?' Danyal asked.

'Certainly not. I think you're the right person for the job. The point is there are others in the Administration over there and even more outside the Administration who would rather he kept his mouth shut. You do know that he has a background in the CIA?'

'I've read his file,' said Danyal. 'He might have a point about Pakistan but I hope he also sees me as a Brit, albeit with an international point of view.'

'I've no doubt he does. Still: watch your back. There are those who would rather the senator was not making quite so many headlines. Washington isn't Westminster, Danyal; everything is megaphone diplomacy, playing to the crowds and the evening news.'

'It's not so different here now,' said Danyal.

'You're right. But one thing I guarantee, Danyal, you will go back a changed man.'

The secondment seemed to go by in a flash. There had been a few choice and decidedly un-diplomatic comments by the senator while he had been there, but by-and-large Danyal had emerged unscathed from his experience. Exhilarating. Yes, that's what it had been and the senator had seemed to listen to Danyal when he had asked for his advice.

There was another issue though on Danyal's mind: the West. His time in America had been high-octane. Thoroughly modern. Anything but the careful and controlled existence of his family life. It had been more North-west Frontier than North-west London. He would have to move back into his parents' house again until he could find another flat to rent. Maybe this restlessness was what the director had been talking about when she had warned about changes. Had she really meant he would start questioning everything about the way he had been conducting his life? He couldn't deny it, it was exciting but also worrying – everything was up for grabs in his mind, everything was debatable. What were once rock-solid certainties were now simply one side of the coin.

To put it bluntly, he had the bug. The glamour of the secular, free market; this capitalist society that he had been enjoying to the full over the past year: now that was something else. What else gives you that kind of buzz? Climbing the ladder of success, driving around in limos with politicians – real movers and shakers, not country cousins from the American backwoods, not local councillors or community leaders from North London. Everyone likes being invited to beautiful houses, receiving acknowledgement from others of your worth because of the company you keep and the feeling of power all around. It's only one life; surely it's got to be worth it? And he was worth it.

There's no end to mankind's desires and Danyal had to admit, it was no different in his case. Artificial or short term it may be; so what? He had been there and tasted the pleasurable fruit. He had shown he could mix it with the best. It had done wonders for his ego. Now he wanted more. But from where would that new cup of success come? All he could see ahead was drudgery where once, briefly, there had been glamour. It was making him depressed. Was he changing?

All his life he had read his faith book every day and said his prayers, although he had to admit that there were times in America when other pressures meant he missed the appointed hour. Then he was consumed with guilt and frustration. Was he any less of a man because he had broken what was increasingly becoming a habit just once or twice? He was simply weak, which didn't make him unique. Surely it was far better to study the book out of a love for it rather than out of custom, or worse – a fear of retribution.

Danyal shifted in his seat, trying and failing to get comfortable. What is this? Why was he beating himself up because he felt tied down by chains of beliefs and habit when what he instinctively felt was the thrill of ... well, a less restricted existence? And yet when he was given that freedom to act, he had felt somehow naked and lonely.

The senator had spotted this tendency towards self-analysis early on.

'Danyal, you need to lighten up a bit. This is America. That's not to say we don't think – although I grant you some would disagree – but once you have had time to think, act.'

What Danyal had learned from America and his time with the senator was the 'can do' approach to life that his friends who had been to the States had told him about. It hadn't completely won him over from thinking about more serious matters, but he thought it had broadened his horizons. The senator had certainly lived a full life. He had even won a purple heart for bravery and probably seen some interesting action during his time at the Agency. Danyal accepted that he was not one of life's heroes, but he was more open to challenges than the day he had his briefing with the Director of the Foundation. Her prediction had certainly proved right.

Gradually the combination of a sleepless transatlantic flight and the steady rumble of the train began to have their effect, and Danyal started to drift off. The battle of conscience would be fought another day.

He shifted in his seat and tried to stretch out his long legs, accidentally bumping into a fellow passenger.

'Oh, I'm sorry,' said Danyal half opening his eyes and immediately tucking his legs under him.

'Don't apologise,' said the passenger in a soft Scottish burr.

'Thank you,' said Danyal looking briefly at the man who had spoken, before shutting his eyes again and twisting in his seat.

'You come a long way?' the passenger persisted. The last thing Danyal wanted to do was strike up a conversation. He sat up and rubbed his eyes.

'Yes. From Washington,' said Danyal glancing towards the stranger who was clearly determined to wreck his sleep. Suddenly he was wide awake: 'My goodness, aren't you?' Danyal looked around for the freesheet he had discarded earlier in the journey. 'I think I saw you in the paper!'

'I'm surprised they managed to get any decent shots at all – it was pouring.'

Danyal could scarcely believe it. Was he dreaming? Why on earth would Jackson Clarke be slumming it on a suburban train to London? He was a star; surely he would have a chauffeur-driven car waiting.

'But ... why are you ... surely,' Danyal stammered as he tried to gather some coherent thoughts. He looked around. There were no other passengers sitting near them and no one else seemed to have noticed.

'I like trains and these days we must all do our bit for the environment. Jackson Clarke.' He held out his hand for Danyal to shake.

'Yes, yes, of course. Danyal Sarwar. What a pleasure to meet you. I'm a big fan, but I suppose everyone says that.' Danyal shook his hand and wondered if he should ask for his autograph. No one will believe him. Jackson Clarke chatting to him on a train.

'I wear this disguise now,' said Jackson stroking his beard. 'Most of the time I pass by unnoticed.'

'Oh, I'm sorry. Would you prefer to...'

'Not at all and you're apologising again. I can't sleep either. I've just arrived back from Washington. We were probably on the same flight.'

'Maybe – although I was at the back of the bus!'

'That is one of the few perks I allow myself. I fly First Class and I can stretch out but I rarely sleep. The way you were tossing and turning there you looked as though you didn't sleep much either. Mind you, the terrible frown on your face suggested you were having a bad dream as well.'

Jackson's deep dark eyes seemed to peer right into Danyal's soul. There was great warmth and understanding, inviting a response. He actually seemed interested which was scarcely believable.

'I was there for a year on secondment,' said Danyal as though this explained his unrest.

'Well was it that bad?'

Danyal laughed: 'No, not at all. It was brilliant. I was just thinking about other things. You know ... what am I going to do now? Not-so-young Pakistani trying to find a job in a world where everyone's first thought is that you are either a terrorist or your first cousin must be graduating from a terrorist training camp instead of a university.'

He didn't think Jackson would be interested in his crisis-of-faith/meaning-of-life kind of thoughts. In fact he didn't really think he would be interested in him at all. Typical of the man though – charming and making polite conversation. After all he had just given one of the greatest film stars a kick, why wouldn't he want to talk to him? Danyal gave a soft laugh.

'What's so funny?' asked Jackson.

'Oh nothing. Just thinking about telling my family when I get home about how I kicked Jackson Clarke – superhero of the movies – on the shins.'

'I'll survive. Are you parents in London? What made you decide to go to Washington?'

Jackson Clarke's interest seemed genuine and flattering, and before long Danyal had given him his life story such as it was. His family had travelled to England, he had completed his secondary schooling and got a decent degree in London. In fact he had hardly been outside London. His had been a typical – even fairly strict – Pakistani upbringing. His parents were both professionals and they expected their only son to do even better. The regime was work, eat and pray with little time for self-indulgence.

The big break was being taken on by the Foundation, who had also helped him through university. It had a fairly broad agenda – part political, part philanthropic – always with an eye on promoting diversity in every field. Fortunately for him, Pakistan was beginning to dominate the news stories about the same time he applied. They didn't pay much but no researcher expected to get rich. Nevertheless it was a job, in fact quite a prestigious job and even his parents were impressed – although he suspected in their hearts-of-hearts they would have preferred him to be a doctor or a lawyer.

Jackson listened intently, occasionally prompting with a question here and there, but apparently happy for Danyal to ramble through what he thought to be a fairly uninteresting story. Jackson's real interest seemed to be in Danyal's family background. He wanted to hear all about Pakistan or what little Danyal could remember from his boyhood. He seemed fascinated by the minutiae of Danyal's everyday life. The food they ate, whether they went out in the evenings, the parties they held, the fasting around Ramadan and the discipline of praying five times a day.

Then in a sudden change of tack he could not hear enough about America and his role as Senator Vance Friedland's resident 'Pakistani Guru' as Jackson called him. Always listening, listening. Talking very little.

'This was how he "got into character" in his roles', thought Danyal. 'He was an observer'.

It was clear Jackson didn't care for politicians whatever their persuasion. In his view they always had some agenda, and the good Senator Friedland would be no exception.

'I can't say I was aware of any ulterior motive in my dealings with him,' Danyal offered in a rather lame defence.

'I am quite certain he treated you very well and why shouldn't he? What I would be interested to know was his unspoken agenda. You may think me a cynic, Danyal – I hope you don't mind my calling you Danyal?'

'Of course not.'

'And you must call me Jackson. I feel we have got to know each other very well in just a short time.'

Danyal thought: 'Well you know all about me. All I know about you is that you are a famous film star who likes trains.'

Jackson continued: 'I was saying: you may think me a bit of an old cynic – which I probably am – but I have been around long enough to realise that every politician has something up their sleeve and we should all be very careful not to miss the trick. Mark my words, your good senator will be no exception.'

The conversation then drifted away into a typical British discussion about the weather, the awfulness of travelling and before long Danyal assumed Jackson had finally lost interest in him. He had picked up the papers he had been reading – it looked like a film script but Danyal couldn't be sure – after all he had had never seen one. Occasionally he underlined a word or heavily scored a passage in the margin.

Just as Danyal was beginning to slip back to sleep, Jackson said: 'If you've got no other special plans would you like to come round to my flat tomorrow? I've invited a few friends over for a drink just to celebrate being back. I'm sure they would be interested to hear about your travels.'

'Goodness. Are you sure? I mean I would be thrilled.'

'Of course I'm sure. Very casual mind you. There will only be a few of us, I've had enough of big parties for a while. That's one of the curses of making movies – keeping the PR people happy. One of the chores.'

'Well, that would be a great honour. Can't start job-hunting until next week anyhow and the fast life of North London can await my return a little longer.'

'Excellent. That's settled then. Here's my card. Why don't you come round about midday? We can all have lunch and chill out as our American friends would say.'

Danyal took the card and read it carefully, remembering to show the proper courtesy of admiring business cards. Unbelievable. Here he was just back from a fantastic if unsettling year with some of the most influential people on the US political circuit and now he had a personal invitation to the private home of one of the movie industry's most famous stars. Just moments ago in his weakness, he had been feeling sorry for himself, wondering what on earth he was going to do next, and now an opportunity beyond his wildest imaginings was before him. He quickly dismissed the fickle mood swings and concentrated on the bright future before him.

His father would be saying: 'Keep your feet on the ground. He hasn't offered you a job and you can't pay the bills hanging around with celebrities'. Well that was all before America. Danyal was now 'going with the flow' and seeing where life leads him.

He looked out of the window and watched the countryside flashing by; the lush green fields of early spring. Yes, his father would be right. He had not made his fortune, he was not running a lucrative business like his cousins and he was even still searching for some sort of personal contentment. America had set new challenges for him: challenged his attitude to life and – Danyal had to admit – even aspects of his faith, but something was happening and for once in his life he was going to allow it to happen.

Yes, there was a chance he may never make it, never hit the big time, but even that recurring thought he was now prepared to ignore for a while. No one knows how, or even if, they will ever realise their dreams. Maybe he was weak; maybe he was a slave to his desires but who needs reminding? He could push these thoughts aside now. Somehow he felt he had a chance to prove to himself that he could deliver.

He felt the card in his hand and closed his eyes. He knew it could only be his imagination but was a heat coming from the card? What more could he say to Jackson and his friends when they met? They were the ones leading the fast life. He would run out of conversation before they even sat down to eat.

'There you go again,' thought Danyal. 'Worrying too much. Remember the senator's advice: "Act, don't think".'

# CHAPTER THREE

After nearly an hour of weaving and dodging – doubling back on their tracks, stopping, panting and waiting in side streets – Jabbar and Sharif finally turned into an alley. There was no one in sight. A dog scratching about in overturned bins looking for scraps was the only witness. The elaborate precautions to avoid being followed had worked – if indeed there had been anyone who wanted to follow. They were just two young men speeding through the traffic on a motorbike – that's what everyone did in Karachi. Once they had reached the city outskirts where the roads had long-since given up the struggle against nature, no one cared much either way. This was not a priority district for any politician. These rutted tracks would never see an official car. No one ever campaigned for votes in these forgotten corners. It was a struggle just to survive, so why would a neighbour turn another one in even if they managed to find a policeman?

Two short beeps on the horn and a rusty corrugated iron gateway opened just wide enough to allow a quick inspection before letting the two inside and then closing quickly behind them. A wooden plank was dropped across the doors and a padlock snapped into place just for good measure. They weren't expecting visitors.

Nothing was said, just a nod of acknowledgement.

This was what the espionage fraternity would call a safe house. There are hundreds more like them in all the major towns and cities of Pakistan – many of them closer to the Afghan border. There was a courtyard, another motorbike and the shell of a car, which looked as though it had been cannibalised for spare parts. The buildings were run down like most others in that quarter. Two old men sat talking in the shade of an old papal tree. They looked up but otherwise did not react. If they suspected what the two boys had been doing, they made no comment. Somehow it was not their business, not their life. The country they had known had changed beyond recognition. It was not the Pakistan they had hoped for after Partition and they didn't want to try and understand the modern ways. It was impossible to follow the goings-on in government. One moment they had a democratic government, and then it was suspended, restored, suspended, amended and restored again. Sometimes the military were in charge, sometimes the politicians. For ordinary people life continued.

Slightly apart from the men was another group – little more than teenagers, who seemed ill at ease. They stared intently at the new arrivals and began talking quietly among themselves.

A door opened and a man in his mid-thirties with an air of confidence emerged from one of the buildings and came over to greet Jabbar and Sharif. There was an embrace and a half smile. They spoke briefly, occasionally glancing across to the teenagers before going inside.

'You have done well today. You have dealt a great blow against the infidel. You must be tired. Here, eat.'

Sharif and Jabbar sat down on the floor where a few dishes had been laid out on a threadbare mat. The room was sparsely furnished, apart from three make-shift wooden cots, an inscription from the Qur'an on the wall and a single light bulb hanging from the ceiling. The green paint on the doors and windows was old and peeling. There were no personal items, no photos; nothing to say that any of the three men in the room belonged here or regarded this as their home. This was just accommodation. The adrenalin that had driven them had long worn off. They were hungry and the plate of daal, plain naan bread and tea were welcome. They ate and listened.

'Tonight you will leave for the north. Everything is arranged. Until then, you can rest. Stay inside and say nothing to the newcomers. They should leave you alone.'

'Brother Khalid, what have you heard?' asked Jabbar anxious that his work that day had not gone unnoticed, seeking recognition somehow to justify the deed.

'The news is already making headlines around the world. The reporter, Awad Fouda, was there within minutes of your attack. The TV is showing pictures all the time. Everyone is talking about it. This time they will pay attention. Of course no one will be able to recognise you.'

'So what if they do,' said Jabbar. 'It is God's work and we are proud of what we have done in his name today.' Jabbar looked across at Sharif and then at the man called Khalid, as though demanding support, even challenging them to think otherwise.

'Allahu Akbar,' they cried in unison.

The meagre meal was finished in silence. Khalid had seen it all before when young men returned from their missions – if they returned. There was bravado, a feeling of invincibility, but also fatigue even sometimes a sense of anti-climax. There would be time enough to explain the escape plan to take them out of the city to the safety of the north. For now they must rest.

'Do the newcomers know what we have done?' asked Sharif.

'No. They only arrived from London yesterday. Most of the time they speak English among themselves – even their Urdu is bad. They have much to learn.' Khalid was leaning against the wall looking out of the window across the small courtyard in the direction of newcomers.

'The reality', he thought to himself, 'was that they would never really learn'.

Khalid Jalil himself was probably a one-off. He had been to London and studied there, earning a reasonable degree in engineering. He saw British society as a collection of disparate groups. There was a lot of talk of integration, but in reality communities lived separate lives. It didn't matter which country you lived in, people from different cultures might work together but they went home to their own communities. While being a good, if not particularly devout, Muslim and a Pakistani, Khalid saw this as an opportunity.

Watching the young men, he wondered what would become of them and if they had any real understanding of the path they had elected to follow. As a man comfortable with Western ways,

Khalid had been chosen to act as chaperone and shepherd to these young idealists. They arrived in Pakistan pumped with passion in their hearts, instilled by long hours in their local mosque but with little else. Sometimes they came alone, sometimes in twos or threes. Occasionally he would travel to England himself to assess whether they were suitable material, visiting certain mosques and talking to the mullahs and teachers in the madrassa schools.

When they reached Pakistan, he would gather them together in a safe house such as this on the outskirts of the city, until the time was right to accompany them to the north where their training could begin. For many it was their first time in Pakistan – a land they called home. For many it was their first time out of England. They had all the passion, but lacked real knowledge. They were sure they knew what they were doing and why they were doing it. They were committed.

As far as Khalid was concerned, this was as a job – not a calling. He knew some of the elders were disapproving of his past and his easiness with the *kuffars'* ways and customs, but they needed him. As far as they were concerned, he was living in a state of *darura*: a necessity – he had to mix with the *kuffars* and at times, even live like them for the greater good. Either way, it suited Khalid. The thoughts of ending his days in a desolate building such as this safe house, far from the delights that in his heart he preferred, were too terrible to imagine. As for the killings and bombings which these young recruits took part in, he was sanguine. Instinctively, he believed the corrupt western culture and capitalism were wrong, but he enjoyed their comforts. He had a small apartment in Karachi away from this house and discretely made the most of the attractions of a modern city. Whenever he travelled to London, the place was so big it was easy to lose himself in its corrupt delights for a few hours. He would discard the traditional Pakistani dress in favour of the modern western look. His clean, dark features and good looks working their charm on the girls he sought out.

While he professed to be against western ways, he genuinely disliked Communism. He was happy to see the work of the Chinese being disrupted by today's killing. But then Khalid could probably rationalise anything in his mind.

He looked across at Jabbar and Sharif. Jabbar was reading a well-worn copy of the Qur'an. Sharif had his copy open but he was looking at Khalid. When he caught Khalid's eye he quickly looked back down.

'There's something about that one', thought Khalid, before saying: 'I am going to talk to the newcomers. I will be bringing them up to the north to join you tomorrow. I think it is best that we travel separately. You rest now. You will leave tonight after *isha'a* prayers.'

From time to time through the afternoon, Khalid would bring reports of the reaction to the killing to Jabbar and Sharif. It was not just another local shooting to be ignored by the outside world. This time international news teams had descended on Karachi to film at the scene and at the power station where work was now at a standstill. Local channels and Al-Jazeerah were leading their bulletins with the story and it was also prominent on CNN, not because another shooting in Pakistan mattered but because this time an important industry had been targeted and one with international connections. Government ministers had predictably condemned the attack as an atrocity that would only set the country's development back. It was regarded by the world as a pariah nation already. Areas such as South Waziristan were effectively separate states within a state where the Taliban and Al Qaeda ruled with impunity. Intermittent assaults by the Pakistan army had failed to dislodge them.

In the safe house, there was no discussion about the merits or otherwise of their action between Jabbar and Sharif. Jabbar simply nodded with approval that the mission had been a success whenever Khalid looked in to check on them and brought some update he had heard on the radio. The mood was subdued. There was no sense of elation; they had done their duty. It was almost history now, as though they were keen to move on to the next assignment.

Later that evening a white Suzuki 4x4 with darkened windows pulled into the courtyard. The driver left the engine running as Jabbar and Sharif quickly climbed in. The driver didn't say a word –

none was expected. He would have guessed that these were the two who had carried out the shooting of the industrialist which was the talk of the city. But there was nothing to be said. His job was to drive through the night and get them to Garanji, near Nawakhali, north of Peshawar. It was all part of a well-funded and well-organised network spread across the country. If fugitives had to be spirited away it was virtually impossible for the authorities to track them down. There were rarely any arrests.

Khalid shut the car door and tapped twice on the roof giving a half wave that only Sharif acknowledged. The car sped out of the gate in a cloud of dust. The newcomers peered out of their window at the late night scene. It would soon be their duty to act.

Once out of the city, past police patrols that barely gave them a second glance and on the road north, the journey was uneventful. They stopped at dawn for prayers and for some simple food at a roadside *jhopthri*. There were no war-stories of how they accomplished their task. It had been their duty, just as it was the driver's duty to avoid all police patrols and deliver his 'package' safely. Occasionally as they bumped through the towns Jabbar would shout in anger if he saw a girl walking without a headscarf, condemning the spread of corruption and modernisation. The driver would blast his horn in admonition, their anger directed at unseen family members who allowed the girl to go out in public uncovered.

Some ten hours after setting out they arrived at Garanji and made their way slowly through the narrow streets with people, donkeys and occasional cars sharing the confined space. Like so many of the villages and even major towns, life and progress seemed to have stalled. Some buildings were still made of mud with occasional unfinished cement structures, electricity wires dangling across the road between them like tangled washing lines. A recent downpour had turned the main road through the centre of the town into a river channel in front of rudimentary shop fronts and homes.

At the far end of the town the driver stopped in front of one of the larger structures. A hand-painted sign on the wall indicated that this was the local madrassa. Jabbar and Sharif climbed down from the Suzuki and pushed open the door. The driver drove off without a word.

For the first time since they had left Karachi, Jabbar smiled – they were home. It had been nearly six weeks since they had set out from the madrassa heading south, not knowing if they would ever return. Once again the adrenalin was pumping – after all he was returning as a victor over the infidel. All the training he had been given had worked. God had protected him on his mission.

As he and Sharif walked into the yard, others began to emerge from different buildings, praising Allah for returning them safely. Even Sharif began to feel something approaching pride. Yes, he had done well. He quickly forgot the horrors of the shooting, the look on the children's faces and his own doubts.

The throng moved across the yard and stopped in front of double wooden doors. They opened and instantly the group hushed as a figure emerged. He was surprisingly short and stocky for someone who clearly commanded authority in the madrassa. He was dressed traditionally in white *salwar kameez*, open sandals and a *pugree* turban wrapped round his head. His beard was full and his eyes sunken and hard. Two assistants stood at his side slightly behind him.

He waited until there was no movement and scanned his audience before saying in Urdu: 'The Holy Book tells us to "fight and slay the Pagans wherever ye find them. And seize them, beleaguer them. And lie in wait for them, in every stratagem." This is what our brothers have done.'

'Allahu Akbar! Allahu Akbar!'

The cries were stilled by a raised hand. The man then signalled for Jabbar and Sharif to step forward. Jabbar went first and bent low to kiss the hand of the leader. 'Teacher,' he said simply. He was pulled upright and embraced.

Sharif then followed his lead. This was a moment to treasure. Not since he had arrived in the madrassa 15 years earlier had he so much as spoken directly to the teacher. He couldn't look him in the eyes, it would have been too intimidating but the teacher's embrace was all the reward he needed.

They were all then ordered to sit on the ground and for more than an hour they heard of the great warriors who had gone before them and were now in the rightful place in *firdaws* with the other martyrs and prophets. Without mentioning them by name, the teacher said that Jabbar and Sharif had taken their first steps on that great journey – but it was only the beginning. There was no joy or triumph on his face. Whatever he felt inside he didn't show it. He wore a cold mask of authority and spoke with a voice that was used to being listened to and obeyed.

These lessons from the teacher were highlights of life in the madrassa. They usually happened once a week on a Friday when everyone was gathered together, but also on the special occasions like this when the moment suddenly demanded an impromptu address.

Sharif's mind wandered as it did during the long lessons that sometimes could continue for hours. If he had thought about it, he wouldn't have considered himself a weak Muslim – but particularly as a young boy when he first arrived at the madrassa, it was hard to concentrate as intensely as the others seemed to be able to do. He was used to walking over the hills with his father and brother as the sheep grazed. All that had gone. His was now a life of constant learning and prayer. There seemed to be time for nothing else although in his quiet moments, as he lay in his bed, he thought about home. Would they be thinking of him? Now in adulthood his life was devoted to the work of God. It was clear from the videos they watched time and time again what the Jews, Hindus and Christians were doing to the world. He now had one solemn duty to perform and he would be brave like Jabbar. 'Allahu Akbar!' Sharif involuntarily cried. Others turned and looked at him for a moment before joining in although it did not seem the right time.

The teacher continued, appearing to pick up Sharif's thoughts and feelings of guilt. He reminded them that it was normal to feel some remorse and even guilt. The victims were after all, humans.

There were one or two new faces in the school that Sharif did not recognise. Jabbar seemed oblivious – strangely focussed again, inspired and encouraged by seeing familiar surroundings.

Familiar it may have been but to the outsider they would have seemed harsh with no creature comforts to distract the people who lived there. During the day youngsters from the town would come and attend classes, but for the likes of Jabbar and Sharif this was their entire life. There were no letters from home, or phone calls to catch up on news from the family. The madrassa, the teacher and his assistants were their family.

Their life was devoted to their duty – their *da'wa* – not only to save their own souls but to save the whole of mankind. In time that passion transcended duty and became an all-powerful conviction; an absolute belief in the righteousness of their role in life. This was where Jabber was – nothing could change his mind and anything that ran contrary to that belief was to be condemned. Just their time in Karachi had been a shock. Everywhere they looked as they prepared for their mission, it was clear to them that the modern world with all its sin and corruption had taken over. Women wandered the streets their heads uncovered, there was loud music and the shops were full of images that were an insult to the Holy Book.

By contrast, the madrassa was quiet and still. There was order and prayer. Like the safe house, the buildings were bare and simple. There was nothing to distract them. There were no comforts because comforts simply led to weakness. They had their faith and nothing else was required. And of course there was training for those chosen to take the fight directly to the heart of the enemy. As Sharif looked around he felt he had changed in so many ways. He was now a man who, with God's protection, had done his duty. There would be more missions and the next time it would be him pulling the trigger.

The address from the teacher over, without a word, everyone made their way back to their rooms for more study.

'Sharif.' One of the teacher's assistants was calling him. 'Tomorrow we will go to the camp. Tell Brother Jabbar.'

'Yes, brother, at once.'

The camp was the training ground they used to practise firing weapons. It was also a place where the harshest of preparation took place and was used to test the students. On his first visit, Sharif had only been required to march and run. Later he was given a gun but it had no bullets. Jabbar, who was older, had been allowed to fire some rounds. Even in the first weeks Jabbar stood apart from the rest of them. He seemed braver, stronger and faster.

When Jabbar heard the news his eyes lit up. His excitement was not about the guns but about the thought of another chance to prove himself and if it was Allah's will, to die. Jabbar returned to his reading. Sharif was neither excited nor fearful. Like many of the others who lived in the madrassa, this was another step in a journey which could only have one ending. They all hoped it would be a glorious ending, but either way it was a journey over which they had long ago given up all control. All doubts had been erased, all questions could be answered by reading the Book and even dreams were about triumph over the *kuffars*.

Sharif allowed himself to think about the coming days. He would pray tonight for courage and the opportunity to show that he was worthy of his own mission. He looked across at the simple, rough-hewn cot between him and Jabbar. It was empty. Brother Falik had been lucky. He had gone to Islamabad with explosives tied round his waist and – Sharif was certain – he was now in heaven, his duty fulfilled. Soon Brother Falik's bed would be taken by another; perhaps one of the newcomers he had seen in Karachi that Khalid would be bringing tomorrow.

There were no close bonds to be made in the madrassa. He had arrived on the same day as Jabbar and he knew him as well as anyone, but he knew nothing about his family. No one spoke about their brothers or sisters beyond a few perfunctory discussions when they first arrived: where they had come from; how they had reached Garanji. But after just a few short weeks their lives became consumed with the daily routine of the madrassa. There were no late night conversations about their futures. There was only one future; one common hope that their lives would end gloriously. The videos they had seen so often were proof enough that they had chosen the right path and the corrupt ways which brought shame on Pakistan and Islam had to be stopped. They were lucky to have been selected. Their families, if they had known, would have been proud.

'So tomorrow come straight to the camp.' The teacher was talking on a mobile phone which seemed incongruous in the stark surroundings of his room. There was a simple cot in one corner, a desk and a chair. The walls were whitewashed with framed religious inscriptions on the wall. There was one worn rug on the floor and a large wooden cupboard at one end of the room. The only object out of place was the PC and keyboard.

'How many are you bringing, Khalid?'

'There are five. But they are very naïve. Are you sure you want to show them the training ground so soon?'

'Yes. We have to take advantage of the news. You say they are still talking about it in Karachi?'

'They speak of nothing else, Teacher. You are wise to seek another strike. Perhaps now they will understand,' said Khalid.

'I have heard from our brothers in the Swat Valley. They are suffering. God willing we can help them by striking hard again soon.'

The teacher snapped shut the mobile and frowned.

The group – consisting of his assistants and two other teachers sitting in silence around the room – were watching attentively. Always ready to respond to their leader's wishes, they could tell something was troubling him now.

Reading their minds he said: 'I always worry about our brother, Khalid. He spends too much time in the city. Remember the teaching that riches come from a contented mind, not an abundance of worldly goods.'

'Teacher, we have always said we need to use all the forces Allah provides us wherever we may find them. Brother Khalid has always served us well and he has to work with the infidel to win their trust.'

'Well, let us see who he brings tomorrow. We may have more newcomers these days but I question their resolve. If we cannot discharge our duty, our work here will suffer.'

The teacher – Abdul Bakri – was aware of the funding that they depended on. He often wished there could be some other way, but even the mobile phone bill had to be paid. He looked at it in his hand and threw it down on the table as though he might be contaminated by its very touch. It seemed to symbolise everything that was decadent and wrong about the modern world and which was leading so many people astray. But the fact of the matter was his madrassa and every one like it, depended on the financial support from the outside world. He could not rely on the donations of the town which were offered in kind – produce from the fields around them. He needed cash to buy and equip his students for the work they were being prepared for, in their fight against the oppressors.

Abdul was in his 50s but looked much older. Until recently he had made almost routine trips to Saudi Arabia, trying to win support and funds not just for his school, but also for all the others in Northern Pakistan. Their cause had been helped by the revival of the *Wahhabi* doctrine of Islam. Abdul preferred its stricter code. He attended conferences where he met other senior representatives of the network. Just like any other business gathering they discussed progress, made plans for the year ahead, but most importantly they came to collect funds. While not the most senior figure at these gatherings, he nonetheless had a growing reputation based largely on the impact his attacks made beyond the confines of his territory. In business terms he would be called a strategist, a mover and a shaker, but like every business he had to work hard at it. In truth he disliked the almost corporate feel of these meetings and the increasing glamour he found in Riyadh with its luxurious hotels and offices, so now he only went when he had to. He longed to get home to the simplicity of the courtyard of his madrassa and to see his own three young children growing in the faith. He found it hard to integrate with the world he saw in the stunning displays of wealth all around in Riyadh. He could only imagine the horrors he would have found in the likes of London or New York.

Abdul was comforted and assured by the ideology he believed in, which he was certain would soon shape the minds of the world.

Those who failed to understand were, in his mind, condemned to ignorance – ignorance he was obliged to challenge. The Islamic heretic Shia were a threat to the true path of Islam, and Western modernisation was a disease spreading through society planted by the infidels.

'The action against the *kuffar*, Haider, was a success and has given our just fight the attention it deserves. We must now think hard about how we can follow this up. We must make the whole world listen not just the authorities here in Pakistan. It is our *jihad* to return not just Pakistan, but the world to Allah. It is written: "Allah has promised those among you who believe and do righteous good deeds, that He will certainly grant them succession in the land." Allahu Akbar!' The teacher's call was answered, 'Allahu Akbar.'

Abdul continued: 'I have decided that I should watch the training tomorrow myself. I want to see these newcomers. Khalid says they are weak but even young Sharif was weak when he first arrived here. Yesterday he showed what the power of study and prayer can achieve.'

His mobile began to ring and the teacher glowered at it for its intrusion, before picking it up.

'It is Karachi,' said the teacher, looking round the room. 'We will speak again later.' He waited until he was alone.

'What news do you have, brother?'

# CHAPTER FOUR

Before dawn a small convoy of vehicles – a motley collection of two lorries and a 4x4, all of which had seen better days, – rattled and bounced its way over the harsh terrain along unmade roads. For the passengers inside it was a rough ride made worse when the vehicles turned off the road and headed straight into the hills following tracks that only the driver seemed able to see.

Eventually they shuddered to a halt and everyone climbed down. Some appeared completely bewildered by their surroundings, cold in the early morning air, rubbing their arms to get the circulation moving again. Others were more familiar with the location.

Jabbar was already unpacking one of the boxes from the 4x4 and with practised ease he checked the mechanism of a Kalashnikov. One had served him well only yesterday.

Sharif noticed the reaction of some of the new faces he had seen at the madrassa – this was clearly their first time at the training camp and at this hour of the morning it must have been intimidating. It was always the same with the newcomers. They arrived with an air of bravado; after all they reasoned they had lived in the far more sophisticated Western world and they would now add the skills of warriors. In truth those who had never travelled far from their villages in Pakistan looked with a certain admiration verging on envy at these 'foreigners' who were welcomed as brothers in their faith and in their dedication to the struggle.

There was not much to see at the camp. There were crumbling buildings that would be their base for the next three days, a stream where they would wash and towering mountains all around. The land was barren and stony with only the occasional bit of scrub to break the monotony. In another context it might have had a rugged beauty but the purpose of this setting was to learn to shoot and to kill. For the foreigners in particular, they would learn the rudiments of explosives. They would not be using guns when they returned to the West; they would become suicide bombers.

Much of the morning was spent sprinting backwards and forwards in an *ad hoc* fitness regime, occasionally crawling for a few yards before crouching and taking aim at an unseen enemy. Only the most trusted – and that now included Jabbar and Sharif – were allowed to work with live rounds.

At the sound of an approaching jeep and another lorry, one of the instructors ordered everyone into a line as though preparing for an inspection. The teacher got out of the jeep and immediately fell into conversation with the instructors, while the newcomers climbed wearily down from the lorry. Sharif knew they must have driven all the way from Karachi. He nodded in acknowledgement when he saw Khalid walk round from the passenger side.

If the training camp had been a shock for the new faces at the madrassa, it must have seemed like an alien planet to the newcomers – some of whom would have been walking the streets of London less than a week earlier. Once over the initial trauma they began to cheer up. This is what they had heard about. This was the sort of action they were ready for, the chance to bring retribution to the corrupt West.

The first training they had to do however was bring food and water to everyone else. The mutterings of resentment at being treated like servants were swiftly silenced by Khalid and a withering glance from the teacher. It was always the same when the foreigners arrived. They thought they were there to fire guns all day and learn about explosives, but the reality was more mundane for much of the time. There were not enough bullets or explosives to allow wasteful practice sessions. As many of them would return to Europe, there was no need to learn how to fire a gun. It was more practical to understand how construct an explosive device from day to day materials. But waiting on others was never part of the dream.

After a frugal meal the instructors laid on a display. Jabbar was asked to give an individual demonstration of his shooting skills and prowess, running swiftly between the boulders, hurling himself to the ground, rolling over and firing again. Sharif then joined him in to show how to work together moving alternately, covering each other before finally destroying what remained of a dummy. As it tumbled in a bundle of shredded rags to the ground, Sharif was momentarily reminded of the bodies lying in the car the day before. He hesitated for a moment before running back with Jabbar, to brandish their weapons in front of the teacher who waved in a gesture of approval. They then all sat in lines as one of their instructors exhorted them to think about their new roles, their future missions and why they should never forget that it was God's will that they should crush their enemy. The message was familiar enough to the likes of Jabbar and Sharif. They had heard it a thousand times. It was repeated and repeated until all doubt had been erased.

Everyone then moved into one of the buildings and gathered in a circle, some sitting on the floor, the teacher on a wooden stool and the rest standing looking on. Then one of the instructors pulled a chicken from a crate and held it flapping and squawking above his head. He told them that this was a test of manhood. Killing a chicken or the ritual slaughter of an animal would be commonplace in most Muslim households – the senior male would often be given the task of cutting the animal's throat with a knife before handing the creature over to a butcher. But this test was different.

Someone would be selected to kill the chicken by stamping on its head with their bare feet. The newcomers visibly flinched and moved back in case they were chosen. The instructor turned to the teacher to decide.

He looked around the group. They seemed young and inexperienced. He was worried that so many of the newcomers who were brought over from the west were too damaged by the corruption of western society. Yes, they had spent time in their mosques and they had learned how to pray diligently but, in his view, they were weak. They had enjoyed the comforts of a world with its many distractions for too long. Each year there were fewer and fewer of them and many of those that did come were too reckless.

Abdul saw his life as disciplined and with a purpose and he recognised that if the missions were to be successful then it required the same sort of discipline. Fanaticism was not a word he even thought about. He wanted conviction but that had to be tempered by care when it came to action. It wasn't that he was worried about his followers being caught; he was worried that they might not succeed. In essence he wondered about their ability to carry the word of God forward. It was a doubt he shared with no one, but it mattered that his madrassa should remain highly regarded. The shooting in Karachi would have been noted. He turned to Sharif.

'Sharif, show our new brothers from London what has to be done.'

Sharif had seen this ritual many times before. Jabbar, of course, had done it but he himself had never been asked. He had often killed animals at home for his father, but he had never stamped an animal to death. These thoughts flashed through his mind for a second before he jumped up and stood before the instructor. The chicken was released but seemed to frozen to the spot, not sure which way to run to make its escape. In that instant Sharif stamped down on it and then again on its head, crushing the life out of it.

He picked up the carcass and held it high to show the onlookers – the cries of approval rang out. Khalid – who was at the back of the room – looked away. He spent too much time in the city to enjoy such displays of manhood. He was looking forward to returning to Karachi and preferred his chicken grilled and served on a plate.

After addressing the group and urging the newcomers to steel their souls for the work ahead, the teacher – accompanied by one of his assistants and Khalid – headed back to the madrassa. It was clear that the teacher wanted to plan another mission and quickly. Those who needed to know would have heard that it was Abdul's madrassa that had produced the gunmen. Khalid understood the motivation. The higher the profile of the madrassa the more support it would receive, and support meant funds. That was good for Khalid as well but his role also depended on the new recruits.

'The newcomers are weak as you feared,' said Abdul. 'Our best people all come from the villages – not from the west. What are they learning over there?'

It wasn't a question Khalid needed to answer. It was a common refrain from the teacher. Everyone who had tasted the decadent lifestyle of the western world was corrupted; condemned in his eyes because they failed to devote themselves to prayer and God's work. Khalid knew the teacher had a television in his rooms and a radio, but they were regarded as essential evils and not for his entertainment. He was well informed and had often surprised Khalid by his grasp of what was happening in the world beyond the confines of Garanji.

In the same way much as the teacher despised the mobile phone it was never far from his side and Khalid was well aware that he was not the only point of contact the teacher used.

'When I go back to Karachi tomorrow I will speak to our friends in London about what you say, Teacher. But we had a good day and it has made headlines around the world.'

'That then, brother, I am thinking about tomorrow and next year and the year after. Even with today's arrivals we are only 25 in the madrassa. Last month, two asked to leave because they said they found the training too hard. Of course they found it hard, they had led a decadent life at home. I had to let them go in case they upset everyone else.'

'Were they the two who were said to be sick, Teacher?'

'Yes. They weren't sick of course, however they thought only of themselves not of their prayers and Allah. But they will be able to encourage others in the struggle when they return to their homes. What we need now, brother, is to follow this shooting with something that will really make the world pay attention. I know we have made headlines, but we have to do more. I pray that Allah will inspire me to find another challenge. When you go back to Karachi you must speak to our brother, Awad. He did well in his report and was quickly on the scene as we had agreed. See what he has heard.'

Khalid knew that the teacher had watched every news bulletin within minutes of the shooting. The reporter – Awad Fouda of Channel Five – was almost too quickly on the scene for Khalid's liking, but no one had commented as they were so shocked by the attack itself. They put it down to a piece of journalistic good fortune if they thought about it at all. It was only other rival bureaux that were suspicious about Awad Fouda's ability to be around with a camera crew whenever major news of this kind broke.

'I will speak to him tomorrow, Teacher. I also had a message to ring a contact in the West but I didn't have time to speak to him before I left.'

'Be careful, Khalid.'

'I know, Teacher. Everyone will be very cautious for some time after yesterday.'

'I don't just mean that, Khalid. You must also be careful about how much time you spend talking and mixing with these Westerners. Remember the Holy Book and its teachings.' He looked across at Khalid. Even in the failing light he seemed to be able to read Khalid's face and his innermost thoughts.

Khalid did indeed need to be careful. Perhaps he should be equally careful about the teacher. Khalid knew fully of his own dual existence: pretending to be at ease with modern ways while at the same time fighting against its spread; and that it was a cause of resentment – even anger and suspicion – at the madrassa, but as long as he had the teacher's support he was safe.

At that moment both their mobile phones buzzed, alerting their owners to incoming text messages. They looked at each other as though they had both made a point. The teacher was prepared to make use of modern technology if it helped him achieve God's will. Khalid was prepared to use it because he could not imagine functioning without it. Neither spoke, neither reached for their mobiles. The 21st Century could wait.

If reaction to the killing of Haider had been received with controlled elation in the madrassa, it was playing differently in Washington.

Some commentators saw it as continuing terrorist aggression that had to be stamped out by whatever means. Although it was no longer politically correct to speak of 'the war on terror', everyone knew what taking tough sanctions against the perpetrators meant.

In Senator Friedland's office reaction was mixed. Friedland was an outspoken critic of Pakistan's increasingly close relations with China. He had even cited the building of the power station as an example of a potential danger in the making for the whole of the West.

'Haider is no friend of ours' was one of his notable, almost sinister sounding comments made in a Senate speech. Others had urged more temperate language.

'At last. Is that you? I have been trying to reach you for more than 24 hours. What the hell happened over there?' The senator was speaking down a poor phone line and his caller was having trouble hearing him. Already the prominent vein in his forehead was throbbing – a sure sign of stress. He loosened his tie to ease the pressure on his neck. Friedland was either full on or deeply relaxed. Full on meant trouble for anyone in his sights. The languid calm emanating from the phone didn't help.

'What do you mean what happened? We did as you asked, Senator. Please speak up, I'm afraid it is a bad line.'

'I didn't ask for that. You knew what I meant. I just wanted you to slow things down. Delay the construction work, organise some sort of a strike or whatever you guys do over there. For Crissake!'

'Well they have been slowed down. Permanently.'

'Have you any idea of the trouble this is going to cause?'

'Senator, you should have made yourself more clear. Didn't the British King Henry have the same problem with his knights? You had a situation, as you have had in the past, and just as we have done before the problem has been dealt with efficiently. We have rid you of your turbulent priest, you might say.'

'Haider may have been turbulent but he was no Thomas Becket and this is no time for history lessons. But you've certainly dealt with it.' Friedland thought for a moment. 'What's the reaction there?'

'There is the usual outcry against terrorism, but the truth is the people don't care for the Chinese. It only suited the government because they were enjoying the funding – nothing ever reaches the people.'

'And work at the plant?'

'Completely stopped. They will have to find a new boss but who would want to take on that job? It carries certain risks.'

'I'm glad you can find some humour in all of this,' Friedland snapped leaning forward on his desk, the garishly coloured braces straining to break free.

'Senator, it is easy for you to stand in judgement from over there. We all have to live with the consequences of our actions.'

'Oh come on! You have your life pretty well sorted out and as I recall you are planning your early retirement on the coast – and that's our Western coast; not the Arabian Sea!'

'What can I do for you now, Senator?' said the caller, ignoring the barbed comment.

'Just keep your head down, keep me informed of any changes and for God's sake don't plan any more stunts like this without warning me. I'm supposed to be the Goddamn senator that knows what is happening in that part of the world. Hell, I even have a special department staffed with interns from your country. In fact where is that guy, just when I need him?' He pressed his intercom and barked: 'Kate, get Danyal on the line will you?'

'Sorry, what were we saying?' said the senator returning to his call.

'There is nothing planned at the moment Senator, but I know there is pressure to follow this up with some other action. I don't think anything has been set up yet.'

'Just try and keep those hotheads calm. This does not help the situation out there and you can forget any funding or aid from our Government while this is still in the news.'

'I don't have that sort of influence, but I will certainly keep you informed.'

'Ok, I better get off this line now anyway. You watch yourself, Khalid. This is getting dangerous.'

'Understood, Senator. We will talk again.' Khalid turned off his mobile and stared out of the window at the slow moving Karachi traffic. It seemed everyone was telling him to be careful these days. Maybe the time was approaching to take that early retirement. The question was how long would he be able to maintain everyone's trust? How long was he going to be able to play this game?

# CHAPTER FIVE

Danyal was outside the Marriott Hotel at least half an hour before the agreed time. He was not going to take a chance on London's public transport letting him down. He had decided smart casual was the right thing to wear. Not too over the top and not so casual that the doormen of the hotel would wonder why he was hanging around in Park Lane.

Just when he was beginning to doubt whether Jackson would show up, Danyal saw the lights of a Range Rover flashing. Jackson was at the wheel. He pulled in, immediately attracting the attention of the doormen thrilled to see the movie star and even more hopeful of a handsome tip.

'Sorry, not staying. Just picking up my friend here,' said Jackson cheerily to a now crestfallen car valet. 'Good morning, Danyal. Jump in quick before they give me a ticket,' exclaimed Jackson.

'Good morning. I hope it was not too inconvenient picking me up.'

What was really going through Danyal's mind was that Jackson had called him his friend. Bursting with pride he settled into the leather upholstery and he fastened his seat belt.

'Not at all. I had to come into Mayfair anyhow to attend a meeting. That's why I'm dressed up like a tailor's dummy. Glad you had more sense.'

Suddenly Danyal felt inadequate again. Jackson looked every inch like the onscreen hero the whole world admired. His suit – a dark blue pinstripe – was beautifully tailored, his black shoes polished to mirrors, his shirt obviously from Jermyn Street was a crisp white, while silver motif cufflinks and a woven silk tie completed the ensemble. Danyal now thought he looked a crumpled mess despite taking so much time selecting exactly the right clothes for the occasion.

Jackson was talking again.

'I'm glad you could spare the time, Danyal. My friends are waiting for us at my apartment, probably already making themselves at home. I hope you're feeling hungry. I asked Katherine to prepare something for lunch. Don't know about you but I'm starving. Talking in those meetings always makes me hungry.'

'Of course, of course,' Danyal stammered, not quite sure what to respond to first. How could he not have found time in his empty diary to meet a film star for lunch? And now that star was talking about his friends as though Danyal was already part of his circle. Who was Katherine? His wife? Girlfriend? Secretary? Cook? He just assumed Danyal knew because after all he was now Jackson's friend.

'Starving, yes, I'm starving. I didn't know you were inviting friends round. I hope I'm dressed appropriately.'

Jackson burst out laughing.

'Relax. You're fine. I'm the one not properly dressed. As soon as we get home I'll get out of this clobber and throw on something more casual. We're very informal. They're dying to meet you.'

The rest of the drive through Chelsea, along the Thames and over Battersea Bridge was in silence. There was nothing Danyal could say. Jackson's friends apparently were waiting in anticipation for his arrival as though it was the only thing that mattered in their lives today. It was terrifying. He was out of his depth. What would he talk about?

Before he knew it they were turning into an underground car park of a modern block of flats overlooking the Thames and were in the lift heading for the penthouse suite.

'One day,' Danyal thought to himself as he tried to build up some confidence; 'one day I will be able to afford such luxuries.' Was it really so wrong to desire the trappings of success?

Danyal was still fighting the constant demons in his mind of God versus Mammon when the doors opened onto a private lobby where a man was waiting. He was slightly shorter than Jackson – a little under six feet Danyal reckoned. His tight cropped, light brown hair suited the roundness of his face, but the beard made him look older than his years. He was wearing a loose fitting beige jacket and no tie. He had a glass in his hand. Danyal began to feel a little more at ease.

'Glad to see you've been making yourself comfortable, Richard.'

'Just following orders. How was the meeting?'

'Long and boring and I could do something refreshing myself. First let me introduce you. Danyal, this soak is Richard West. Richard, this gentleman is Danyal Sarwar.'

'Danyal, Hi come on in and meet the rest of the gang. Jackson has been telling us all about you. I gather you have been trying to talk sense to those Americans. Poor you.'

'Nice to meet you,' said Danyal shaking hands. 'It wasn't that bad actually.' It seemed as though Jackson had portrayed him as some sort of roving ambassador rather than an intern on a work experience visit. So now the bar had been raised and he had to sound like a diplomat but there was no time left to worry. Jackson ushered him in.

To Danyal it looked like the scene from a plush movie set. Everything was perfect: bright and beautifully decorated. The focal point across a vast open plan floor was the wide double glass doors leading out onto a balcony with a commanding view up and down the river.

'Right. Let me do the introductions and then I will change.' Jackson led him across the room to the modern kitchen area. 'Danyal, this is Katherine Tait: my muse, my soul mate and my...'

'And your cook at the moment,' said Katherine drying her hands. 'How do you do, Danyal? Welcome to one of Jackson's typically chaotic lunches. It's a bit of everything so I hope you will find something you like to eat.'

Katherine was a beauty: tall; probably about 40 but looked 10 years younger. She had long auburn hair and warm hazel eyes. Her smile melted any worries Danyal had in his mind. He was indeed among friends. He still didn't understand why or how but he felt he was safe.

'Jackson: you didn't say he was so good looking; you should find a part for him in your next movie.'

'I don't need any competition at my age, thank you very much,' Jackson called through the open door of his bedroom.

Danyal blushed. 'You are very kind to invite me. I hope I have not made things too complicated. I feel I might be gate-crashing.'

'Nonsense,' said Richard taking Danyal by the arm; 'Katherine is a genius with a piece of lettuce. She's just like one of those celebrity chefs – they make everything look simple while the rest of us flounder over boiling an egg. Now let me introduce you to Nicky. And then you will have met the two most beautiful women in the world. But be careful: all men are mere putty in their hands.'

'Behave yourself, Richard. Hello, Danyal. I'm Nicky. Nicky Freeman.' She reached out her long elegant hand. Her look was sultry and alluring. This was pure Hollywood.

'Come and sit next to me and ignore the rest of them.' Nicky unwrapped her long legs and slid along the leather sofa. Her skin – unlike the modern style of a perpetual tan – was like porcelain, delicate and white.

'Don't say I didn't warn you, Danyal,' said Richard as he poured himself another drink. 'Who's for a top up?'

'What about offering something to our guest? Danyal, what can this rude man get you?' purred Nicky softly touching his arm. Forget putty – Danyal was already melting like butter in the hot summer sun.

'Just a Coke with lots of ice, please,' said Danyal.

'Only a Coke,' called Richard, slightly surprised. 'Anything with that?'

'No, thank you. Just a Coke.'

Jackson walked back into the room, moving like a panther in elegant black slacks and a long, loose shirt that was styled like a *kurta*.

'Are they looking after you properly?' he asked.

46

'Very well, thank you.'

'Come over and admire the view, Danyal, if you can drag yourself away from Nicky's clutches. I never get tired of looking at her either.' Jackson playfully stroked Nicky's blonde hair as he walked past and out on to the balcony.

'It's stunning,' said Danyal struggling to his feet and giving an apologetic nod to Nicky as though to beg forgiveness for abandoning her. Nicky feigned disappointment but then smiled a bewitching smile of understanding.

'Stunning,' Danyal repeated himself in his fluster.

'I take it your referring to the view,' Jackson gave a broad grin to Danyal and winked. 'I'm glad you could come. I would value your opinion on a project I'm working on. If you're good enough to advise a US Senator you're good enough for me.'

'Oh, I wouldn't say I was an adviser. I was really only there on secondment. Sort of work experience really.'

'Well perhaps I can second you for a few days,' said Jackson. 'Come on, let's have something to eat.'

As they walked back inside Richard was standing looking at a CNN report on the large flat screen TV.

'Looks like some trouble back in your home country, Danyal,' he called over his shoulder.

'Actually England's my home country,' Danyal murmured as he stared at the screen.

'What's happening now?' asked Jackson glancing momentarily at Danyal who seemed to have been startled by the pictures.

'I only caught the end of the piece. It seems an industrialist has been gunned down in broad daylight in Karachi. Wouldn't normally make the news but this guy was working on a big project for the Chinese. Everyone's jumping up and down including the Yanks.'

'Well, let's turn it off for now and enjoy our lunch. Richard's a documentary producer. I don't think he can walk past a TV without turning it on to see what's happening in the world. Come on, Danyal; you sit over here. I'll protect you from Nicky and Katherine,' said

Jackson. He had noticed the tiny frown on Danyal's face when he saw the report and wanted to keep the mood light.

Katherine picked up the signal from Jackson almost telepathically and put an arm round Danyal's shoulders.

'He's perfectly safe with us and needs no protection,' she said.

The large circular glass dining table was colourfully laid with a variety of dishes. Danyal panicked for a moment, too embarrassed to ask which of them did not include meat in case one was pork, until he saw a very obvious fish dish and relaxed again.

'Have a glass of wine?' Katherine asked, reaching out for a bottle in the middle of the table.

'Not for me, thank you,' said Danyal. 'I'll stick with the Coke, thank you.'

'Don't you drink at all?' asked Nicky.

'No, I don't actually. Never have.'

'But you do smoke.' Nicky remembered him having a cigarette out on the balcony when he was talking to Jackson.

'Everyone has a few vices,' Danyal said rather defensively, but trying a joke as he began to feel more at ease.

'The drinking, or rather non-drinking: is that for religious reasons?' Nicky asked again, seemingly with innocent curiosity, but her question had caught everyone's attention and they all strained to hear Danyal's reply. What Danyal had noticed most – more than the question – was the peculiar way in which Jackson was awaiting his answer, keeping his eyes down on his plate, but he could sense his hidden curiosity. He had also chosen a soft drink: whether it was in deference to him or for some other reason, Danyal didn't know.

'Yes, that is the reason,' said Danyal waiting for more intensive questions. 'But that does not mean others should not enjoy it. You might say abstaining from alcohol is just one of the rules of the club I have joined.'

The truth was, although he usually kept his personal beliefs rather hidden, explaining them to curious people was something he quite enjoyed.

'Not the sort of club I'll be joining then,' said Richard reaching across and helping himself to another drink.

'I'm quite sure even you, Richard, would be forgiven your many sins if you chose to repent,' Jackson raised his glass in a mock toast to Richard.

'Not a chance,' said Nicky. 'I know him too well! But tell me Danyal: I assume you are a Muslim; why is your religion so opposed to drinking?'

'Actually, most religions prohibit alcohol on some level; Islam has just taken a stronger line on this issue than others.'

'Why?' persisted Nicky. 'What is really wrong with it in a religious context?'

'Well, besides all the negative tendencies it usually seems to bring out in those under the influence of it, it also reduces sanity of one's mind; a condition which under the Islamic belief contradicts the state of mind we are required to maintain.'

'But why is one required to have a certain state of mind anyway?' asked Richard. 'Sounds too much like control and what do you mean by negative tendencies?'

'I think we can safely say you know all about negative tendencies after a long session filming on one of your assignments.' Nicky gave Richard a knowing look.

'There's an old story which may illustrate what I mean,' said Danyal getting into his stride and increasingly feeling more confident in his surroundings. 'There was a man who was riding a chariot with five horses, he was holding the reigns in his hands and all the horses were trying to run wildly in their own directions. Imagine this man's head to be his intellect and his hands with which he is holding the reigns to be his mind and now imagine all the horses to be the five senses of touch, smell, sight and so on. Although the horses would want to run wildly in their own directions it would be the intellect which would control the mind – the hands – to control all the horses or to let them go. Alcohol can sometimes make us let go.'

'Alright, occasionally I let my hair down but this is something different. It is not about values it is about a religion demanding something of an individual. I don't mean to sound offensive but the position taken by most people in the west is that the ideology of Islam is mostly fundamentalism, aggression and suppression. Just look at the shooting in Karachi.' Richard waved a hand towards the TV. 'Now even though some of us like a drink or two, these are not the values practiced by the west.'

'Richard, stop having a go at our guest,' Katherine admonished.

'Please, don't worry,' said Danyal. 'He makes a good point. What has happened in Karachi and what is happening even here in London among some sectors of the Muslim community has nothing to do with Islam. Don't confuse the faith of Islam with the political Islamist view. Such acts of aggression are born out of ignorance of the faith; not the true teaching of it. But it is worth remembering I think that while here in the West we treasure our freedom of speech, we should not forget that the ideology of Islam is equally precious to its believers. Both sides should tread carefully so that they don't push their own agenda so hard that it offends the other point of view.'

'Nicely put, Danyal – and diplomatically handled if I might say so. I am certain you taught those Americans a thing or two while you were in Washington,' said Jackson who had been listening to the exchange closely. 'Of course, Richard is just being argumentative for purely investigative reasons. He wants to do a documentary in Pakistan and needless to say, he is not finding it easy to get permission to travel to the country with his camera crew.'

'I quite understand. And there is no need to worry. If a faith cannot take a little questioning, then it is a weak faith and regardless of faith, in the end everyone of is responsible for their own actions. If we look closely at the real motives of those actions, too often they are rooted in self-interest. Do we really want to protect an oppressed people or control them? Are we more interested in their mineral wealth or strategic geographic position of their country than the well-being of their people?'

'Quite right, Danyal. Now I have been asked to take a part in a movie which the lunatic director of ours wants to shoot in

Pakistan.' Jackson reached across to a side table and picked up a bundle of papers, the same ones he had been reading on the train from Heathrow the day before. 'This is the script. I'd like you take a look at it after lunch and tell me what you think.'

'I would be delighted, but I'm not sure what I could say about the merits of a film script.'

'No, but you can see it through the eyes of a Muslim of Pakistani origin. I noticed by the way that you regard England as your home country. Interesting.'

The rest of the meal continued in a light hearted vein, with Jackson carefully steering the conversation away from more contentious issues like religion. But Danyal was still puzzling as to why he was there. The company was exhilarating and their stories of Hollywood, movie sets and international jet setting were all a million miles away from Danyal's humdrum life.

However it was as though Jackson was probing not to unsettle his young guest, but out of a spirit of inquiry. Of course there was nothing Danyal could say about the script, apart from the obvious point that getting permission to film in Pakistan would be difficult, let alone the physical dangers. People were beginning to talk about Karachi as the new Beirut. Everyone had a gun and everyone it seemed was prepared to use one.

They discussed the fragile political situation in the country, which was torn not only by political division but also religious tension. Suicide bombing – a tactic normally exported to the west – was increasingly being used in Pakistan's major cities, where before there would have been shooting like with the industrialist. People had even become refugees in their own land, driven out of the beautiful Swat Valley by Taliban fighters struggling with government forces. As usual it was the innocent families trapped in the middle that suffered the most, until they could take no more and had to flee to the rapidly growing shantytowns and camps springing up around Karachi.

Sitting alone with Jackson on the balcony watching the boats meander their way up and down the Thames, Danyal thought he occasionally saw something else in Jackson's gaze. It was as though the film he was planning was really of secondary importance. There were other things on his mind. Jackson seemed pensive, almost apart from the lavish surroundings. Katherine brought him a glass of wine, which he held for a moment nestling in his hand and seemed to be studying its contents. He then quietly put it down – its contents untouched.

He was interested in Danyal's education and experience as essentially a Westerner, but one who crossed the boundaries both in his religion and his upbringing. He said Danyal was clearly an Englishman in so many ways by tradition, by habit, by dress and by inclination. And yet he was a Pakistani by skin colour, by birth and a Muslim by religion. How had he managed that seemingly impossible transition?

They talked late into the afternoon while the others slept off their lunch in front of the TV. Katherine was attentive, bringing cups of tea and coffee, not wishing to interrupt Jackson's train of thought. Religion was foremost on his mind, although he was careful not to make Danyal feel uncomfortable with his probing. The strange thing was that it was as though the questioning was in pursuit of knowledge. He was not trying to put doubt in Danyal's mind; rather he was trying to make sense of the issues in his own mind. It was a search for knowledge.

Danyal glanced down at the abandoned script lying on the floor between them. He had only glanced through it briefly since lunch, as Jackson seemed more intent on talking – as though he was exploring Danyal's faith.

'Of course', he suddenly realised. 'Jackson was just trying to get into character as actors do'. He flattered himself by thinking he could teach Jackson anything about his faith. But he shivered involuntarily; there was something else he didn't understand.

Jackson looked across.

'Sorry, it's getting cold and you must be fed up with all my questions. Let me get you back home. But I don't even know where you live...'

'Please don't worry, I can catch a bus and it's an easy journey back to North London.'

'Certainly not. I'll call the mini-cab firm I use. They're better than most and very reliable. It's on account – I'm sure it is tax deductible.'

Katherine noticed them stirring and came over.

'Jackson, I've had an idea. Why doesn't Danyal come down to Cedars for the weekend? Patrick has pulled out because he has had to go back to LA and we are one short. What do you think?'

'Brilliant idea. I should have thought of it myself. Katherine you're a genius and Danyal and I have lots more to discuss. What do you say Danyal? Fancy getting out of London for a couple of days?'

Danyal was stunned. 'Oh, that's very kind but surely you want to ask...?'

'No, there is no-one else and in any case, you have been seconded to me, remember?' said Jackson patting Danyal on the back. 'Katherine, why don't you give Danyal the directions before he changes his mind and get a car to take him home? It is the least we can do after the grilling the poor chap has had. Cedars is my bolt hole in Kent. You'll love it. We sit around and do absolutely nothing.'

Was there no end to the surprises Jackson was going to pull? Danyal was not just a friend of a movie star but also now a fully-fledged member of his weekend set. He realised he was not in control but there seemed no point spoiling the party. If nothing else he would be able to dine out on this with his friends for years to come.

The Intercom at the door buzzed. It was the mini-cab firm. Danyal looked once more round the apartment in admiration, and at Richard and Nicky curled up sound asleep on the sofa.

'What were you saying about the negative effects of alcohol?' laughed Katherine.

'Oh I hope you don't think I was being critical,' Danyal spluttered.

'I'm only teasing. Have a safe journey home.' Katherine pecked him on the cheek and Danyal blushed again.

'I have had a wonderful time. Please thank Richard and Nicky too.'

Jackson put his arm round Danyal's shoulder and led him to the door.

'I'm glad you could come. I enjoyed our chat and look forward to picking up where we left off at the weekend. The car will be waiting downstairs and will take you home. Everything has been taken care of so there is nothing to pay. See you on Friday evening.'

With that the lift doors closed and Danyal caught sight of his reflections in the mirror.

'This must be a dream,' he thought. He had started the day full of trepidation and he had ended it as an adviser to a film star, adored by his beautiful friends and would soon be hobnobbing at his country retreat.

The lift bumped to a stop and jolted Danyal from his daydreaming.

'Oh God,' he thought; 'what do I wear at a country weekend? I have seen Brideshead Revisited, is it like that? What will the butler think when he unpacks my suitcase? Will there be a butler? What do we wear for dinner?'

Danyal looked down at the note Katherine had given him with the directions to Cedars. She had written at the bottom: 'Very casual. We'll provide the Wellies. We don't wear dinner jackets in the evening!!'

'Was there anything Katherine did not think of?' Danyal wondered. And being a weak man, he started thinking about Katherine: her beauty, her elegance. And Nicky; such a delicate piece of china, she looked as though she would break in half if handled too roughly.

'So much for negative tendencies,' he said out loud.

'What was that, sir,' asked the mini cab driver.

'Oh nothing, just talking to myself.'

# CHAPTER SIX

In the crowded and noisy newsroom of Channel Five, Awad Fouda was still basking in the glory of his latest scoop. Once again he had been first on the scene at a major incident; this time the shooting of the industrialist Haider and his story had made CNN. For a local news reporter that was success indeed. He was sitting on the corner of a desk holding court. The younger reporters were suitably impressed and jealous in equal measure.

Awad Fouda was enjoying that limelight. He knew he was no different to every other journalist. Like them he wanted to get that big story – that scoop, which would make his name. Each one may well have a passion about their chosen speciality, but in the end it was the admiration of their peers that counted. It is all about ego. Fouda also looked the part – handsome features, tall with a swagger which come with confidence and pride.

His editor – Salman Siddiqui – was more old school journalism. He had made it before mobile phones and satellites and he had even spent time on an evening paper in England learning his craft. No one had time to learn a craft today, to do their apprenticeship. Everyone was rushing to make it in their chosen field.

But there were differences in Pakistan. There were different pressures: very few professional editors – and those that tried to steer a balanced path were invariably whipped into order by their owners, who would insist on some particular political line. Journalism was a tough and poorly rewarded vocation in most parts of the world but in Pakistan, Salman Siddiqui knew it was harder than many westerners could imagine. There was no pension scheme, no insurance policy for journalists who got injured in their work – which was becoming increasingly dangerous as they tried in vain to investigate terrorist attacks. In reality there was no investigation to be done.

Usually their offices were drab rooms on one floor of a large apartment block; not the glittering glass palaces which most people would expect of a broadcasting station or even a newspaper office. Channel Five was no exception. Every corner was piled high with boxes and papers. If you were lucky you sat near one of the three fans that stirred the warm air in the large open planned room. All the windows were left open but that didn't help – the temperature in the newsroom was always high.

But Siddiqui knew his time was nearly over at the TV channel. He was getting tired of the sort of stories he had to run in his bulletins. In short they were usually a catalogue of murder and mayhem as he would have put it. He also didn't entirely trust his current star reporter. Of course the Channel's popularity was on the rise, but that was another reason Salman Siddiqui had had enough. It had become a ferocious game of chasing ratings – at any cost.

There were more than 100 private channels in the country now and when they weren't fighting to stay on air during the days of military rulers who pulled the plugs when they didn't like the news, they were fighting each other – and that meant cutting journalistic corners. The reporters seemed to think that just because the news was broadcast first it was right. Nobody wanted to check facts any more. There was precious little, if any, independent news coverage outside the main cities in the districts and provinces where the various feuding factions could easily intimidate real investigative journalism by local reporters.

The concept of verifying sources was alien. The motive of sources was seldom challenged and the willingness of news outlets to be manipulated was widespread. But it was a freedom of expression of a kind. The media had become a significant force in Pakistan politics. It could sway public opinion as it had done over the imprisonment of leading judges forcing the government to capitulate. No politician dared ignore the increasingly popular political chat shows. The presenters of the most influential shows were becoming immune from the sort of intimidation that governments in the past had tried to threaten.

Awad Fouda was of the new breed. He was slick, fast and popular with viewers. The only question for Salman Siddiqui was: 'How did he do it?'

As he watched him through the glass doors of his office, one of the secretaries shouted across the room to say Fouda had a call. They wouldn't give a name but sounded English. He broke away from his admirers and picked up the phone. He was happy to take calls from his fan club.

'Hello?'

'Awad Fouda? Hello, my name is Richard West; I am calling from London.'

'Hello, how can I help?'

'I have been watching your reports on the shooting. Very impressive.'

'Thank you, but what can I do for you? I am in a hurry I have a news bulletin coming up.'

'I understand. I'll be brief. I am a TV producer and I am planning a trip to Pakistan but it is proving difficult to get some permissions. I wonder if you can help me in return for a little bit of information which I am sure your viewers will be interested in.'

'I am listening, Richard.' Fouda sat down at his desk and picked up a pencil and notebook and pushing a chaotic pile of files and old newspaper cuttings to one side. It wasn't every day he took a call from London and this one sounded promising. He was ready to help a fellow TV man if it meant another lead story.

'I assume you have heard of Jackson Clarke?'

'The film star? Of course.'

'Well he is also interested in Pakistan and I don't think he just wants to make a movie there. This will make headlines around the world.'

Fouda slowly replaced the receiver, looking at it while trying to decide what he should do with the information he had just received.

This had nothing to do with entertainment and he would certainly not be passing the tip off to his colleagues on that desk. No, this one had to be handled carefully and if he got it right he would soon be out of this local TV station and heading for one of the big national channels where he would be able to command a good salary. They already knew his name, even outside the country where private Pakistani channels were picked up in large parts of the Middle East and South Asia. But this story was different.

He caught Siddiqui watching him from his office and quickly looked down. His editor was not the person to talk to about this, at least not yet. This almost had a political connotation and there was one guy who would know what to do. If they played this well together they would both be made.

Picking up his notebook he headed out of the office. He could feel Salman Siddiqui's eyes boring into his back, and without looking round, just shouted to one of the PAs that he was going out for the rest of the day. He didn't really have a bulletin to prepare – that was just to sound busy to an international caller.

In fact Fouda made his way straight to the station. He planned to catch the Sindh Express to Rawalpindi and then by bus to Islamabad, the capital. He would be gone for at least 48 hours but his new-found fame had given him some leeway. Siddiqui could curse and shout as much as he liked about his absence, but he had to follow the story – that's what Siddiqui himself always preached.

Asif Khan first met Awad Fouda when they were at university together. They had kept in touch as their paths took Khan into politics while Fouda went for the glamour of TV, as Khan jokingly dismissed it.

Khan was a rapidly rising star in the Ministry of Information. He was in his early 30s, ambitious, well groomed and knew how to use the media to promote his main interest – himself. He regarded his present position as only a temporary stop as he made his way up the precarious political tree in Pakistan where it was mainly a question of who you know and not what you know. He was always ready to give a quote or be interviewed making the most of his photogenic looks and way with words. He had his own website which meticulously recorded all the photo opportunities he attended. Khan enjoyed his life. He knew politics was the same in every country and so long as you understood the game anyone could play.

It was usually worth meeting Fouda and hearing his snippets of information. This time he had seemed more anxious than usual to get together at their normal meeting place: a crowded café near the National Assembly on Jinnah Avenue. It was popular with politicians, professionals and the media. They all needed each other.

'I'm surprised you have time to meet me, my friend: you are so famous now,' said Khan getting up to shake Fouda's hand.

'Enough of that. Did you order me a coffee? I need to keep awake. I shall have to move to Islamabad soon. That journey is too long and the trains are more crowded than ever – if that is possible.'

'Coffee is coming,' said Khan waving at one of the waiters. 'What are you working on now? I'm not sure I should be too close to you. Whenever you step outside someone gets shot or a bomb goes off.'

'Only when I have a camera crew with me,' said Fouda enjoying the backhanded compliment. 'But this is even more explosive and I think we could do well with this story.'

He leant forward in a conspiratorial fashion. Khan was intrigued. Fouda wasn't frightened but he seemed to be on edge. He had never seen him like this before and it must be important otherwise he would never have made the long journey up from Karachi.

'First of all I need you to arrange for a British TV journalist to get his papers approved to come over here,' Fouda continued trying to keep his voice as low as possible and yet be heard above the din. He stopped abruptly when the waiter brought his coffee before continuing. 'He wants to do a piece about the north. Yes, I know he will never manage it, but at least if we can get his visa through for him and his crew he can get into Pakistan. After a week or so of kicking his heels in Karachi, seeing the sights and getting nowhere, he will soon leave. Then I will have kept my side of the bargain.'

'Pakistan seems to have become the most popular destination

in the world for journalists now that Iraq is all but over. Here and Afghanistan. Ok, no problem, I will see what I can do. But I hope you have something good for me?'

'Do you go to the movies?' asked Fouda obliquely.

'Sometimes. Why?'

'I assume you have heard of Jackson Clarke?'

'That's like asking if you have heard of James Bond. Yes I have heard of him, of course.'

'Well it seems he is planning to visit us.'

'Really? That would be nice. I shall mention it to the Ministry of Culture. Is that it? I thought you told me you were on to something big.'

'Patience, my friend; you are always in a rush. I'm surprised you are not a journalist. It appears that our Hollywood hero has taken a liking to our country and might want to make a film here.'

'A little more interesting but still something for the Ministry of Culture. I will of course try to facilitate everything for him and I might get a few headlines standing next to the great man but –'

'What if I said to you that Mr Clarke is having a crisis of faith?'

Fouda looked around to make sure no one was eavesdropping on their conversation. The noisy café was an ideal place to have a discreet conversation and the sight of a politician talking to a journalist would not have raised any suspicions here. The waiters were buzzing around attentively but everyone else seemed to be absorbed in their own conversations or newspapers.

Khan asked sarcastically: 'Do you mean he has finally realised that all his movies were just action and make-believe without any depth? That's what everyone liked about them.'

Fouda shook his head and looked straight into Khan's eyes.

'No, he is having a crisis of his own faith and it seems he rather likes ours. Islam. He might be planning to announce something when he comes over here.'

Khan could not hide his surprise. He also quickly looked round.

'Now that is something for the Ministry of Information. When is all this likely to happen?'

'As far as I know, he is trying to arrange a private visit with one or two close associates. I gather he likes to do this sort of thing to soak up the local atmosphere whenever he takes on a new role. Only this time he may be planning to adopt more than just the facade of his character. What you need to do is make sure you handle all the arrangements – not the Ministry of Culture. And of course, as it is a private visit, you will not need to make a big announcement. Only let a few favoured journalists know – if you follow me. I will make sure there are plenty of good pictures of you with the star.'

Khan nodded and absentmindedly began imagining the scenes when it was announced that Jackson Clarke – under the guidance and with the assistance of Asif Khan – had decided to become a Muslim.

'Are you sure about this, Fouda?'

'I don't know about the timing and I don't know for sure that he is planning to make any sort of announcement here – in fact I would bet he is not – but that won't stop me asking the question. I do know he is going to make a movie and the director wants to shoot it here in Pakistan.'

'But what about wanting to become a Muslim, Fouda? How do you know he is not just trying to understand our ways just for the sake of the part he is playing? What do they call it – getting into character?'

'What's the problem? Even if he says he does not want to become a Muslim we will have a story...'

'You're forgetting, dear brother,' interrupted Khan; 'it may just be another story and a denial for you but if I am the politician standing by his side I might be made to look foolish.'

'You have nothing to lose. When he arrives at Karachi Airport you will be there to welcome a distinguished visitor. If it turns out that he wants to adopt our faith then you are the hero of the hour.'

Khan sat back in his chair and became thoughtful again. There were possibilities – that was for sure – but there were also potential risks. He would need to be wary. On the plus side, Awad Fouda did seem to be in the right place at the right time these days and he could do with a little of Fouda's magic at the moment. There were some important promotions coming up and he wanted to be sure that he would get one of them. Showing Pakistan in a good light by welcoming high-profile visitors was always a good bit of PR and to be seen to be instrumental in persuading one of the world's best known movie stars to adopt Islam would be a triumph.

'Let me have the details of when your TV producer friend wants to come over. You are right, of course; we cannot allow foreign journalists to wander around the country. It would not be safe,' said Khan leaving the question of who would not be safe the journalist or Pakistan's reputation hanging in the air. 'Still we can welcome him and eventually I assume he will leave out of sheer frustration. I must get back to my office. As usual, Fouda, it is interesting talking to you. Have a safe journey back.'

Fouda finished his coffee, allowing Khan to leave alone. It was a silly tradition they had – wanting to leave separately. Everyone in the café – which was guaranteed to be packed at that time of day – knew they had been talking. In fact, people often went there to be seen talking to other influential figures – but they agreed not to flaunt their friendship on the streets.

Sitting with his back to their table, another customer was deeply engrossed in his newspaper. Fouda was pleased to see he was reading about the shooting and he noticed a picture of the scene with him and his camera crew. He smiled and left. Fame indeed.

What Dr Tariq Mitra was not remotely interested in was the article full of useless speculation about who was responsible for the attack. What was far more troubling was the conversation he had just been listening to. The thought of a Hollywood star claiming he had found the true faith and wanting to convert to Islam was a horror in his eyes. It was also totally unbelievable. He was certain it was just a publicity stunt, but would the star really want to try that in Pakistan of all places? It was an insult to Islam that a man whose whole life and career had been built on the evils of the film industry could think that he would be welcomed into the faith.

Dr Mitra had studied long and hard in London. He had achieved his medical qualifications and become a senior consultant in record time, but he had also been studying his faith. When his fellow medical students had been out drinking, he had been attending his local mosque in East London. He had seen the corruption in the West and as soon as he was able he had returned to the land he regarded as his real home: Pakistan. Drink, loose living and a loss of faith even among his fellow Muslims he blamed on advertising and the entertainment industry. But he could barely disguise the anger that he felt when he saw that same collapse of morals creeping into life in Pakistan as well. In the meetings he attended every week it was the same discussion: the world is insulting the teaching of Allah who should guide all our actions, our desires, our lives.

Hollywood was an abomination and this film star was now claiming to have found Islam, and yet was still planning to make a film. It could not happen. The teacher Abdul would know what needed to be done.

How he longed for the simple life he had enjoyed in Garanji. A number of times he had asked the teacher if he could return to the small town and devote the rest of his life to providing medical services to the poor people there, but the teacher had insisted that his real healing should be done in the big cities. His task, his mission, wasn't a case of healing the sick – it was a matter of ensuring that those who had lost the faith or were threatening the faith should be healed – by whatever means.

Dr Mitra folded his newspaper carefully and studied the faces around him. He wondered what was on their minds and he feared the worst: politicians on the make, journalists picking up gossip and professionals enjoying mixing with the powerbrokers. He came here once a week because that was what the teacher had told him to do – not because he enjoyed it.

'You are our eyes and ears,' the teacher had told him. 'You have been trained in the West and they regard you as a sophisticated medical man who has seen the world. No one will suspect for a moment that you are anything other than a successful professional mixing with others like yourself.'

Mitra had protested in vain and in particular had hated the suggestion that he was too ill to continue. It showed weakness and he had never demonstrated anything of the sort. One day, the teacher had said, 'you will hear something that will be important in our *jihad*: you will see.' And, of course, he was right. Today he had heard of plans to insult Islam to its face, but what was he to do about it? He was a man of faith – so much so that he had left his own parents in London. They had been heartbroken and could not understand his feelings. They worried that his intense interest in religion would jeopardise his medical career. He loved them as a son could love his mother and father but they simply could not see that there was more to be done. Sometimes it took extreme measures – even violent measures. Yes, he was a medical man but it was all in the service of Allah. He had even drifted apart from a girl he thought one day he would marry, and finally decided to leave the UK and live in Pakistan. All he knew about his real family background was that his parents came from Garanji and soon after arriving in Pakistan he had made his way there as a some sort of pilgrimage. He had visited the madrassa where his father said he had studied. That was when he had met the teacher. Abdul Bakri didn't remember his father but he had taken Dr Mitra under his wing. After six months, the teacher had explained the role he wanted him to play and the excuse for leaving the madrassa.

With his medical qualifications he quickly found work in the central hospital and had also become a regular in a small mosque near his home. Sometimes he felt the imam was not forceful enough in his condemnation of what was all around them in Islamabad, never mind the West. But Mitra kept a low profile as he had been advised, occasionally attending lectures by some of the younger and more radical members of the mosque. Mitra felt that this was likely to be more fertile territory to find like-minded people.

From time to time he had also been called upon to treat young men with terrible injuries but this work had to be done away from the main hospital, away from too many questions. He had saved a number of lives and had lost some as well, because he did not have all the facilities of a proper hospital. But Mitra reassured himself that these few were not lost to Allah. They had fulfilled their dream in the struggle against the infidel. He had even asked the teacher if he could be allowed to travel to the Swat Valley – where in Mitra's view the Pakistan Government forces had committed grave atrocities – but such heroics had been vetoed by the teacher. He said he had a different role to play and his time would come to serve Allah. He must have patience.

Now he knew it was time to act fast. He would call the teacher to get his instructions. For some reason he was certain that this was important – possibly even the most important task he had ever had to undertake. Although he had never seen any of Jackson's films, he knew the sort of movies they were, and importantly he knew that Jackson was world-famous. Some might say it was a wonderful thing that he had seen the light by choosing to follow the true faith, but this was unacceptable because he intended to go on making films. The character he usually portrayed was a hard-drinking womaniser. It would be a mockery of everything he had learned. He was certain the teacher would be as outraged as he was.

For now though he had to return to the hospital and treat what he regarded as unworthy patients: some were just overweight and suffered from diabetes; others had cancer from smoking too much, from taking drugs or increasingly even alcoholism, which was – until recently – unheard of in Pakistan, a Muslim country. As far as Dr Mitra was concerned they had no-one to blame but themselves. Smoking was a drug just as bad cannabis or cocaine, alcohol was the drink of the Devil and over eating showed a lack of discipline. He did his duty as a clinician and treated their ailments but what he wanted to do was show his displeasure, which he could not. He had seen all this in the hospitals where he had worked in London and he was dismayed that the same symptoms were increasingly showing up in Pakistan. It was as though they had no shame. Some even still called themselves Muslims, but this wasn't the Islam he knew. The Qur'an was clear: "O ye who believe! Strong drink and games of chance and idols and divining arrows are only an infamy of Satan's handiwork."

The thought of 'idols' reminded Mitra of Jackson. Somehow his publicity stunt – for that was all it was to promote a film – had to be stopped.

# CHAPTER SEVEN

Danyal drew back the heavy curtains and the morning sunlight flooded into his bedroom. From his window he could see for miles across the Kent countryside: idyllic scenes of horses grazing in the fields and dotted on the hills, sheep like fluffs of cotton wool. So this was the Garden of England. It had all been pitch dark when he arrived late the previous evening and he hadn't been able to see much of his surroundings. Some of Jackson's other weekend guests had arrived; others apparently were due that day. Supper round the kitchen table the night before had been very informal, as everyone seemed tired after the week's work and were looking forward to an early night. Jackson had promised good weather, good company and lots of good food the next day. So far he had delivered – the weather could not have been better. Danyal was starving, his appetite stimulated by the delicious smells coming from downstairs. Breakfast was ready.

Cedars, Jackson's house, was exactly as Danyal had imagined – large and rambling, a creaking wooden staircase leading down to a large flag-stoned hall. He stood for a moment at the front door, which was open, leading on to a gravel driveway. He could hear a dog barking in the distance and a tractor was at work turning hay in the fields.

'I hope you don't suffer from hayfever.' Danyal turned to see Jackson walking towards him with a mug of coffee in his hand. This was definitely going to be an easy-going weekend and Danyal instantly relaxed.

'There is not much hay making in Southall so I don't really know. What a wonderful scene.'

'It helps me keep my sanity amid all the nonsense of my working life. I don't think the man who looks after all this for me has even seen one of my films. I tried explaining the plot of one movie to him a long time ago but I could tell he was really more interested in coping with what nature threw at him down here every single day. Real life, in other words. I doubt that he's even been to London. I suggested he should go up one day and he asked me why. I couldn't really think of an answer. What could compete with all this?' Jackson waved his arm across the scene.

'I see his point,' said Danyal.

'Come on now, you're probably ready for some breakfast. As you see I have already had my first caffeine hit of the day.'

The centre-piece of the dining room was a large polished oak table. Places had been laid with silver cutlery and there was a sideboard with every conceivable dish. Most of it was off Danyal's menu – sausages, bacon and black pudding but the scrambled eggs, toast and coffee looked perfect.

Jackson caught Danyal's worried glance at the food.

'Sorry about all the meat but I think you will be alright with the eggs or I highly recommend the kedgeree. Have you ever tried it? Very traditional English breakfast made of fish, rice and eggs. I know sounds odd, but try it. You may like it.' Jackson lifted the lid off a dish and allowed the steam to rise in his face.

'Jackson always tries to force feed his guests. Don't be afraid to say no.' Katherine walked into the room in a long, flowing robe wearing dark glasses. 'Did you sleep well, Danyal?'

'Yes, thank you. Very well.' Danyal couldn't stop himself admiring her. Even in a dressing gown, Katherine was stunning.

'Forgive me. It's a small weekend indulgence. I get up very slowly on a Saturday, dress after breakfast and hide behind dark glasses until my eyes are ready for the sunshine.'

'Not at all,' stammered Danyal. 'I thought you looked very ... smart. I love the robe.'

'You're too polite. Come on: have a coffee at least to get you going. The others will be down soon. I think Richard and Nicky are in a bad mood. I heard raised voices last night. Ignore them – they're just over-excited television types.'

'Who else is coming for the weekend? You mentioned others would arrive today.'

'An old Foreign Office friend of mine named Rory McLeod is staying, and some others will be over for dinner,' said Jackson as he tucked into a plate piled high with the kedgeree he had been recommending. 'Rory would have been down last night but there was some crisis he had to deal with. I hope he'll give us all the dirt when he gets here.'

'So what have you got planned for us, Jackson? Nothing too energetic I hope.' Katherine pushed her dark glasses to the top of her head and winked at Danyal.

'I thought a brisk country walk, some tennis and then lunch.'

'Lunch is the only part of that list which appeals to me.' Richard West came into the dining room followed by Nicky who certainly looked a little subdued.

Remembering his manners, Danyal pushed his chair back to get up.

'Relax, Danyal, we don't stand on ceremony here,' said Jackson stretching out his arm and urging him to remain seated. 'The trouble with you, Richard, is you don't take nearly enough exercise.'

'The only fit people I know,' said Richard, 'are always suffering from some injury or another – sprained ankles, pulled muscles and the like. Now I never suffer from any of those. Ah, kedgeree, this is the only time I get to enjoy this treat. What about you, Nicky?'

'Just a large black coffee, please. I'll think about food later.' Nicky sat next to Danyal and gave him a tap on the shoulder in greeting.

'Good morning, Nicky. You must try the scrambled eggs.'

'Urrgh! No thanks! Too early.'

'Well, I am going to give Danyal a little tour after breakfast, if you're up to that Danyal?' said Jackson. 'And then let's see if we can persuade Rory to make up a doubles match for tennis when he gets here. Do you play Danyal?'

'A little but I'm not very good and I haven't brought anything to wear.'

'Don't worry,' laughed Katherine. 'It's not Wimbledon. We just run around in jeans and trainers. If you play a little you're probably better than the rest of us. Rory's the one you have to watch though. He has a very sneaky drop shot.'

After breakfast Jackson showed Danyal round the grounds: mostly lawns and shrubs which, he explained, were easy to maintain; the famous tennis court; some outbuildings and, all around, acres of fields. As far as Danyal could see there wasn't another house in sight.

'I don't blame you for wanting to escape down here. It's beautiful.'

'I was lucky. It never really came on the market. It used to belong to an aged aunt of Rory McLeod's and when it got too much for her, Rory arranged for me to buy it. I've been here nearly 20 years. Come on – let's sit on the terrace and get our breath back.'

'Who is this Rory McLeod? You mentioned he worked at the Foreign Office.'

'Well, when people say the Foreign Office, Danyal, as you know that covers a pretty wide brief. I've no doubt he is some sort of spook. He travels a lot mostly in the Middle East as far as I know. But I don't ask too much because, of course, he won't tell. Let me get you another coffee. You sit here. I'll see what I can find in the kitchen.'

Danyal sat back, shut his eyes and soaked up the morning sun. This was a life he could enjoy.

'Well, I don't care. I just don't think you should have said anything about it.' Danyal – startled – opened his eyes wide. He could hear Nicky's raised voice from the bedroom window above his head.

'So you have said. Several times. It was just a tip off and it may help me get that visa. Nicky, you know what it means to me. It will be a great piece. The networks will love it.'

'Let's not discuss it any more, Richard. It will spoil the weekend. Come on I think I can hear Rory arriving.'

Before Danyal could make sense of what he had just overheard, he saw a car pulling up in front of the house. At the same moment Jackson emerged through the French windows with two steaming mugs.

'At last, Rory's made it. Here, bring your coffee with you and let's make the introductions. Rory, welcome! You're just in time for tennis.'

Danyal did not disgrace himself and Rory was every bit as dangerous at the net as billed. Katherine and Nicky decided it was far too hot to run around and let the men take what the ladies said was some much needed exercise. Despite his earlier refusal to exert himself, Richard proved to be a very determined player. No one seemed to worry too much about the score and by the time lunch had miraculously arrived under a huge parasol on the terrace, everyone agreed that honours were even.

It still all seemed a little unreal to Danyal, who felt he had strayed into some country house party. He was being made very welcome but he was still not sure why he was there. Rory McLeod managed to talk about the drama he'd had to deal with in London without actually saying anything at all. It involved something in Iraq and it was all quite serious but he had been vague about the details – no doubt deliberately so.

Nicky had apparently recovered her humour and she and Katherine danced attendance on the men much to their delight. There was lots to drink for those who wanted it and nothing was made of Danyal's special requirement for iced Coca Cola this time. He thought he caught Rory glancing at him in an inquiring way once or twice, but he might just have been imagining things.

After lunch, which extended into the late afternoon, most of the party were content to enjoy the final warm rays of an un-typically warm summer's day. Jackson was again working on the script of his new movie and the others slept off the excesses of a good lunch. As Danyal surveyed the scene he began to feel there was something rather unreal about the whole setting and yet he was sure there had to be some purpose. In his mind events did not just happen there was usually a logical flow to them even if the logic itself was obscure.

Jackson looked up from his papers and smiled at Danyal.

'Fancy a walk? I have got to work off that meal. It will soon be time for dinner and I won't feel I have earned it.'

They headed off in silence across the fields, Danyal happier to be doing something. When they reached the top of a small hill they turned to admire the view. Cedars was set in a small valley, somehow protected from the outside world. This was the life he really aspired to – a comfortable even luxurious home, beautiful friends and, yes, riches. In his mind he knew he should aspire to greater ambitions – less worldly and more worthy – so why was he so weak? Already this weekend he had missed the prayer times. Maybe he was allowing himself to be led astray by the habits of his new friends. His usual life as a good practising Muslim was a million miles away from Cedars. He wondered if Jackson could even understand the gulf between their worlds. The truth was he knew that he wanted to be more like Jackson and he feared he might lose his friendship if that gulf was too wide.

'What do you make of it all, Danyal?' Jackson's question startled him. It was as though Jackson was reading his mind.

'It's magnificent. Fantastic view in all directions.'

'I didn't mean that, I meant this existence of mine. These friends.' Danyal turned to look at Jackson who seemed remote now. Danyal shivered involuntarily not sure how to answer.

'They're great. I mean they're beautiful and fun to be with. They're all obviously very fond of you. Katherine especially.'

'Yes, Katherine is extraordinary,' replied Jackson sitting down and plucking a piece of long grass. 'If you start sneezing we'll head back.' He laughed but Danyal thought he looked troubled.

'I'm quite sure I don't have hayfever. I don't really know what you mean by...'

'Have you heard of a man called Kutub Reza?' interrupted Jackson.

Danyal was stunned. How could Jackson possibly know of Kutub Reza and why bring him up now?

'Yes, I know of him. He is a very devout Muslim scholar and teacher. I have never met him. Why do you ask?'

'I know him quite well. In fact I have been meeting him every month for the past year or so. I am very interested in learning the philosophy of Islam, Danyal.'

'Yes I realise that. I assume it is important to understand the part you are going to play.'

'No, it's not that, although you're right: you have to get a real feel for the part you are playing. No, what I mean is that I am studying Islam in some depth. I want to understand its teaching and philosophy. I am certain that what we see on our televisions has nothing to do with real Islam.'

'I entirely agree. The fanatics have somehow hijacked our religion.'

'My only problem,' said Jackson, 'is can someone like me really get to the bottom of a religion which is really so alien to my life. Can't imagine a mosque around here, can you?'

'The locals might have something to say.'

'So might some of my friends. I sometimes wonder if everyone is really on my side.'

'What do you mean? They all adore you.'

'Some do and some just adore what I am and what I can do for them.'

'Surely you don't think...'

'Oh there is nothing sinister. Just human frailty. We all suffer from it from time to time. We all think we are so liberated but I think most of the time we are shackled by our own desires. We are only really free when we focus entirely on other people.'

Jackson lay back in the grass but his eyes remained open. Danyal sat cross-legged, trying to understand what could be troubling a man who seemed to have so much. Occasionally they could hear a cry drift up from the house. Katherine and Nicky were playing tennis and getting some crowd support from Rory and Richard. It hadn't crossed Danyal's mind that Jackson's friends would have had any hidden agenda. And what about Jackson's interest in Islam? Here was a man who had achieved everything Danyal secretly desired – success, wealth, fame and the good life – all of which he seemed to be suggesting he would happily sacrifice for others. Jackson wanted to do the right thing, while he was obsessed with achieving his fortune – in short quite the opposite. Why was he so driven by money and possessions? Danyal felt even more inadequate.

'Time to head back,' said Jackson getting to his feet. 'They will be wondering what's happened to us.'

As they walked back Jackson talked about his plans for the estate, the old buildings he wanted to replace and the new tree-planting programme he was starting. Danyal listened but he was really thinking about what Jackson had been telling him on the hill. He was clearly not content? Why was he taking such an interest in Islam? And why did he not trust the beautiful people he gathered round him? For the first time Danyal felt uncomfortable.

Dinner was a more formal affair than lunch and Jackson had invited another couple – General Michael Grant and his wife, Mary – whom he introduced as his neighbours, although they lived five miles away. He was a retired army officer – typical military bearing and delightfully unimpressed by the whole movie industry or television. The general had served all over the world and there was not a danger he had not faced – from Northern Ireland to conflict zones throughout Africa and the Middle East. He was now an adviser to a security firm, which was fully occupied with guarding business executives in hot spots. Mary was the dutiful army wife who had found herself in unfamiliar and uncomfortable postings around the world. But like all dutiful wives, Danyal suspected she was the rock on which the marriage was based.

To the general, everyone was either a potential target or a potential enemy. In his view the whole world was at war to a greater or lesser extent. He had little time for politicians and even less time for American politicians. He burst out laughing when he heard that Danyal had just been on secondment with one in Washington.

'I only hope you managed to knock their heads together while you were in America. There's always some agenda with politicians and they usually ask the military to clean up the mess afterwards, if you don't mind my saying so, Danyal.'

'Not at all, General, and in many cases I think you're probably right. But we have to go on trying to understand.'

'Exactly,' said Jackson joining in the exchange. 'We have got to try and understand one another as a first step.'

Jackson got up to serve wine to his guests – his own glass was full and, Danyal noticed, had not been touched all evening. His outfit was one of the finest *kurtas* Danyal had seen – black, high-collared jacket with a delicate embroidery motif.

'I must compliment you on your *kurta*, Jackson,' he said. 'Where did you get it?'

'It may surprise you, Danyal, to know that I had it made in London. I saw something similar in a magazine and a tailor took just three weeks to make it for me. So it's not entirely authentic but it seemed to go down well at the film premiere last week.'

'You could pass for a distinguished Pakistani gentleman any day.'

'Thank you, Danyal. I shall take that as a particular compliment coming from you. Now while we are on the subject, as some of you know, I have been offered a part in a new film and I thought I would take myself off to Pakistan to see things for myself. What do you think?'

'Is that altogether wise?' asked Rory who was sitting across the table from Danyal. 'Things are a little uncertain there, to put it mildly.'

'I would have thought you are pretty well briefed already aren't you, Jackson? You spend quite a lot of time with that funny preacher fellow and you seem to have gone fairly native with your dress sense.'

'Ouch! Do I detect some criticism there, Richard? And that's coming from someone who wants to shoot a documentary about the Taliban.'

'Hardly the Taliban,' retorted Richard. 'I'm trying to look behind all the rhetoric that is flying about. And I'm not planning on going native.'

Jackson shot a glance towards Richard. 'Like you I am just exploring and investigating in my own way. As for the clothes, I think they suit me.'

'Here, here,' piped up the general's wife, Mary. 'I think you look perfectly splendid. What do you think, Danyal?'

'Oh, I agree. Most splendid. I think people get too fixated about clothes and often associate them with religion. We should not need to wear our religion on our sleeve so to speak. But tell me who could possibly object to a film about the real people of Pakistan?'

'The Pakistani politicians for one,' said General Grant brusquely.

'Not to mention the religious element,' Rory added more quietly apparently concentrating on his food but all senses clearly bristling like receiving antennae. 'I would advise caution to both of you.'

'Surely, if it's understanding that you are both after there can be no danger. Jackson is a man of the world but he is still searching it seems to me. True understanding comes only after going through a lot of phases in one's life. The very big question which arises in everyone's life at sometime or the other is to find out the meaning and reason of this life. Some people live, failing to comprehend or even trying to comprehend. Others make their own approaches in discovering. Some even go to extremes and yet the importance which could rightly be called obligation is mostly taken for granted.' Danyal fell silent, worried that he had spoken out of turn.

After a moment's pause, General Grant said: 'Well he seems to have worked you out pretty quickly, Jackson.'

'Forgive me.' Danyal looked down apologetically.

'Nothing to forgive, please go on,' said Jackson.

'I was just thinking that most people believe in God and in life after death. But if this is to believe that this life is only temporary and the life after is eternal, then surely the meaning of this life remains nothing but a test. If we really believed that for everything we do here we would be accountable in the eternal life, then it follows that the wisest thing for us to do is to prepare for the test. Part of that preparation is exploration and inquiry.'

'And that really is my motive for going,' said Jackson. 'Yes, Andy Lucas wants to set his film in Pakistan and you all know what I am like about trying to make my characters realistic and believable but I am also interested in going from a spirit of understanding as Danyal says. If we don't constantly question and search for answers then what is the point of it all?'

The general 'harrumphed' as only generals can. 'From an intellectual point of view – academically speaking – that's all very well, but sadly in the real world away from the groves of academe, or even the rolling fields of Kent, there is something much more sinister going on. We are at war in many parts of the world and it is just not acceptable to wander around in a spirit of inquiry or exploration. And unfortunately what you wear does matter to some people. Wouldn't you agree, Rory?'

'Sadly, General, you are right. There are plenty of people out there who would rather we didn't dig too deeply into their motives. For them Islam is not a religion but an ideology, which is altogether different. And I regret that in this country we pretend we are tolerant about Islam in particular and yet in reality people are afraid. Afraid to speak their mind and say they don't agree. Women draped from head to foot in *burqas* are seen as a threat to our way of life. Along with intellect, God – if you believe in him – has given us a choice. Choice between right and wrong. I would say that intellectually, it might well be fascinating to understand what is happening in Pakistan or some parts of the Middle East but it would be the wrong choice to visit those places at the moment to find out.'

Katherine – who had been silent throughout these exchanges, busying herself passing round food and making sure all the guests were well looked after – quietly asked: 'Do you really think you have to go, Jackson?'

The question was simple enough but there was something about the tone that brought a sudden silence to the table. It was as though someone had dropped a plate. Jackson looked at Katherine and said reassuringly: 'Don't worry I'll be discreet and try to keep a low profile. However I think I must.' There was a long pause then he added to lighten the tone: 'After all, what can a mere Scot know about playing the role of a Pakistani? I can't learn everything from Danyal here. Anyhow he is practically an Englishman now. He is the one who has gone native.'

They all laughed. Danyal felt both embarrassed and proud to be accepted as one of them and the awkward moment quickly passed. But to finely tuned ears, particularly those of Rory McLeod, there was a potential problem.

Dinner over, everyone moved into the large drawing room. Mary helped distribute coffee. She had been a guest at many diplomatically awkward dinners and to her mind this was a mere squabble between partners, which could be easily remedied. She found Katherine and Nicky in the kitchen tidying up.

'I'm sure everything will be fine, Katherine dear. Jackson knows what he is doing,' she said putting a consoling arm round her shoulder.

'I've been trying to tell her that,' said Nicky. 'Personally, I hope he doesn't go. It's just another film and they could probably shoot the whole thing on a set anywhere in the world. Richard tells me it is all about authenticity.'

'I know he'll do what he feels he must,' said Katherine as she carefully tidied the dishes away. 'I would never question his decision; I just worry about the consequences. Right, let's leave the rest of the tidying up. It can wait until the morning.'

The following day the heavens opened and the torrential rain seemed to signal an early end to the weekend. Rory said he had to go back to London straight after lunch and Richard and Nicky decided they would follow him up. There would be no chance of a return match and Katherine was declared the tennis champion of the group, on the basis that she had managed to get at least some of her first services in.

Danyal accepted Richard's offer of a lift back to London and slept most of the way. As he drifted off in the back of the comfortable BMW seats, the strangest thought crossed his mind. He was convinced that they would never have another weekend all together again.

# CHAPTER EIGHT

All one could see was the glow of computer screens and people sitting in silence listening intently to the sounds on their headphones. There was no day or night in the room. Round the clock the listeners just listened. It had all the appearance of a rather ghostly call centre but there was none of the two-way conversation that you might get in such an office. No one was trying to sell anything. The purpose of this office was to listen not speak. This was one of the world's most famous collection points and the operators were collecting information – careless conversations going on not only in the UK but around the world.

Since 1919 the British Government has spent time and effort learning how to break codes and eavesdropping on what the enemy or potential enemy is saying. The ability of the team based in Bletchley Park to crack the German Enigma Code became the stuff of legend and was even turned into a movie. Their success is said to have shortened the Second World War by two years. The department used to be called the Government Code and Cypher School and then in 1946 it adopted the name Government Communications Headquarters, better known as GCHQ. As one of the British Government's three intelligence agencies it works closely with MI5 and MI6.

The focus of attention tended to shift as tensions across the globe rose and fell. The 'chatter' from Pakistan and Afghanistan had intensified in recent years as all governments and nations became directly and indirectly affected by the manoeuvrings of the Taliban and Al Qaeda. Mobile phone traffic had increased the workload but mobiles also left telltale footprints that could be traced and people were more casual, more careless about using them. Just because they were out walking in the street or even sitting in a hotel lobby they thought they were safe from eavesdroppers. They were not.

Language skills were always at a premium in the world of the spooks and in the 21st Century speakers of Pashto, Hindi, Urdu, Punjabi and the multitude of other popular dialects were in the greatest demand.

Key words triggered special interest but equally important were connections and links between words and their users. The team listening in on traffic from Karachi were on their guard following the murder of an industrialist called Haider and his family. The Pakistan Government had put in a special request for any assistance Britain could offer in trying to track down not only the actual killers, but also the masterminds behind the killings.

From time to time one of the operatives would break off and draw attention to a supervisor about something they had heard. After a brief conversation the operator returned to his screen and the supervisor reported to his superior. Their job wasn't to interpret the information they picked up, but to listen intelligently for the unusual or unexpected. It was the unexpected phone traffic picked up from a newspaper office in Karachi that on this occasion had raised concern. A reporter who was making a name for himself for being first on the scene at numerous attacks – and was therefore under particular scrutiny – had just received a call from London about a British film star. The connection was unlikely to say the least.


Rory McLeod liked to be in his office early – very early. He hated getting caught in the London traffic and it allowed him to get through his own paperwork before the typical daily round of meetings, crises and emergencies which now seemed to be routine in 'The Office' – no one spoke about MI6.

By the time he had worked his way down to the file, he had already been at his desk for an hour, making small notes on top secret documents, initialling them as read and putting them in his out-tray ready for his secretary, the ferociously efficient Lizzie.

McLeod stood up to take off his jacket. The pile of documents seemed to be bigger than usual and he would have to roll his sleeves up to get through it before the day started in earnest. The next file waiting for his attention was unusual. The difference was the informality of the sticker, which simply read: 'Don't you know this character?' Whoever had passed it on to him had decided not to enter any formal note with the paperwork. It was rare, if ever, that a personal contact should appear in these documents. Someone was obviously being sensitive and wanting to keep McLeod's name out of the official loop for now.

It was a transcript of a conversation picked up by GCHQ, and at first McLeod didn't see the relevance until he got to the name: Jackson Clarke.

'What an idiot,' McLeod said, just as his PA walked in through the door.

'I hope you're not referring to me.'

'Oh, Lizzie. Good Morning. No of course not, just something here which I was not expecting to read.'

'Well that's the nature of the beast, I'm afraid – the unexpected. Is there anything I can do?' she asked, collecting up the files waiting for her in the out tray.

'No, thank you. I'll have to think a little more about this one. Slightly personal actually.'

Lizzie Stroud knew better than to inquire any further. She had worked in The Office for nearly 30 years and had seen people come and go. Rory McLeod was one of the most able men she had worked with and she liked his diligence. She knew he would not break the rules and his obvious intelligence meant he could be allowed some leeway.

Lizzie herself was a legend in her department – some suspected she had direct access to whomever was running the Service such was her stature. She would have dismissed that as gossip but rumours persisted. She had a photographic memory and seemingly the ability to recall every document that had crossed her desk, its relevance and what she had done with it. She had of course mastered the new-fangled computer which she had been forced to accept, but she never had to refer to any database when quizzed on a subject. Next year she would retire to the holiday home she had recently bought in Hastings. She would sell up her neat two-bedroom London flat and say goodbye forever to the world of intrigue. As she prepared a black coffee for her boss, she wondered what could possibly have upset his composure. In all the years she had worked for him, she had never known a personal issue to interfere with the job.

The issue as far as Rory McLeod was concerned was two-fold: his good friend Jackson was now of interest to a reporter in Pakistan who had a reputation for being near murderous encounters. To put it bluntly everyone in the intelligence world remotely connected to Pakistan assumed he was being tipped off. They just couldn't prove it. The hope was that eventually someone would make a mistake and a trail would lead back to the people behind the killings.

McLeod's other problem was Richard West. What on earth was he doing talking to this reporter? Judging from the transcript that was incomplete due to a poor phone line, he was trying to offer some sort of carrot – a bit of information about Jackson's travel plans – in return for a visa. There was more, but it was lost in transmission. However, it didn't take a genius to see the risks that West was running. There was nothing illegal about what he had done – it was just plain stupid. The real problem was trying to avoid letting Richard know that his phone call had been overheard. Richard was a prickly customer – the sort of person who might think his rights had somehow been infringed even if he had been getting too close to potential terrorists. Freedom of the press would be invoked before McLeod had been able to explain that the war against terror was probably a higher priority.

'Thank you, Lizzie,' he said as she quietly placed his coffee on the desk. 'Can you see what you can find about Jackson Clarke's plans to make a film in Pakistan of all places? Just unofficially for the moment, if you would.'

'I believe there was something about that in one of the evening papers just the other day. I'll look it up.'

Lizzie left the room without another word. She knew perfectly well that her boss had just spent the weekend with his very old friend, Clarke, and that McLeod was honest as the day was long. On this occasion it seemed he wanted to try and protect a friend but she knew friendship could only be stretched so far and once a line of inquiry was started it would soon become official.

In less than half an hour, Lizzie had produced a single typewritten sheet about Jackson's possible role in a new film to be made by an American director called Andy Lucas. He was something of a maverick in the industry and the word was that his next film was going to be his most controversial – not least because he planned to shoot entirely on location in Pakistan. It seemed everyone apart from Lucas thought it was a lunatic idea, possibly even dangerous.

McLeod pressed the intercom button.

'Lizzie, what's the name of that senator in Washington who has been sounding off about the Taliban? Vance somebody?'

'Senator Vance Friedland, sir.'

'That's him. As soon as America wakes up could you try and get him on the line?' McLeod wasn't sure how Friedland could help but he knew the senator was interested in Pakistan and McLeod wanted to keep his inquiries low-key for now. It was around lunchtime when Lizzie Stroud got through.

Vance Friedland was another early starter and he was used to taking the first few calls of the day himself; usually they were important at that hour.

'Senator, good morning. This is the British Foreign Office, I have Mr McLeod for you.'

'Hello, Senator Friedland? This is Rory McLeod, sorry to call so early.'

'Not at all, I think better at this hour. What can I do for you Mr McLeod?'

The Foreign Office didn't just call a senator to make polite conversation and usually it would have been through more official channels, so this call intrigued Vance Friedland. Someone was about to ask him a favour and that meant a possible advantage. He would have to choose his words carefully. First thing was to say nothing and listen carefully.

Rory McLeod was also on his guard but he had his brief in front of him, carefully and rapidly prepared by the ever-efficient Lizzie. It seemed that the senator liked the sound of his own voice but was also something of an expert on Capitol Hill when it came to Pakistan. At least that was how he portrayed himself. McLeod decided to start on a completely different tack.

'I would like to pick your brains about Hollywood, if I may?' McLeod smiled to himself – he could almost hear the senator's confusion at the other end of the line.

'I'm not with you there, Mr McLeod. Hollywood is not my field.'

'No of course not, but I wonder if you have heard of Andy Lucas. He's an American film director.'

'Ah, I see what's on your mind. Lucas is telling everyone who'll listen that he wants to make a movie in Pakistan. He'll never get permission of course.'

'That's rather what I thought. Is he likely to find any difficulties at your end or is it just a question of obtaining a visa to enter Pakistan do you suppose?' McLeod asked in a disinterested tone.

'We don't stop our citizens flying out, Mr McLeod. It's the ones flying in we are little more cautious about.'

'Indeed, it's just that Pakistan as you know is hardly the safest place in the world to choose to make a film. What is this man Lucas like?

'Hothead from what little I know. Makes a lot of blood and guts movies but now he seems to be taking up causes.'

'Yes, it was the causes part which concerned me. I understand that he is trying to line up Jackson Clarke as one of his stars,' said McLeod vaguely.

'Sounds to me that you don't want to let your man get mixed up in a fight.'

'It would be unfortunate. I would be grateful if you could let me know if Lucas's plans get any closer to fruition. If I hear something at my end I'll let you know right away.'

'Sure thing. I'll do a little digging here. Have a nice day.'

'You too, Senator.'

Needless to say neither man would let the other know anything until they really had to, but the call to Washington would have stirred things up. Friedland would shake the bushes and something might emerge. In the meantime McLeod was increasingly worried about his friend Jackson. He decided to call him on the pretext of thanking him for the weekend, taking the opportunity again to advise him not to travel to Pakistan. Even India was decidedly uncomfortable with new dissident groups springing up overnight, all thinking they could emulate the bombing of the Mumbai hotels that had left more than a hundred dead.

Typically Jackson had remained sanguine about the whole issue. He thought he would simply take a quiet holiday and hope to slip into Karachi unannounced, try and get a feel for the people and the place and leave without anyone knowing he had been there.

McLeod suggested that Jackson Clarke could not go anywhere without being noticed – with or without his beard as a disguise but the implied warning was either unnoticed or rejected. There was little McLeod could do without revealing that Jackson's friend had guaranteed that any discreet holiday trip was out of the question. What he could do was forewarn the British High Commission in Pakistan when they were likely to expect a VIP and hope there was something more newsworthy to catch the eye of the local press.

Lizzie came back into the room with another pile of papers to distract him.

'Is everything alright, sir? I never had a chance to ask if you had a good weekend.'

'Yes, thank you, it's always good to go back to Cedars. And in answer to your first question I hope everything is alright, Lizzie. I just have that nagging doubt in the back of my mind and sadly when I get it I am usually proven right. Still, what have you got for me here? Has another minister just out of puberty upset diplomatic relations somewhere?'

'I'll get you a fresh cup of coffee, sir, I think it is going to be one of those days.'

'It already is Lizzie, it already is.'

In Washington, Senator Vance Friedland was contemplating how best to use the information he had just received. He had read all about Andy Lucas' plans for his new movie because he was an avid film buff. In fact he wished Lucas would stick to the old formula of big action, big explosions and big fight scenes and leave the special cause type of film to the French and the Swedes. He didn't understand those films, as there was usually too much talking and too much looking meaningfully into the middle distanced boring the pants off the viewers. At least that was the way he interpreted what he dismissed as heavy-message movies.

But the message he believed he had just received from London was quite another matter. If someone in the Foreign Office was interested he knew he should be too. He didn't think there would be too many tears shed if Andy Lucas got imprisoned for shouting his mouth off in Pakistan – in fact it would probably raise a bit of a cheer not to mention help his waist-line. But he could just see Lucas blundering into Kashmir and causing an international incident by trying to solve a centuries-old feudal conflict in a few glib and probably rude phrases.

Of course the Foreign Office wouldn't want to get their movie star mixed up in any diplomatic row either. It wouldn't take much to fan the flames which were burning well enough on their own without some blood and guts movie making it worse. No one trusted anyone else – Pakistan didn't like India and the feeling had remained mutual since Partition. They both claimed Kashmir but the tribes scattered through the mountains didn't like either of them. Throw in Al Qaeda and the Taliban crossing the border between the two at will, with a dash of mayhem in Afghanistan which no invading nation has even been able to tame and you have precisely the sort of heady mix that you would do your utmost to prevent the maverick Lucas imbibing.

It was a forlorn hope though – if his mind was set on going he would go. Friedland decided to let the Foreign Office take the lead on this one for a while. Lucas may well be a US citizen but Jackson Clarke was undoubtedly the box office draw. He would wait and see who walked into the spotlights first – superstar or director.

# CHAPTER NINE

Jackson Clarke never used his normal mini-cab firm for his regular trips to Norwood. It would have been too tempting a story even for the most loyal of drivers not to tip off the press that he was visiting the neighbourhood. Before long reporters would be hanging around trying to find out what he was up to so far from the more glamorous parts of town. Instead he took a black cab to Richmond and made the rest of the journey by mini-cab out to South London. He always asked the driver to drop him off a short distance from Stockley Road and walked the rest of the way. Mini-cab drivers were less likely to notice who was sitting in the back of their car. To them it was just another monosyllabic fare wearing dark glasses and not interested in talking much. Internationally renowned movie star he certainly wasn't.

Stockley Road was a non-descript tree-lined road that once upon a time might have been quite gentrified. Most of the original British inhabitants had long since moved out making way for the new influx of Asians.

'So much for integration,' thought Jackson as he walked slowly past the unkempt gardens and questioning glances of the passers-by. It may well have been London but white folk did not often venture into the neighbourhood.

There was nothing remarkable about Number 27. It had a tidy, if slightly overgrown, front garden – the hedge needed trimming and the roses had missed their seasonal pruning. However this was the home of Kutub Reza, a wily old scholar who for the past two years had been teaching Jackson the history of Islam. They had met by chance at a book launch they both attended. There had been the usual mix of celebrities and hangers-on as the author tried to promote his latest volume. Jackson had been on the verge of making his excuses and leaving, when he turned and nearly knocked a glass out of the diminutive Reza's hand. What appealed to Jackson most of all was the long silence and penetrating look Kutub Reza had given him when they were introduced. For some seconds he did not respond to Jackson's formal words of greeting and despite his age (early eighties Jackson guessed as no-one really knew), he had a vice-like handshake.

Instead of saying 'hello' or 'how do you do?' or any other typical pleasantry, Reza simply said: 'I think we might have a great deal to talk about together.'

The only possible answer it seemed to Jackson was: 'I think we might.' He didn't know why he had said it but the words just came out and within days he had found himself in Stockley Road as if he was sitting at his tutor's feet back at Edinburgh University.

A housekeeper opened the door and showed him into a study. Every surface was piled high with files and other documents; the walls were lined with books and a desk was covered with papers waiting for attention and family photographs of children and grandchildren. The only thing missing was a computer. It seemed that he could manage without such modern distractions.

Reza walked into the room, sprightly as a 40-year-old and bristling with enthusiasm.

'You're looking well, sir,' said Jackson. 'In fact I would say fighting fit. You must tell me your secret.'

'I have no complaints. And just because I am a scholar does not mean I should not be ready for battle. Remember Imam Ali was a warrior as well as a holy man. The two are not incompatible. But then you know that already.'

Indeed Jackson had enjoyed the stories about Ali ibn Abi Talib, who the followers of the Shia branch of Islam believe was acclaimed by the Prophet Mohammed to be his successor.

Reza and Jackson – master and pupil – had talked for many hours about the conflicts of more modern times. Conflicts not just between Muslim and non-Muslim peoples but even between Shia and Sunni sects within Islam and the wave of terror instigated by the Taliban and the disparate groups loosely said to represent Al Qaeda. Initially there was no real focus to their meetings; just two men exploring each other's interests in gentle rounds of mental sparring. Eventually when it became clear that Jackson wanted to pursue his inquiries and had devoured the books Reza had lent him, they developed a more formal structure, beginning with Reza's favourite: the history of all religions. Only by understanding all points of view could one reach any sort of tranquillity and balance, he believed. On this occasion he could sense that Jackson was neither tranquil nor balanced.

'Come, sit down. You look a little troubled today. What is on your mind?'

Jackson explained about his plans to travel to Pakistan; both from a professional point of view in preparation for his film, but also because he felt an even stronger urge inspired no doubt by all that they had been discussing. He also wanted to try and make sense of why the region was a hotbed of terrorism and yet its people followed a religion that the two men understood to be essentially a peaceful one. It was as though there was some calling, some imperative, which meant he had no choice in the matter.

As usual Kutub Reza sat and listened. At times like this Jackson felt the great scholar already knew the solution and that he was just letting him talk it through to see if he reached the same conclusion. Occasionally he did but on this occasion there was some obstacle.

Finally Reza said: 'You remember we talked about intention? If what you truly intend to do is right, then even if you make a mistake or even don't achieve your goal, you will have done the right thing, taken the wise course because you will have followed your conscience. Too often we try and justify wrong actions by ignoring our conscience and allowing our ego to pull us away from the right path. I know you have already reached a state in your life where you don't desire any more material things. I know you are grateful for all the good fortune that has come your way and I know that your every action is founded on that gratitude. It does not matter that you are a Christian, Jew, Shia or Sunni, it doesn't matter if you fail to achieve what you are aiming for – if your intention is pure then you are already a victor. You might say that Imam Ali could not be beaten in battle as he had already succeeded even before he had picked up his sword and his shield, because his intention was simply to do the right thing. He did not want to inflict harm or pain on anyone. He did not want any riches or spoils of victory and he showed mercy to those he defeated. At the same time we must beware of arrogance and superiority. We can't say: we are Shia and we are safe because we are followers of that faith. This ignorance just means the true message of humility and sacrifice gets lost. We are all searching and following a path – that is no reason to condemn any other human being. It brings us back to intention.'

Jackson relaxed in his chair the words of comfort beginning to settle his troubled mind as Reza continued.

'Now you are searching for something new – something beyond wealth and recognition but you are having doubts. These are not spiritual doubts but I believe your doubts are much more about your friends. You are not concerned about your own safety but about their future well-being. In the end you must take your own decision and if it is based on truth, on gratitude you will take the right decision. What I do know is that whatever your decision, it will be taken for the good of others. We are warned repeatedly by Imam Ali against the vice of pride. God alone has the right to be proud. But you have burned away any pride you may have had in your past and for that reason you should not worry about the consequences of your actions. Let your friends worry for themselves.'

'I know you are right but my weakness is my humanity,' said Jackson. 'I fear what might become of them after I have gone.'

'Or is it that you fear what might become of you if you go on this trip?' asked Reza.

The joy of these 'conversations' as Jackson called them, was that they allowed for long periods of silence. Kutub Reza knew the answers of course but he allowed time for his 'pupil' to catch up.

Jackson started thinking about Danyal and why he had stumbled into his life. Pure chance some might argue; others would say nothing happens without purpose. Danyal it seemed was travelling in exactly the opposite direction to him. Although he was Muslim, Danyal was dazzled as any young man might be by the baubles of Jackson's success – the homes, the car, the beautiful people. He was losing direction. And here he was – a man who had everything who was contemplating another existence, which if taken to its logical conclusion would mean giving up all the treasures he had gathered in all his homes.

He looked up and saw Reza smiling one of his serene smiles, encouraging him it appeared, to go on battling with his doubts. Reza was already there. He was not an imam but he had worked it all out. He had no time for the zealots and the bullies and the empty noise coming from some of the mosques calling for justice, or worse – *jihads*. So many religious leaders seemed to enjoy the power of their position instead of living the simple life. Imam Ali was a poor man and yet rich in everything that mattered. He would have been appalled by the divisions in Islam and wondered how people so close in faith could be so violently opposed to one another; they were following the words of the Qur'an literally and failing to understand its spiritual meaning.

For more than three hours they talked but it always came back to the battle going on in Jackson's mind about his trip, the conflicting obligations to his closest friends – Katherine in particular – and the compulsive desire to find answers.

'My friend,' Reza continued softly, 'we all have to follow our conscience, which is guided by a strange force, and our intellect, which has the ability to choose between right and wrong. To me that force and the ability of our intellect is the work of God, which in a secular society bears hardly any meaning. But to understand my point lets presume it does. Materially one can evolve very well in the secular society – as you have done – but if you would want to evolve spiritually, I am afraid that one needs a lot more than that which the secular system offers. There are much deeper insights into life and the implications are far more than just a social and political system. You already understand that and you know what you are going to do.'

'I am going to go to Pakistan,' said Jackson almost to himself, but out loud.

'I know you are,' replied Reza quietly. 'We spoke about your real intention. I believe your intention – the purpose of your journey – is one of inquiry, of discovery. As an academic I would applaud any pursuit of knowledge. In fact for some people it is an irresistible urge. Even if I were to advise against it for whatever reason, you would still find it necessary to go.'

'You're right. I will have to send you a postcard!' said Jackson standing up.

'I look forward to receiving it. Come, let me walk you to the door while I tell you one final thought.'

'I trust it will not be final. You make that sound almost terminal. I hope we will be able to have many more chats.'

Reza held Jackson's forearm as they made their way into the hall.

'Of course we will have more chats. I hope we manage to talk even when we are not together. Sometimes I can almost feel you in the room. Now I just want to you to remember this as you leave on your odyssey. I think you are already along way down the path of understanding and discovery. You have the virtues of humility despite all the great good fortune that your acting talents have bestowed.'

'I don't know about that – I just stand in front of a camera and spout the lines someone else has written,' said Jackson bashfully.

'Ssh, you spout them very well, as you put it. No, you understand your gift but you recognise that that is exactly what it is – a gift. Where it comes from who can say, but let's say it is from God. All I am suggesting is that we must understand that we all should use our talents for the right purpose. I happen to believe there is a God and our job on this planet if you like, is to interact with one another in a just way and to pay the dues owed to all our fellow beings – and to me this is encapsulated in the belief that God is justice himself. A Jew and a Christian and a Muslim can all do this with equal success. That is how we can achieve what you might call sacred justice in this life. When everything is in its right place, in our minds, then there is nothing that can really harm us.'

'I don't think I need fear any danger on this trip.'

'You are quite right,' said Reza stopping and looking directly into Jackson's eyes. 'Of course you have nothing to fear because I am sure you have everything in its right place in your mind. Everyone regardless of their position in the secular world has equal standing in the spiritual world order of things. Whether a man is a powerful leader or just a humble labourer, in God's eyes both are of the same stature, and if the leader recognises that he must serve his people just as the labourer serves him with justice then there will be no conflict. Remember we have talked about the word 'ahd which appears frequently in the Qur'an and reinforces our duty to act fairly and kindly to our fellow beings.'

Reza held open the front door and said: 'Remember not to worry about things over which we have no control. You are the ruler, my dear friend Jackson, and you have learned humility and gratitude so you already wear the armour to protect you on your real journey. Your visit to Pakistan is merely a stopping-off place.'

'I'm beginning to have second thoughts. Your words are both generous and full of foreboding.'

'If you don't go then I will never get my postcard and that would be a pity,' said Reza stepping back into the house. 'I wish I had the strength to travel with you but my jet-setting days, if I ever had them, are long since gone and I would just hold you up.'

'On the contrary, I would struggle to keep up with you.'

'You're already ahead of me but you just don't know it yet. Give my good wishes to my old home.' And with that he shut the door.

Jackson felt his journey had begun. It was like waving goodbye to a family friend at the airport. He was now heading for the departure lounge and there was no turning back.

As he made his way along Stockley Road he found himself looking round as though he was committing the scene to his memory. He wished he had brought a coat as the wind was getting up now and there was a distinct chill in the late afternoon air. He stepped up the pace and began to regret that he had not driven himself, as there might be a problem getting a cab.

Visits to Kutub Reza always left him thinking hard, trying to analyse what he had been told but there was just one thing troubling him today. What had Reza meant by saying: 'You're already ahead of me but you just don't know it yet'? No matter how many visits he made to the good man's house, he felt he could never compete with his wisdom. So in what way could he possibly be ahead of him?

He laughed out loud. This was typical of Reza, he always managed to say something just as Jackson was leaving the house to set his mind spinning once again. It was his homework until the next time they met – only this time it was a tough assignment. He picked up the pace as it had started raining. Hopefully the sun would be shining when he made it to Pakistan.

'Taxi!'

# CHAPTER TEN

About the same time as Awad Fouda was starting his long journey back to Karachi, the 4x4 Suzuki that had spirited Jabbar and Sharif out of the city only a few days earlier, was returning and going through the same elaborate routine to ensure they were not being followed. 'Dry cleaning' the security people call it: making sure you leave no trail or trace of your existence.

This time it was particularly important because Abdul Bakri did not want anyone to recognise his face and link it in any way with the safe house. He had only been there once before when the place was a deserted, rubbish-strewn building which had clearly been neglected for years. Nobody cared who came or went and nobody asked questions. It was ideal for Abdul's purposes. Again the rusty corrugated iron gate was opened and closed quickly to allow the car in and prevent inquisitive eyes peering into the compound. There weren't any, but it was a routine drummed in to all who worked there.

It was rare for Abdul to leave the sanctuary of the madrassa these days, preferring instead to dispatch his forces into the field of battle. That was how he saw it: a holy war against the infidel – the crusades in reverse although he wouldn't have appreciated the irony. But the teacher did recognise that on this occasion he needed to hear at firsthand what his informant had to say and it was not something he wanted to trust to a mobile phone connection.

As soon as he heard the car arrive in the compound in a cloud of dust, Dr Mitra came straight out to greet Abdul like a long lost uncle. They hadn't met face to face for more than five years, not since Dr Mitra had left the madrassa an apparently sick man, too frail to continue the training. He had wanted to return to the village to meet there. He felt he belonged in Garanji and the madrassa with its simple, strict codes. But Abdul knew it was important to maintain the story that he had not been well and had left their organisation altogether. There was no need for the other instructors in the madrassa even to know that the doctor was still involved in any way. The gatekeepers at the safe house had been forewarned to expect a visit from a man who would introduce himself as Dr Mitra and give the teacher's name as a reference. He was also to say that the teacher would be arriving the same day. The story for the gatekeepers was that Abdul needed to have a check-up. At the madrassa they had simply been told he was going to Karachi and would be gone a few days – no excuse or explanation was necessary. None was given and no questions were asked.

An hour later there was another arrival. Khalid Jalil had also been instructed by the teacher to make his way back to the safe house to meet him there. He wanted to give him new instructions.

As Khalid walked into the room he saw the teacher deep in conversation with Mitra and stopped in his tracks.

'You look surprised to see me, Brother,' Mitra said to Khalid who was rapidly making connections, trying to undo assumptions he had nurtured for so long and wondering how someone he had considered almost as a traitor to the cause could now be sitting sharing a meal with his leader.

'I thought you had –' Khalid hesitated as he tried to find the words to describe a failure and probably a coward who had walked out of the madrassa training camp on the grounds of ill health.

'Come brother, sit down and let me tell you all about our little subterfuge,' said the teacher patting the mat at his side. 'Even you can't know everything. It was for your own safety.'

The teacher explained how he had asked Dr Mitra to work in Islamabad nearer to the seat of political power and to keep his ear very close to the ground just to see what idle chatter he might pick up. Their patience, and the doctor's humility in being publicly rejected as a failure by so many, had paid off. The doctor reported to the teacher that a British film actor was planning to visit Pakistan and to make a film in the country. But worse than that he was thinking of converting to Islam; and yet he still intended to go on making films and presumably continuing to live the lifestyle of so many westerners.

The purpose of the meeting was to devise some sort of protest to coincide with the visit, if it really went ahead. Whatever was decided, Hollywood had to realise that it had no place in Islam.

Quite the opposite attitude was being taken by Asif Khan in the Ministry of Information some 700 miles away in Islamabad. A visit from one of the movie industry's most popular and famous actors was an excellent photo-opportunity in itself and would look good on his personal website, but the potential of a sensational news story about that most glamorous of stars becoming a Muslim was the sort of thing which could make a career. It could even lead to a ministerial appointment.

The most important thing was to keep the story under his control because every other politician would see the same potential. It did not take long to discover the status of Richard West's visa application and to fast track it with a generous six-month tourist approval; after all he wasn't going to make any films, he just wanted to look around and that would be the stipulation.

So far, however, there had been no application from Jackson Clarke – but that would get immediate approval anyhow because of his status and the good publicity it would bring the country – which was increasingly regarded as off-limits to any tourist, let alone one with his background. All Khan had to do was ensure he was informed as soon as the application was received and divert all inquiries about it to his office. And the first news about the details of any visit would come via his friend, Fouda.

He dialled his mobile number and affected a disinterested tone when Fouda answered after two rings.

'I have taken care of that matter for your friend, Richard West. He is getting notification of his visa approval from the High Commission even as we speak.'

'Excellent,' said Fouda. 'I will call him now and make sure he realises I was instrumental in getting it pushed through – that should also help me find out when our other distinguished visitor is likely to arrive.'

'Oh, yes. Now be sure to let me know so we can arrange an appropriate welcome.'

'Don't worry, you'll be the first to know.'

'I just want to be certain that we handle his visit properly, Fouda.'

'Yes and to be sure that you are the one to welcome him,' he laughed. 'As I said, you will be the first to know and I will make sure you get plenty of coverage.'

'Well that would also be nice,' said Khan smiling broadly to himself while still trying to sound calm about the prospect of so much publicity. 'Of course what will lift this from just another celebrity passing through is some admission – or should I say, announcement – that he plans to do more than just travel through an Islamic country. I'm sure you understand what I mean.'

'Naturally. I will try and find out some more on that when I speak to Richard. But I don't want to frighten anyone off.'

'By the way, the visa application was also for someone called Nicky Freeman, who is described as a production assistant. She is presumably also his partner, as the two applications have always been made together. Anyhow, all the obstacles to their visit have now been removed so your new friend Richard West, should be suitably grateful and be talkative about his plans and those of his other friend.'

'Very good. I'm quite sure he will be most informative. I will call you later.'

Khan was already picturing the scene at the airport – Fouda's TV crew and him standing beside the great movie star, welcoming him to Pakistan and then the revelation. It would be a world-exclusive for Fouda, but in every picture that would be shown globally within minutes of the announcement, he – Asif Khan – would be at his side, somehow instrumental in pulling off this amazing coup. It would just be assumed by the millions of viewers that he had been the one who had helped Jackson Clarke – superstar – to convert to Islam. Some might even think he was Jackson Clarke's mentor.

Richard shut the door and threw his keys and a bundle of newspapers onto a side table. He hadn't particularly enjoyed the weekend. Nicky had been giving him grief for tipping off the Pakistani hack about a possible visit from Jackson, which struck him as being harmless enough. It was worth a try and Jackson would not have been too worried about it had he known. After all he was a film star and was used to getting mobbed.

'Do you want the good news or the bad news?' Nicky called from the bedroom.

'I'll take either – better give me the bad news first.'

'The Pakistan High Commission has just been on.'

'And? And? Don't keep me in suspense.'

'And they have said "no" again to a working visa.'

'The bastards. What's the good news?'

'The good news is they have said yes to a six-month tourist visa for both of us and they have arranged for a meeting while we are over there to discuss your documentary in more detail – a sort of working holiday, you might say.'

Richard almost ran into the room and swept Nicky up in his arms.

'Fantastic. I told you it would work calling that journo. And no harm done. Jackson may never even go to Pakistan to make a movie. You know how slow these feature films can be. Terrific. Am I forgiven?'

'You're forgiven,' said Nicky planting a big kiss on his lips. She was delighted that at last Richard's mood had lifted. He had been stomping around the apartment ever since they had got back from Cedars and truth be known, he had been in a foul mood for weeks beforehand. The Pakistani officials had obviously decided to compromise. They knew perfectly well why he wanted to go to the country and this was a way of facilitating the visit without formally giving permission to film. That was fine by him. All he needed to do was get a foot in the door and the rest he would blag by himself.

The only slight doubt in Nicky's mind was why had they decided to be so cooperative, even to arranging a meeting to discuss the project – a meeting Richard had been pressing for over the past few months without success?

If Richard had any doubts he was not sharing them. This was the breakthrough he had been waiting for and if he now had some sort of official backing – maybe even someone who wanted him to succeed at a government level – so much the better. He was not so naive as to think he would just be able to tip up in the country with a load of camera gear and think he was going to be able to wander off on his own. There would have to be some sort of backing whether it came from the military side or the government side he still didn't know. Even within the country's own intelligence community there seemed to be a long-running rift. The Federal Investigation Agency had long been regarded with suspicion by the military's Inter-Services Intelligence. It all looked a little like professional jealousy.

None of that mattered to Richard now. He had got permission to visit so the first hurdle had been crossed. He was about to call his cameraman with the good news when his mobile rang.

Richard snatched it out of his jacket pocket, now a bundle of energy – all the lethargy which comes with worry and uncertainty instantly lifted.

'Hello!'

'Richard?' asked a foreign sounding voice down a slightly crackly line. He thought it must be the High Commission.

'Yes, who's this?'

'Awad Fouda, calling from Pakistan.'

'Oh, yes. Hi. By the way I don't know how you did it but somehow my visa has come through. Brilliant job. You must have some good friends.'

'So you have heard. Good. I was just ringing you because I too had been informed that the visa application had been approved.'

'Yes fantastic. Good work. I hope we'll be able to get together when I come over so I can thank you personally.'

'Sure. That would be good. Tell me, any more on the possible visit of Jackson? We are all very excited about getting such a big star over here.'

Richard's heart sank. It was as though he had done some sort of pact with the devil and now his debts were being called in. He couldn't just fob this guy off because he obviously had some well-placed friends. The visa could be cancelled just as swiftly as it had been granted. But at least he was just treating it as a celebrity visit and the whole religious thing seemed to have been forgotten.

'He hasn't confirmed when he is going over but I think he is pretty determined. In fact we're getting together this evening so I shall try and find out. I've got your number. I'll call you tomorrow morning, my time.'

'Very good. I look forward to hearing from you and I'm glad I was able to help with the visa.'

'Yes, thanks for that. Chat tomorrow.'

Richard clicked off the phone and wondered about his new best friend in Pakistan. Was he going to be a problem? Would he want his pound of flesh for using his contacts to push the visa through? If all he wanted to know was when was Jackson planning to come that would not be an issue – after all eventually word would get out. He shrugged away his worries. It was no big deal, he would check with Jackson tonight what his plans were.

Jackson was also in an upbeat mood when they met for supper and it did not take long to find out why. He had decided finally that he would be going to Pakistan. It would be a private visit – low profile – and he would only be going for about a week.

'Look, I know you all think I'm barking mad but even Katherine has accepted that I need to go and see the place and the people for myself.'

'Very reluctantly accepted I should add,' Katherine piped up. 'I have agreed to go with him just to make sure he doesn't do anything

I might regret! I'm still hoping they will refuse his visa for being a cantankerous old Scot.'

'Actually I think you will find they are in a particularly accommodating frame of mind at the moment,' said Richard.

Jackson spun round from a table where he had been glancing through some papers.

'I don't believe it. Do you mean to say after all this time they have finally let you in?'

'Yep, as a tourist mind you,' said Richard grinning from ear to ear unable to contain his pleasure. 'They don't want me to bring any heavy gear and Nicky is also coming. I think we should make a party of it.'

'Well, I don't know about that,' said Jackson as he handed a glass to Richard. 'If they are letting all kind of riff raff in I don't think I'll bother.'

They all toasted the success of the visit and Jackson agreed that he and Katherine would apply for their visas in the morning. They would have to go to the High Commission in person.

'When shall we go?' asked Richard. 'I'd prefer to go before they change their minds. I've waited long enough for this. I know it's not exactly a licence to recce the country but it's a start and I can try to make a few contacts.'

'I'm ready to go as soon as I get my visa,' said Jackson looking across at Katherine, who still seemed doubtful about the whole trip.

'The sooner we go the sooner we get back,' she said quietly. 'I can't say I'm thrilled about the idea but I know you're determined to go. I'm sure we'll have no trouble getting a flight – I can't imagine it's exactly on the popular tourist trail.'

'Splendid, that's agreed. If they have no objection to my handsome countenance or my lack of a proper job – let's see if we can get over there next week.'

Katherine got up: 'Come on Nicky, let's go and prepare supper and talk about what we are going to wear. I suppose we can leave our bikinis behind.'

'I believe the camouflaged look is all the rage at the moment,' said Nicky, winking at Jackson as she walked by.

News of Jackson's visa application soon reached Asif Khan. It helped to have an informer in most of the offices of Government. The document said he intended to visit for just one week although he had been granted a six-month visa and he anticipated arriving in Karachi within the next two weeks. He seemed to be in a rush.

Khan immediately contacted Awad Fouda at Channel Five and told him that Jackson's trip was definitely on and he should find out from his source when exactly he was coming. In any case, Khan's office would keep a careful watch on all flight manifests so he would soon know when Jackson was due. Once again he reminded Fouda that he should keep the visit under wraps – he did not want anyone else at the airport. Fouda gave his word but it said it was highly likely that news of the star's arrival would leak out. There were too many unknown elements: the star's own PR machine which Fouda assumed he had; the airline he was flying on would want to extract the maximum publicity; and of course there was the whole Pakistan Government apparatus. If Khan knew then it would not be long before everyone would find a way of being in the greeting line to welcome him.

The fact that Jackson was planning a low key trip, did not have his own PR machine and was oblivious of the publicity storm about to break around him never crossed Fouda's mind. He could not imagine anyone not wanting to be in the limelight and just assumed that superstars actively courted it at every opportunity.

He was in a very good mood that night when he met up with his best contact, which he only knew as Khalid. As usual Khalid was at one of the more racy private clubs in the centre of Karachi. It was more a private residence than a club. Discretion was the watchword. It never advertised, but everyone knew it was there. For the very special customers everything was available. This was Khalid's favourite haunt even though he pretended to be a fine upstanding Muslim; Fouda assumed that most of the clientele led a double life – outside they were respectable but in here they liked to play.

Khalid was unusual because he was clearly not a businessman – at least Fouda had never heard him talk about business although he did travel to Europe frequently. But Khalid's biggest strength as far as Fouda was concerned was he was exceptionally well informed. Khalid was the one who advised Fouda where and when to be with his camera crew and it was thanks to those scoops that Fouda was certain he would soon be on his way to one of the big national channels.

Fouda had decided after the first tip off had proved correct that he would never ask Khalid how he knew. It was obvious he was connected in some way either with the network carrying out the attacks or the intelligence services. Either way he did not need to inquire and he had no intention of stepping out of line: either group could have cut short his career – permanently.

Fouda was bursting to tell someone about his latest news and it seemed Khalid was the safest bet. He was certainly not a journalist and news about a superstar was hardly likely to interest him.

'For a change I have some news for you Kal.' Fouda liked to indulge Khalid's tendency to adopt westernised nicknames and in these surroundings they all felt like international players.

'What have you heard? I always like a little gossip.'

'We have a movie star coming to town. Jackson Clarke. And I have the scoop on it.'

Khalid pretended it was all news to him and affected a mild interest: 'Well done. Why is he coming? Just for a holiday?'

'I think he is planning to make a movie here and is on a sort of reconnaissance trip. You know finding out what we're like, how we talk, how we dress.'

Fouda decided that he would not share the real purpose of the trip – to get a deeper knowledge of Islam and probably to announce his conversion.

'Do you think he will be allowed to make a film in Pakistan – particularly the sort of films which include sex and drink?!'

'That's not my problem, but I will certainly ask him about that.'

'I shall look out for the story. When do you think he's coming over?' asked Khalid casually, not wanting to show any real interest.

'From what my sources tell me, he is likely to be here in the next two weeks. I know that his visa application has been approved,'

Fouda added just to show how highly placed his own contacts were and of course to impress Khalid.

'It's all a bit off your usual type of story isn't it – Hollywood, movie stars. You're not losing interest in hard news are you, Fouda?'

'No, not at all, but let's face it who doesn't like a bit of glamour from time to time. After all, we both enjoy it in here don't we?' said Fouda archly, catching Khalid eyeing up a beautiful client of the club as she sashayed past their table.

'We do indeed. Two weeks you say – any idea where he is staying?'

'Certainly coming to Karachi but I don't know which hotel. Why do you ask – want to get his autograph?'

'I might try and meet him and see if he can get me a walk-on part in his movie.'

They both laughed but both had their own private thoughts. Fouda was mentally working on the script of his big story. Khalid was wondering exactly how the teacher planned to use the event for his purposes. One thing he was absolutely certain about – it would not turn out as his Fouda was expecting.

# CHAPTER ELEVEN

It didn't take long for the information that Jackson was going ahead with his trip to reach Rory McLeod. It was understood by all parties that a discreet and permanent watch was kept on all embassies 'of interest' and the Pakistan High Commission was certainly of interest. Most of those who came and went were of no interest but when a movie star turned up on the doorstep – presumably contemplating a visit – that deserved to be logged and passed along the line.

He was thinking how he could advise Jackson without making it too obvious that he knew all about his plans when his phone rang: 'Sir, I have Katherine Tait on the line.'

Maybe there was a chance to dissuade them from making the trip after all. Perhaps Katherine was having second thoughts.

'Katherine, hello. I meant to call you to thank you for the weekend. It is always a great break going down to Cedars.'

He would let her make the running in the conversation. He didn't want to sound too anxious because he knew Katherine was worried, but they needed to realise this wasn't just another tourist destination. Pakistan was at the very centre of every government's counter-terrorist agenda. It had impossible borders to monitor and leaked like a sieve with terrorists coming and going at will. There was little the authorities could do about it.

'Rory, Jackson and I are going ahead with this trip. It's completely mad. What do you think?'

'I would agree.'

'Well, do you think we should call it off?'

'I don't think anything I could say would make Jackson change his mind. He's clearly determined to do it so the only thing is to be sensible while you're out there. The Foreign Office's official line is stay in the major cities. For goodness sake don't venture up to the North-west Frontier region and places like Peshawar. How much research does an actor need to play in one of Jackson's type of movies? I don't mean to be rude, but he's not exactly making a documentary.'

'No, he's not but Richard might be,' said Katherine quietly.

'Oh no, he's not going there too is he?' Rory quietly riffled through his papers to see if there was a Richard West listed. 'I thought he was struggling to get a visa?'

'He's just been given his and Jackson and I got ours yesterday. There was no delay we just sailed through. I thought it would take a few days.'

'Normally does,' said Rory frowning. 'Must have given you VIP treatment. When are you and Jackson going?'

'We're all going out together: Richard, Nicky, Jackson and I. Probably next week if we can organise some flights.'

'Sounds like a jolly party. I hope Richard is on his best behaviour. I really can't see them allowing him to wander about with his cameras. How long are you going for, Katherine?'

'Just for a few days and Richard is not bringing his cameras – it's a sort of recce.'

Rory found Richard and Nicky's names on his list and marked them with a yellow highlighter pen.

'Well, I'm quite sure everything will be fine. You have got my number and my mobile so if you have any concerns while you are there, call immediately. Where are you staying? Islamabad or Karachi?'

'Karachi,' said Katherine without much enthusiasm. She knew Rory had to sound upbeat but she shared his real misgivings about the whole venture. 'And you know what F.I.N.E stands for, don't you Rory?'

'I would never describe you as frustrated, insecure, neurotic or emotional. I will let the Deputy High Commissioner in Karachi know that you're in town. He might even arrange a car for you.

There'll probably be a scrum at the airport. Superstar visits and all that – I can see the headlines.'

'Oh, I hope not,' said Katherine quickly. 'This is a private visit. I don't think Jackson has even told his PR people that he's going.'

'Well these things have a tendency to get out. Look, don't worry. Have a good trip and tell me all about it when you get back.'

'I will. Thanks.' Katherine put down the phone just as Jackson walked into the room. 'I was just telling Rory that we were going to Pakistan. No harm keeping him in the loop. You never know.'

Jackson walked over and put an arm round Katherine as he said: 'There is nothing to worry about. We just fly in have a look round town, pay attention to the people and how they walk and talk and fly home again. Anyhow we could do with a break. Change of air, change of food – it always helps. And you're quite right. Rory will make a few calls and I'm sure some of his mysterious friends will keep a discreet eye on us so we don't get up to any mischief.'

'Ok, but Rory said we must stay in town and not go wandering off piste even if Richard decides to do his own research. Agreed?'

'Agreed. Scout's honour. I've booked return tickets so we will only be gone four days. Maximum.'

It was another blistering hot day in Islamabad but that was not going to stop the affluent young of the city cruising the Jinnah Super Market area on their sports bikes. The even better-off enjoyed the admiring glances as they drove their open-top sports cars aimlessly back and forth, occasionally stopping to greet a friend, music blaring from the cars' ostentatious speakers.

This was youthful Pakistan at play. For them the priority was looking good, listening to the latest music and hanging out with their friends. In short, exactly the same as youngsters anywhere. They were not concerned about cross-border tension with India, or terrorist threats or even any political issue. They were determined to have fun; they would leave the 'serious' concerns to their parents.

The other similarity with the affluent anywhere in the world was that the so-called 'little people' and the poor in particular, did not even register on their radar. They simply did not exist so why should they be noticed.

Jabbar was well aware of this as he walked in the shadows with his head down, not wanting to attract any attention. Walking with him – although not as calm as Jabbar but with the same steely focus in his eyes – was one of the young men who had arrived in Garanji just a few short weeks ago: one of the newcomers. Despite his youth and inexperience, the teacher had been impressed by his dedication and had singled him out for special duties.

He had learned quickly and nothing had dented his conviction. The real test had been when he tried on the white waistcoat for the first time. He hadn't hesitated for an instant as he lifted it off the hanger and adjusted the straps round his waist. To begin with they had just put weights in all the pockets, front and back, adjusting it to his slight frame. On the day the weights would be replaced by explosives, charges and a firing mechanism.

That day had arrived.

As they made their way past the shops selling exotic Chinese silks, the latest CDs by the latest bands, the most expensive watches all the better for wearing with the expensive suits, neither of them looked left or right. If ever a road was designed to inflame Jabbar, this particular stretch in the Jinnah Super Market was the one. Opulence, vulgarity, self-obsession, suggestive fashions – they all were condemned in Jabbar's mind. He wore a watch. A simple watch. It told the time. There was not long to go now. Soon this would all come to an end.

Tahir matched Jabbar stride for stride. Occasionally a breath of wind tugged at his billowing shirt, threatening to reveal what lay beneath. He quickly folded his arm across just as Jabbar flashed a warning look at him. It didn't matter. They were little people. The passers-by only had eyes for the merchandise hanging invitingly in the windows and in the open shop doorways. Inside, the shopkeepers waited patiently for another rich customer. They didn't notice the little people walking by. They were just like fleeting shadows, gone in an instant, before allowing the sunshine of the wealthy to burst in again.

At last they reached the centre of the market. In full view and yet still invisible. A motorbike sped by, the rider racing his engine for maximum attention and blasting his horn at the two little people in his way.

'You're clear now brother,' Jabbar said right into Tahir's ear so he could hear above the noise of Satan's temptations all around. 'In five minutes you will be in Paradise. You are lucky, brother, God is Great.'

'God is Great,' Tahir mouthed in response.

With one last glance back, Jabbar left Tahir standing alone in the crowded square. It was not Jabbar's time, the teacher had said. You are his guide so just lead him to the place, give him courage if he needs it and move away to safety. Those were his instructions. That was his duty for this day. A greater duty would surely come for him soon, he prayed.

As he reached the western corner of the square – the one where a music shop blares out the latest songs accompanied by videos which filled Jabbar with fury – a red sports car (it was a Jaguar but Jabbar would not have been able to identify it) swept by. The driver was a man about Jabbar's age with slicked-back, jet-black hair, his shirt open to the waist with the inevitable gold medallion. His passenger allowed her hair to blow back in the wind as she draped an arm languorously round the driver's shoulder. She looked at Jabbar as though to say: 'pathetic, little man'. As the car raced into the square the driver hit the horn letting out a shrill multi-toned blast.

So no one heard Tahir call out: 'Allahu Akbar.'

Those nearest to him just brushed him aside as they hurried to admire the Jaguar. No blast. No flash of light. Just the latest rock music and another multi-toned horn answering like some mechanical mating call.

Tahir looked around panic stricken. The explosive vest he was wearing had failed to detonate. What should he do? He flicked the trigger mechanism again and again. Nothing.

From his vantage point, Jabbar had waited for the sound. The triumphant blast which would have put an end to this abomination.

111

He walked warily back into the square to see what had happened. Coming straight towards him was Tahir. His face fixed in panic.

Jabbar tried to signal to him to go back and try the trigger again, but Tahir kept walking towards him, thinking he was calling him over. Jabbar would know what to do. Jabbar always knew what to do.

'It didn't work. What has happened? It didn't fire,' said Tahir as he reached the edge of the square.

'Go back brother, go back and try again. It can happen sometimes.'

'I think a wire must have come loose,' said Tahir, pulling at his shirt. 'Can you check?'

'No, don't do that. It might...'

Jabbar never finished his sentence. In a blinding flash the detonator, which had jammed in the folds of Tahir's shirt as he tried to stop it blowing open when they crossed the square, came loose and the connection was made. Perfectly.

The corner of the building took the full force of the explosion. Windows were shattered and the beautiful people in the square were screaming, but none of them was hurt. Only Jabbar and Tahir died that day. The little people.

For once Channel Five were not the first on the scene and Salman Siddiqui wasn't sure if he was pleased that they had been scooped by the opposition. He looked for Awad Fouda in the newsroom but his star reporter was nowhere to be found. A PA said that she last saw him two days ago.

According to the police version, two people had died in the attack and it was assumed that the bomb had gone off prematurely, killing the terrorists. The square had been crowded with shoppers at the time. A few moments later, if the bombers had actually reached the centre of the square, it might have been a disaster. Eyewitness accounts were sketchy. The driver of the Jaguar was more concerned about the scratch that a flying piece of brick had caused to his paintwork. One glamorous witness said that she saw someone who looked suspicious standing on the corner where the blast happened but could not really describe the individual. How do you describe someone who makes no impact on you, who doesn't exist in your eyes? The police dismissed her account as an attempt to get on television. Fame for five seconds; never mind five minutes.

Whatever the police thought of the description, it was clear enough to Abdul Bakri who was flicking between the Pakistani TV channels that the girl was talking about Jabbar. It didn't take long for him to guess what had happened. For some reason the bomb had gone off in the wrong corner of the square; the corner where Jabbar should have been standing alone and not with Tahir. Either Tahir had panicked at the last moment or the bomb had failed to go off in the correct manner and he had come over to Jabbar for guidance. Abdul didn't like using suicide bombers. The tactic was indiscriminate and as such counterproductive. It was always easy to show a picture of an injured child afterwards lying in agony in a hospital bed surrounded by tearful relatives, that would immediately turn public opinion against whatever cause you were fighting. Targeted assassination was more effective and more surgical. Now he had lost an experienced brother, wasted for no benefit at all.

Abdul called his assistants together. It wasn't a failure, he insisted – they had brought panic to the streets once again as a warning to the authorities and the people that they should change their ways. Brothers Jabbar and Tahir had been heroic and now they were enjoying their reward in Paradise. That was the message the students in the madrassa should understand.

Nevertheless he wanted to strike at the heart of the corruption, which Abdul now felt was eating ever deeper into life in Pakistan itself. He told his assistants that it was time to let the world know that there was only one true faith and only one true way to Paradise. The world had to learn that lesson.

It may have been leading the Pakistani news, but this time the attack didn't make the international news channels. There were bigger and more deadly explosions to report in Afghanistan as the death toll for the coalition forces fighting an elusive enemy continued to rise. Everyone accepted that the blast near the Jinnah Super Market had only succeeded in killing the bombers themselves and it was more a feeling of good riddance. It never made the news bulletin running order on CNN.

But Rory McLeod did notice the brief Reuters announcement on his screen. There was no point trying to talk his friend Jackson out of going, so all he could hope was that the bombers would think again before launching another attack. With luck there would now be a few weeks of calm, which would be time enough for the trip to be made and everyone could return home in one piece.

He thought he would touch base with Senator Friedland to see what he had heard and to let him know that the star of the movie was on his way to Pakistan. Friedland was shocked and asked if there was any way the trip could be stopped.

'You know he'll be a nice juicy target for some madman to try his hand,' said Friedland in a typically reassuring fashion.

'I'm hoping at least two of those madmen have just gone to meet their maker.'

'Yeah, I saw that but the trouble is that just leaves several million more waiting in line.'

'I don't think every Pakistani is anti-Hollywood, Senator. At least I hope not.'

'No, you're right. The trouble is, it just takes one and suddenly the whole world thinks we should go to war again. I think Iraq and Afghanistan are quite enough for one generation.'

The senator had not heard that the director, Andy Lucas, was thinking of following Jackson to Pakistan, so they assumed this was just a private fact-finding trip by Jackson and his friends. Every effort would be made to keep it a low-key visit but the senator promised to let the US Embassy in Islamabad know that Jackson and party would be in Karachi in the coming days.

They agreed that there was little more anyone else could do. It wasn't illegal for a British citizen to travel to the region if they wanted to and the argument would always be made that one shouldn't allow the terrorists to win. New York and London had both suffered. The universal reaction was to fight back and the best way to fight was to behave normally.

Normality was exactly what Danyal's life had become. His mind was still in the clouds after his weekend with Jackson and his friends, but his day to day existence was more humdrum, normal and – if he was being honest with himself – it was boring. He felt he was marking time turning up for work in his father's business every day. There was nothing for him at the Foundation, which was struggling financially with the recession and finding it hard to find financial backers or grants. It seems there were too many think-tanks.

He'd called Jackson to say thank you for the weekend, but really to see if there was something he could offer which had a little more excitement than he could find in Southall. Jackson must have been out because all he got was his answer phone. A day or so later he got a text from Jackson saying he was following Danyal's advice and going to Pakistan for a short visit. He would be in touch when he returned.

Advice? What advice had he given Jackson? All they had talked about was what Danyal saw in Jackson's life – the excitement, the beautiful people, the movies. Yes, he had spoken a bit about his faith and why he always drank Coke not alcohol, but surely Jackson could see that what he, Danyal, admired was everything about Jackson's world – the success and the achievement?

Danyal was almost embarrassed about what Jackson would find in Pakistan, a country struggling to match the progress of its more affluent neighbour, India; a country where people lived in fear of constant attack. Some – a very few – were successful and enjoyed a privileged life but he knew Pakistan was the problem child in the region. This surely wasn't what Jackson was in search of or needed to improve himself. What did he need to improve?

He resolved that as soon as Jackson returned from Pakistan he would meet up again and ask his advice. In his mind Danyal had decided that the future lay in America. He had taken to reading *USA Today* so he nearly missed the single paragraph report from

Islamabad buried on the inside pages of the international news section. It was just a filler item squeezed in by the sub-editor to complete a corner of his page:

> Two men thought to be suicide bombers exploded a
> bomb in the centre of Islamabad. Police said the bomb
> went off prematurely. No one else was hurt.

Danyal called Jackson's mobile again to warn him to be careful, but mobiles do not ring at 36,000 feet.

# CHAPTER TWELVE

Nine hours cocooned in a metal tube – albeit with first class comforts – is no pleasure. A long stopover in Dubai before the last haul to Karachi hardly makes the ordeal any easier. There is just so much you can do after you've flicked through the in-flight entertainment, read and re-read the newspapers and tried in vain to sleep. In the end all that is left is to shut your eyes and wrap yourself in your own thoughts. Jackson didn't like what he was thinking.

Perhaps he had been too selfish in insisting on making the trip. He felt he had been unreasonable in his demands and felt guilty that he had almost coerced Katherine into coming along. He was certain that if Richard and Nicky had not insisted on coming with him, Katherine would have stayed at home. He wished she had.

The first class cabin on the first leg of the Emirates Airways flight to Dubai had been half full – it was no longer the destination of your dreams. The Dubai property bubble had burst as it had done around the world. It just seemed more acute in a city that had been built precisely on the property boom. Palm tree shaped islands created in the middle of the sea from sand imported to a land that in living memory had itself been no more than a desert. Hubris colliding head-on with irony. It seemed inevitable to Jackson as the plane had made its final approach that it would all end in disaster. A noble tribal people intoxicated by the lure of 21st Century frippery.

'The sooner the sand consumed it all and the tiny emirate embraced once more its past, the better', he thought. Impossible pipe-dream of course, but where was the nobility in endless shopping malls selling more unwanted baubles, and properties with every conceivable luxury which in turn made such delights commonplace? People had even flocked to snap up apartments – some of which had not even been built. They had been bought purely on the strength of the glossy brochures and the plans. But as the gloom of the financial decline strengthened its grip round the neck of every economy in 2009, the traffic was all heading one way – out of Dubai. The airport car parks were now littered with luxury cars, abandoned by their owners with the keys left in the ignition. No wonder the first class cabin was virtually empty.

On the second leg of the journey there was only Jackson, his friends and a Pakistani couple in first class. The cabin crew seemed delighted to have something to do and of course there was the added coup having a film star on board.

Jackson looked across at Katherine who couldn't sleep either; she was staring at him with a mixture of compassion and apprehension. He knew there was tension growing among all his friends, with the exception of Richard. He had that journalist's confidence that somehow he was immune to what he was reporting on. The bullets and the bombs were for others; he was just an observer. Yes there was always risk but he was not the enemy, so if there was a choice he hoped that the gunmen would not be aiming at him.

As the flight approached Jinnah International Airport in Karachi – named after Pakistan's founder, Muhammad Ali Jinnah – the crew began fussing about their duties, checking seat belts were fastened and stowing away loose items. Jackson smiled at Katherine and held out his hand in reassurance.

'We're just a bunch of tourists. No one will even care that we are in town and before anyone knows it we'll be on our way home,' he said giving Katherine's hand a squeeze.

'I'm quite sure you're right, but I'm going to be prepared for a reception committee just in case,' said Katherine checking her make-up in a small hand mirror. 'We girls have to look our best, don't we, Nicky?'

'Quite right,' said Nicky who had managed to sleep for most of the flight and looked her stunning self despite the discomfort.

The only problem with Jackson's plans for a low-profile visit was that news of his arrival was even being talked about in the control tower at Jinnah International. The captain of Emirates Flight 609 was proud to have such a famous passenger on board and thought he would share the news with the controller guiding him through Pakistani airspace. That meant the local news photographer who made the airport his personal beat would be waiting in the arrival lounge. But he was not going to be alone.

Awad Fouda and his cameraman arrived early at the airport that morning, which as the flight was due in around 5.00am meant very early. He was confident that he would have the story all to himself. The airport's own cameraman might be bothered to get up for a few snatched shots but apart from that he would have the story to himself. So the swarm of newsmen waiting at the entrance to the arrivals lounge was a shock. And then he saw Asif Khan himself busy talking to the journalists. He just couldn't keep his mouth shut, Fouda thought to himself. He had told every newspaper, radio station and TV channel about Jackson's visit. What else had he told them? Fouda pushed his way through the melee and managed to drag Khan away to a corner.

'I thought we had an agreement? Did you tip everyone off?'

Khan smiled a typical politician's smile, all unction and insincerity. 'Word just got out. You know how it is. This place just leaks.'

'It only leaks if someone makes the holes,' snapped Fouda. 'What else did they just happen to find out? Do they know why he's really coming?'

'No. Not from me.'

'Ok, but with all these people I cannot guarantee to get you in the shot, so you'll have to make sure you are close by him when I ask the question. Is there anyone else coming to meet him – I mean anyone official?'

'No. I certainly wouldn't have told them. I am the official welcoming party,' said Khan puffing himself up in anticipation of his big moment. Fouda just raised his eyebrows in contempt and elbowed his way through to the front of the waiting news crews.

As the Emirates jet gently touched down and taxied slowly towards its allotted parking bay, no one had any idea of the reception committee awaiting them. Richard was looking out of the window, mentally picturing himself filming in the surrounding countryside. Nicky was adding the finishing touches to what looked like perfection in her appearance and Katherine and Jackson were just wrapped in their own thoughts – one hopeful and content that at last he was doing what he knew he was compelled to do and the other wishing she was thousands of miles away walking through the fields around Cedars in the Kent countryside.

One of the cabin crew leant over and asked Jackson if he would mind signing his autograph for her nephew who was a great fan. Jackson happily obliged while hoping that that would be the last 'public' duty he would have to perform. The airhostess hurried back to her post giggling to her colleague and admiring the trophy as the engines finally stopped.

The captain came on the tannoy to welcome everyone to Pakistan and to thank them for flying Emirates Airlines. He hoped the passengers enjoyed their stay and looked forward to seeing them again soon.

'Very soon,' Katherine muttered under her breath.

A blast of hot air rushed through the cabin as the door at the front of the aircraft was opened. Despite the early hour, the temperature outside was in the low eighties and the air conditioning in the plane was no match. The Pakistani couple were already at the door, waiting impatiently to be allowed off as Jackson and his friends were still gathering themselves together.

'What was the rush'? Jackson thought. 'They would still have to wait for the customs clearance'. These things always took time.

The usual group of airport officials in their fluorescent jackets were waiting at the entrance to the walkway leading on to passport control. Maybe one or two more than was strictly necessary, Jackson thought, but he kept his head down which meant he didn't see the grainy photograph of him on one of the clipboards. Needless to say he didn't understand the language being spoken on the radio: 'Yes, he's coming now.'

Passport and customs clearance were surprisingly swift and just before they walked out into the main arrivals area of the terminal, two men hurried up to him. They seemed flustered, almost anxious.

'Welcome to Pakistan, Mr Clarke. I'm David Benson from the British High Commission and this is my colleague, Victor Jones.'

'How do you do? I wasn't expecting a reception committee. This is a private visit. I'm sorry you had to get out of bed so early to come and meet us.'

Jackson introduced Katherine, Richard and Nicky. There was lots of polite handshaking and typical English courtesies, with inquiries about the flight and the hardship of such a long journey. What was perfectly obvious was the diplomats seemed to know them all at least by name and Jackson was quite certain they were all listed on some document that the man called Victor Jones was carrying in his briefcase.

'We're just here to ensure your safe arrival and we've got a car waiting to take you to your hotel. Perhaps on the way we can give you a little briefing about Pakistan from a diplomatic perspective. We understand Mr West, that you have some meetings to discuss the possibility of making a documentary.'

'You're well informed,' said Richard slightly taken aback that the Foreign Office should be taking such an interest in his documentary.

'Well, if there is anything we can do to assist. Or any guidance please don't hesitate to call me during your stay. Mr Jones here will give you our contact details. There's just one other thing.'

'I don't think I like the sound of that,' said Jackson.

'It's nothing really and I'm quite certain you have encountered this sort of thing before.'

'I think you better tell us,' said Jackson, sensing Benson's hesitation to break what might be bad news. There was just so much courtesy and politeness one could take at this hour of the morning, particularly after no sleep.

'Yes, of course. Well it seems that word of your arrival has slipped out and there are some press people waiting.'

'Well nothing quite like a dawn news conference to get the mind working. I wonder how they got to know?'

'Don't worry, sir, we'll get you through them as quickly as possible. No need for any press conference. I did notice that there was one of the local politicians here too. It might be polite just to shake his hand.'

'In that case we better get it over with.'

The tinted glass doors at the end of the customs hall leading into the arrival lounge slid back and the flash-guns opened fire. The noise was deafening. Katherine slipped her arm into Jackson's. He touched her hand for comfort.

'Just smile, they only want a few pictures.'

Meanwhile Richard and Nicky moved to one side leaving their friends in the limelight.

'I hope you're pleased with your handiwork,' Nicky snapped accusingly.

'They've gone a bit over the top. It will soon pass.'

'Let's hope so – for your sake Richard. Poor Katherine, she looks terrified.'

By now the crowd of journalists, camera crews and photographers had surrounded them; everyone shouting questions urging Jackson to turn their way. Some were even calling in a language Jackson didn't understand but it didn't seem to matter. He couldn't hear the English either. It was time to take charge.

'Gentlemen, one at a time please,' shouted Jackson, just as a smartly dressed man stepped up to him and held out his hand. The combination seemed to work and the shouting subsided.

'Jackson Clarke, welcome to Karachi. My name is Asif Khan from the Ministry of Information. As you can see you are a very popular figure over here too.'

'I'm delighted to meet you, Mr Khan. This is all most unexpected. I'm just here on a private visit.'

'Well, it's not every day such a famous international film star comes to Pakistan, so on behalf of the government we wanted to give you a warm welcome.' Khan turned to deliver a beaming smile to the cameras as he shook Jackson's hand vigorously. The fact that he was not representing the government or was there in any capacity other than to promote Asif Khan was of no consequence. His name and face would be in all the papers and on all the news channels. It also helped that it was he who had tipped off every journalist in town about Jackson's arrival.

'You've certainly given me that,' said Jackson managing to offer a smile to the cameras looking left and right.

With his height, he was able to see over the heads of the news crews and saw the two men from the High Commission looking on anxiously. They were talking to another man who – judging by his crew cut and extravagantly coloured shirt – Jackson took to be an American. He obviously wasn't a tourist, which meant he was some sort of US official. What on earth could they be interested in? But he didn't have time to think about his answer; a slick looking TV reporter was standing right in front of him.

'Mr Jackson, I am Awad Fouda from Channel Five News,' the young reporter said, quickly looking behind to be sure his cameraman was filming. 'It's a pleasure for everyone to have you here. What are your first impressions?'

'Terribly hot!' Jackson replied cautiously.

Fouda laughed but no one picked up the slight nervous tremor.

'Mr Jackson you're a long way from the bright lights of Hollywood: would you like to tell the viewers what has brought you here?'

He was a sharp young man with straight quick questions. Jackson decided he would just play it calmly and he'd soon be away from the press.

'As some of you may know I'm thinking of making a film over here and I always strive for authenticity. I had some free time, so my friends and I thought we would come over and visit and get to know the people and the country a little better.'

'Pakistan has been getting a bad press internationally. What are your thoughts about that?' Fouda probed a little more closely.

'Whoa there! I'm not a politician – I just make movies. But since you ask, I hope that this movie – if it ever gets made – will go some way to showing audiences around the world what Pakistani people are really like.'

'What experiences do you hope to get during such a brief visit staying in a luxury hotel?'

Jackson chose to ignore the barbed side of the question: 'I am here to get a closer contact and to talk to anyone I can. It is not always easy to move around as one might wish and, as you rightly point out, Pakistan is not getting many high profile visitors because it is perceived as, how can I put it? A troubled country.'

'Brilliant,' thought Jackson: he hadn't been in the country five minutes and already he was having a political row on national TV.

'Let's be frank, Mr Clarke – most people think Pakistan is a hotbed of terrorists and are worried about extreme religious fanatics. Is that your view?'

'Those are your words not mine,' Jackson retorted, a little too sharply for his liking.

'And if you were to meet such people what would your message to them be.'

'Awareness of others, peace and tolerance,' replied Jackson briefly. 'Now if there are no more questions...'

'Just one more, if I may,' Fouda interrupted, blocking Jackson's path as he tried to move away. 'Is it true that you are thinking of becoming a Muslim?'

There was uproar. The other journalists did not know whether to film Fouda or Jackson. Police with wooden batons who had been idling against the wall watching the impromptu press conference with subdued interest were suddenly galvanised into action, taken by surprise by the sudden outburst of shouting and pushing. Benson and Jones from the British High Commission were unexpectedly agile as they pushed their way through to Jackson. They hadn't heard the question but the uproar was not a typical news conference and it was clearly getting out of control. The unnamed American moved in, hurling cameramen aside like toys. Katherine was panicking and claustrophobic as the bodies pressed in around her. She clung on to Jackson as though her life depended on it.

'Are you planning to make some announcement about your conversion while you're here?' Fouda shouted above the clamour.

Jackson stared at him but made no answer. He felt as though he had been ambushed – set up – and he was worried that he was not handling it well. He was anxious not to offend his host country but also worried about his friends. Wrapping his arm round Katherine's shoulder he used his superior height and strength to push his way towards the exit of the terminal building.

It had not gone as Asif Khan had hoped either – his big moment disintegrated into chaos. His tie was crooked and his hair, normally scrupulously groomed, was dishevelled. In vain he tried to establish himself as the voice of calm.

'I think we should allow Mr Jackson to leave now and we are all very pleased to hear that he has come to Pakistan to visit and perhaps even find a new faith.'

But no one was listening to his words, which he had carefully rehearsed a thousand times in front of the mirror. He was nearly knocked over by the mob of journalists racing after Jackson, who was now surrounded by police as he was escorted towards a waiting mini-bus.

Fouda held back, allowing his cameraman to snatch some more pictures outside the terminal that would make up the final sequence for what would undoubtedly be his next lead story. It had gone better than he had hoped. He had obviously touched a nerve with Jackson – at least that was how he would play it in his report entitled *Superstar wants to become a Muslim*. The fact that Jackson hadn't said anything one way or another was irrelevant. Not only did he have a scoop, but also he himself was an integral part of the story all the other news programmes would run. Perhaps it had not been such a bad idea of Asif Khan to alert the rest of the media.

No one said a word until the mini-bus was clear of the airport.

'What was that all about?' Jackson asked to no one in particular.

'It seems you were set up, I'm afraid, sir,' said Benson, who was also trying to decide how he would be able to downplay the whole incident. He too could see the headlines and he didn't care for them. 'Do you mind my asking, sir, is there anything in what that reporter was saying?'

'I don't think that is any of your business and nor is it his.'

'If we were in the UK I would agree. Unfortunately in this part of the world they take their religion very seriously and if I were a betting man, I would say someone has decided that they are going to make your interest in Islam – however true or false – an issue. So while you're a British citizen – and a high profile one – and you're in this country, it makes it my business. Sir.'

The 'sir' was added much as a British policeman has to address a drunken thug as 'sir'. The respect was just the right side of politeness with heavy overtones of irritation. Some so-called superstar had strolled into the most volatile part of the world – Benson's world as he saw it – and now there was a half-brain suggestion that he was thinking of taking up the local religion, much as he might consider taking up golf.

'You're right, I'm sorry. Just a bit tired and I wasn't prepared for that reception committee. Be sure to thank your colleague and that American. I take he was American. I suppose he was an official and not a tourist? It was good of him to wade in to help back there.'

'CIA actually.'

'What was that?'

Benson turned round in his seat and looked straight at Jackson. 'I said he was CIA.'

'What has any of this got to do with the CIA?' asked Jackson, now completely dumbfounded.

'For some reason, your visit was so well telegraphed and has caused so much consternation that they even managed to get Frank Miles, the Karachi bureau chief, out of his bed to come and make sure everything was in order. And to be frank, sir, I don't think everything is in order. Do you?'

It wasn't a question that either man thought required a reply and the rest of the journey into the centre of Karachi was completed in silence. Sitting in the seats immediately behind Jackson and Katherine were Nicky and Richard. They didn't bother talking either because there was no need. Nicky realised that Richard must have done much more than simply tip off the local press about the trip.

He must have also discussed Jackson's interest in Islam. Presumably the reporter who had asked the direct question at the airport was the one Richard had spoken to from London. What had just been a way of getting a visa to visit was now turning into an international incident. What on earth was the CIA doing at the airport?

As for Richard he thought the best option was simply to stare out of the window and say nothing. He had abused Jackson's trust and now the whole object of the visit as far as he was concerned could have been jeopardised. The press would be crawling all over the hotel. On the other hand, he smiled to himself, it was Jackson they were interested in not him. After a couple of days he would be able to slip out of the hotel and follow up on his meeting. One thing though, as soon as he had a moment alone he would call that Awad Fouda and give him an earful for the mayhem at the airport. Yes, perhaps everything was going to work out for the best after all.

Khalid Jalil also thought he saw a lucrative opportunity as he watched the Jackson convoy of mini-bus and black Mercedes with British diplomatic plates speed away from the airport. Jackson was now certain to be a valuable commodity. He needed to get close to him and see what the screen hero could do for him, Khalid Jalil.

# CHAPTER THIRTEEN

The news alert Rory McLeod had set up on his Blackberry beeped insistently.

*'Jackson Clarke to become a Muslim – report.'*

'Dear God,' Rory muttered under his breath as he read the full account on the various news outlets and carefully compared each version. Cutting away all the hyperbole it was plain that Jackson had never actually said that he wanted to become a Muslim: it was just the interpretation the journalists were putting on it, so that at least was a plus – albeit a very flimsy one.

What was more worrying was that the journalist had even asked the question in the first place. How could he possibly have known unless someone had tipped him off? And that someone had to be very close to Jackson. Rory McLeod's suspicions immediately fell on Richard West. Katherine could be ruled out as she had no possible interest in telling anyone and in any case she would not have had the contact in Pakistan. So it had to be a journalist and that meant Richard. There obviously had to be something in it for him. It wouldn't have been money so presumably someone would have pulled a few strings and managed to get his visa pushed through the bureaucracy after all the months of stonewalling. That explained how they had all got themselves into this situation – the question now was how to extricate themselves? And in particular how to extricate Jackson.

Rory didn't claim to be an expert on show business but he could see no upside for Jackson 'coming out' and declaring himself to be a supporter of Islam. Whether anyone liked it or not, Muslims everywhere were being tarred with the same brush thanks to the activities of a lunatic minority. There was no point in saying that the teachings of the faith condemned murder or the mistreatment of innocent people, women and children. If one took a poll in New York or London Rory suspected that the vast majority would heap the blame for the world's terrorist ills on Islam.

Now here was Jackson Clarke declaring himself a believer. It would certainly get publicity for the film he was hoping to make but he doubted whether even Jackson's global fan club would be rushing to buy tickets. And it was not only the impact on box office that troubled Rory.

'Well, you've certainly made a big impact on local TV,' said Katherine as she flicked through the channels in their hotel room. 'I can't understand a word they're saying but your face is all over it.'

'This wasn't exactly what I planned. I'm sorry about what happened at the airport. Somebody blabbed and I have got a pretty good idea who it was.'

'Richard?'

'Who else? Who else would benefit? But I don't blame him. He was just using a bit of leverage as the Americans would say. He obviously thought by tipping someone off it might help his chances for his visa and his documentary,' said Jackson quietly.

'You're staying remarkably calm about the whole thing. Why not go next door and shout at him. That's what I would do.'

Jackson stared out of the window watching the chaotic traffic nine storeys below wind its way through the streets.

'What would be the point? I think I will just let him stew for a while. What's done is done anyhow and we must use the time we have here constructively.'

'You don't think Andy Lucas is going to want you in his movie now do you?' Katherine was not so ready to take Jackson's laid-back approach. '9/11 is still a little raw for most Americans. I don't think they're going to be too happy that the star of the film has gone over to the other side, as it were.'

'No one's gone over to any side. I'm just trying to understand. You must realise that?'

Katherine threw the TV remote onto the bed and came over to

wrap her arms round Jackson's waist. Looking up into his eyes, she said: 'It's not what I realise that matters. For some reason people are taking too much interest in our little visit. We, you must be careful.'

'I'll be careful don't worry so much. Now, tired as I am, I fancy some lunch. I don't really want to risk going down to the lobby in case there are photographers hanging around. Let's get something in our room.'

'Good idea,' said Katherine. 'I'm starving. Nothing like a good tussle with the media to work up an appetite.'

'That's the attitude. Now do you mind turning to a channel which doesn't mention me?'

Just as Jackson was about to dial room service the phone rang.

'Mr Clarke, it's the switchboard here. Sorry to disturb you. I have a Mr McLeod calling from London. Shall I put him through?'

'Yes, please do.'

'Oh, Mr Clarke, I should just advise you that there are some photographers outside should you be thinking of going out this afternoon.'

'Really? No in fact I was just about to order something on room service. Could you send up some sandwiches and coffee?'

'Very good, sir, I shall put the call through now.'

'Photographers outside,' Jackson whispered to Katherine covering the phone with his hand. She raised her eyebrows as though to say I told you so. There was a brief click on the line and then Jackson could hear Rory McLeod giving orders to someone in his office in London.

'Hello Rory is that you?'

'Jackson, I was just calling to make sure you had arrived safely at your hotel. I notice that you made CNN already. Nice discreet arrival.'

'Well, I am supposed to be a superstar, you know. I would hate to think people are ignoring me. Thanks for organising transport for us by the way. I assume that was your doing?'

'I didn't want you getting lost,' said Rory. Then after a pause: 'Interesting line of questioning, I thought.'

Both men were aware that the call was probably being listened to by others, both in the hotel and probably further afield.

'What would journalists do without their rumours? I'm just hoping they will leave us alone long enough to have a look round town, although I gather one or two are still hanging around outside.'

'Well, try and keep out of the headlines for the rest of your stay. And if there's anything else, call me. Now put Katherine on the line if she's there, I want to make sure she has you under control.'

Jackson laughed and held out the receiver to Katherine: 'Rory McLeod wants to make sure I'm behaving.'

'Rory, hi. Have you ever been to this town? It's very exciting.' Katherine was also well aware that there would almost certainly be other people listening on the line.

'Too hot for my delicate skin, I'm afraid. But I think you've met a couple of my chums, so be sure to call them or me if you're – how shall I put it? – unsure of anything.'

'We're being well looked after, so don't worry. Even your Uncle Sam came to meet us,' said Katherine mischievously.

'I'm glad the whole family were there in force. It was the least we could do. Have a good stay. I can't wait to hear all about it.'

'Thanks Rory. And thanks for the call, it was much appreciated. Bye.'

So that was clear then. Katherine was terrified and the sooner she got home the better. Rory was pleased the CIA had turned out – he thought the person in the flowery red shirt was one of the brothers when he saw the pictures on TV. Most viewers would have missed him but Rory always paid close attention to the people on the fringes or in the background of photos. They were the ones always slightly out of focus but often the key figures in the game. He would call Friedland in Washington and thank him – that would have been on his advice directly or indirectly.

The real issue though was the content of the impromptu news conference at the airport. A reporter doesn't just blurt out a question like that without some prior information and of course Richard West was the source – as McLeod recalled from the GCHQ transcript.

The difficulty in these situations was to predict what the enemy – and anyone other than your friend in that part of the world should always be regarded as the enemy – now planned to do. This was an orchestrated event. It might just have been a journalist trying to make a name for himself, but in that region there were usually several strands to the story. Rory McLeod hoped his good friend would have enough sense to cut short his already short visit in the light of all the press interest and return home, but he was all too well aware that Jackson had a mind of his own and he wasn't easily ruffled by an awkward news conference.

The presence of the junior official from the Ministry of Information was a puzzle, but he had not been a significant player. There were no sound bites from him, at least none was used in any of the clips Rory had seen which suggested it was not a government-sponsored event. The official must have been trying to muscle in on the story and get some press exposure with the star. It hadn't worked, so he could be discounted. In fact the more he analysed the situation, the less immediate danger Rory saw, apart from some explaining Jackson might have to do with the producers of the film when he got home. He decided he would get his PA – Lizzie – to monitor every mention of Jackson and his interest in Islam. He hoped that the whole story would just fade away as another piece of gossip for local consumption, but he had his doubts.

Khalid Jalil sauntered casually into the lobby of the Sheraton Hotel dressed for the cosmopolitan clientele the management encouraged. He held his mobile close to his ear and chatted as we walked past the receptionists, taking care not to catch their eye. As far as they were concerned he was either a guest or meeting a guest. He was elegantly dressed and looked as though he belonged. There was no one on the other end of the phone. He was talking to himself but it meant no one asked if he needed help, so there were no awkward questions to answer about whom he was meeting or why he was there.

All the time his eyes were scanning the other guests hoping to recognise at least one person from the Jackson party. He had memorised all their faces from the TV coverage, which he had replayed a dozen times. Jackson of course he would know immediately, but he was really hoping to spot the other man whom he now knew from Awad Fouda was called Richard West. They had agreed that there was no point in Fouda trying to get another interview – in any case the hotel had a strict ban on local journalists trying to doorstep guests without their permission. So Khalid would be the one to find out their plans. He would present himself as a young independent businessman with good contacts who knew his way around town. Just the sort of person Richard West would need if he were to make any headway with his documentary. Fouda just wanted to be tipped off about Jackson's plans and any possible meetings he intended to have. Khalid was still not sure what he would get out of the meeting but he was playing it by ear. On this occasion the teacher wanted him to make full use of his suave, westernised techniques to get close to anyone in the British party.

Unfortunately all the restaurant and lounges were empty, so Khalid headed for the poolside, slipping off his jacket to look more casual. At one end of the pool, sitting under a parasol and sheltering in its shade from the midday heat was Richard West – alone, nursing what looked to Khalid like a Bloody Mary.

Richard had failed to calm Nicky down after the fiasco at the airport and decided to console himself with a drink. There was only one other guest busy doing lengths of the pool.

Khalid settled himself into a chair two tables away from Richard and ordered an iced fruit juice from the waiter. He let out a loud sigh and threw his head back.

'Hot enough for you?' said Richard amused to see that even the locals found the weather unbearable.

'It's always bad this time of year. How about you? Are you on holiday?' asked Khalid casually stretching out his legs and leaning back his arms behind his head.

'Sort of,' said Richard non-committedly. 'Only a short visit.'

'You should come back in our spring and get out of the town a bit. The countryside is beautiful, but sadly most tourists just fly in and fly out.' Khalid took the drink from the waiter and asked Richard: 'Can I get you a refill? After all you're a guest in my country.'

'Thanks a lot. I would love one. Same again please,' said Richard, handing his glass to the waiter.

'May I join you?' asked Khalid. 'My guest has just cancelled our meeting as he has been held up in town.'

'Please do,' said Richard. 'My name's Richard West.'

Khalid walked over and shook hands. 'Khalid. How do you do? So what brings you to Pakistan, Richard? May I call you "Richard"?'

'Of course. I make documentaries. This is really a preliminary visit to see what chance I have of travelling around a bit. You know; seeing more of the country than just the big cities, exactly as you suggest. Trouble is there are some security issues in this part of the world.'

'Yes, I'm afraid there are. We live in troubled times. But that's fascinating. What sort of documentaries? Are they wildlife?'

Richard laughed. 'In a manner of speaking. I make news documentaries – the wildest sort of wildlife and for some time now I have been trying to get access to some of the tribal areas. I'm not taking sides, I just don't think the world is getting a very balanced coverage.'

Khalid raised his eyebrows in apparent surprise: 'That sounds very dangerous work. Who are you talking to over here? I assume you have some local contacts – they would be essential.'

Richard took a long drink from his ice-cool Bloody Mary and drew a finger down the chilled glass.

'To be frank, I'm rather busking it. I have an official meeting in the next day or so, just to outline my plans, but I don't expect too much to come from that. If you happen to know someone I would be very grateful. To be honest, the way this trip is shaping up I think I might be wasting my time. We had a real bust up at the airport.'

Richard looked over to Khalid taking in the well-cut trousers and jacket, his highly polished shoes and expensive watch. He didn't think his new friend would be much use doing anything outside the confines of a five star hotel.

'What happened? Did you have trouble with customs or something?'

'No, the local bloody press. I'm over here with a guy called Jackson Clarke. You may have heard of him. Film star.'

Khalid sat up pretending to be surprised: 'You don't mean the Jackson Clarke? Wow, is he here too?'

'Yes, staying in this hotel up there on the ninth floor.' Richard waved an arm vaguely in the direction of the floor he meant. 'Unfortunately, there was quite a reception committee waiting for us when we arrived. Lot of pushing and shoving. I think he's keeping his head down at the moment.'

'That's incredible. Jackson Clarke here.' Khalid thought for a moment. 'Look it's not really my territory, but I do know someone who's always telling me how well connected he is with these sort of people. Why don't we call his bluff?' said Khalid, cleverly making himself part of West's team by suggesting they were in on the game together. 'What's your room number? I'll see if I can get hold of him and call you back tonight. I can't promise anything.'

'That would be fantastic. Frankly I'm happy to take whatever help I can get. Tell you what – if you have some good news why don't you come round tonight and I'll introduce you to Jackson. He wants to meet some real locals himself. He's got a new movie he's about to start shooting and he likes to make his characters as authentic as possible.'

'I'd be thrilled to meet him. Should I dress up as a local?' They laughed and both silently thought that things could not have worked out better.

# CHAPTER FOURTEEN

Langley decided that the incident at Karachi Airport as reported by their bureau chief, Frank Miles, was purely a British matter. It was noted but frankly there were bigger issues for the Agency to worry about. A US drone had taken out another Taliban leader on the Pakistan-Afghanistan border while he was attending a family wedding. The collateral damage of women and children had been high, but as far as Washington was concerned, it was yet another case of ends justifying the means.

Needless to say on the ground they were claiming that the leader who had been targeted was nowhere near the scene. It was impossible to prove one way or another. Local law enforcement did not exist and was hardly likely to be able to get DNA evidence even it did. The territory was strictly off-limits to coalition forces. Their only contact with the area was to strike silently by drone guided from a computer control centre thousands of miles away in the Creech US Air Force base in the Nevada Desert outside Las Vegas.

Later there were counter stories to say that not only had the leader been killed, but there was now feuding to among the tribal people to decide who should be their next leader. Like so much in the territory, reliable intelligence was in short supply, which meant worries about whether or not a 'limey' film star was going to upset the locals by possibly adopting the Islamic faith did not even register on the CIA's collective radar.

Miles said he was happy to offer back-up support if there were any real difficulties, but David Benson agreed that it might all soon blow over, and in any case it really was a problem for the British High Commission. God preserve us from thespians with a conscience, Benson said to himself.

'Victor, get over to the Sheraton would you and pay Her Majesty's kind regards to our important guest. See if he can be persuaded to keep his mouth shut for the rest of his stay.'

'Yes, sir,' said Jones, relishing the chance to meet the star properly and perhaps talk about life in Hollywood. Victor Jones – while being a talented operator, hence his appointment to a posting as sensitive as Pakistan – was nonetheless a little star-struck. He always made a point of going to see Jackson Clarke's films as soon as they were released. They bore no relation to the mundane duties of everyday life for real operatives in the Office but the movies were thrill-a-minute stuff and Victor Jones – a 3rd ranking officer in the High Commission, Karachi – enjoyed them.

Abdul Bakri was still not sure what opportunity had landed on his plate, but he was clear that the arrival of Jackson Clarke and the uproar that had followed the impromptu news conference at the airport was something he should exploit. Khalid Jalil had reported in detail what had happened out of sight of the cameras – the obvious involvement of the US embassy as well as the British diplomats.

Contrary to David Benson's wishes, the story had not died away and not only was it the top news story throughout Pakistan, but it was also leading many of the British tabloids. Jackson Clarke had crossed some invisible line, which the editors assumed was unacceptable to their readers. And as usual they had tapped into that vein of xenophobia that could always be relied up to sell newspapers. The essentially conservative-minded British public did not want their heroes becoming Muslims. It wasn't that they were anti-Muslim; it was just that it was not a very British thing to do. There was no point arguing that many thousands of UK-born citizens were Muslim and regarded themselves as British first and perhaps Indian or Pakistani second. The commentators fanned the flames of public opinion and the issue was even raised in the House of Commons. The story was going to run and run.

The teacher decided to send back up for Khalid, partly because he thought his normally reliable lieutenant would need help in a plan as yet un-formed and partly because he didn't entirely trust Khalid to act purely in the best interests of the madrassa and its teaching. He knew Khalid was an opportunist and the Jackson Clarke visit might be too tempting.

As for Bakri himself he chose to keep his options to himself for now at least. He would not be in control of all the circumstances, so it would require quick reactions depending on how the players in his game reacted. For that matter, Khalid Jalil did not trust Dr Mitra and Dr Mitra loathed the pseudo-western posturing of Jalil. It was a potent combination. Bakri understood his psychology and now planned to create circumstances where they would have to work together. However events unfolded, the teacher became increasingly convinced that Jackson Clarke had a new starring role to play.

Bakri punched in some numbers on his mobile: 'Go to the meeting now. Remember, whatever you feel about this man is irrelevant. You must now do your duty. You know what to do. This is what you have worked for all these years.'

The hotel staff were preparing the reception areas and restaurants for the first early diners. The ornate lounges with marble floors and five star furnishings were beginning to fill with groups of people – mainly men – sitting around talking over endless cups of tea and coffee. A sprinkling of Europeans were enjoying the foreigners' dispensation of alcohol. Victor Jones, 3rd ranking diplomat at the British High Commission, felt slightly more important on these occasions visiting foreign visitors in their upmarket hotels, because it put him in the driving seat as he was the local expert; he was the one who could give even the most important VIPs the low down on the country. This visit would be even better because he, and he alone, was meeting Jackson Clarke on behalf of Her Majesty.

The only problem was Jackson Clarke had told the reception desk that on no account should he be disturbed until at least 7pm, which meant Victor Jones would have to cool his polished diplomatic heels for another hour. It also meant that he would have to refrain from having a beer and settled instead for a local coffee, which he had come to appreciate over his three-year posting. He would have preferred something stronger. He settled himself in a corner of one of the lounges with a good view of the reception area and flicked through an old copy of *Newsweek* magazine, taking none of it in.

Just as he was beginning to wonder how much more caffeine he could stomach, he heard the 'ping pong' tone signalling a lift arriving in the lobby, and glanced up to see Richard West emerging alone.

'At last,' thought Jones, deciding that he would give the message from his boss to West and then head home to his apartment – unless of course his screen idol appeared, in which case he had all the time in the world. He folded the magazine neatly, sipped his final mouthful of coffee and called for the bill. He wanted to catch West before he disappeared into the night. He seemed to be expecting company, as he kept checking his watch and looking towards the main door.

Jones paid for his three coffees and was about to hurry over to pass on Her Majesty's greetings courtesy of his boss, when West gave a beaming smile and walked over to greet an elegantly dressed Pakistani. Much as Jones was ready to go home, he thought he would just watch and wait for a moment and sat back down again. Discreetly he snatched a shot of the young man with his mobile and sent it back to the office for identification.

The face didn't register on any database, which made the meeting all the more intriguing. As far as Jones was aware, West knew nobody in Karachi. He had an appointment with an official in a local branch office of the Ministry of Information, but the man now chatting animatedly to West was a private citizen and did not show up on any British records.

Khalid Jalil had always been careful to keep off any register. He was a freelance in all senses of the word; he worked for himself and took payment from the highest bidder. He had never even been questioned by a police officer. Khalid Jalil – the name on all his paperwork, passport and identification papers – was to all intents and purposes, invisible. To achieve that special status he had changed his name several times, bribing key officials along the way and now all those officials had moved on to other departments. No one cared about Khalid Jalil officially, and that was exactly how he liked to keep it.

'So you think this friend of yours will be able to introduce me to some of the tribal leaders?' Richard West was saying.

'Absolutely. But you can ask him yourself when he comes tonight. He keeps late hours, but he should not be much longer. By the way – did you manage to speak to Jackson Clarke? I would be honoured to meet him,' Khalid Jalil asked, maintaining the pretence of an admiring fan.

'Yes, he'll be down shortly. But tell me more about this contact of yours. What does he do?'

'Normally he lives in Islamabad, but fortunately he happens to be in Karachi at the moment. He's a doctor, which means he meets all sorts of people. Ah, there he is.' Khalid jumped up and signalled across the lounge.

For Dr Tariq Mitra – staunch Muslim and staunch opponent of all things western – the Sheraton Hotel was an abomination. Everything about its lavish surroundings appalled him and he could scarcely contain his disgust when he heard a young woman in a group of Europeans laughing out loud. Where was her modesty? Where was her shame? Then he saw Khalid Jalil, dressed in modern Western clothes waving to him and he had to force himself to smile.

'Could the man not dress as a Pakistani?' he thought to himself.

'Ah, my friend, *As-Salaam-Alaikum*. It is good to see you again after so long,' said Dr Mitra deliberately mixing his English with the traditional greeting of Muslims the world over.

Richard West stood up and like all people was making instant judgements about the man, based purely on his appearance. He was dressed in traditional Pakistani style of *salwar kameez*; he wore glasses and was clean-shaven apart from a thin moustache. He looked serious and alert. Every inch the medical man. West immediately felt certain he could be trusted.

'*Wa 'Alaikum As-Salaam*, brother,' Khalid replied, amused at

140

Mitra's pretence that they had not met for some time. He had clearly been briefed by the teacher to be on his best behaviour. 'I would like to introduce Mr Richard West who is visiting us from England. And this is Dr Mitra.'

'Welcome to Pakistan, Mr West. Have you been here before?' Mitra asked politely.

'No, this is my first time but I have been meaning to come here for a while.'

'I gather you are a journalist working in television. Am I right?'

Mitra waved away an attentive waiter who asked if he required anything. This was not a social gathering as far as Mitra was concerned. He would do what he had to do to win West's confidence, but he refused to put money into the coffers of a decadent hotel.

'Yes, I make news documentaries. I'm hoping to be able to film something of the real life of Pakistan, not just the main cities. It's a country which has captured the world's attention over recent times.'

'Indeed it has, Mr West, but sadly it is a country which is misunderstood.'

'That is precisely why I want to make a documentary. Khalid here thought you might be able to point me in the right direction; maybe even introduce me to some people I could film.' He looked across at Khalid, inviting some support.

'Dr Mitra knows the country well and I'm sure if anyone can help you he can,' said Khalid reassuringly.

'Have you brought a big team with you, Mr West? I imagine making documentaries is quite difficult.'

'No, in fact I'm officially here on a tourist's visa. I'm travelling with some friends. It's a sort of recce – trying to see who and where and what I can film. I'm expecting to meet some official while I'm here to get a formal permission, but I have to say it is all a bit vague and I'm still waiting when that meeting will happen.'

'Yes, the wheels of bureaucracy can turn very slowly I'm afraid. I believe it is the same in England. I studied there a long time ago.'

'Really?' said Richard who was keen not to be side-tracked down memory lane of a medical student. 'Tell me, do you think I will be able to get out of the city a bit? Perhaps travel to the northern territories?'

'As I'm sure you know, that is very unsafe. To be honest a European would become a very tempting target. There are so many dangerous people in that part of the country that even the authorities are careful where they go. Is that something your travelling companions would like to do?'

Richard laughed out loud. 'Oh, I doubt that. Although my friend Jackson does want to meet some Pakistanis and get to know something of their way of life. He's an actor and might be making a film here.'

'That sounds fascinating,' said Mitra, sitting forward as though he was surprised by the news. 'Would I know his name?'

'Very good', thought Khalid as he watched the Mitra's performance and exchange of words: 'Very polished and convincing'.

The only question was what did Mitra intend to do? Khalid had been told by the teacher to get close to the Westerners, and if possible to find a way of introducing Mitra but there had been no further explanation. No reason had been given and nothing was discussed about what he should do after the introduction had been made.

Khalid was not listening to Richard West's stories about Jackson Clarke, superstar and hero of the movies. He was beginning to feel left out and he started to resent it. But that was only because Khalid had resolved in his own mind that Jackson and his party would somehow be his exit plan from the double-life he had been living. If the teacher no longer trusted him enough to be included in the planning, then so be it. He liked meeting people in smart hotels; he liked dressing in Western clothes – in short he liked the fast life. He had had enough of skulking around in the shadows. He had no qualms about the role he had played, which had led to the deaths of many people. They were expendable – Khalid Jalil was not.

A bellboy from the hotel came over and handed Richard a message. He frowned and said: 'Well I'm afraid any plans we may have to travel outside Karachi will have to be put on hold until the day after tomorrow. I have finally got my meeting with the Ministry of Information at midday tomorrow: too early to go anywhere in the morning and get back in time, and too late to set off in the afternoon. Is there any chance of organising a trip the day after tomorrow?'

They began talking about the various options, when Richard noticed Jackson in the lobby.

'Brilliant. There's Jackson. I'll get him to come over and meet you. At least you can chat about what life is like for Pakistanis today. I don't suppose he'll be interested in going on any trips but I'm sure he would like to meet you.'

What West really meant was: 'if I do you guys a good turn and introduce you to a movie star then the least you can do is fix me up with a day trip away from the city to meet some real people – possibly even some of the movers and shakers in the conflict which had placed Pakistan and Afghanistan at the heart of global terrorism'. He hurried across the vast expanse of the lounge and waved to attract Jackson's attention.

Jackson saw Richard flapping his arms and drawing lots of attention, which was not what Jackson wanted, but he smiled a weary smile and came over.

'Look Jackson, I'm really sorry about that scene at the airport,' said West rapidly. 'I suppose you guessed that I tipped off that idiot reporter. Thing was, he managed to swing it for my visa and –'

Jackson put up his hand and said: 'Richard, forget it. What's done is done. They would probably have found out anyhow that I was in town.' Jackson paused for a moment then added: 'Didn't think you really had to mention the Islam stuff though. That really is a private matter – or at least it was. Now it seems to be an international issue.'

'I know, I'm sorry. I just had to get the guy's attention.'

'Ok forget it. Now who are those unsavoury looking fellows you're talking to over there? You seem to be awfully pally.'

'Stroke of luck really. I met one of them when I was having a drink by the pool earlier trying to console myself about the possibility that you would never talk to me again. The other guy is his friend.

I thought you might like to meet them. Genuine Pakistani types. One fancies himself as a European but the other fellow is the real McCoy. Dresses like a native. He's a doctor by the way.'

'Better get over and meet them in case they think we're being rude and just standing here talking about them.'

Watching the gathering from the corner of the lounge, Victor Jones was getting concerned. Jackson Clarke had arrived which was good news, but the information he had received back about the second Pakistani he had photographed on his mobile was confusing and the Foreign Office did not like to be confused.

Jackson Clarke was deep in conversation with one Dr Mitra. He was a registered doctor at a hospital in Islamabad, so was a long way from his home base and he just happened to be talking to the one man making all the news. Jones did not like coincidences and he could also see his opportunity of having a friendly chat with his screen hero evaporating.

Across the room, at Jackson's table the conversation was relaxed enough and Jones needn't have worried. They were talking about past films and Hollywood gossip, which was a strain for Dr Mitra, although he didn't show it.

'Jackson, I was talking to Khalid and the good doctor here about trying to get out of the city and meet some of the local people. I can't go tomorrow, as that meeting I've been waiting for has been scheduled for midday tomorrow. I don't know if you would like to do a bit of sightseeing with them. It's always better to have a local guide. What do you think?'

'Well, I don't know. I don't think I can impose on them. I'm sure Dr Mitra here has more pressing duties.'

'In fact I'm having a short break myself from my hospital in Islamabad. I am free in the morning tomorrow. We wouldn't be able to go very far. Perhaps if we made an early start. What do you think, Khalid?'

'I think that would be a good idea. It would be better to start before the temperature gets too hot. We could aim to get you back to the hotel by about midday.'

'Great,' said West. 'You go off and see what you can learn about the place. I'll be over meeting these officials by the time you get back, so can we get together a bit later. I don't want Jackson to have all the fun.'

Dr Mitra stood up and said: 'Very good. I will be here about 6.30 am, if that is not too early, Mr Jackson? Perhaps it would be an idea if you asked the hotel to make up a small packed meal for you. You'll need some bottled water.'

'That's very thoughtful. An excellent idea. I'll ask the concierge to organise that. Well, until 6.30 tomorrow then.'

Jones watched in dismay as the meeting broke up. He thought about going over to snatch a quick word with Jackson, but something made him think better of it. He called the office and found David Benson still at his desk.

'Any idea what they were discussing?'

'No sir, but I got the impression they were arranging something. They were all looking at their watches while they were talking and Clarke has gone back up to his room. West is eating in the restaurant.'

'My guess is they have set up another meeting,' said Benson. 'I think the best thing is to go home now but be back at the hotel first thing tomorrow and one way or another get a word with Clarke. I don't think there is anything more we can do tonight. We might have some more background on this doctor in the morning.'

'Very good, sir,' said Jones, somewhat deflated by the way the evening had turned out, but his professional sense told him there was something else at stake. He would be back at the hotel the next day and insist on a meeting with his hero.

# CHAPTER FIFTEEN

Katherine barely heard Jackson whisper that he would see her for lunch and kissed her softly on the cheek. Picking up his camera and, out of habit, slipping his passport into his hip pocket, Jackson quietly clicked the door shut and made his way down to the lobby.

Only one or two cleaners were about at that hour of the morning, plumping up cushions and polishing already highly polished surfaces and mirrors to ensure everything was exactly as their guests would expect.

Jackson made his way over to the concierge and was immediately handed a hamper.

'Your tiffin box, Mr Clarke. Have a good day. Where are you going today?' the night duty officer inquired politely.

'Frankly, I have no idea but this should keep me going. Thank you very much. By the way has anyone come for me?' Jackson asked.

'No, I don't think so. Can I get you a coffee or tea while you're waiting?'

'Still a little early for me ... Ah, there he is.' At that moment Khalid Jalil walked through the glass doors of hotel.

'Good morning, Mr Clarke. I see they've provided you with something to eat,' said Khalid admiring the tiffin box in Jackson's hand.

'Yes, I think they must believe I am going to be away for days.'

A doorman saluted them as the two men made their way outside into the already draining heat of a Karachi day. Waiting to greet them was Dr Mitra.

'I'm afraid it is going to be another hot day,' said Mitra, holding open the door to the white 4x4 Suzuki.

Katherine, Nicky and Richard were having breakfast when Victor Jones came into the dining room. He was looking anxious as he made his way straight over to their table.

'Good morning. Sorry to interrupt. My name is Victor Jones from the British High Commission – I was at the airport to meet you.'

'Good morning, Mr Jones,' replied Katherine. 'Yes, we remember you and thank you very much for your assistance. Have you had some breakfast?'

Katherine had calmed down after the drama of the past 48 hours and was looking forward to an easy day by the pool. She wasn't interested in sightseeing, although she and Nicky had decided they might venture out to do some shopping later in the day when it was a little cooler.

'Yes, thank you very much. I have had breakfast. Er, I wonder if Mr Clarke is coming down to join you?'

'Sorry, you've missed him,' said Richard. 'He's already gone out. He went early trying to beat the heat. Should be back for lunch though. Anything we can do?'

'Oh dear, I was hoping to have a word with him before he left. Any idea where he is going? Not alone I hope?'

'Couldn't say where he's going but he's with a couple of people we met. One's a doctor, so he should be in good hands,' said Richard, cheerily tucking into a piece of toast.

Katherine caught Jones's slight frown that brushed across his brow before vanishing again in a diplomat's practised insouciance.

'Is there a problem, Mr Jones? You look a little concerned,' she asked.

'No, I'm quite sure everything is in order. I would just have liked to have spoken to him first. Pakistan can be a difficult place.'

'You mean dangerous, Mr Jones. What did you want to talk to him about?' persisted Katherine.

'How well do you – does he – know this doctor if I might ask?'

Jones looked around the group and his eyes settled on Richard – not exactly accusingly but it was a look that could not be mistaken and the question could not be ducked.

'We were introduced by someone – a businessman I think – I met here in the hotel yesterday. He'd offered to take me actually to meet some people for my documentary, which as you know I am planning to make. Unfortunately I couldn't go as I have a meeting at the Ministry this morning. The doctor – his name is Dr Mitra – came along last night and offered to show Jackson around. You know – it's all part of his getting into character for his film.'

'Yes, Mr West, but do you know where he might be taking Mr Clarke and what do you know about either this Dr Mitra or the man you met in the hotel yesterday? What was his name by the way?' Jones enquired. He was beginning to make Katherine worry again as she looked first at Jones and then accusingly back at Richard West.

West caught her look and flushed, saying: 'I think his name was Khalid something. Yes, Khalid Jalil. Not sure what he does, but he looked like a pretty serious businessman.'

'Look, what's all this about, Mr Jones?' Katherine asked with increasing concern. 'Jackson told me he would be back at lunchtime as I said. I'm sure if you come back then he will be able to explain exactly who this Dr is and the other fellow, Khalid whatever his name is.'

'Yes, I have no doubt. We just want to make sure that he doesn't –'

'Doesn't what, Mr Jones? You're really beginning to worry me now.'

'I'm sorry, Miss Tait. I did not mean to do that. There really is nothing to concern yourself about. I will do as you suggest and return here at midday and perhaps I will be able to have a word with Mr Clarke then. If he returns earlier would you call me? Here's my card. I'm sorry I interrupted your breakfast.'

Victor Jones gave a little bow and walked away. The day had not got off to a good start and now Jackson Clarke had decided to take himself off on a sightseeing tour with two men he barely knew. He dialled the High Commission to report the news.

'I thought we would look at some of the major landmarks of the city and then head out of Karachi a little way to see a more authentic Pakistan, if that would suit you?' Dr Mitra called over his shoulder.

The car windows were open to allow what little air there was to blow through the car. There was no air-conditioning.

'That sounds fine. It really is good of you to take this trouble,' said Jackson, who was sitting in the back next to Khalid.

'Not at all. Khalid there is the local man so he can be our guide. Then we'll drop him off and go out of the city for a short drive.'

This was news to Khalid who caught Dr Mitra's eye in the wide rear-view mirror. But now was not the time to argue and he began his impromptu-guided tour.

'As you know, Karachi is the financial capital and largest city of Pakistan. Islamabad became the capital of Pakistan in 1960. Like New York, Karachi is known as 'the City that Never Sleeps' or 'the City of Lights'. There are around 20 million people living here. We're just coming up to the principal landmark: the Quaid-e-Azam Mausoleum. This is where the founder of Pakistan – Quaid-e-Azam Mohammad Ali Jinnah – is buried. It was built between 1960 and 1970 and stands 43 metres high.'

Khalid continued his fluent commentary as they drove round the city sights, taking in the Aga Khan University, the so-called Tooba mosque the largest single domed mosque in the world, and when in the commercial city-centre they passed the Mereweather Tower on the ll Chundrigar Road. They had only been driving around for about half an hour when Dr Mitra tapped the driver's arm and sig-nalled to him to stop. He turned in his seat and address Jackson.

'Khalid has to leave us here, but we'll be able to catch up with him later when we return to the hotel. We'll continue now out of the city and – how do you say? – get to meet some of the locals.'

Mitra gave a broad grin, pleased with his turn of phrase.

Once again Khalid was surprised, but knew better than to question the decision. He had hardly had a chance to talk to the film star properly so he quickly handed him a personal card.

'Yes, I'm sorry I have to leave you now, but I hope we can talk again later.' Khalid shook hands with Jackson and then with Mitra looking at him closely.

'We'll talk again tonight, brother,' said Mitra, almost pushing him out of the door. 'We must hurry now because it is already getting hot and Mr Clarke wants to see more than just the city sights.'

'Thank you for the tour,' said Jackson. 'Very professional. I look forward to talking again and maybe you can tell me a bit more about the history of this city.'

'It will be my pleasure,' said Khalid through the open window, but already the Suzuki was pulling away. Once again he felt as though he was being kept in the dark. A plan had been worked out and he was not part of it.

Lunch came and went but Jackson had not returned. Katherine checked several times at the desk. There was no message so she assumed his day trip was going well. At least that's what she thought initially. The visit from Victor Jones was beginning to prey on her mind. He had a point: Jackson had arrived in town, had a fairly hostile reception at the airport and had now gone walkabout with a couple of people Richard had just met out of nowhere.

Nicky tried to reassure her that there was nothing to worry about. Jackson was a grown man and perfectly capable of taking the right decisions. She suggested that they go on their planned shopping expedition and practise their haggling skills, but Katherine was no longer in the mood. She decided to call Mr Jones and ask his advice.

'I thought I should let you know that Jackson has not returned yet. Should I be worried?'

'No, I'm quite sure everything is ok. He's probably got carried away with his sightseeing and not noticed the time passing.'

'That's not like him. He's normally pretty reliable about that sort of thing. Of course, his mobile might not be working, although he has international dialling.'

'I'm afraid mobile reception can be a bit problematic over here. Not a hundred per cent reliable. He's probably tried and failed to get through. If he still isn't back by about 4pm give me another call.'

Missing nationals was staple business for British High Commissions and Embassies around the world. Usually they were backpackers who had simply failed to call their parents at an agreed time because they were having too much fun. But embassies didn't often lose superstars, usually because they travelled with an enormous entourage catering for their every need.

It was not the news David Benson wanted. The High Commissioner himself would have to be told and that would mean dropping everything else until Jackson Clarke turned up or something else. It was the 'something else' bit that troubled Benson but he refused to be rattled.

'We can't go searching for him, Victor, so all we can do is wait for him to return. I agree it was bloody stupid of him to go wandering off with a couple of people he didn't know but it's no use worrying about that now. And you say he gave no indication about where he was going?'

'No, none at all. It was supposed to be a bit of sightseeing and then what was vaguely described as "going out of the city to meet some people". He was supposed to be back by midday or lunch at the latest.'

'Terrific: you would have thought someone like him would have known better. Ok, Victor, let's wait until four. If we haven't heard anything by then we'll both get down to the hotel and talk to these people,' said Benson. 'I take it none of the others are planning any excursions?'

'No, sir. Richard West went for his meeting, which seems to have been predictably unproductive. Miss Tait and the other woman, Nicky, have called off a shopping trip they were planning. I think Miss Tait is beginning to get a bit concerned. He has been gone quite a while.'

'Right, well I'll go and inform the boss. I knew this was going to end in tears.' Benson pushed back his chair and straightened his tie before going through the connecting door to the High Commissioner's office.

Victor Jones checked his watch it was 3pm. Jackson Clarke had now been gone for 8 hours.

Shortly after dropping a bemused Khalid off in the middle of Karachi, Mitra had suggested to Jackson that they head out of the city a little way into the surrounding countryside and head out along the coastal road. After a while they pulled over to enjoy the view and sample some of the hotel's picnic hamper. Jackson took the opportunity to stretch his legs and take some photographs. Mitra had been a good guide and proved to be a fount of knowledge about the country's politics and religion, even if once or twice Jackson thought he sounded a little strident in his views.

It might have been the combination of the heat, the sea air or the long car journey but Jackson suddenly felt tired and suggested to Mitra that it was time they turned back. Katherine and his friends would be worried that he hadn't made it back for lunch as agreed. Unfortunately, Jackson's mobile phone didn't work and Dr Mitra said he never used them so they had not been able to call about the change of plans.

'I think you're right,' said Mitra who was sitting on the rug they had laid out for the picnic. 'Let's pack up. You probably haven't really recovered properly from your flight and this heat takes some getting used to.'

'Yes, that must be it, but it's strange I can normally cope with it. I'll just sit down for a minute.' Jackson's voice trailed off as he almost collapsed on the ground. After a moment, his breathing short and his eyelids growing heavy, he struggled to get to his feet but his legs wouldn't obey the commands from his mind. Even the commands were now garbled. 'Can you help me up, I –'

'Yes, I think the heat has really got to you.'

Mitra stretched out his hand but Jackson couldn't reach. Jackson thought he saw him smiling, but all seemed blurred as he slipped back on the ground and everything went black.

Mitra waited a moment and then went over to the Suzuki, opened the passenger door and took a mobile phone out of the glove pocket. It was his own phone, which never left his side. Jackson would have been surprised to see it.

'This is Mitra. Yes, everything is under control. We should be there by 9 o'clock. Yes, he is asleep. Like a baby, as they say.'

He switched off the phone, replaced it in the glove pocket and then with the help of the driver, tidied up the picnic and lifted Jackson into the backseat.

'How long will it last?' asked the driver.

'Long enough to get us back. I put quite a large dose in the coffee when he was taking his photographs. Fortunately, the hotel use a strong flavour and he never noticed the taste.'

Mitra laughed as he polished his glasses, pleased with his work. The sedative was fast acting. Ahead of them now lay a long drive but so far the plan was working out perfectly and the teacher had sounded pleased on the phone. It would be good to return to Garanji.

By nightfall, Victor Jones had already notified the authorities that Jackson had still not returned to his hotel and that the British High Commission was officially concerned about one of their citizens. The description of the car did not help – a white 4x4 Suzuki in a land full of white 4x4 Suzukis. From the hotel CCTV it was possible to make out the number plate but the car had been registered to a man who had sold it ten years earlier – present owner unknown.

The face of the man holding the door open for Jackson to climb in had been obscured by an overhanging banner advertising an IT conference which was due to be held that weekend in the hotel. The man was either deliberately keeping out of shot or it was just bad luck. The younger man accompanying Jackson, whom hotel staff vaguely recalled but could not identify, was not known to anyone. He had no records, he had given no name and any refreshments he had taken in the hotel had been paid for by others, so there was no credit card trail.

Richard West – who had a good eye for faces – gave a clear

description of the two men they had been speaking to the previous evening but no one knew where to start searching.

Any reassurance from Mr Jones – who by now had been joined by his immediate boss, David Benson – that there must have been a problem with the car and he would very soon be walking through the door, sounded weaker with every passing hour. Katherine was convinced something much more serious had happened and was getting increasingly irritated by the professional calm of the British diplomats. They'd organised a meeting room at the hotel where they could all sit round a table and not be overheard. But endless supplies of tea and comfort were doing nothing for Katherine. She decided to go back to the privacy of her own room and call Rory McLeod in London where it was still early afternoon.

McLeod answered the call on his mobile after one ring as soon as he saw Katherine's name flash up on the display. He let her vent her anger on the incompetence of everyone around her and then said: 'Katherine, I was called by the High Commissioner personally four hours ago. I spoke to Mike Grant about it. You recall he wasn't too thrilled about Jackson going when we discussed it over dinner at Cedars the other weekend. He has one of his best people on standby to fly out by chartered jet tonight, if we don't hear from Jackson before then. He is half-Pakistani and half-British, so he is totally familiar with both cultures and was actually born in Karachi.'

'Thank you,' said Katherine, immediately reassured both by the familiar voice and that the some concrete plan was being put into place. But then the penny dropped. 'What sort of expert is he, Rory?'

'I'm not going to beat about the bush, Katherine. He's their top hostage negotiator.' Rory could hear the gasp at the other end of the line. 'Katherine, this is just a contingency plan. I always plan for the worst and hope for the best. David Benson – who is a good man by the way – will call me at exactly midnight your time if Jackson still hasn't come. Mike Grant will then send his man over. He's literally waiting at RAF Brize Norton now and the aircraft is ready to fly.'

'Rory?'

'Yes Katherine, I'm here.'

'Tell me honestly. What do you really think has happened to Jackson?' The silence between question and answer seemed eternal before McLeod replied.

'Worst case? I think he might have been taken hostage. But as your decision to go on this trip was all so last minute no one could have planned this. I would say it was a purely spur-of-the-moment idea.'

'What does that mean, Rory?'

'It means that they're opportunistic. You hadn't planned your visit much in advance so they're probably after a quick buck. They'll hold out for a ransom, which will be ludicrously high to start with and then settle for a few thousand dollars.'

Katherine sat on her bed, her eyes red with tears, scarcely believing that just a couple of weeks earlier they had all been enjoying a tennis game and a beautiful weekend in the tranquillity of Kent and now this – kidnap, ransom, fear and danger in a land where life seemed to be worthless particularly if you didn't fit.

'Rory, am I going to see him again?'

'Of course you are, and stop thinking like that. I suggest you go back downstairs and have a good stiff drink with Nicky. Better still, set one up for Jackson, as I'm sure we're all probably worrying unduly. He'll walk back in, be full of his stories about who he's met and where he's been and deeply apologetic about all the fuss.'

'And yet Rory, you've arranged to have a top hostage negotiator on standby ready to leap into a Lear Jet and fly half way round the world to help find him.'

'That's because I'm British. Belt and braces. And as I say, while I plan for the worst, these things invariably have a happy outcome.'

Rory hoped he was sounding convincing but in his own mind he was already planning to take a fast car to Brize Norton and get on the jet himself with Grant's negotiator. If nothing else, he would be able to keep the peace among his friends. He knew how these things played out. In the agony of the waiting it was not long before those on the same side starting fighting with each other. This was not how he wanted it to end.

# CHAPTER SIXTEEN

S alman Siddiqui for once was happy with the latest story Awad
Fouda – his high-flying reporter – had delivered. There was no
carnage, no death and no shooting. It was a genuinely interesting
angle on an internationally recognised figure and it was happening
in his town.

Whether or not Jackson Clarke wanted to become a Muslim
was not the issue – he had not denied it, which in itself was
intriguing. The story had been picked up by every news outlet in
the West and Channel Five was getting the credit for breaking
it. The next step would be to try and get a proper interview –
an exclusive – which was why he had agreed that Fouda and his
cameraman should hang around the Sheraton Hotel and see what
they could find out.

The answer to that was not very much. There was no sign of
Jackson, or indeed any of his British colleagues. Gradually the rest
of the press corps got bored or had been reassigned to other more
immediate stories and apart from one or two crews left outside the
grounds of the hotel to grab any quick shots, Fouda was soon the
only journalist actively looking for a follow up. He was beginning
to get bored himself and was even questioning the accuracy of
his tip off, when he noticed the British diplomatic plates of a car
parked near the entrance. He was more intrigued when a second
embassy car pulled up and two men he didn't recognise from the
airport greeting party got out and disappeared quickly into the
hotel.

One car was understandable – two was interesting. So Fouda
decided to wait and put in a call to Asif Khan at the Ministry. They

hadn't spoken since the airport news conference, which hadn't gone exactly as Khan had hoped.

Khan was a little cool on the phone – no doubt upset that he had barely featured in the reports Fouda had filed.

'You shouldn't have invited so many other reporters,' Fouda was saying. 'It was impossible to control such a large group. If it had just been me it would have been better.'

'You didn't even use my welcome to Jackson in your story,' Khan moaned.

'It was unusable. There was too much shouting and it could not be heard. But never mind that, what has happened to Jackson now? I have been waiting all day outside the hotel and there is no sign of him inside – I got one of the staff to check.'

'I have heard nothing. The only thing that has happened is that Richard West had his meeting – of course he will never be allowed to make a documentary.'

Fouda was not interested in West. 'Why are there so many British embassy cars at the hotel? They have been coming and going all day? Is there some function here?'

'No there is nothing planned. I can only assume it is related to the Jackson story. It is all over the newspapers in Britain and America, I understand.'

Fouda smiled. Whatever the truth of the story his reputation was made.

'As you are the only official Jackson has met, why don't you pay a courtesy call on him at the hotel? You might be able to find something out?'

Khan thought about it for a moment and liked the idea.

'I think I probably should. You are right. In an official capacity of course.'

'Of course,' said Fouda laughing to himself at the delusions of grandeur Khan gave himself. 'And when you come out you can tell me what he said ... off the record.'

In less than half an hour, Khan walked into the hotel lobby and straight up to the reception desk.

'I'm Asif Khan from the Ministry of Information. I have come to pay a courtesy call on Mr Jackson Clarke. I wonder if you could see if he is available?'

The desk clerk said she would check and picked up the phone. Her call did not go through to Jackson's suite but directly to the meeting room, which had been set aside the hotel. It was answered immediately.

'Sorry to disturb you. I have a Mr Asif Khan from the Ministry of Information in reception who would like to see Mr Clarke.'

A quiet English voice said: 'Please ask him to wait. Someone will be straight down.'

Charlie Barnes put the phone down and turned to Victor Jones who was now on permanent duty at the hotel.

'Anyone know someone called Asif Khan? Says he's from the Ministry of Information and wants to speak to Jackson?'

Jones said he had been at the airport to meet them but High Commission checks showed that he was just a junior member of the Ministry. Not a significant official. Barnes decided he would go down and meet him.

Barnes was the negotiator who had flown in with Rory McLeod on the orders of General Mike Grant. He was the top hostage negotiator at International Risks but you wouldn't give him a second glance. He was medium height, medium build and of sallow complexion, which came from his mother's side. She had been a Pakistani who had died in childbirth. His father – Patrick Barnes – had been a career soldier but had died on operations in Iraq five years earlier.

Charlie Barnes had also done a short service commission, but his real talent was spotted by a representative from International Risks and he joined the company as soon as he left the army. Barnes was calm, had a voice that sounded like honey and he could speak four languages apart from English – including Urdu and Punjabi. His special skill was unlimited patience and a voice that could settle any nerves. He had 'talked' down more than a dozen potentially dangerous kidnappers, helping recover the victims. Some reckoned his voice alone was enough to diffuse a bomb.

No one knew if this Mr Khan could help – but he was the first contact from outside the hotel. It may or may not be significant. Charlie Barnes was interested in even the slightest piece of information.

The concierge pointed Asif Khan out to Barnes, who unlike most people could instantly read a person from their clothes and bearing but never jumped to any conclusions. A poor man may be wise and unlucky, a rich man maybe exactly the opposite.

'Mr Khan? How do you do? I understand you have come to see Mr Clarke. My name is Barnes and I represent him. Could you tell me what it is in connection with?'

'This is purely a courtesy call. I was at the airport to meet Jackson Clarke and his party the other day. There were quite a lot of press people so we didn't really get a chance to talk properly. I hope everything here at the hotel is satisfactory and he is enjoying his stay.'

'Yes, thank you. The hotel is very satisfactory. Unfortunately Mr Clarke is not able to meet you at the moment. Perhaps you could give me your card and I shall make sure he sees it.'

Barnes was studying the politician's eyes and facial expressions to see if he detected any signs that Khan knew more than he was letting on but there was nothing. Whatever he was thinking he did not know where Jackson was.

'I quite understand, perhaps another time. Please give my regards to Mr Clarke.'

'I will of course.' Barnes held out his hand. 'It was quite a crowd at the airport. Surprising really, for a private visit.'

'Er, yes. Quite a crowd. It is good for Pakistan to receive such important guests.'

There was just a flicker across Khan's brow. Undetectable if you weren't looking for it, but Barnes was. The first piece in the jigsaw had landed on the table.

He watched Khan leave and discreetly followed to look through the glass doors as the politician walked away from the hotel, stopping briefly to talk to a small gaggle of waiting newsmen.

As Barnes was heading back to the lifts a bellboy handed him an envelope addressed to 'MISS KATHERINE TAIT, c/o THE JACKSON SUITE'. The words were spelled out in capital letters. Barnes carried it carefully back to the meeting room like an unexploded bomb.

Jackson woke with a blinding headache. His neck and back were aching as though he had been sleeping in an awkward position. Slowly his eyes adjusted to the dim light. He was in a small room with bare whitewashed walls and a tiny window that let in the first rays of morning light. He had been lying on a wooden bed with a blanket, thin mattress and a solitary chair. There was no other furniture in the room. He rubbed his arms to get the circulation moving as he tried to work out what had happened.

Instinctively he got up and tested the low wooden door but it was locked. It didn't take much to realise that he had been drugged and kidnapped. He felt his pockets but of course they were empty. His mobile was gone along with his wallet and passport.

He tried hammering on the door to attract attention but there was no response. If there was a guard outside, he was clearly under instructions to ignore the prisoner. For that was what Jackson now was. He stood on the bed and tried to look out of the high window, which was too small to climb through. All he could see was some rough terrain and hillside in the distance. He was very much alone until his captors decided to return.

For a while Jackson just sat on the bed going over everything that had happened in the past 24 hours as far as he could remember – the meeting with Richard's new acquaintances, who clearly had not just wandered into the hotel by chance. The studious Dr Mitra with all his history about Karachi and his interesting anecdotes about life as a doctor had obviously administered the drug to knock him out. The coffee. It had tasted unusually bitter. The good doctor must have slipped it into his cup while he had been taking photos of the scenery.

The other guy: Khalid, Jackson couldn't recall his other name, he had obviously been sent to trap Richard when he had bumped into him apparently quite by chance at the poolside. It must have all started when they were still in England. Jackson was trying to remember the details but his head was still pounding.

Richard had suddenly got his visa after months of waiting. Somehow the journalist he had contacted was connected but he didn't know how. How was the strange politician who had met them at the airport involved?

Jackson was still trying to piece the whole story together when the door opened and a plate of bread with, what looked liked, beans and a bottle of water were quickly pushed onto the floor. The door slammed shut before Jackson could say anything or even see clearly what his jailer looked liked. He hammered on the door again and called out but there was no answer. Jackson looked down at the humble meal he had been offered. He might as well eat it, he thought – who knows when they would return.

He had no recollection of the journey and no idea how long he had been out for – must have been hours. Judging by his aching arms and legs he had probably spent most of that time in the back of the car which meant he could be virtually anywhere in Pakistan.

The question was, why had he been kidnapped in the first place? His arrival had not been exactly discreet, so anyone with a grudge against the West could have seen him as a likely target – but there was a degree of sophistication. The drugs and the elaborate charade of giving him a guided tour of Karachi all suggested that this had not been the work of some hotheads. There was a mastermind of sorts behind it.

Jackson was not so much worried for himself, as for the fear that must be going through Katherine's mind. In a sense it was alright for him – he knew where he was and he knew he was alive. She didn't. Then the serious, darker thoughts began to crowd in: did they just want money or did they want his head as a trophy. He consoled himself with the knowledge that a dead hostage was of no value, so somehow or other they would keep him alive. He allowed himself a wry smile – at least he might lose a little weight if beans, bread and water were to be his staple diet.

Jackson bent down and picked up a small white feather – possibly from a chicken he thought. That would be good right now, some roast chicken. It didn't look much like the place you would keep chickens in, but anything was possible he reasoned. He rubbed the end of the feather against the wall to make a sharp point.

'I have my quill; now all I need is some ink and paper,' Jackson said out loud. He scratched a little line on the bed: 'Day One,' he said to himself and wondered how long his captivity might be.

Katherine, Nicky and Richard were sitting on one side of the large table with David Benson and Victor Jones on the other. Rory McLeod and Charlie Barnes were standing at the head of the table. They all were staring at the piece of paper lying in front of them.

It was a photocopy of Jackson's passport with the words: 'HE IS ALIVE' written underneath. McLeod broke the silence.

'What is important now is that we focus all our efforts and energy on getting Jackson back. The whys and wherefores are for later. Any statements for public consumption will be handled by David here, after agreeing all content with Charlie. Charlie over to you.'

Charlie was silent for a moment looking at everyone then back to the image of Jackson on the table.

'Now we have to wait for them to contact us. There is obviously no point trying to find him ourselves. After so many hours he could be anywhere – probably well out of the city. What we can do is focus on the people we know something about. The first person we should do a bit of digging on is the slippery little politico who came to the hotel asking to meet Jackson. I didn't like him and I think he knows something about all this – indirectly at least. He left his card, so once we have all the background info on him I suggest we invite him back to the hotel for a chat. I'm only guessing but I would say he doesn't know that Jackson is missing. I would also like to know a bit more about the journo at the airport who asked the questions. Richard didn't you–?'

'Yes, he was the guy I contacted. Awad Fouda is his name. He works for Channel Five and has been making a name for himself covering the recent bombings in Karachi. Katherine, I'm really sorry...'

'Ok, what's done is done,' said Rory jumping in before tempers were raised. 'Remember our focus. David, can you find out any more about this reporter?'

'Not a problem, but we have to be very careful. We can't give the press the slightest idea that Jackson has been ... is missing.'

Somehow the word 'kidnapped' sounded too threatening and everyone wanted to opt for vocabulary that suggested the situation was no more worrying than a set of lost keys.

'Just let me know where I can find him and I'll see what turns up,' said Barnes. 'Can someone fix me up with some local clothes? It's time for me to become a Pakistani again.'

Katherine – who had been silent throughout – asked: 'Shouldn't we involve the police in this? Can't they send out search parties or something?'

'Our best course is to wait for them to contact us with their demands. Neither the police nor army would be able to track him down – this is a big country and Jackson has been gone for some hours. But you can be certain someone does know where he is and while we're waiting for them to call us, we can start with the people we do know something about. We have the reporter, the politician, the doctor and the slightly more elusive Khalid Jalil character. While we are waiting I shall just scout around a bit and see what I can find out and I can best do that looking like a native.'

What Charlie Barnes did not say, was that he feared the kidnappers would soon find they had bitten off more than they could chew. Jackson had seen all their faces, so had Richard West. If this were a publicity stunt for some lunatic terrorist group who wanted to make a point, they would not really be after money whatever their first demand might be.

The first demand soon arrived.

It was in the form of a package that contained Jackson's own mobile phone and instructions to listen to a recorded message. Barnes, McLeod, Benson and Jones listened to it alone, having sent the others to their rooms to try and get some rest.

The voice said: 'We are holding Jackson Clarke for crimes against Islam. We demand an end to Western attacks and bombings on innocent civilians in Northern Pakistan and Afghanistan. All future contact will be made on this phone. *Allahu Akbar!*'

'Well that's all suitably vague,' said Barnes, trying to downplay the implied threat. 'The first thing we better do is get the charger connected so the phone battery doesn't run out. It must be in Jackson's room. Obviously the demand has been plucked out of the air and they don't seriously think anyone is going to agree to a change in strategic engagements with terrorists because an actor has been kidnapped.'

Barnes was silent for a moment. No one else spoke. This was his world. He was the expert. The best outcome would only result from careful practical planning. 'The boring stuff' Barnes called it.

'Rory, you better tell the others that the kidnappers have made contact again. Interestingly they have not demanded money – at least not yet. In one sense that is a little worrying because it suggests they are more interested in making a political point then raising funds, which is the usual motivation. But, as you know, this is very early days – we are just in a stand-off phase at the moment so we need to make some domestic arrangements with the hotel. We could be here for weeks possibly months. The biggest difference in this situation is Jackson himself. He is famous and I'm quite sure the hostage takers will want to play that card at some point. My guess is it will be sooner rather than later – they'll want to take advantage of Jackson's publicity value.'

There was a knock on the door as one of the staff delivered a package from a local store. It was the clothes Barnes had ordered. They were neither too cheap nor too expensive. In a moment he had changed and had transformed himself into an average Pakistani; just as in his western attire, no one would have given him a second glance.

'What do you think?' Barnes smiled.

'Quite the native,' said Benson. 'Now let's see if we can track down that journalist. This is where Channel Five are based,'

McLeod handed him a slip of paper with the address.

'It's not far from here but that's the best we can do. How you get in or meet him is up to you. Richard could simply put in a call to him but we don't want the press to get involved if we can help it.'

'First thing I've got to do is get out of this hotel without being noticed and see if I can talk to those photographers hanging around outside. I saw that politician speaking to some of them when he left so they might have some ideas. In the meantime let's see what we know about either of them.'

Barnes pulled on a cotton *kufi* skull-cap and somehow visibly shrank before their eyes. The man who had taken charge and given instructions moments earlier, had transformed himself just in his posture into a modest nobody. There was nothing distinctive about him at all.

'Rory take a look in the corridor. I don't want to be seen leaving here. I don't think we are going to get any more calls for a while. Just like us, they are feeling their way. I am certain nothing specific has been planned. Better keep the TV on, tuned to Channel Five – they're not just going to drop this story.'

McLeod checked there was no one in the corridor: 'All clear, Charlie.'

Barnes paused for a moment at the door and said quietly to McLeod: 'You do realise that Jackson can identify some of these people, particularly the doctor?'

'The thought had crossed my mind. It's going to be hard for them just to let him go.'

'Agreed,' said Barnes, who then like a shadow slipped through the door and in an instant had vanished from view.

Just as McLeod was closing the door, Katherine Tait burst into the room, the tears welling up in her eyes again.

'What does this mean? How can Jackson's kidnapping stop the war? Rory what are we going to do?'

Rory held her in his arms and placated her: 'Katherine, they don't really expect anything to change. I think they are just playing for time while they try and work out what to do themselves. In the end, I'm certain they will simply ask for money. At this stage we must just wait. Charlie Barnes is having a look round. You must rest.'

'Rory, I've been resting. I want to be doing something. Who can we get to help? What about the Americans, those CIA people?'

'The fewer people that know anything about this the better, but I will now call Frank Miles. He should know what has happened. It is only a matter of time before the news leaks out.'

# CHAPTER SEVENTEEN

The teacher carefully rolled up his prayer mat and returned to his desk. The only change to the routine in the madrassa was that a visit to the training camp had suddenly been cancelled and the students, as Bakri liked to consider them, had been told to spend the day in their studies. Of course, no reason had been given and no one would have guessed that the camp buildings had a new guest.

Bakri had driven out to the camp just after dawn prayers to see Jackson Clarke the day he had arrived. He needed to see his hostage with his own eyes. At that time, the drugs had not yet worn off and Jackson was still asleep. Dr Mitra had checked his pulse and reported that apart from a headache, their captive would be in good health.

Lying on the bed, the screen-hero seemed humbled in Bakri's eyes. So much for all the adulation, so much for the presumption that he could just become a Muslim as easy as picking up a bag of sweets in a shop. Here was the man whose very life was a rejection of the purity of Islam – the cinema, the entertainment, the wild living.

A quick search of Jackson's pockets had revealed a wallet with some cash and assorted credit cards, along with his passport. This thoughtful precaution of a foreigner travelling abroad provided the teacher with the necessary proof that they were holding Jackson and it was easy to get a photocopy delivered to the hotel where Jackson and his party were staying.

Khalid Jalil had phoned several times but Bakri had either ignored his calls or told him that he was too busy to talk. Bakri knew why he was ringing. He was feeling left out – possibly even exposed because his was the face all the Westerners could identify. Mitra would also never return to his hospital, but he was happy because finally he would have his wish to live in Garanji at his teacher's side.

By now, Jackson's photograph and phone would have been delivered to the hotel and the Westerners would know that Jackson was a hostage and their demands had been made. But Bakri was also a realist. He knew that nothing would change as a result of the kidnapping, so Jackson was only of value to him to make a point and to attract world attention to the folly of Western interference in Pakistan and – most importantly – to the insult to Islam that Jackson's world represented.

The next step was to let the world know that Jackson Clarke was being held hostage for these crimes.

The teacher's call on Khalid Jalil's mobile had been the brightest moment in Khalid's day. For nearly 48 hours he had wondered what he had done wrong, how he had offended him. Although Khalid wanted an end to the double-life he had been leading, he was still enjoying the regular payment he received through convoluted banking routes to his account. He needed the money; after all he had a lifestyle to maintain.

What he heard on the other hand was worrying. You don't just kidnap a superstar and expect the world not to react. In Khalid's selective mind he could see a distinction between helping gunmen escape after a shooting in Pakistan; after all he knew that virtually all of the killings would quickly be forgotten by the outside world. But when a prominent figure like Jackson Clarke was kidnapped, there would be repercussions. He began wondering just how easily he might be traced. And now he was to tip off Awad Fouda at Channel Five of another world exclusive. Protecting your sources was not a concept Pakistan was familiar with, and it would only take a few moments in a police cell for Fouda to say where he got his information.

There was no choice. He had to do as the teacher demanded, but he would have to do it in such a way so that he would not be held responsible.

'Fouda? This is Khalid. We must meet, where are you?'

Awad Fouda was still outside the Sheraton Hotel, having spent a fruitless morning trying to get some information out of the hotel staff as they came and went. All he could establish was that the Jackson Clarke party had taken over part of one floor. There were a number of Westerners coming and going, but no one had seen the film star. He had not eaten in any of the dining rooms and had not been seen in the lobby or any of the lounges.

Fouda himself had spotted the diplomatic number plates on the cars; so the Westerners the staff had seen arriving and leaving must all have been embassy people. Something was happening – maybe Khalid Jalil had some information; he had proved a reliable source in the past. Fouda pushed his way passed the small group of locals who had been attracted by the camera crews outside the hotel and made his way to a nearby café. His cameraman would call him if there were any sign of the Westerners and Jackson Clarke in particular. It would only take him a couple of minutes to get back.

'Go on,' he shouted shoving another local out of his way. Although his job was to inform the people, Fouda had a remarkably low tolerance of what he called civilians. They were always in the way when he – Awad Fouda – was trying to get his story. Charlie Barnes politely stepped aside and like a silent shadow, discreetly followed unnoticed.

The café was crowded and noisy, so it would be impossible for Barnes to hear what was being said, but it was easy enough to snatch a photo of Fouda and his friend deep in conversation and forward it to McLeod. The text reply soon confirmed that Fouda was the journalist who had door-stepped Jackson at the airport and that Barnes was also looking at the man Richard West just happened to bump into by the pool. He had also helped set up the trip for Jackson. It was Khalid Jalil.

It was another small but important link in the puzzle but judging by all the shrugging of shoulders, neither man knew what was happening.

'I keep telling you, I haven't seen Jackson Clarke since yesterday. We were on a sightseeing trip around Karachi and I had to leave half way through,' said Khalid, giving the impression that it had been his decision to leave the group as opposed to being virtually thrown out of the car by Dr Mitra. He thought he would not mention Mitra's name to Fouda – at least not yet.

'Where were you when you left him?' asked Fouda.

'Near the banking sector. How does that help?'

'I don't know. Brother, did you leave him with the driver alone?'

'No, of course not,' Khalid shot back as if that would be the craziest thing in the world to do. 'He was with a guide – someone I know well. Why do you ask? What are you suggesting?'

Fouda looked up from his notebook, his brow furrowed.

'All I'm suggesting is that it is that no one seems to have seen this man for more than 24 hours after he set off on a sightseeing trip with someone he didn't know. What was his name by the way?'

'I can't tell you that.'

'Why not? It might help.' Fouda pressed.

'I'm not at liberty to say and anyhow you wouldn't know him.'

'Well, unless someone sees this Jackson Clarke soon I'll run a story saying he is missing.'

'Just because he has not come out of his room, does not mean he is missing, brother.'

Khalid was not convincing himself and he could tell from the smirk on Awad Fouda's face that he was far from convinced either.

'Do you know something more about this?' The journalist's nose for the truth was now twitching.

'There is nothing more I can say.'

'What have you done, Khalid? You realise that he is an international figure?' Fouda's eyes were now burning with passion. If he had guessed right, he had a sensational story on his hands.

'Brother, you should say nothing ... at least not yet. As usual I promise you will have the story exclusively.'

Fouda said nothing and just stared at Khalid. Just as the teacher had predicted, the effect of the conversation would no doubt work.

Simply by asking Fouda not to run a story about Jackson Clarke would guarantee he would do the opposite. The game was on.

Barnes had not heard a word, despite moving a few tables closer, but he could read a great deal into the body language. The conversation had not started well for either man. Both seemed to be searching for answers to a question that in the circumstances could only have involved Jackson in some way. Then as they both explored the topic, the man Barnes now knew was Khalid Jalil must have said something that had set the journalist's juices flowing. It was written all over his face. It didn't take a rocket scientist to work out that Khalid Jalil was the key and he had to be grilled.

But neither Barnes nor the Foreign Office, nor even the CIA, had any jurisdiction in Pakistan – so whatever action had to be taken would have to be off the record. Nothing official. No police. No formal British or US operation.

Barnes quickly phoned in his report to McLeod with Benson and Jones listening in on the speaker-phone. McLeod trusted Barnes' instincts totally. Before he had flown out from RAF Brize Norton, he had been given a briefing on the man by his boss, Mike Grant, who said if there was any doubt about what to do next in an operational context Barnes could be trusted implicitly.

It was agreed that Barnes should stick with Khalid Jalil, while McLeod put out his feelers. His first call was to Frank Miles. His message was simple: Jackson Clarke had been kidnapped was there anything the CIA could do without letting the news slip out? In short the answer was not much. They would see if there was any talk about foreigners missing in Karachi but usually they would have heard something by now. They would keep looking and listening and lend any manpower necessary.

McLeod tried another tack. He hated to admit it, but Senator Vance Friedland was one of the best-informed people on Pakistan, even though he was thousands of miles away. He had influence in the country, which was both political and commercial and at the same time his name was hardly ever mentioned. He had helped out by ensuring there was some unofficial CIA support when Jackson had arrived at the airport and there was no harm keeping him in the loop now. His network would pick it up soon enough anyhow.

There was no risk of Friedland leaking the news that Jackson was missing to the press. Quite the reverse in fact – as people would want to know how he was involved. McLeod thought it was worth a shot.

Vance Friedland was expecting all sorts of calls that morning relating to new healthcare and housing bills fighting their way clause by clause through Congress, but he was not expecting to hear again so soon from Rory McLeod of the British Foreign Office. He was even more surprised to learn that he was being called from Pakistan.

'You choose some dandy vacations, Rory – if I may say so. But let me guess: you haven't called me to discuss your travel plans.'

'You're right, Senator. I–'

'Vance, you must call me Vance.'

'Thank you. Vance, you remember our conversation a little while back about Hollywood?'

'I do indeed. Don't tell me you've got a walk on part and that's why you're there.'

'Not exactly. My role is slightly different. You see our star has gone walkabout as our Australian friends would say.'

'You mean walkabout as you haven't the slightest idea where he is?'

'Precisely.'

'Jeeeesus!' said the senator, which seemed to be the one most inappropriate words to choose in the circumstances. 'Have you any leads at all?'

'We have a couple. And we have had some communication from – shall we say his travelling companions. So we know he is still–'

'I get it,' said Friedland, saving McLeod from having to spell out that he knew Jackson was at least alive. 'What can I do?'

'Well, I think I am right in saying that you have some good contacts in this part of the world and I wonder if I threw a name or two at you, something might ring a bell.'

172

'Shoot. But it's a big place.'

'We think a journalist might be involved in some way: Awad Fouda. He took the lead in the press circus when Jackson arrived. It seems everyone and his auntie knew Jackson was coming.'

'Yeah, I know that guy. He's been making a bit of a name for himself covering all the bombings over there. Everyone assumes he has an inside line to the bombers, but nothing can be proved. Anyone else on your list, Rory?'

'We have one mystery customer who met this Awad Fouda character a short time ago and according to our sources they are pretty friendly. We think there might be a link. His name we believe is Khalid Jalil, but it might be a false name.'

There was silence at the other end of the line. Friedland had gone ghostly white. 'Jeeesus,' he said again, this time almost in a whisper.

'I take it that rings some bells?' said McLeod.

'Look, Rory, all I know is that there is a guy called Khalid. I have spoken to him on several occasions. I have never used a surname and of course Khalid is pretty common but—'

'But like me you don't believe in coincidence. How do you know your Khalid?'

'Shall we just say he has been helpful to us down there. He's a sort of fixer but he's also a bit of a loose cannon. You cannot always be sure he will follow orders – or at any rate understand exactly what you mean. Sometimes he gets his wires a little crossed.' Friedland paused for a moment and McLeod wasn't going to interrupt his flow. The senator continued: 'I can't describe my Khalid to you because I have never met him but I would say he is a young thirty-something. He likes the good things in life and I don't think he is a particularly devout practising Muslim. Bit flashy, I think you Brits would call him.'

McLeod was still quiet. The description that Friedland had given seemed to describe Khalid Jalil perfectly. He liked his western clothes, smart shoes and expensive looking watches.

'I think we are talking about the same man.'

'I was afraid you might say that. If it is the same guy, he will sell his soul to the highest bidder. He is quite prepared to play one side off against the other, so watch him. I don't know where he lives but I do have his cell phone number.'

McLeod took the details and began to evaluate what he had. A fixer used by America for undoubtedly illicit reasons in Pakistan had met up with a journalist who had a reputation for being on the scene of numerous atrocities before anyone else. The two had just been seen together not long after Jackson Clarke had been kidnapped. It was clearly time to talk frankly to Khalid Jalil.

Barnes had followed him to a private address and assumed as night fell that his quarry was now at home – or one of them at least. He decided to return to the Sheraton and resume his normal identity. Benson gave the unenviable task of sitting up all night to keep an eye on the building to one of the High Commission's security teams, while a plan was worked out. If Jalil tried to leave the building, they were under instructions to seize him and take him to a British safe house. Nothing was to be said.

In fact Khalid Jalil had no intention of going out that night. He was too busy preparing to leave the country. He had to pack his bags and decide what he was prepared to leave behind in Karachi forever and which of the forged passports he would use to travel to Europe. London would be his eventual destination but it had to be by an indirect route, probably via Germany. Later he would try and move to the States.

All Khalid knew for certain was that this time the teacher had gone too far. Jackson Clarke was too big a name. He was certain that Dr Mitra had somehow kidnapped him and in all probability taken him to Garanji. He – Khalid – would be implicated in the kidnapping and it would not be long before he was arrested. He did not want to spend the rest of his life in prison and least of all a Pakistani prison.

Money was not a problem as he had made good use of the electronic banking system on the Internet and moved his savings around so often that they would be hard to trace by anyone other than a determined investigator. He also had some useful insurance material in the form of recorded telephone conversations with a US senator. If he were arrested, he would make sure he got the best defence Vance Friedland could afford. He wiped his computer, having downloaded vital records onto a 16GB memory stick and turned out his light.

The baby sitters from the High Commission security team, watching from a car outside, finally relaxed.

In a cold room the only light Jackson Clarke was enjoying was from the moon. He turned over on his bed and pulled the thin blanket up round his shoulders. He looked at the lines he had scratched in the soft plaster on the wall and wondered which would give out first – the sharpened stem of his feather or his willpower not to allow his captors to win.

He was being fed but so far no one had asked him anything. He hadn't seen anyone or anything apart from the shrouded figure that pushed his plate through the door with his single meal for the day. Occasionally he heard the noise of car pulling up close by, some voices he didn't understand but presumably asking about him and then silence. He tried humming to himself to break the monotony of sleepless moments but decided silence was probably better.

In the morning, or when he could sleep no longer, he did some exercises. If the worst came to the worst, at least he would die fit. Jackson felt stoic Scottish humour would be his strength and began thinking about Andy Lucas, whose bright idea for a film in Pakistan was at least in part responsible for his being here – perhaps a dramatic kidnapping could be worked into the plot. He tried to picture Lucas trying to survive on a single plate of prison gruel with some bread and water. Lucas would probably have simply shouted so loudly at his guards that they would have let him go just to get some peace. And strangely, that was all that Jackson was feeling – against all logic for a man being held captive in a foreign land, he was at peace.

If Lucas would have bellowed, how would his dear old friend Kutub Reza in Norwood have reacted? No question, he would have been totally calm. He wouldn't have pushed for answers he would have allowed answers to come to him. Jackson was grateful for the time he had spent in his company. He seemed to sense Reza's presence and gradually Jackson knew that one way or another everything would unfold as it had to – he knew he was not angry about the kidnapping, he knew he was indifferent to what might become of him. Was this the homework that Reza had set him when they last met?

He remembered all the spiritual and realisation books he had read which were written with the sole aim of showing people how they should know themselves and learn about themselves to achieve peaceful and successful lives. But now he realised that all those books were like the driver's manual of a car that had thousands of functions; the manual just showed how to use those functions but it never said where the driver should go. He had to discover the correct route for himself.

If his guards had been watching they would have been surprised to see not a humble, terrified captive but a man completely relaxed. His daily exercises complete, Jackson lay back on his bed staring up at the ceiling and smiled.

# CHAPTER EIGHTEEN

News that Khalid Jalil had decided to leave home reached Charlie Barnes just before dawn.

'Instead of completing his first prayers of the day to save his soul, he was making a run for it to save his skin', thought Barnes as he made his way quickly to the meeting room. It had now become something of a nerve centre. It had been block-booked from the hotel and all room service was left in an adjoining room, so casual eyes could not see any of the paperwork, street-plans or photographs that were pinned to the walls. When Barnes reached the room, Benson and McLeod were already there.

'He's being followed,' said McLeod. 'Do we pull him in for a chat?'

'We have no choice. He's our only positive lead or contact with the kidnappers,' Barnes confirmed what everyone knew. 'Do you have somewhere suitable for him?'

'Yes. It was all set up just in case he decided to skip town.' McLeod hit a speed-dial number on his mobile and said simply: 'Bring him in as arranged.'

Khalid Jalil was too preoccupied with his own plans to pay any attention to anyone who might be following. The sun had barely risen and in the dark shadows it was easy to move unnoticed. A car pulled up alongside and Khalid half-glanced at the driver. Their eyes met which immediately panicked Khalid, but as he turned to run in the opposite direction, he was expertly held by a second man, who then bundled him into the back seat of the car. A swift punch on the nose was enough to persuade Khalid that it would be pointless struggling.

The two men looked European but they had said nothing in the seconds it had taken to snatch him from the street. He asked in Urdu what was happening and then tried in English but he got no answer. The car sped through the streets, heading into a residential area that Khalid knew was popular with the diplomatic community. So this was official and not just a random robbery – that much was clear. They had not even bothered to look through his shoulder bag. He tried to figure out who might be behind this – English or American he guessed, possibly even both.

Judging by their build, the driver and the man sitting in the back next to him were obviously security so there was no point in trying to ask any questions. There would be others higher up the food chain that would be waiting to question him or worse. These men were the hired help. If he tried to speak he would probably get another punch for his troubles. They had not even tried to hide their faces, which was both worrying and reassuring; either they didn't care because he was about to die, or they had diplomatic immunity and he would be released after they had got whatever they wanted out of him.

The car turned into a gated compound and he was manhandled up a short flight of stairs into a house. Half-walking, half-hopping because he was virtually carried along a corridor, Khalid was taken into an empty room and made to sit on a chair in the middle of it, facing the window. The sun was now up. It was going to be a hot day.

'Is your name is Khalid Jalil?'

Khalid turned to the door to see who had spoken. Charlie Barnes was back in Western-style clothes but his sallow complexion was enough to make Khalid still wonder who was really holding him.

'Yes. I'm Khalid Jalil.'

Barnes looked hard into Khalid's eyes. 'I only have one simple question for you and depending on how you answer you will be free to go or we might have to go on talking for some time.'

Khalid wanted to believe him but his nerves were still jangling. Nothing was quite so simple. He said nothing.

'What I would like to know is the whereabouts of Jackson Clarke.'

Barnes made the question sound so matter-of-fact. It almost sounded like an inquiry about directions. There was no threat, no malice – just a softly spoken request for information.

'I don't know. I really don't know anything–'

'Let me stop you there. You see, we know you know something, so why don't we try again. It would be much easier.'

Barnes glanced across at the two unsmiling security men who had snatched Khalid. They were standing with their hands hanging by their sides just waiting it seemed, for a command to inflict damage. Khalid's nose had stopped bleeding but it still hurt. He wasn't a hero and he did not wish to try and resist the sort of interrogation he imagined they could inflict. As usual, his prime concern was Khalid Jalil.

'Alright. I met Jackson Clarke in the Sheraton Hotel two nights ago. He wanted to do some sightseeing and I introduced him to someone I know. We drove round the city looking at sights for a while. I got out and left them. That's all I know.'

'Very good,' said Barnes softly. 'Now we're getting somewhere. Would you like a glass of water?'

'Thank you.'

Khalid had already decided his life was not in danger from these men. If there was anyone to fear it was the teacher because he knew he was about to betray him.

Jackson was lying on his bed, his mind re-tracing the steps that had led him to this moment. The door opened. For the first time he saw the face of the shrouded figure who had been delivering his meals. He seemed young and there was an almost innocent look in his eyes. He looked at Jackson then back at the door as an older man came in, stooping slightly under the low doorframe. He was dressed in a long black *jubba* coat over a white *galabiyya*. He wore a turban and had a black beard. He stopped just inside the room and stared at Jackson. There seemed to be nothing but scorn on his face. Jackson smiled back. Then he noticed Dr Mitra behind him.

'Ah, Doctor. We seem to have wandered a bit off-course from

our sightseeing trip. Perhaps someone can tell me why I'm here or even where I am?'

Mitra was bemused by Jackson's apparent good humour and glanced at the teacher waiting for his lead.

'Where you are doesn't matter. You are here because you represent the insult and arrogance the West continues to show towards Islam.'

Jackson was a little surprised by his fluent English but he was determined to remain resolutely upbeat. He stood up and stretched out his hand.

'How do you do? My name is Jackson Clarke, I don't believe we have met.'

'Sit down Mr Clarke,' snapped the teacher, ignoring Jackson's gesture. 'My name is Abdul Bakri. You think you can simply come to Pakistan and announce that you intend to become a Muslim despite everything you have done and the life you continue to lead?'

'Actually I have made no such announcement. It is all—'

'Be quiet. You will speak when I say.'

For the teacher there was no justification for anything Jackson represented. His fame was founded on multiple evils: the depiction of sex in his films; the immodesty of dress of the women; the drinking; and for the entertainment industry itself. In the teacher's mind, Jackson was the very embodiment of everything he abhorred. Then on top of this list of heinous crimes against Islam, he professed a desire to become a Muslim. While the lecture was delivered, Jackson fixed him with his gaze. Finally the teacher asked: 'What do you have to say to all this?'

'I have been an actor all my life and much of what you say was depicted in some of the scenes in my films. I don't even say they were all good films but I have grown older and my journey is nearly over. What I am trying to do now with the rest of my life is simply to understand and learn. I have never said I want to become a Muslim, but I do say there is something we can all learn by studying other religions.'

As he talked Jackson looked closely at his new audience, knowing it may become the most important speech he had ever made. The difference this time was that his words were his own – not from some scriptwriter.

The man who called himself Abdul Bakri remained unmoved. Mitra didn't say a word throughout, always looking to see how Bakri would react first. And then there was his silent jailer. He probably didn't understand a word that was being said but in some strange way Jackson felt he was communicating more directly with him. Where the man called Bakri was filled with anger, the silent jailer at least seemed to have some compassion in his eyes. The doctor was in thrall to Bakri – there was no way of reaching him.

The thought actually surprised Jackson himself: why was he trying to reach any of them. He was the prisoner. Why should he be trying to win them over? But he knew he had no choice – they were all human beings. If he had learned anything from his time with Kutub Reza, it was the absolute requirement to show compassion to your fellow man – particularly when he wished you most harm.

Bakri was responding: 'At the airport you said you wanted to become a Muslim.'

'At the airport a reporter asked me if I was going to become a Muslim – which is different. But I don't deny that I have been studying Islam now for some years. There is much I admire, just as there is much I admire in other religions. Surely our purpose in this life is to understand first and foremost? If some people can grow to believe in something passionately then they are very fortunate. I am still at the learning-to-understand stage.'

Bakri didn't answer. There was nothing to be gained by getting into a debate with the actor. As things were at the moment, he had a prized hostage – one that the world thought wanted to become a Muslim. So far the story running on the international news channels was that he wanted to convert to Islam and the debate was hotting up. In the west, the coverage was almost universally hostile. Why had he done it? What about all the suffering from 9/11? The horrors of Afghanistan where so many lives had been lost? How could he be so insensitive? Some said that they would never go and watch another Jackson Clarke movie. By contrast, coverage in the Asian press and debates on the TV channels was a mixture of hostility and bemusement. A few commentators welcomed him to the faith but warned that it would spell the end to the style of films he normally acted in.

For Bakri, any film was to be condemned but that was not his issue now. It was time to move the talking about the rights or wrongs of Jackson Clarke's decision to the more significant announcement that he had been taken hostage.

'Understanding is very important, I would agree,' said Bakri. 'Which is why I intend to help the world understand more clearly what I mean.'

Turning to the silent jailer he gave some orders in a language Jackson didn't understand but he thought he could make out a name: 'Sharif'. About an hour after they all left, Sharif returned with some soap and water. Evidently, whatever they had in mind, Jackson assumed that they wanted him looking his best. At least he didn't have to shave in a country where facial hair was the norm rather than the exception.

If he was being prepared for something, Jackson was ready. The initial fear of the kidnap and waking up in his makeshift prison cell had quickly worn off. He was calm and certain of what he would – and more importantly – what he would not do. He would not give them the satisfaction of begging for mercy if that was their plan.

He smiled at Sharif as he placed the basin of water on the chair. Sharif smiled back before he could stop himself. Sharif was uncertain about the stranger. This man represented the devil – or so the teacher had said. Sharif had never heard of him but he knew he was an actor. In films. Films were evil – so the teacher had said. And now this actor was a prisoner, so he should have had nothing to smile about. Why was he smiling?

'Thank you,' said Jackson politely, as though a waiter in a restaurant had just delivered a finger bowl to wash his hands in between courses. Sharif looked at him and guessed what he must have said.

Sharif smiled again briefly. As he closed the door he turned and glanced once more at the tall man, sitting on the bed still looking at him gently.

'Go on wash,' Sharif said in the Pashto language, rubbing his face to explain what he meant. He shook his head and closed the door behind him. Either the stranger didn't care about what was to happen or he was too stupid to understand.

It soon became apparent why he was being encouraged to clean himself up. It wasn't the sort of film set up Jackson was used to, but the small video camera, the masked men and the guns were clear enough when they burst into the room some two hours later. There was one rudimentary light. Jackson was made to sit in the low wooden chair while a banner no doubt proclaiming some cause was attached to the wall behind him.

When all was ready, Dr Mitra returned followed by Bakri.

'You will sit and say nothing, do you understand?'

'It's the easiest role I have ever had to play,' replied Jackson.

'There is nothing to joke about I assure you. By now your friend, Katherine Tait, and your other colleagues know you are our guest. How they react will determine your fate.'

The mention of Katherine's name momentarily knocked Jackson off his stride. He didn't like the fact that they seemed to know so much about him and his friends. They must not get involved but he had to get a message to them that he was in good spirits.

Recovering his composure he asked: 'May I ask what the message of this production is?'

'It is simple – leave Pakistan and Afghanistan and you will be freed. If they do not, you will suffer the consequences,' said Dr Mitra, who seemed to enjoy delivering the news to Jackson that his life was in danger.

'So much for the Hippocratic Oath, Doctor. Do you wish harm on everyone who disagrees with you?' Jackson fixed him with a stare.

But Mitra did not matter. It was Bakri who called the shots and Jackson said to him: 'You don't really think my life is worth that much to the western government forces fighting here do you?'

Bakri held up his arm, cutting Mitra short before he could get into an argument. 'That is for the western governments to decide after they have watched your latest starring role. Now be quiet.'

With that, one of the masked gunmen standing on either side of Jackson launched into a speech that rose to a crescendo as he shook his gun in Jackson's face. Jackson didn't understand what was being said but the tone was perfectly clear.

'Now you must read this,' said Bakri, handing Jackson a sheet of paper. The message was simple and crude. Jackson looked at Bakri then straight at the camera, the red recording light went on.

'My name is Jackson Clarke and I am being held for insulting Islam and for the insults America and Britain are showing to the people of Pakistan and Afghanistan. This is something I regret. If after three days an announcement that coalition forces are to be withdrawn immediately has not been made, I will be killed.'

'Very good,' said Bakri. 'How do you say in Hollywood – one take? Good.'

'I've had a bit of practice.'

Jackson was determined to keep his composure and not let his kidnappers think they were winning. He also didn't want them to listen too closely to the recording he had just made. Otherwise they might pick up the message he was trying to send.

Jackson recalled reading about the training special-forces receive when they were being forced to make such recorded statements. There was no choice but to read the material put in front of them, but by slightly slurring some of the words anyone who was watching – particularly those who analysed every frame – would immediately realise that the prisoner was fighting back, was still in good spirits and of course did not believe a word they had been forced to read out.

Bakri ordered the gunmen and the cameraman to pack up their things and leave the room. He turned to Jackson: 'Don't worry Mr Clarke; your last performance will be viewed worldwide.'

'Oh, I'm delighted ... but I hope it won't be my last performance.'

'That depends on how your friends react, Mr Clarke. If they make some positive gesture then who knows – maybe you will be able to perform again. Now we must leave you. I'm sorry this room is not up to the standard of the Sheraton – is there anything you need.'

'Perhaps the key to the door?'

'I'm afraid not,' said Bakri, privately admiring Jackson's good humour.

As he and Dr Mitra left the room, Jackson called out: 'Doctor, I hope we can continue our discussions about the history of Pakistan sometime.'

Mitra said nothing and swept out of the room.

'Perhaps another time,' Jackson muttered quietly to himself. The taped message was meaningless and he had not only succeeded inserting his own secret message into the recording, but he had also kept calm throughout.

In the silence that descended, his thoughts turned first to Katherine. If he was to keep his sanity through this ordeal he would need to draw strength from somewhere, while Katherine would probably be worrying alone in their room. If ever there was a time when mental telepathy was needed, now was the time. He had to tell her that all would be well. He was certain the High Commission would be doing all they could and he hoped Rory McLeod was contributing in some way. He knew Katherine would not be alone, so he concentrated on being positive because he was certain some higher force would transmit that energy to her.

Jackson laughed. Perhaps this was the first sign of his own madness – thinking that he could transmit his own thoughts to another person, who for all he knew might be hundreds of miles away.

And what of his captors? What should he make of them? He didn't think he would be able to reason with the good doctor – he was a zealot – but strangely, he reckoned he could work with Bakri. If he was to be held here – and it might be weeks, months; even years before he was released – then he wanted to try and win Bakri over. He wanted him to understand the journey he – Jackson Clarke – was on. Surely that was the whole point. Life was nothing if it not a journey of discovery. If he had made mistakes along the way – if he had really insulted Islam, which Jackson emphatically denied – then Bakri should point it out to him. If there was a difference of interpretation then could it not be left that way as a difference, even a disagreement? Surely there was nothing to be gained by resorting to violence. His own life was irrelevant but if he died there would be a backlash, not for who he was but what he represented: the West; entertainment; possibly even freedom of speech and maybe freedom of belief. It wasn't such a crime to make people smile – even laugh – because of something they saw on a screen. It was all make believe.

Who were the self-proclaimed guardians of religion – any religion? Who was making up the rules that proved so hard for ordinary people to keep? The rules were God's – love is the answer.

'Kutub Reza at home in Northwood would be enjoying this', Jackson thought. A world gone mad where a world-renowned actor was locked up in a cell, agonising about religion, trying to see not only how he could send messages of support by telepathy to his friends but also seeing how he could help his jailers. He had often told Jackson that he had still not found a role worthy of his talents. Jackson fondly reckoned he was referring to his movies, but here he was playing a new role. His speaking part had been short and hardly compelling – instead he was acting out mind games. It was a worthy enough part to play. He refused to get angry with his tormentors. He would set himself the task of convincing them that it was possible to find a balance in life without knowing all the answers, and even more importantly without trying to impose his view on anyone else.

Ever the perfectionist, he wondered if he could have delivered his lines in the video in a more convincing fashion – convincing that is to get his own message across. He gave himself seven out of ten but wished he had been able to do two takes.

That night as predicted by the teacher, Awad Fouda ran an 'exclusive' story on Channel Five, asking what had happened to Jackson Clarke. No one had seen him since his high profile arrival in Pakistan. Why had he made no public appearances? Why was his hotel refusing to comment beyond saying he was still a registered guest? Why was there so much diplomatic activity at the Sheraton? Was Jackson Clarke missing ... or worse?

# CHAPTER NINETEEN

Charlie Barnes' mobile interrupted his chat with Khalid Jalil. He listened and simply said: 'Understood.'

He turned to Khalid: 'It seems your reporter friend has just run a story saying he is worried that Jackson Clarke is missing. Perhaps that was something you and he were discussing yesterday when you met at the café?'

'You were there?' Khalid looked surprised.

'Yes I was there and the problem for you is that not only do I know you have something more to do with his disappearance than you are letting on, but so do the people who are holding him. On top of all that, I know you have been particularly well informed about various bombings and shootings in this fair city. Now how is it, I wonder, that you have been able to predict so accurately when the next terrorist event is going to happen?'

'I have had nothing to do with any killing,' Khalid protested.

'Oh you have never pulled the trigger or pressed the button, but you know who has or at least who ordered the attacks.' Barnes pulled up a chair and sat directly in front of Khalid. 'Now it is time for you to tell me everything you know or I will have to release you on to the streets and let it be known that you are a stooge of the British and US secret services. I would give you less than 24 hours before...' Barnes left the implied threat hanging in the air.

'All I know is that I get a call when something is about to happen and I tip off Fouda so he is ready to report on it.'

'And who calls you, Khalid? You must have a name?'

Khalid thought he saw a way out and said: 'All I know is that he is called Abdul. He is somewhere in the north – I don't know where. I have never met him.'

'I think some of what you are saying is partly true, but I think you could do better. You see, I know that you get instructions from America to carry out jobs from time to time.'

Khalid's lips tightened momentarily: a telltale sign of guilt. His most closely guarded secret – not known to anyone else, and certainly not the teacher – was out in the open.

Barnes continued: 'Yes, you see we know that you enjoy the lifestyle you do because not only are you being paid by your terrorist masters here, but you have also been enjoying some remuneration from Uncle Sam. Now that would not go down well with your friends here in Karachi.'

'Well, they benefited as–' Khalid stopped himself in mid-sentence.

'You were going to say they benefited as well. All very cosy. But that's not how I'm going to put the message out on the streets. As soon as you walk out of this building, people with a short fuse will want to know why you are working for the evil American empire, against the interests of your own people.'

Khalid could see his world rapidly crumbling. His plans to slip quietly into Europe and then make his way to America to enjoy the dollars he had stashed away in his numerous bank accounts were disappearing before his eyes. He would not climb the Statue of Liberty; he would not drive in an open top car along America's open highways – in short he would not be free.

Barnes said nothing, knowing full well that Khalid was weighing up his options. He was already talking and given time – one way or another – he would reveal everything. But time was probably not on their side.

'I could phone my contact and see what is happening, but I can't just ask him if he is holding Jackson Clarke. That would be too obvious.'

'Listen Khalid: you know perfectly well that your 'contact' has Jackson somewhere; probably not in this city. Now all you need to do is to tell me where that somewhere might be.'

This was the tipping point. Khalid knew he would never live in

Pakistan again. 'Can you arrange for me to leave the country and go to America if I help you?' He had crossed the threshold; he was now negotiating.

'I can't guarantee that America will take you, but I'm sure we could lose you somewhere in Europe,' said Barnes coolly, not wanting to spook his quarry but desperate to get the information.

'I know there is a house on the outskirts of the city which they sometimes use. It is how do you call it–?'

'A safe house,' said Barnes.

'Exactly: a safe house. I have been there and it would be easy to hide him. No one goes there. I could show you where it is.'

'Good. We can go right now. But first, why don't you call your friend, Abdul, and check in? He might be worrying about you. Your mobile is over there on the table. See what you can find out. But Khalid: be careful what you say.' Barnes pulled back his jacket to reveal a shoulder holster and gun. The message was plain enough.

Khalid dialled the teacher's number. After the usual greeting he said: 'It was just as you said: Fouda did the story. Did you see?'

'Yes,' said Abdul carefully. It was unusual for Khalid to want to confirm that he had done what he had been ordered to do. 'Is everything alright with you, brother? You sound different.'

'Everything is very good, master. Everything is fine.'

The teacher had no choice but to move to the next phase of his plan, but he chose his words carefully: 'You should check your home for any messages, brother.'

'Messages? Oh yes, I see. I am not at home now but I shall go straight back.' Khalid looked across at Barnes who was listening in on an earpiece connected to the mobile. He nodded his approval.

The message waiting for Khalid when he returned to his apartment, discreetly followed by Charlie Barnes and two minders, was a single brown envelope containing a CD with instructions to deliver it to Awad Fouda at Channel Five.

There was a choice for Khalid of course: he could pretend there was nothing at his apartment – but the teacher knew it was there and would wonder why he was not watching its contents on the news that night. Or he could do as he was ordered. Whatever the CD contained – and Khalid could guess – it would have to be broadcast or the teacher would realise that Khalid had been got at. On the other hand, if he handed it over to Barnes and his friends at the British Embassy they may refuse to release it – in which case Khalid was in the same mess.

Barnes had a similar predicament and it was not made any easier when he watched the CD with McLeod and Benson. It was no surprise to see Jackson with armed guards on either side. There was the usual condemnation of the West and the threat to Jackson's life, which Barnes translated simultaneously as the gunman spoke.

'Interesting,' said Barnes. 'Just play the Jackson section again.' The three men listened once more to the impossible demand for an announcement by the West that it would pull out its forces. 'Did you hear that?'

'Yes, Charlie, we heard it. Crazy – how could we possibly meet that deadline, even if we wanted to?' said Benson.

'No I don't mean the words, but the way he said them. Jackson is a professional actor. Happily, he doesn't look too stressed. In fact I would say he's remarkably calm in the circumstances; that makes it all the more peculiar.'

'What's peculiar, Charlie?' asked McLeod.

'Did you notice how he slurred his words? He is telling us that he doesn't believe a word he is saying and that there is plenty of fighting spirit left in him.' Barnes played the words again and the unmistakable lisping was clear.

The difficult part was playing the message to Katherine, Nicky and Richard. It didn't matter how much warning and preparation Katherine was given, inevitably she burst into tears at the sight of Jackson and they left Nicky to try and calm her.

It was agreed that Khalid would contact Awad Fouda at Channel Five and deliver the CD. The hand over would be in the street, to make it easier for Barnes and his team to ensure Khalid stuck to the plan.

Awad was so intrigued by the new package that he failed to notice Khalid's reticent, almost nervous, demeanour. As far as he was concerned Khalid was simply the messenger and he was about to break another big story – possibly the biggest of his career. Khalid had not seen the contents of the CD but he had been told to inform Awad that it was directly connected to the strange disappearance of Jackson Clarke.

As Awad returned to his office, Khalid looked around, half hoping that there might be a chance to run – but Barnes in Pakistani clothes again was already at his side, gently but firmly guiding him to a waiting car. The next part of the plan had to move fast before Channel Five broke the news.

It was one thing applying a little pressure on an individual; it was quite another raiding a house without police permission. So Benson had no choice but to brief his local contact in the Pakistani Intelligence Community – the Inner-Services Intelligence (ISI) about what had happened. A British citizen – who happened to be a household name – had been kidnapped by suspected terrorists who were threatening his life unless impossible demands were met.

After the obligatory annoyance that Pakistan security had not been informed sooner, a coordinated swoop with the police and army was organised on the safe house where Jabbar and Sharif had earlier sought sanctuary.

It was a professional attack and the corrugated gates offered no resistance as the reinforced police Land Rover smashed its way into the compound. The police and troops swarmed through the buildings but found nothing of interest. There appeared to be some sort of sleeping accommodation for a number of people, but there was nothing to suggest this building was anything out of the ordinary. It was strange that there were so many beds and so few people but there was no evidence of criminal activity being been planned there. The teacher's instructions had been followed to the letter. Nothing should be kept that would indicate the real purpose of the buildings.

The bemused permanent residents could offer little help. They recognised Khalid and confirmed that he had been there on numerous occasions but they could not even identify a photograph of Jackson Clarke. So much for Hollywood fame. They were all rounded up for questioning, but there was little information they could give beyond the fact that foreigners would suddenly arrive and then be taken away after a few days never to return.

So far, all that had been achieved was the closure of a terrorist safe house – just one of hundreds in the city. It was hardly a stunning success.

Khalid knew Jackson was not going to be there, but hoped this might be enough to prove he was being cooperative. It took just one glance from Charlie Barnes for Khalid to realise that he was not off the hook. The information about how the compound had been used as a safe house and staging post was interesting enough for the local police, but it did nothing for Barnes, who was given permission to keep questioning Khalid. This time there would be an officer from the ISI listening in.

Awad Fouda was also a little uncomfortable working on his story for broadcast on the evening news with a Pakistani security man standing at the back of the editing room. Channel Five's editor, Salman Siddiqui, was also unhappy, but there was no choice. The story had to go out, otherwise Jackson Clarke's life might be at risk if the kidnappers suspected someone had talked.

Siddiqui had been briefed about how his star reporter was always first on the scene so soon after the various terrorist attacks which had hit the city. If he was lucky, he would stay out of prison but no one would employ a terrorist accomplice. Awad Fouda didn't know it, as he was putting the finishing touches to his world exclusive report, but the only live appearances he would be making from now on would be in a court of law. His dreams of a high-flying career at CNN in America or Europe would very shortly be terminated. For now at least, Channel Five had a world exclusive. Siddiqui returned to his desk, sat down and looked out across his newsroom. As soon as Jackson Clarke was found – alive or dead – he would retire.

For once Andy Lucas was at a loss for words. As he sat in his cliff top home overlooking Los Angeles, he just stared at his 63-inch plasma TV screen with Jackson's face looking back at him. Over and over again the networks were running the clip of his friend and the star of his next movie, virtually begging for his life. Lucas thought he sounded nervous and his delivery was a little rough round the edges but in the circumstances he supposed it was not surprising.

'What was he doing there in the first place'? Lucas kept asking himself. 'Was it anything to do with his film'? Jackson was always a fanatic about authenticity but Lucas hadn't really believed him when he had said he was going to visit Pakistan.

'No one goes to Pakistan for a holiday, Goddamn it,' Lucas said out loud to himself. His phone was ringing off the hook as everyone caught up with the news. They all knew that Jackson was in the frame for a starring role in Lucas's next film. The film itself was now in real jeopardy. No star would be prepared to travel to Pakistan to film any of the scenes, which Lucas was determined had to be shot on location.

'Thanks for nothing, Jackson', Lucas thought as he mentally began reorganising his schedule. They would have to try and film in India instead. It might be a bit politically sensitive but at least it would be safer – after all, it was now a popular location for many movies. It was just that his film might try the patience of his hosts. Lucas shrugged the thought off – they would be grateful for the money.

Senator Friedland was even more distraught. In some way he felt partly responsible. If his contact Khalid Jalil was involved then he, Friedland, had been keeping a terrorist in play for the past three years; satisfying Khalid's appetite for the good life while all the time giving him what Friedland fondly called 'assignments'.

There was another more pressing concern for Friedland – what if Khalid talked too much about their relationship? It wouldn't matter too much to the networks that he had been working in the best interests of the US if a globally popular film star was killed as a result – direct or indirect – of what Friedland had asked him to do over the years. It was clear to Friedland that Khalid Jalil had become a liability. As soon as he led the search party to Jackson he would be expendable.

Danyal Sarwar had been walking near his home when he saw Jackson's face on a TV screen in a shop as he passed. He stopped and smiled at first, assuming it was something to do with the new movie – and then he saw the clip of Jackson with two gunmen on either side. He ran into the shop and asked an assistant what had happened.

Kidnapped? Threatened with death? How could that have happened? No wonder he had not been able to reach him, but why had he gone to Pakistan? Jackson should have told him that he was thinking of making the trip. Would he have warned him not to go or would he have seized the opportunity to act as his guide? Was this the end of the new dream he had been constructing for himself; somehow spending more time with his new Hollywood friends?

Danyal immediately started feeling guilty – a habit he was getting into. Here he was thinking about his own future while Jackson was being held captive and facing death. He stood transfixed by the screens in the shop – every one now showing Jackson's face; his eyes staring straight at Danyal – or so it felt. In spite of his plight Jackson managed to look calm. Of course he had been forced to say the words handed to him, but his eyes were smiling; yes they were smiling at him – Danyal – as though saying 'Everything will work out in the end. Don't worry about me.'

'Come on mate: either buy a TV or go and watch your own one at home,' – the sales assistant in the shop cut short Danyal's imagined conversation with Jackson.

'Sorry, yes, I'm leaving. It's just that I know this guy.'

'Yeah the whole world knows him, mate; he's a film star. Silly bastard went on holiday to Pakistan or something. Idiot.'

'No, really. I have met him.'

'Good for you, now are you going to buy a TV or not?'

Danyal left the shop, looking again at the screens in the shop window and then at the assistant who was shaking his head as though Danyal was mad – a dreamer.

At Number 27 Stockley Road, Kutub Reza focussed his mind exclusively on his friend and pupil. What Jackson Clarke needed now was mental and spiritual support; he needed the strength to endure whatever his captivity threw at him. In one sense he thought that all their meetings had been a preparation for this ordeal and he was confident that Jackson already had the necessary strength. In fact he had arrived with it on the first day he came to visit. Reza always said his role had simply been to open Jackson's heart to what was already there.

Reza closed his eyes and brought the image of his pupil to the front of his mind. He tried to picture him sitting alone in his room – perhaps in the dark – undoubtedly alone, probably cold. This was all he could do, but Reza was a firm believer in the power of the mind and he knew there were greater forces at work in the world than humans could comprehend. The whole world and its security services would certainly be scouring the land for his friend; what he could do was to transmit his message of comfort. Whatever fate lay in store, no one was readier than Jackson Clarke.

Day and night were a blur for Jackson. It didn't much matter whether he slept all day and stayed awake all night. When he was awake, he certainly felt guilty of the inconvenience he had caused. 'Inconvenient' – who had put that understated word in his mind? He knew everyone was busy thinking about how their own lives and plans and future had been disrupted one way or another and all he could do was send out a mental apology and hoped they would pick up the vibes. He would have to throw a big party down at Cedars for them all to say sorry. Maybe this was all a dream and he would soon awake to find himself lying out on the veranda soaking up the last rays of a British summer afternoon. But the dream continued. This was not make-believe.

As though to emphasise the point, the door opened and another bowl of dall with bread and water arrived. This time the boy (Jackson felt he was old enough to be his grandfather) came right into the room and placed the food on the bed.

'Sharif?' Jackson ventured. Sharif turned acknowledging his name and quickly looked away. 'Thank you, Sharif.' Jackson smiled and waited for Sharif to respond. He couldn't resist and smiled back, guiltily glancing at the door in case the second guard had noticed,

'Jackson Clarke,' said Jackson holding out his hand.

Sharif wasn't sure how to respond but shook his hand all the same, confused at the complete lack of anger or hostility from the prisoner. The thought entered Sharif's mind that maybe this man was not bad. He even wondered why the teacher wanted him to be held as a prisoner. Was this man evil? He was always smiling; always saying something – which he guessed was thanking him whenever he brought him food – and never showed any signs of resentment. It was almost as though he was happy to be there with them.

Jackson noticed his frown as they shook hands and continued to smile. It was the only way of communicating. The boy probably had no understanding of why he was being held; he was just following orders. Jackson wondered how long he had been doing that: following orders... Probably all his young life.

The second guard shouted something from the door; it was a hurry-up call. Sharif quickly snatched his hand back as though he had been caught fraternising with the enemy and the moment had passed. But a link had been made. Jackson had taken the step across to Sharif's side of the invisible barrier and for a few seconds Sharif had crossed over to Jackson. Jackson knew that if only he had been able to speak the language, he would be able to find at least some common ground – he was sure of it. That is what Kutub Reza always urged him: look for the commonalities between people, not the differences. The differences are easy to see, while similarities are much harder but infinitely more rewarding to find.

What Jackson was refusing to think about was the three-day deadline – there was only a day left before time had run out.

# CHAPTER TWENTY

Khalid Jalil was not returning his calls, which made Abdul Bakri worry. The broadcast had gone out so he knew Khalid had delivered the CD but it would soon be time to move to the final phase. There was a certain inevitability about it, but for his plan to succeed he needed to ensure it got the maximum publicity. Khalid had a role to play in that strategy and now he could not be reached.

The missed calls were not being ignored. Barnes, who had enlisted the help of the local police to try and trace the incoming messages, was carefully monitoring them.

Tracking a mobile phone was relatively easy in a modern built-up area where triangulations between several masts could establish the location of the phone. But in rural areas where there were fewer masts, that was not so easy and it was assumed Bakri was holed up somewhere in the mountains. The other method was simply to track the GPS signal being transmitted by more modern handsets, but it seemed that Bakri was using an old model.

Barnes's only other option was to wait for a call from the kidnappers on Jackson's own mobile, which they had thoughtfully provided with the original message. He knew the waiting game could not last forever.

Khalid was still insisting he did not know where Bakri was based. He assumed it was in the north of Pakistan – somewhere near Peshawar – but claimed he had never been there. Some residue of loyalty towards the teacher meant he was still holding out. Barnes suspected that was the case, and wondered how long Jalil would be able resist some strong-armed tactics. A little waterboarding would have worked wonders, but even the American military avoided such techniques now and it wasn't Barnes's style anyway.

The meeting room that the team had commandeered in the Sheraton no longer appeared quite as smart as when they first moved in. The boards were plastered with notes, cuttings and photographs. Half finished coffee cups lay forgotten. Housekeeping had been over-looked but no one seemed to mind. They had other priorities. This was all part of the long drawn-out game of cat and mouse that kidnappers and hunters played. Each side was waiting for the other to make the next move.

The shrill blast of Jackson's phone shattered the silence. For a fraction of a second Barnes, Benson and McLeod looked at one another, then Barnes leapt to his feet and flicked his fingers pointing at the digital recorder. With the machine running he answered the phone, his voice betraying none of the anxiety they all felt.

'Hello, this is Charlie Barnes.'

'You have just 24 hours left. If we hear no announcement on Channel Five and at least one international TV channel then you will have left it too late.' The voice fell silent waiting for a response.

'We understand,' said Barnes calmly. 'But it is a question of contacting various governments to get them to agree some joint statement. This is going to take much more time. I hope you will be able to give us—'

'There is no more time. There will be no extension to the deadline. We are serious. Twenty-four hours; no more.' The phone line went dead.

Barnes looked at McLeod and Benson – the caller had sounded uncompromising and he knew that something had to give. Just then Victor Jones came in with a face matching the bleak atmosphere in the room.

'The High Commissioner is worried. He has been taking calls from London and from various embassies. The US ambassador has offered any help we need. Oh, and the world's press is now camped outside the hotel.'

'For a change, that might actually help us,' said Barnes. 'There is no way we can get any sort of announcement about troop withdrawals, but we could announce that every diplomatic effort is being made to bring the situation to a peaceful close. Governments have been approached about the issue of coalition forces in Pakistan and Afghanistan. It won't amount to much but it might buy us some time.'

'Let's do it,' said McLeod. 'We need to get Awad Fouda – he still sees it as his exclusive story – and one other TV crew who can pool the coverage with everyone else. We don't want a media free-for-all.'

'Agreed,' said Barnes.

David Benson was already making notes: 'Right Jones, see if the hotel can fix us up with a small room where we can make our statement. You also better get our friend Awad in here and I suggest the BBC reporter covering the story and explain the pooling arrangement. Let's try and get it done in about an hour. I'll work on the text and confirm it with the High Commissioner.'

'Who's going to give the press conference?' asked McLeod.

'I'll ask the boss when I show him the text, but as Jackson is a Brit I think it should be the High Commissioner. I will liaise with the local authorities because we don't want to upset them. But my guess is they will want us to make the running on this. If something goes wrong they will be able to point the finger and say we fouled up,' said Benson, a little ruefully.

It seemed like positive action was being taken but Barnes was worried that events were not following the usual course of a typical kidnapping. He was increasingly concerned that someone just wanted to make a point – a big point. There had been no demand for money. The kidnappers were sticking to the original demand, which they must have known was impossible to meet. So what did they really want to do? He caught McLeod's eye and signalled him to come to one side of the room.

'I think you better check on the others and let them know what's happening. Best not go into too much detail about the call; just say the kidnappers have been in touch and we are putting out a statement,' said Barnes.

'Katherine will be at her wits end. Nicky is with her but she can't bring herself to speak to Richard or even have him in the same room. I knew it would come to this. They'll soon be turning on one another unless we can–'

Barnes held up his hand and stopped McLeod in mid-sentence. 'You have got to know that this is not going as I hoped. I don't think they are even considering letting Jackson go. Our best hope is to find out where they are holding him and I think we have run out of options. I'm going to apply a little more pressure on Jalil. Do you agree?'

'Do we have any other choice?' asked McLeod.

'No.'

Khalid Jalil was being moved constantly from one address to another in case his whereabouts were discovered and someone chose to bring his cooperation with the authorities to an abrupt halt.

The Pakistani ISI operative could not understand the interrogation technique being used by the British. Something a little more forceful was surely required and when Barnes burst into the room, he thought at last they were going to get some results.

Barnes had other plans.

'I'm afraid we have run out of time, Khalid, which means you have also run out of time. Your friends have called again. Now you and I both know that we cannot meet their demands, which only leaves us with the option of finding out where they are holding Jackson and rescuing him. Do you understand?'

Khalid nodded, not quite sure what the consequences of the British inquisitor's statement meant for him. The Pakistani ISI officer was certain he knew – at last they would beat the answer out him. What was the delay?

'I must ask you one more time: where are they holding Jackson? Where is this Abdul Bakri based? I know you have been there – I specialise in reading people's faces and voices. I know when someone is lying to me. Where is Jackson?'

'I am telling the truth. I have taken you to the other house. I was sure he was being held there. He must have gone to the north.'

The ISI man could barely restrain himself and it was only the firm hand of one of the two British minders that stopped him lunging forward to strike.

'You see,' said Barnes glancing across at the Pakistani; 'my friend here is running out of patience too and I'm inclined just to hand you over to him. They have different techniques.' Turning to the local officer, Barnes asked: 'Did you know that this man was also being paid to inform on Pakistanis by the Americans?'

'That's not true. I–'

'Maybe, but it could easily be seen that way and you can tell by our friend's face over there that he's not pleased.' The veins on the ISI man's face were bulging. Why would these English people not just get out of the way and give him five minutes alone with this filth?

Barnes went on: 'I am going to do one of two things, unless you start telling the truth. My British colleagues and I are either going to leave the room while your countryman has a quiet word with you, or – as I mentioned earlier – I am going to release you on to the streets, having briefed the world's press that Khalid Jalil has been helping us with our inquiries as a suspected US informant. Of course I'm sure something will be lost in the translation and you will be branded a US spy by all the local papers.'

'We had a deal. I took you to that house. How was I to know he wasn't there?' Khalid blurted out looking frantically between the ISI man, the two British security guards and Barnes.

'You were stalling and you know it. We checked the building forensically and Jackson Clarke had never been there. You on the other hand were a familiar figure. Oh and by the way, one of the old men we found at the house has been very helpful. I believe there was a shooting not so long ago. Some industrialist I'm told. The old man told the police that two young men had arrived on a motorbike the same day as the shooting and he said you had met them at the compound. Any idea how that might have happened?'

'I... I was just–'

'So they were the gunmen and you just happened to be there at the time. Sorry my friend, that won't wash. I have to go to a press conference now so I'll leave you to think over what we have been discussing. When I get back, we'll see how your memory is doing.'

As expected, the pooling arrangement had not gone down well with the news crews waiting outside the hotel. Each one wanted to be chosen to do the filming but Barnes was adamant that he did not want the session to get out of control. There would be a statement by the High Commissioner as agreed, and everyone would share that footage. There would be no discussion on the matter.

The High Commissioner arrived at the hotel in one of the un-marked bullet-proof diplomatic cars. By the time the cameramen realised who it was, he was already inside the building being swept along by his security detail to the hastily arranged press-conference room.

Two cameras had been set up and the room was already warm from the artificial lighting. The High Commissioner had been well briefed and he just held Awad Fouda's gaze a little longer than would have been normal – to say he knew exactly who he was and the role he had been playing – then smiled across at the BBC correspondent.

'Gentlemen, if you are ready, I will read a short statement. I will not be taking questions afterwards. Please ensure that copies of my statement are distributed promptly to your press colleagues waiting outside.' He paused, then looking directly into the cameras added: 'A man's life could depend on it.'

The High Commissioner delivered the text Benson had prepared, stood for a moment to allow the cameramen to get some additional shots of him and then left as swiftly as he had arrived.

Within the hour, his words were being shown around the world along with background reports on Jackson Clarke. Many of his friends and colleagues from the film world appeared on news bulle-tins, appealing to the kidnappers to release Jackson. They protested that he had never done anyone any harm and he could not be held responsible for the military or political action in Pakistan or Af-ghanistan.

Sitting in Garanji, the teacher was less than impressed. He rightly dismissed the High Commissioner's statement as an attempt to play for time, and as for the appeals from the people of Hollywood, they made no impact. If anything they angered him even more. He felt insulted that some actress who should have been more modestly dressed could even think he would be swayed by her words.

He turned down the sound of his TV and looked at his watch. Around him sitting cross-legged on the floor, his assistants waited for their instructions. All were aware that the deadline the teacher had set was about to expire. All were also aware that the foreigner's fate lay in their leader's hands, but they had never been in this situation before. They knew that young men had left the madrassa on missions – some never to return – but this was the first time they had taken a hostage.

Abdul Bakri smiled at the faces in front of him and reached for one of three mobile phones on his desk. He knew of course that the Westerners would be attempting to trace his calls and understood the danger of repeated use of the same handset.

He signalled to Dr Mitra to come to his side. 'You will tell them that the deadline has expired. Whatever happens now is a consequence of their actions and their refusal to cooperate. Say nothing more.'

Mitra dialled Jackson's number and Barnes answered. He listened to the message he had been expecting.

'We have made an announcement that discussions are underway. That is a big step–'

Mitra couldn't resist getting into an argument: 'You have not done what we requested – you only have yourselves to blame now.'

Barnes tried to keep him talking: 'How do we know that Jackson is still alive? What proof do we have?'

There was silence at the other end of the line as Mitra looked at the teacher, wondering what he should say in response. Bakri was thinking. This was another opportunity for even greater publicity. He whispered an instruction.

'We will give you proof that Jackson Clarke is still alive. We will call in one hour and you will hear his voice.'

'Dr Mitra is that you? I'm Charlie Barnes,' said Barnes, trying a new line. He had gained a little more time and he wanted to try applying his own pressure by personalising the exchanges using Mitra's name. 'Dr Mitra, as you know, we are doing everything we can to accommodate your demands and those of your leader. You must understand. You're a doctor and–'

'Mr Barnes, be ready to answer the phone in one hour.' Mitra rang off and looked at the teacher, just as a student might wait for his master's approval. For the first time Mitra felt exposed. He was no longer just the anonymous voice at the end of the line. They knew who he was.

Bakri touched him on the arm, reading his mind: 'Brother, there is nothing they can do to you. They don't know where we are.'

'You are right, Teacher,' he hesitated for a moment; 'but what if Brother Khalid brings them here. They have arrested everyone in the house in Karachi.'

'The actor has never been here. He was taken straight to our camp, remember? There is no sign of him. Be strong.'

'Yes, Teacher. You are right.' Mitra looked down, ashamed at his own cowardice and weakness.

'Now we must go to the camp. Bring the recorder.'

Jackson had already settled into a routine of sorts, with Sharif bringing him his food and the two of them trying to communicate through signs and the odd shared word. Sharif stayed a little longer each time and Jackson thought some sort of link had been established between them. He didn't believe that Sharif really wished him harm but after years of brainwashing by his elders, he assumed the boy no longer knew right from wrong.

This evening the routine was disrupted by a second visit – the heavy mob as Jackson had decided to call them: Bakri, Dr Mitra and minders.

Abdul Bakri spoke: 'Your friends at the Sheraton seem to think you are no longer alive, Mr Clarke.'

'Well that's disappointing. What are you proposing – shall we all go back to the hotel?'

'That would take too long.'

'So we are a long way from Karachi. I guessed as much. It was a long trip Dr Mitra; a pity I couldn't enjoy more of the view.'

Mitra flushed with anger but said nothing. Bakri continued: 'Yes, we are a long way from Karachi, so I just want you to say a few words into this recorder. You will say the following.' He handed Jackson a piece of paper.

'Ah, another script, what have we here?' Jackson read the words. 'I take it from this that there has been quite a lot about me on the news. That's encouraging. I'm glad someone's noticed my absence.'

'Just read it,' snapped Bakri beginning to get irritated himself by the actor's continuing good spirits. Mitra flicked on the recorder and held it to Jackson's face.

'Very well.' Jackson cleared his throat and read: '"I know the British High Commissioner has made a press-statement, but this does not go far enough. It fails to deliver what is required and prove that the West takes seriously the demand that coalition forces leave the region. The deadline to meet this demand has expired and un-less a statement is made immediately, I will be killed." Is that good enough?' asked Jackson, refusing to be unsettled by the words.

'Yes,' said Bakri and signalled for everyone to leave.

'You do realise of course, that it won't have any effect,' Jackson called out after them. 'The British don't make deals with terrorists.'

Bakri turned on his heel: 'We are not terrorists. What your government is doing in this part of the world is terrorism – killing innocent women and children.'

'Oh come on, don't give me that old story. What do you care about women and children – you hide your women away, refuse to give them education and you corrupt the young minds of lads like Sharif over there.'

Bakri flashed a glance at Sharif who quickly looked down at the ground. He didn't understand what was being said but he knew they were talking about him. He wondered what he had done wrong. He could sense the teacher was angry about something. The Westerner had raised his voice for the first time; what did it all mean?

Bakri recovered his composure: 'Mr Clarke, I don't need to take any lectures from a film actor about corruption of young minds. What we teach here in the madrassa is religion and belief in God – not sex and drugs and drinking.'

'Now we're getting somewhere. I am being held in or near a madrassa – the place where right-thinking Muslims should be learning about their faith – not fine-tuning the art of kidnapping and murder.' Jackson reckoned he had nothing to lose by some honest talk. Strangely his focus had shifted from his friends in the Sheraton hotel, who could take care of themselves whatever the outcome, to his young jailer, Sharif.

In the past three days Sharif had been his regular visitor. Jackson was positive that the boy's attitude towards him had shifted. He, at least, could be saved. He laughed to himself: what was he thinking? He was the prisoner – not young Sharif – and yet here he was trying to save his jailer.

'You are not helping yourself talking to me in this way,' said Bakri.

'What happens to me is unimportant, but all I see around you is fear. Everyone is frightened of you. Too scared to speak freely. Is that what you want – their terror? Would it not be better to command their respect? Maybe even their love? Everyone can change their ways. I am changing. You could change – change is not impossible, you know.'

'Enough. You talk too much. Let's see if the sound of your voice will make your friends see some sense and they could also change their minds.'

'Oh, I doubt that,' said Jackson laughing. 'They all think I talk too much anyhow.'

'Well, let's hope you're wrong. For your sake.' Bakri snapped an instruction at Sharif who hurried out of the room.

'Poor boy,' said Jackson out loud. Bakri heard him but didn't turn back. The door slammed shut and Jackson was alone again.

Exactly an hour later the call came through. For Katherine it was almost too much to bear but Barnes was determined to focus on the positive aspects. To begin with, Jackson was alive and knew about the broadcast, even if he hadn't actually seen it. On top of that, his voice sounded strong and there were still the telltale lisps in his speech patterns. He still had the mental capacity to send out his own signals, even if the words themselves were grim. The next few hours were critical.

He had also decided to let Khalid loose.

# CHAPTER TWENTY-ONE

If Asif Khan thought his connection with the Jackson Clarke kidnapping had passed unnoticed he was mistaken. The Pakistani secret police – acting on information helpfully placed by the British High Commission – smashed the door of his apartment off its hinges with ease.

In less than a minute he had been roughly manhandled into the back of unmarked car and driven away. To his neighbours in the apartment block, Khan was a high-flyer. They were used to seeing him appear on TV regularly at various functions; he always had a snappy sound bite and always looked immaculately turned out. Some of his neighbours thought his effortless rise was a little too easy and they couldn't resist a small smile of pleasure at his comeuppance.

In some parts of the world, politicians enjoy a degree of immunity from the powers of law and order; in other parts, the privileges of power can be swiftly removed. Pakistan was one of the more volatile nations in the latter category, where even the head of state could find himself or herself summarily removed – sometimes violently. The dry wit of some commentators observed that it was not the sort of place your life insurance company encouraged you to visit.

As Khan sped through the streets past the Ministry of Information, where he had carved his small powerbase, he realised his time in the fast lane of political influence, such as it was, had just ended. The question was: why?

He had bent a few rules as he ruthlessly feathered his own nest, as well as those of his supporters, just to get where he was. Others had done much more, broken bigger rules, made even larger donations to helpful causes. He had hardly committed any crimes worthy of an early morning raid on his home.

Neither the British High Commission nor representatives of the US Embassy were present while Khan was 'talking' to the Pakistani authorities. Sometimes it was better not to know the techniques used – it allowed for complete deniability. In a world where freedom of information allowed the media to dig deep, many people found it convenient to look the other way. Benson was impressed when he received a detailed report of the interrogation from Islamabad within an hour of his arrest. Their methods might have been questionable, but they were certainly efficient.

Khan had confirmed he knew in advance that Jackson Clarke was planning to come to Pakistan and make some sort of announcement about becoming a Muslim, and yes, he had organised the press reception for Jackson when he arrived in Karachi.

He was also able to confirm that once again, the man with all the information was Awad Fouda, who in turn had spoken to Khalid Jalil. But as Khan protested he knew nothing about any plans to kidnap Jackson; it had purely been a bit of self-publicity. Fouda was the one who had the best contacts, he insisted. He was always the one ready with his camera crew whenever there was a terrorist attack – that's how he had made his name.

The only problem for Khan was that he was invariably close behind Fouda; on hand to give a telling comment condemning terrorism or taking whatever particular line suited him at the time. This of course meant that he knew in advance when – and to some extent where – the next attack was going to be, even if he didn't know the target. Instead of waiting to give a statement to the cameras, the Pakistani authorities wanted to know why he had not tipped them off that an attack was imminent.

'That is something Khan can discuss with the police', Benson thought as he made his way over with their debriefing report to the Sheraton. They knew for certain that Khalid was the principal point of contact. He must have had direct access, not only to Jackson's kidnappers, but also to the people behind many of the recent attacks in the city – they might even be the same people. The Pakistani police were now doubly interested in finding Jackson. And the fastest way to finding Jackson was to break Khalid Jalil, which made the suggestion to set him free all the more baffling.

In his office in Washington, Senator Vance Friedland was also more than interested in Khalid. He assumed that the British or Pakistani authorities would have picked him up by now. Sooner or later, he would start singing his heart out. If that led to them tracking down the missing limey actor, all well and good. The problem was Khalid might also have something to say about the connections the two of them enjoyed.

Rescuing a superstar actor was to be hoped for, but he was damned if it was going to be at his expense. It was time to terminate their relationship – permanently.

He dialled a number simply listed as 'Jack' on his mobile phone. 'Jack' stood for 'Jack of all trades', which was Friedland's own little joke. Jack could take care of anything anywhere.

He had only met Jack once. Ex-military, not an ounce of spare flesh on his bones – all sinew and muscle and very mobile. After they had met in the middle of a crowded Washington Dulles International Airport arrivals lounge, he had said his goodbye and like a ghost had simply vanished into the crowd of passengers. He didn't bump into anyone – he just seemed to glide past the rest of the jostling multitude like a wisp of smoke. There were a lot of men like Jack after years of recent combat in the Iraq and Afghanistan wars. Civvy Street held no attractions – most of them preferred action, even the danger of war was better than being trapped in an office environment. Not all carved out as lucrative a niche as Jack, but Jack and those like him knew theirs was a short career with no generous retirement package at the end.

Friedland didn't know if Jack operated alone or had a team of people he called on. He was encouraged not to ask any unnecessary questions. Just explain what the job was, make the 50 percent deposit and once the job was complete, pay the balance. There were no unsettled accounts, no bad debts; because of course Jack always knew where to find his clients. They always paid.

'I have a job for you, Jack – quite urgent and overseas. Might be a little tricky this time.'

Jack answered: 'No one calls me when it's easy.'

'No, I guess not. I'll leave an envelope at the usual place with some details and your normal fee for an overseas assignment.' Friedland hesitated for a second: 'There might be a small wrinkle. The subject is currently a guest of the British.'

'Any idea how long he is staying with them?'

'As far as I'm concerned, he has already overstayed his welcome and I don't really think it would help me if he stayed any longer.'

'Understood. Keep me updated if the subject has any change in travel plans.'

Friedland knew better than to inquire how Jack would complete the assignment or even how he would track his target down, but he would and the matter would soon be closed.

Fortunately for those who worked in the information-gathering field, generally speaking, data was surprisingly easy to come by. People often talked too much and too carelessly or they needed funds or all three. This was just grist to Jack's particular mill.

No sooner had he collected the package of information – a plain envelope with photographs and every piece of background available about Khalid Jalil – and more importantly, had he confirmed that 50 percent of his fee had been transferred to his bank account, than the process began.

His first call was to an ex-colleague from the British Parachute Regiment – 3 Para – they had been in the several firefights together in Afghanistan. 'Baz' Rahman was Pakistani and was committed to his country. As soon as he left the regiment he signed up with the Pakistani secret service. But Baz – Jack never mastered his unpronounceable real name – was not averse to supplementing his meagre wage with some extra-curricular work. It was easy for him to brief Jack on the latest activity in the search for Jackson Clarke.

He quickly confirmed that the British were holding Khalid Jalil and that he was being moved around constantly – always accompanied by a member of the Pakistani ISI so there was no difficulty keeping track of him. Baz was not complimentary about Jalil and thought if he was being questioned, they were taking their time about getting the information out of him.

'Watch your back on this one, Jack,' warned Baz. 'There's a lot of interest in this subject. Everyone wants to get in on the act. The Brits, the Yanks, my side and freelancers like yourself. Curiously most of them want the same thing, which makes your subject the most popular person in town. Just watch yourself in the cross-fire.'

'Thanks for the warning – I'll keep my eyes open. I'm on a flight over tonight, Baz – I will call you as soon as I arrive. Try not to lose him before I get there.'

'You're welcome to him, Jack – he's not doing anything to help this country. Talk soon.'

Salman Siddiqui felt strangely concerned about his fallen star. He hadn't approved of his methods but the once idol of the newsroom, Awad Fouda, now sat ignored by his colleagues. He was somehow now an untouchable. Rumours built on rumours, but all knew that he had crossed some line. He had got his scoops by talking to terrorists. Some said he had direct links with Al Qaeda and they were nervous even to be seen talking to him in case they too were picked up.

The glowering presence of a security officer in the newsroom didn't help. He was there just to watch Awad Fouda. The strategy was to allow him to remain in the newsroom just to maintain some element of normality. No one could be sure who was watching and on Charlie Barnes' instructions, nothing was to be done that might spook the kidnappers. No one was to be formally arrested or any suggestion made that the net was closing in. The fact that Khan had been picked up in such a heavy-handed way was precisely the public event he wanted to avoid, but on the plus side, they hadn't wasted time in extracting information – so he could not be too critical.

Barnes' caution was well placed. It wasn't just the authorities that were well informed. Every move being made was being relayed back to the teacher. He knew now that the British were interrogating

Khalid; he assumed the techniques used would be at least as brutal as he would employ so he also assumed that Khalid would eventually break – if he had not already done so.

The teacher was not so concerned about the clumsy arrest of Khan, because he had never been to Garanji – they had never met and the politician would have no knowledge of the work Bakri masterminded from his madrassa.

Nevertheless, he needed some protection even from his closest followers. The situation with the actor had to be concluded.

Jackson himself seemed to sense a change in the atmosphere, even though he was quite alone. There was even a renewed nervousness about Sharif when he brought the same frugal meal. As usual, they had exchanged greetings, but for some reason the boy was not his usual self.

Jackson wondered what had changed and thought that perhaps he was just imagining things. The weather outside had even turned gloomy – back home in Britain that was enough to depress everyone. He was certain that there was going to be a storm of some kind. But these visits from Sharif were all that broke the monotony and he refused to waste an opportunity.

It was difficult to communicate when they had no common language beyond a few basic words, but Jackson did not want to lose the tenuous link with humanity that he felt he had established. Something told him that he had a chance to help Sharif. He was certain that given different circumstances and different opportunities, the boy would not have been guarding kidnap victims. He would have been at college learning to be a doctor or a teacher – not a soldier. As he watched Sharif place his food down carefully on the bed, instead of just throwing it quickly through the door onto the floor as he had done at first, Jackson thought about his own childhood.

He might easily have been a criminal, growing up in the rougher parts of Glasgow – had it not been for a chance encounter with a Catholic priest who ran a youth club. He had notice Jackson's acting potential and had encouraged him. By contrast, Sharif was under the influence of Abdul Bakri – a man who no doubt regarded himself as a cleric, but what path had he set the boy on? Could he even think clearly for himself? Jackson had heard that some madrassas could virtually brainwash young impressionable minds. This was clearly what had happened to Dr Mitra. There was nothing that could be said or done to make him change his views, but there was still an independent spark in Sharif.

Jackson stood up and walked over to the boy to thank him once again for his food. They now had a ritual where they would shake hands every morning and every evening in greeting, but only if the other guard on the door was not watching. On this occasion Jackson shook his hand a little longer looking deep into his eyes. This was what Kutub Reza often did during Jackson's visits to Stockley Road. Words were not necessary; just listen to the silence he would urge.

The silence on this occasion was full of foreboding. Was that a slight frown he saw on Sharif's face? Did the boy know something? What was about to happen? Of course there was no answer, no word from the boy who soon left him alone again.

As quickly as the questions came, Jackson deliberately drove them from his mind. He would not allow himself the luxury of wallowing in self-pity. How would some of the heroic characters he had played over the years have reacted? 'Laugh in the face of adversity' was the great cliché – maybe now was as good as time as any to draw on some of those clichés. This thought made Jackson laugh out loud.

On the other side of the door Sharif and the other guard stopped and looked back at the locked door. They were baffled, but Sharif was beginning to admire the strength of character in his prisoner. All his young life he had admired others – his father, then the teacher and Jabbar.

Just then, he realised that he hadn't thought once about Jabbar since the foreigner had arrived. He was confused. Jabbar had once been his hero. He wanted to emulate his every move. He was strong. He always knew what to do. And now he found himself looking forward to taking a meal to this stranger – the man the teacher hated so much. When faced with gunmen threatening to kill him in the video, he simply smiled. He always smiled. And now he laughed. What did he have to be so happy about? He might be about to die. Did he realise?

Sharif looked at the other guard who was shaking his head in disbelief. He asked him what he thought, but the guard just said the foreigner was going mad. Sharif didn't think so – although he still didn't understand what he should believe.

This strange man was kind when he should have been angry; he was fearless in talking to the teacher when he should have been terrified; he spoke a language Sharif did not understand but his eyes told him that the words he uttered were not violent words and contained no anger. The stranger was not a threat. He wondered what he had done that had made him such a bad man as far as the teacher was concerned. Of course, he had never seen the films the teacher spoke of and he wondered what they could have shown that was so evil. The stranger did not look like he would do anything that was evil. Sharif resolved to listen even more carefully to what the teacher had to say when he spoke to the whole madrassa later that day.

He wondered what Jabbar would have thought of the stranger. Would he have liked him? Would he have shaken the stranger's hand? Certainly not – but what would his father have done? Would he have been prepared to smile at the stranger? Sharif smiled himself – undoubtedly yes.

# CHAPTER TWENTY-TWO

Khalid had been left alone, allowing him to think about his options and to worry about what might happen if he did not cooperate. As his British interrogator had made clear, his choices were limited. He could tell them everything he knew – which Khalid realised meant revealing all about the teacher, about Garanji, the training camp and the shepherding services he provided for the newcomers to the madrassa. Or he could keep his mouth shut.

Option one meant he would almost certainly be killed by the teacher's associates and option two meant he would have the information beaten out of him by Pakistani interrogators. If he survived that questioning, he would still face the wrath of the teacher. Khalid wasn't one of the foot soldiers happy to lose his own life for the sake of a cause – religious or otherwise. The only question was what would be best for Khalid Jalil? It was time to make a deal.

On cue Charlie Barnes walked into the room and sat across the table from Khalid. 'Now is the hour, Khalid. If you were the kidnapper where would you be holding Jackson Clarke?'

'I don't where he is being held – but I could guess.'

Barnes looked at Khalid, reeling him in carefully: 'Let's start with a guess.'

'I have been up to the north of Pakistan. It's a small town and well away from any main routes. You would only go that way if you wanted to get to the town.'

Barnes said nothing as Khalid inched closer to naming some names, then he seemed to hesitate again. The fish was wriggling on the line.

'We have a deal, don't we? I'll be taken to Europe and given a new identity. A new life?'

'Don't worry, you will have a new life. Now where would you take someone if you wanted to hide him?'

'Hypothetically, you mean?'

'Time has run out, Khalid. I don't intend to play any more games.'

'There is a town called Garanji. I have been there once.' Khalid caught Barnes's look and added: 'Several times. This would be a good place to hide someone.'

'Why did you go to Garanji? How do you know this town?' Barnes probed. He knew the conversation was being monitored in the adjoining room by Victor Jones, who in turn was to pass any information on to Benson. But no moves would be made until Barnes gave the word.

'As I say I have been there before to take–'

'Let me guess: you have taken new recruits up there. Is it some sort of training facility. Perhaps a terrorist camp?'

'No ... well ... There is a madrassa there. It is a religious school,' Khalid spluttered.

'Really? And what sort of teaching do they receive in this school? How to murder? How to make bombs? How to kidnap even?'

'How do I know what they learn? I take them there or I arrange for them to go there.'

'And the place we raided the other day – the little diversion you organised for us – that was what a sort half way house?'

'Yes,' said Khalid simply. He was past fighting.

'And when they were suitably educated you contacted our friendly journalist, Awad Fouda – and he just happened to be on the scene when the next bomb went off. Is that how it worked?'

'I just helped people get to the north. I wasn't responsible.'

'I think we both know that's not true. And what about the special assignments you carried out for your American client? Were you not responsible for those either?'

Khalid made one last attempt to fight back: 'It was in the interests of the West.'

'Well, that's a matter of opinion. Now from whom do you take your orders? I think you mentioned a name? 'Abdul'?'

218

'Abdul Bakri. He is the head of a madrassa in Garanji. He gives me instructions.'

'And of course, he was the one who sent you the video of Jackson?'

'Yes.'

'Well why the bloody hell didn't you tell me that in the first place?!' Barnes exploded standing up sending his chair flying across the room. 'If anything happens to him – if he has so much as a bruise on his body – then I will hold you personally responsible!'

'But we had a deal!' Khalid protested.

'You, my friend, are a terrorist in all but name. I don't do deals with terrorists.'

Barnes stormed out of the room banging the door, which swung back open on its hinges. Khalid saw the two security men who had snatched him off the street standing unsmiling outside in the corridor. One stepped forward and quietly closed the door.

Katherine was thrilled and hysterical: 'Well what are we waiting for? Why don't the security people – the police, army, whatever – go to this Garanji place and find Jackson?'

'A raid is being organised right now and Barnes is making sure it is done right. They can't just go crashing in all guns blazing, which is probably how the locals would like to do it.' McLeod was trying to persuade Katherine to sit down, but rational thought and behaviour wasn't easy when those nearest and dearest to you were at risk. Every second that ticked by seemed to be a second wasted.

'The problem is this guy, Khalid, has led us on a wild goose chase once before. There's no knowing he is doing the same thing again. The other problem is we are not dealing with the SAS here. The local militia are not trained in this sort of search and rescue operation.'

It made no sense to Katherine, who now felt she was so close to having Jackson back. Surely she would not lose him again.

As for Barnes, not only did he have a military assault to conduct on a target located a thousand-plus miles from where he was now standing (which was the Pakistani ISI headquarters in Karachi), but he also had local politics to contend with and all the local tensions. The police felt they should be handling it; the military said only they were trained for such an operation; and the ISI felt only they had the undercover skills necessary.

None of this helped Barnes who just wanted to get up to Garanji by helicopter with the best half-dozen men he could muster. Anymore and it would have turned into a crapshoot with innocent people being caught in the crossfire – possibly even Jackson himself.

After a lot of raised voices, everyone finally calmed down and it was agreed that one ISI officer would accompany a small contingent from the military. A helicopter would be made ready and they would leave at dusk, aiming to land near Garanji and make the final approach on foot. No one said so but it was clear that Barnes would be in charge of the operation, even though the army would only be taking direct orders from the most senior officer among them.

Needless to say there were only rudimentary plans for Garanji, which meant Barnes would have to have another talk to Khalid to establish the lay out. Before he left he was introduced to the men he would be leading.

The military looked competent enough but Barnes doubted that they had been in a real firefight in their lives. At least an attack on a madrassa should not provoke too much resistance.

'And this is Officer Rahman. He will be representing the ISI. He has a lot of experience. He used to be in your British Parachute Regiment,' said one of the officials briefing them.

Barnes looked round at the only man who had remained silent throughout the noisy exchanges. He had piercing blue eyes, which was rare for a Pakistani, and a dark swarthy complexion. Barnes reached out to shake his hand.

'Ex-para, eh? Well that's a surprise. Welcome to the party.'

'Thank you, I look forward to it,' was all Rahman said.

Officer 'Baz' Rahman was thinking that he would just have time to brief Jack on the last location he had for Khalid Jalil before they left on the mission.

In fact Khalid had – on Barnes' instructions – been moved again to a new location in the heart of the city. He was in a small room in a seemingly deserted apartment building. Panic was quickly setting in. The only person he thought he could rely on had turned on him. At this stage, just getting out of the city safely would be acceptable.

He almost jumped when Barnes pushed open the door. The ISI officer and the two British security men took up their positions by the door and the window.

'Just one thing Khalid: can I be absolutely certain that I will find Jackson in this madrassa?' Barnes placed a rudimentary map of the location on the table and stabbed a finger at a line of buildings.

Khalid thought he had another chance; his last chance. This wasn't the time to negotiate – it was the time to tell them everything he knew. He might still be released.

'It is an old map but I think that is the madrassa. It will be obvious from the sign when you get there. But it is possible that–' Khalid hesitated. What he was about to say clearly placed him at the heart of the terrorist network, but he had no choice.

'What is possible?' asked Barnes.

'This road leads out of the town to the north – there I think that is the one,' said Khalid, tracing a single line away from Garanji. 'There is a place in the hills about quarter of an hour away by car where we ... they do some training. There are some buildings – just sheds really – I think that is the most likely place they will be holding him. They would not keep him in the madrassa itself.'

Barnes was silent, weighing up his options. He only had a small team: somehow they would have to hit both locations at the same time.

He looked at Khalid and decided that this time he was telling the truth. A foreigner in the middle of a town like Garanji would have been too obvious. He would have stood out and someone would have said something. The man called Abdul Bakri had so far played his cards carefully and Barnes concluded that he would not have taken such a casual risk.

Finally he said: 'I think you're right. What you have got to do now is try very hard indeed to remember everything you can about this training camp. Think about how you would get there by car and just perhaps we will be able to work out where it is on the map.'

Half an hour later they had narrowed the options down to just two possible locations. Assuming Jackson was being guarded day and night, it should be possible to overfly both places and look for telltale lights or fires being burned by the guards to keep warm.

As Barnes made to leave, Khalid tried one more appeal: 'I have told you everything I know. I am not a terrorist. Maybe I am weak, but I am not a kidnapper. I want to leave this country. I don't want to see these people again. I have never killed anyone I swear.'

Barnes looked at Khalid: no longer the smooth operator with ambitions to lead the fast life in the West; no longer the one who could rise above all the blood and the bullets never wanting to get his own fingers dirty. For years, Barnes assumed, he had been happy to arrange for young impressionable men to be transported around the world to training camps where they would be turned into suicide bombers and killers.

'You really don't care about anyone else, do you Khalid? It's always number one. I don't even suppose you care about your religion that much either. At least fanatics like Dr Mitra and your Abdul Bakri – what did you call him? 'Master'? – at least they have some passion and belief. I abhor what they do in the name of that belief which has nothing to do with their so-called faith, but at least they think what they are doing is right. Why should I treat you any differently to the way I fully intend to treat them when I get to Garanji?'

Khalid had no fight left. His focus had always been on himself: getting rich; rich enough to live the life he briefly tasted when he travelled to the West himself. The teenagers he selected from the mosques in London and nurtured until he could deliver them into the hands of Abdul Bakri and his assistants were blind, ignorant or stupid.

He had managed to justify the killing of industrialists like Haider to himself by saying he was anti-communist and that it was for the greater good of his country, but he knew what his real motivation was.

Khalid could not answer.

'You are not a dangerous man yourself, Khalid,' said Barnes; 'but you live off the misery that others cause while they proclaim what they are doing in the name of religion. You're a parasite, Khalid, and in my book no better than the gunmen themselves. But your biggest problem now is that your people have upset some of my friends and that in turn has upset me.'

Barnes folded up the map and signalled for the others to leave the room.

'I don't know what is to become of you, Khalid, and frankly I don't really care. I am not a policeman and I am not a judge. This is not my country. If you and your fellow countrymen want to carry on killing each other in the name of some god I personally don't believe in, good luck to you. But you cross the line when you start attacking my people. I have one simple task: to rescue Jackson Clarke and get him safely back to England. And that's what I intend to do.'

'What happens to me now?' asked Khalid desperaely.

Barnes stopped at the door: 'Frankly, I don't care. As far as I'm concerned, you are not a threat and you are of no value. I don't think you will want to make contact with your friends in the north because I shall make sure that everyone knows all about our discussions. Your role as a fixer for terrorists is over. No one will trust you any longer. What the local authorities have to say about all this is up to them.'

Without saying another word, he turned and left the room leaving the door wide open.

'This is Jack.'

'Welcome to Pakistan.'

'Is the package still available?'

'Yes, but it may not be for long. It might be moved. Interest in it is mixed at the moment. Some of us have lost interest as we have extracted all we need, but I wouldn't be surprised if others would still like to have a close look at the contents.'

'How much time do I have?'

'I suggest you get to the location as soon as possible and collect it or dispose of it as you wish. I have got to leave town shortly. I don't suppose you'll still be around when I get back.'

'Understood. Your Christmas present will be posted as usual regardless of the state of the package when I find it.'

The line went dead and Baz Rahman got up from his desk to prepare for the flight to Garanji.

Jack just had to make one stop before heading to the address Baz had given him. It was a pharmacy run by Baz Rahman's uncle.

'I wonder if you sell inhalers for asthma?' Jack asked the elderly man behind the counter.

'You are very lucky sir, we have just had a delivery. Do you have a note from your doctor?' the old man asked.

'No, I'm sorry. I have just arrived in town and realised that my own inhaler has run out.'

'That won't be a problem. I wonder if you could just come into the office and sign for it.'

Jack nodded and walked round the counter to a back office.

'Baz told me to expect you. I didn't think you would be here so soon,' said the pharmacist shaking Jack's hand.

'It was a bit of a rush job. Is it all here?' asked Jack looking at the small hold-all the pharmacist handed him.

'I haven't looked inside, of course, but Baz said it was everything you asked for on your ... er ... prescription. I gather it is quite difficult to get this medicine through customs.' Jack opened the bag. Everything he needed – two small handguns and a throwing knife.

'Thank you. I won't keep you any longer. This is for your trouble,' Jack pushed a bundle of dollar bills into the pharmacist's white coat pocket and left by a back door.

# CHAPTER TWENTY-THREE

Khalid sat staring at the open door. It was either an invitation to make a run for it or it was a trap. He tried to peer round the door without getting up from his chair, to see if the security men were still on guard in the corridor. He couldn't see them. He couldn't hear them, but they might still be there.

If he gave them an excuse they could claim to have been trying to stop a fleeing suspected terrorist. Who would have complained? Who would even have known?

The silence continued and he began to hear the sounds of the street outside. Somehow he had muffled the volume of the outside world, which he knew was only the other side of the window during his interrogation. That world had not mattered for days. It was only he and his inquisitors. They were his world; the rooms he was kept in his only existence. Even when he was being transported from location to location, he was still apart from the everyday life his fellow Pakistanis were living.

Now he thought he could return to the real world, but then he remembered: he would never know who had been informed about his background. Who was waiting to kill him for the work he had done – not only for the teacher but also for the American?

'The American,' he said softly to himself. 'Friedland.' It was only then that he remembered his insurance policy – the recordings he had made of his conversation with Senator Vance Friedland. If he could not work as he had done any longer, then it was in part because of the senator and he would have to pay for his early retirement.

Khalid suddenly perked up. Perhaps his prospects did not look so bleak. All he had to do was leave this building. The door was open. He was certain he had been left alone. All he had to do was walk out of the apartment block into the sunshine outside. For once, even the heat of a late Karachi afternoon seemed appealing.

Slowly he stood up and edged towards the door. He pulled it back, fully expecting to be shouted at or hit by one of the security detail. Nothing. There was no one immediately outside and there was no one in the corridor. He waited, not daring to believe his luck.

His old confidence was beginning to return. Yes, Senator Vance Friedland of Washington would ensure he had a long and comfortable life. He might even be able to arrange for him to go directly to America. Of course, that all depended on the miniature tape still being there. It should be, as it was well hidden in a wall cavity in his kitchen which he had found accidentally when he first moved into his apartment. The builders must have thought it was easier to board it over and plaster rather than deal with an awkward corner. Khalid had redecorated the corner himself and was quite proud of the work he had done.

At the top of the stairs he stopped and looked down into the stairwell at the landing below. There was no one – he had definitely been abandoned.

Now on the ground floor, he inched towards the front door, which was also ajar. It seemed they had wanted him to escape and were showing him the way out. The street noises were now back to their familiar din – he had allowed them back into his mind and was letting himself dare to believe he had a second chance.

It was time to rethink his position. At least now he had might live. He had an insurance policy to survive on. He assumed the teacher would guess who had led the raiding party to Garanji, when eventually it struck – presumably that night – but even if the teacher survived, he would be long gone.

Along with the tape he had stashed his false passports and a supply of dollars – not enough to get to America but enough to get out of Pakistan. If he could access his on-line banking account, he would have enough to survive for some months – but he assumed they had been frozen or at least being watched electronically. He wouldn't make such a simple mistake. He would leave those alone until he was sure he was clear of danger. Who would bother chasing after him once they had rescued the actor? They would probably arrest the teacher or he might even be killed in the raid. Without the teacher to guide them they would all be lost. There would be no one to run the madrassa. There would be no one to organise a hit on him.

With a deep breath he opened the door onto the street. Nothing. No shot. No screams from the passers-by that he was a traitor, that he was a spy for the Americans. No one gave him a second glance. It had all been bluff. He shut his eyes and let the welcome noise of the street sounds wash over him. Dusk was beginning to fall and everyone was thinking about enjoying the evening after the heat of the day.

Suddenly there was a roar from a motorbike. Khalid spun round to see two men racing down the street in his direction. He froze. Impossible. How could the teacher know he was here?

He put his hand out behind him to push the door of the apartment building open but it had slammed shut. They were already on to him. He put his hand up to his face bracing himself for the blast but the motorbike sped by. One or two people looked at the strange man sheltering his eyes from something and walked quickly past. Had he never seen a motorbike before? Crazy kids. Crazy man.

Khalid leant back against the wall panting. Was this how his life was going to be from now on? Constantly jumping every time he heard a loud noise and always looking over his shoulder waiting for the attack? He tried to pull himself together, still holding on to the wall as though he would fall over without its support.

'Calm down,' he said to himself. 'Think rationally. You're in the clear. No one is after you. You have your insurance.' *The Vance Friedland Fund for Khalid Jalil* – it sounded good. He could leave this country and this life forever. No more clandestine meetings, no more taking misguided teenagers around the world on a one-way ticket to certain death.

The street was right in the centre of Karachi, close to the Saddar Bazaar. 'Clever', thought Khalid as he recovered. 'A secure house, hidden in full view'. It was one of the most crowded parts of the city at all times of day where everyone was too busy thinking about their own affairs to see what might be happening right in front of them.

The afternoon light was beginning to fade, which suited Khalid as he skulked along the pavements with his head down, not wanting to catch anyone's eye – or worse still: see anyone he might recognise. In 24 hours he would have vanished from the city and be forgotten. Only one or two of the private club owners would wonder what had become of one of their best customers, but even they would soon stop thinking about him. He had no history anyhow. No one knew what he really did. He travelled and everyone assumed he was a private businessman – although he never discussed what line of business.

But Khalid was not a forgotten figure. From the moment he stepped out of the apartment block he had been watched. Jack looked like just another of the bargain-hunting tourists – mostly backpackers who were prepared to take a chance with Pakistan's volatile political climate. He had allowed himself a quiet laugh when Khalid had been startled by the boys on the motorbike. A traffic accident would have been too easy.

A hand reached out and touched Jack's sleeve. He turned sharply but it was just another shopkeeper with another must-buy bargain. He looked back again in time to see Khalid disappearing down a side street.

Jack ran across the road, ignoring the blaring horns of the undisciplined flow of traffic, every driver forcing and pushing their way looking for the smallest advantage. It was the old favourite adage about the Asian Highway Code: all you need is good brakes, a good horn and good luck.

Good luck was something you made for yourself in Jack's book and that came from total all-round awareness. It didn't matter how crowded a room or even a street scene, your quarry or even your hunter moved at a different speed to the rest of humanity. If you looked for the signs you could see the difference. And Jack knew he was not alone in this hunt.

Just occasionally there would be a movement which was out of synch with the rest of the crowd – slightly too quick, slightly too jerky. There was someone else who was either following him or following Khalid. As far as Jack was concerned, that meant he had two preys – until he could establish who else was in the game and why they were there.

Baz had warned him that there was others interested in the package. 'Don't get hit in the crossfire' he had told him.

Khalid was moving faster now, trying to put good distance between himself and the apartment building.

The increased speed helped Jack. Darting round a corner, moving erratically between the shop fronts, he saw the other target. He looked like a Pakistani in traditional dress, indistinguishable from everyone around. Jack was impressed. The man was maintaining a good distance, manoeuvring until he could pick his moment. His only fault was he was totally unaware of Jack's presence. He was so fixated on his target that he could not see the danger he himself might be in.

But then the man didn't mind. The teacher had told him he was in no danger. Once he knew for certain that Khalid had been held for questioning, the teacher had used his own informants at the city police headquarters to locate Khalid. It was then simply a case of biding his time. He assumed that Khalid would be imprisoned, but as he was actually being questioned by the British he couldn't be sure so he had entrusted Shaheed – one of his most devoted students who was born and bred in Karachi – with the task to watch and wait. If the chance presented itself, he knew what he had to do. If he was caught he should fight and never surrender.

Shaheed knew Khalid from his occasional visits to the madrassa and he had been surprised when the teacher told him that they had all been betrayed. Khalid Jalil had turned against them; corrupted by the life he had been leading not only in Karachi but also on his trips to the West. Everything they stood for was in danger because brother Jalil had forgotten his duty to Allah.

He picked up the pace again. This was the best place. The street was narrow and dark. Khalid was just 20 paces ahead, his head down. Shaheed felt the knife in his jacket pocket and tightened his grip on the handle. He quickly looked up and down the street. There was no one – only a small group of tourists too far away to be able to identify him.

He called out: 'Khalid. Is that you, brother?'

Khalid stopped dead, his heart pounding. Who could know him in this street? What should he do? He turned and tried to make out the face of the man in the gloom.

'Who is that?' he asked

'Brother, it is me, Shaheed. From Garanji.'

The mere word Garanji made Khalid want to bolt. It was a million miles away – another place, another lifetime. He struggled to place the name 'Shaheed', as the youth got closer.

'Shaheed, yes, I remember. What are you doing in Karachi?'

'I have come to see you. The teacher asked me to give you this. Allahu Akbar.' He pulled out his knife and lunged clumsily at Khalid's stomach but missed his target, striking him in the ribs.

Khalid lashed out in self-defence, striking Shaheed on the shoulder and both fell to the ground scrabbling for the knife, which lay just out of reach. In a frenzy of blows they punched and kicked. Panic gave Khalid added strength as he pushed Shaheed away crawling to pick up the knife. But he never saw the other blade slashing down from behind cutting through his carotid artery. He died instantly.

Shaheed rolled over to see a figure standing over him. His face obscured in the half-light.

'Who are you? What are you doing?' Shaheed asked in Arabic.

'A pity you didn't do a better job for me. You could have got away with it,' said Jack leaning over. And with a backhand strike his knife flashed across Shaheed's throat.

Jack looked up and down the street. There was no one in sight. If someone had seen anything from one of the windows they were not reacting. Why get involved? Jack wiped both knives, just in case there were any fingerprints and threw them back into the gutter. It would go down as just another fight in the street that would remain unreported and unsolved. There were bigger crimes to investigate.

Just as silently and swiftly as he had arrived, Jack was soon out of the street and mingling with the crowds. He called Vance Friedland: 'Two for the price of one. The package has been dispatched along with a secondary item, which happened to be attached. I am leaving town.'

'Very good. I shall arrange for the rest of your present to be transferred today. Have a nice day.' Friedland smiled one of his smug self-satisfied smiles. Another loose end had been tied up. There was nothing that could connect him to any of Khalid Jalil's assignments. The Pakistan chapter could be closed.

As Jack made his way back to his hotel he called ahead to the helpful secretary who took care of the guests on the exclusive 'club floor': 'I'll be checking out today. Could you arrange for my bill to be made up and call ahead to Emirates Airlines to confirm my reservation for tonight?'

'Of course, sir, and would you like a car to take you to the airport?'

'Thank you, that would be kind although it sounds as though I'm at the airport already.'

'It does indeed, sir. We will see you later.'

Jack glanced up at the low-flying Chinook as it banked away over the city heading north its navigation lights flashing in the dusk.


Katherine looked exhausted as she came into the meeting room. Only Victor Jones and Rory McLeod were in there, studying maps and talking quietly. It was as though there was nothing more to be done. All the decisions had been taken, the rehearsals were over and it was now up to others.

'Will they have left yet?' she asked.

McLeod looked at his watch: 'Just now, I'd say. It will take them some time to fly up there and then make their way to the location on foot. You should get something to eat and rest. Charlie will call us as soon as they have Jackson.'

'If they have Jackson, you mean.' Katherine had nearly given up all hope and alone in her room she had even started contemplating life without Jackson. It would be impossible.

'Don't think like that Katherine. All the evidence, all the intelligence, points in this direction. I am certain they are going to find him. He might be a little thinner but he will be alive, I have no doubt.' McLeod led Katherine to a chair. 'Can I get something sent up for you? You've got to eat.'

'I'm not hungry, Rory.' She hesitated then asked the question which had started gnawing away in her mind: 'This Khalid – are we sure...?'

'Katherine, of course we are sure. Charlie is the best. He reads people like a book and he knows when they are lying. He said he was absolutely convinced that he would find Jackson in this town.'

'And what if it is another wild goose chase – what will this Khalid character tell us then?'

McLeod looked at Jones who nodded briefly. 'Well, that's why we are absolutely convinced that he was telling the truth.'

'What? What's happened now?' Katherine was on her feet, her hands clasped round her shoulders, fear once again in her eyes.

'The local police found Khalid Jalil's body in the street not far from the place where he was being questioned. He had been stabbed. There was another man dead beside him. It appears there had been a fight and they killed one another. At least that's what the police think, although judging by the wounds, I think we can safely say there was a third person involved, but we don't know for sure and we don't know his agenda.'

Katherine gasped holding her hand up to her mouth: 'Oh, God! So we have no more contacts. No more leads.'

'I'd say it's the reverse. The fact that someone – possibly more than one person – wanted him dead so badly must mean that he was telling the truth about Garanji. Someone wanted to stop him talking. But they were too late.' McLeod's voice tailed off. He knew that Katherine was right. If Charlie Barnes and his team failed to find Jackson there was nowhere else to go.

'What if they get there and it's too late? They might have already–' Katherine started sobbing and sunk back down into her chair.

'I refuse to believe that Jackson will not make another film. By the end of tomorrow he will be sitting with us. He will be safe and the whole affair will be over. In another 48 hours you will be at home in Cedars, sitting by a fire. It will just be a bad dream. Come on – not long now.' McLeod bent down and held Katherine's hands in his. 'Not long.'

Jones hoped McLeod was right and looked back down at the paperwork on the table. Jones was a details man. He liked to be sure everything had been taken care of: all the unanswered questions at least explored if not satisfactorily answered.

The mystery assassin who had taken out Jalil and the second victim would probably never be identified, but there was one puzzle he would like to get to the bottom of before the story finally closed. He underlined an entry on the list of items recovered from Khalid Jalil's home. Apart from the false passports that had been found hidden away in a wall cavity and the large quantities of US dollar bills, there was a small cassette tape. In itself of no real value, and yet Jalil had thought it was significant enough to hide away with his false passports and cash.

All efforts had been focussed on the rescue mission for Jackson but Jones made a mental note to ask for the transcript as soon as it was ready after everyone had returned safely. It looked like Jalil had been saving the tape for a rainy day. It might be connected – it might not – but Jones was prepared to bet that whoever was speaking on the tape would rather it was not broadcast too widely, if at all. Maybe Khalid had a little blackmail on his mind. Something incriminating was on that recording and someone would be keen for it not to be found, assuming they knew it existed in the first place. He got his red pen and put a circle round the letter 'F' followed by a question mark. The letter was the only distinguishing feature on the tape. Jones wondered what the letter stood for – or even for whom did it stand?

# CHAPTER TWENTY-FOUR

Abdul Bakri said nothing. He had been sitting silently for several minutes, occasionally asking a question to clarify some point. Dr Mitra and the other assistants knew better than to interrupt his thinking. The news had been unexpected and while one problem had been resolved another had been created.

Khalid Jalil was dead and no one could identify his attacker. They might if they had put some additional effort into the investigation but it was low-priority for the police. The worrying part for Bakri was that Shaheed – who was almost like a son to Bakri – was also dead. It would have been impossible for them to kill one another, which meant there was a third party involved. Assuming no one was interested in Shaheed, it meant someone else wanted Khalid dead. And if they knew so much about Khalid – that he was a threat to them – then it was probable that they could follow a trail back to the madrassa.

For all his adult life, Abdul Bakri had lived and worked in Garanji building up the school. It was his entire existence and he had no intention of giving it all up. Jackson Clarke was the answer. It was a difficult path to tread: he wanted his paymasters in the Muslim world to acknowledge the coup he had managed to deliver, but he wanted none of the security attention which would follow if his name got out.

The teacher's informant had told him that there was an unusual amount of activity at the army base in Karachi. He didn't know for certain but he thought some sort of military operation was being planned – it wasn't a police raid because they had been specifically excluded which had upset the station chief.

Raids were a regular occurrence against the Taliban bases as the Pakistan government struggled to fight the insurgents – many of whom had direct links straight into the heart of the most sensitive buildings. Attacks on police stations and even intelligence headquarters in the major cities had become commonplace. With every assault by terrorists came a counter by the Government, so the informant could not say what this particular operation was targeting. Bakri did not want to wait to find out.

He pushed a phone across the desk to Mitra: 'Brother, we must tell them that we have run out of patience. Their time is up. Say nothing else.'

Mitra dialled Jackson's mobile number and waited.

The phone rang and vibrated on the desk in the meeting room, but as agreed neither Benson, Jones nor McLeod answered it. Charlie Barnes had been clear there would be nothing either side could say to bring about any change in Jackson's fortunes. By not answering any calls it would at least create some uncertainty among the kidnappers. It was an unorthodox strategy, as the normal rule was to keep hostage-takers talking but Barnes reckoned the silence might buy them some precious moments.

Mitra looked at the teacher, holding out the phone so he could hear the ringing tone. Bakri signalled to turn it off. The silence made him nervous. It was time to move to the action he had known all along he would have to take. He said to one of the assistants: 'Tell Brother Sharif to come here.'

If they wanted confrontation, Bakri thought he was prepared to deliver. Once and for all he would make a statement about the disease spreading from the West and the strength with which it would be opposed. The path was clear – it had always been clear – and the foreigner Jackson Clarke would be the one who would be used to get that message across. His only regret about Garanji had always been that he had not been able to reach the thousands of people being led astray in cities like Karachi and Islamabad. But now he had his audience; the world was watching and waiting to see what would happen to their idol, Jackson Clarke. Well, they would not have to wait much longer.

Sharif had been taken off his Jackson-watching duties. The teacher had seen what was happening. He didn't think the actor could change Sharif in his beliefs, but he saw that the Jackson Clarke was gaining strength and energy from their exchanges. It was giving the foreigner hope and it was giving him some purpose and Bakri refused to provide his prisoner with any comforts.

Jackson was sorry not to see Sharif when his next meal arrived; not for himself but because he thought the boy was being punished for showing too much friendship towards him.

'The Stockholm Syndrome in reverse', thought Jackson. The jailer was sympathising with the prisoner rather than the other way round. He wondered why kindness should be seen as a sign of weakness. It was the very opposite: it was much harder to do something for a person you hated. Abdul Bakri wanted to have the respect of his students and followers, but all he did have was fear. Jackson remembered his own teachers from the tough Scottish schools he had attended as a boy. The ones who achieved the most and got the best results, were the teachers who had ruled by authority blended with kindness and understanding. What was the purpose of so much animosity and, at times, hatred between religions – even within a single religion like Sunnis and Shias, Catholics and Anglicans?

Sharif sat on his hard wooden bed with a copy of the Qur'an open on his lap, wondering what had happened. He knew he had upset the teacher but didn't know how. Should he have not have shaken the foreigner's hand? Was that what he had done wrong? Had his brother guard reported him to the teacher? And what about the foreigner? Was he an evil man? He didn't look like one. What had he done in the past – before he came to Garanji – which had angered the teacher so much? Why was he so troubled by all these things? Everything had been so clear until the stranger had arrived. He resolved to ask one of his instructors about it, but he should not show his weakness. He was having the same thoughts as he'd had after they killed the infidel Haider. Nothing was clear anymore and he started thinking of his father and his family. He hadn't thought of them for a long time and wondered what advice they would all be giving him now. His father would want him to be strong and to do the right thing.

Sharif looked up as the assistant pushed open the door and told him the teacher wanted to see him. His heart leapt. The teacher would know the answer to all these questions, but just as quickly, Sharif realised that he would never be able to ask them. He had never addressed more than a few words directly to the teacher so why should he now waste time with a lowly creature like himself? Why did he want to see him? He had been summoned personally to the teacher's house. He had never even seen inside after so many years at the madrassa.

Sharif jumped up and brushed the front of his *salwar kameez* as though he was getting ready for a formal gathering. What would he want? What would he – Sharif – say when addressed directly by the teacher?

He hurried across the courtyard behind the assistant, as other students in the madrassa watched him with envious eyes. Then Sharif realised why he must have been summoned. It was because of what the stranger had said, although he hadn't understood the language. Whatever it was it was clear that the teacher had not been pleased. Would he be thrown out of the madrassa? Where would he go? Back to his village? But he had no skills: he had forgotten what little he knew about looking after the animals for his father.

He would try to explain if the teacher let him. He tried to fill his heart with courage. He would say that the stranger tried to trick him by smiling, by trying to say a few words in Urdu or Pashto. But he would assure the teacher that he was strong. He was strong like Jabbar. The stranger was an infidel.

Nervously Sharif entered the teacher's room. He looked around in awe. There were many books, unlike his own room where all he had was his worn copy of the Qur'an. He was surprised to see a TV turned on in the corner. He thought the teacher was against all such things. The last time he had seen a television was in a shop in his home village – it was the only one and all the men used to gather round it in the evenings when work in the fields was done. Sharif never really understood the programmes they were watching.

The teacher was standing at one end of the room talking quietly to one of his assistants. He glanced up at Sharif and then continued talking for a few moments before coming over. He looked solemn and Sharif felt certain he had done something terribly wrong.

'Brother, you have had a difficult duty watching the stranger and I know he has been trying to mislead you.' He held his hand up when Sharif tried to speak up. 'I do not blame you. It is just what I would expect from the western culture – their poisonous ways. But it is now time to show your strength.'

'I will, Teacher. I am strong and with Allah's will I will be able to do my duty. What can I do?' Sharif was relieved and now he wanted to show he was worthy of everything he had learned.

'The foreign infidel must pay for his insults against Islam and I have chosen you, Sharif, for the task.'

Sharif began to feel less certain. He knew the stranger was an infidel but what did the teacher expect of him? Surely he would not think of...

'Sharif, the foreigner must pay with his life and it is your honour to defend Islam. You will execute him.'

The words echoed round his head: 'Execute him. Execute him.' It was his duty; his honour; but Sharif suddenly realised too late that the stranger had somehow become a friend. He had shaken his hand every morning. He had even smiled at him. He had looked in his eyes. Were they really the eyes of the enemy?

The teacher was talking but Sharif was not listening: '...this will show the Westerners that they cannot come to our land and spread their disease. This will be seen around the world. No one will ever dare challenge our faith again. Do you understand brother? This will be an important day. You will be remembered like Brother Jabbar.'

'But, Master, how ... when do I...?'

'Everything will be arranged. But we do not have much time. Brother Khalid has been killed in Karachi and others may be on their way to stop us in our legitimate struggle. We will go to the camp immediately. You must make yourself ready to do this sacred thing. Prepare yourself.'

'Yes, Master,' said Sharif as he was ushered from the room.

The sun's afternoon rays still burned down from a clear sky, but Sharif felt none of their warmth. Was this how it had been for Jabbar when he had been chosen to kill the man Haider and his family? Had he hesitated when he had been handed the honour of the task? Had he felt fear when he looked into the faces of those he had killed? Sharif was struggling to understand why the shooting of Haider and his sons seemed easier than what he had been told to do a few moments ago.

And who had killed Khalid? Who did the teacher think would be coming to Garanji to stop them? For Sharif, the teacher was the law and the authority. He could not even conceive of anyone being able to threaten him.

With a heavy heart Sharif returned to his room. The other students looked up but said nothing. They could tell from his face that he had been shocked. They wanted to know if he had been punished or if he had been given the ultimate honour – a chance to fulfil his duty. They guessed he had been rewarded for his faith and he would soon be in Paradise.

Sharif did not say a word. He sat on his bed and held the Qur'an in his hands. He didn't open it. There wasn't a passage of prayer he could think of which would help him now. All along he had assumed he would be given the chance to fight against an enemy of Pakistan; an enemy of Islam. He would know the righteousness of his actions. He would be proud. But now he would have to kill the stranger who had shaken his hand, who had been kind, who had smiled at him every day.

The others returned to their studies in their faith books – it was not for them to question what had happened or what might be about to happen. The teacher would have taken the wisest decision and now brother Sharif would have to obey whatever instructions he had been given. He was lucky.

Later, as dusk fell, the door opened and one of the teacher's assistants simply looked at Sharif. He stood up. It was time.

Once they had left the lights of Karachi behind them there was little to see from the small round windows of the Chinook helicopter. Barnes looked at the group of 20 men he had been assigned – he'd blagged some extra support because they were now going to strike at the madrassa and training camp at the same time. They didn't look that impressive. Some even looked a little worried. He wondered how many of them had actually been in a helicopter before, let alone a raid. He comforted himself in the knowledge that there would probably not be much resistance. A little light small-arms fire but against the overwhelming might even of this small force, he thought the action would be over quickly.

He scanned the line of faces. Only one – the man from the ISI – looked remotely capable: Baz Rahman, ex-Para. It was a strange career path he had chosen but he was clearly dedicated to his country. Barnes decided he would rely on him to lead the assault on the madrassa.

Then his thoughts turned to Jackson Clarke. He wondered how he would be coping – probably well enough if he was anything like his screen persona. Barnes had a quiet laugh. He would actually be quite honoured to meet him. He clearly had enough strength of character to try and get messages back to his friends, so as long as they reached the camp in time, he was sure Jackson Clarke would make it through his ordeal.

Baz Rahman caught his smile and nodded back in acknowledgement. Both men were ready for a fight – Baz probably more than anyone. He had a passionate loathing for all religious fanatics and particularly those who were harming his country. He himself was completely agnostic. He took the view that anyone could believe in anything they liked, but he drew the line when they tried to inflict those beliefs on anyone else. He reckoned that just getting through life was complicated enough, without muddling it up with religion. And when people of the same faith started killing one another in God's name, he was convinced that the only right path was the code of honour that he had learned in the military. Every man was prepared to die to save one of his colleagues, quite simply because every man knew his colleagues would do the same for him. Wasn't that what was said in the Bible? 'No greater love has a man than to lay down his life for another.'

Out of habit he re-checked his assault rifle – perhaps that would really be his closest ally in the coming hours. In combat it was never out of reach. If you cared for your weapon it would look after you. The same simple rule could be applied to everything in life, Baz reasoned; he did not require any further rules or explanation.

He also began thinking about the man they were going to risk their lives to rescue. Of course he knew he was a famous actor, but actor or not he was also a fool wandering blindly into Pakistan. Was the mission worth the lives of the people who would certainly die that night? That was the beauty of soldiering: you took orders, did your duty and you did not question. It was slightly different for him because he had volunteered for his role with the ISI. However, he had the additional privilege of fighting for his country of birth. He could have stayed in the British Army but he knew that he had to help Pakistan. If the needs of Britain and Pakistan happened to coincide from time to time, as it did on this occasion, so much the better.

He knew his former colleague Jack took a different, more fatalistic approach –as many people did in life. Jack had always told him that his life would be like one of their training assault courses. It would be run at speed, it would be difficult even hazardous at times and it would be short. However, it would be exhilarating. Jack said he had been trained for one thing and one thing alone – attack the enemy with maximum force. It did not suit the kind of life that many ex-military people found in the office or management environment. This was all he knew. He would let someone else judge him. Baz wondered how Jack's mission had gone. By now he would surely be on his way home.

Baz put his rifle down, happy with its state of readiness, just as he was happy with his own certainty and conviction. He had been trained but he wanted to devote his training to his country; sometimes if that meant bending the rules to remove the parasites and the vermin such as Khalid Jalil he was more than ready. As for the kind of people who were holding Jackson Clarke – they would receive no mercy.

The pilot switched the cabin lighting to red to help the men adjust their eyesight to the night vision they would need and dropped the aircraft to hilltop height.

Below them countless eyes looked up, wondering if it was worth a shot. It was obviously a military flight and to many in the northern territories that alone made it a legitimate target. On this occasion they decided against – either that or they missed.

'About half an hour to target,' said the pilot into the headphones Barnes was wearing. He passed the message along the line.

Charlie Barnes and Baz Rahman looked at each other and had the same thought: 'It's going to be a long half hour. Let's get this bird on the ground where at least we stand a chance of defending ourselves.'

It was certainly safer but there was even less that could be done back at the Sheraton Hotel. Rory McLeod had insisted on Katherine taking a sleeping pill, as he knew there would be no news for several hours. It would be first light before they were likely to hear anything. Nicky and Richard were barely on speaking terms and she had decided that sleep was the best option, so she also had taken a pill.

Rory watched as the meticulous Victor Jones tidied the papers together. He was right. One way or another they would know in 24 hours what had happened to Jackson: either he would be safe or he would be dead. One way or another, he would be on his way back and there would be no further need for the room. The keys could be handed back to the hotel and, no doubt after redecoration it would be let out to some business convention or other. The delegates would never know what had been going on inside these four walls.

Jones opened a brown envelope that for some reason had been ignored or simply over-looked as the preparations for the attack on Garanji were being finalised. He sat down and began reading intently. It was the transcript of Khalid Jalil's sound tape, which he had hidden away.

It ran to just two pages of single-spaced text but it very quickly became clear why Khalid had kept it safely. Jones looked across at McLeod: 'I think you better take a look at this.'

The typist had headed the document: *Transcript of conversation between unknown male and man identified on the tape as Senator Friedland*. The typist didn't know to whom the 'unknown male' referred, but McLeod and Jones knew it was Jalil.

It appeared that on one occasion Senator Vance Friedland had let his emotions get the better of him and he had been careless. It was incontrovertible proof that he had asked Khalid Jalil to arrange for the work of the industrialist, Ali Haider, to be disrupted. 'Permanently' was the word the senator had used. He had then launched into a vitriolic attack on the intentions of the Chinese, determined as he saw it to win friends and influence people in one of the most sensitive regions on the planet.

'Just stop him. I don't care how you do it, but I want that operation closed down immediately. Do you understand?'

Khalid Jalil had said he understood perfectly and the rest of the conversation was about Jalil's payment and the expenses he would incur. He spoke of the difficulty of trying to sabotage the building work at the plant and his contacts in the north demanding more than before. Khalid had been a good haggler and the senator had agreed a ten percent increase in 'the usual fee', but for that he wanted the job done quickly, adding: 'If you want to cause the maximum of disruption in any organisation, go for the head and the rest will simply follow.'

US Senator Vance Friedland was to all intents and purposes, sanctioning a hit on a foreign national on foreign soil. He was conducting his own illegal foreign policy programme and Khalid Jalil had him cold. No wonder he had treasured the tape so carefully.

It had not done Jalil much good in the end, but McLeod thought his counterparts in Washington would be most interested in the tape's contents. Another thought crossed his mind – if Friedland had been prepared to order the murder of the industrialist, then he wouldn't have hesitated long in arranging for Khalid Jalil himself to be erased from the picture. He must have known that Jalil could identify him, even if he didn't know about the recording. In this day and age, just making an accusation was enough to destroy a reputation.

The more McLeod thought about it the more it made sense. The third man in the alley would have been on the senator's payroll. It might be difficult to prove, but he wouldn't need to – thanks to the tap. McLeod had no compunction in sharing it with Washington. Friedland had financed Khalid Jalil and Jalil had been instrumental in trapping Jackson. Good riddance to both of them. He did not expect the senator to be considering re-election and he would be lucky to escape prosecution.

'Victor, I might have a word with the good senator when I get back to London and ask him just how close he was to our friend Khalid Jalil. I think he might seek early retirement. If something has happened to Jackson then I will push for an equally painful solution.'

# CHAPTER TWENTY-FIVE

Jackson stood up as three men clad in turbans and full-length black robes came into the room carrying a camera, tripod and lights. He smiled in greeting but they looked away and got on with their tasks. He had not seen them before and he thought he detected an air of menace about them.

Jackson stood back as 'the set' was being prepared. He had had plenty of time to reflect on the possible outcome of his captivity and he seemed to realise that today would bring some sort of finality. He was powerless to fight and it was impossible to escape. It appeared that his own life was about to come to an end, but Jackson accepted whatever the future held for him. His sadness was for his captors: the futility of what they were doing and the life they were leading. They placed their own young lives at risk and for no good purpose.

The mere eagerness they had for dying, driven by hatred, just reinforced the stereotype of Islamic militant the rest of the world envisaged. On the other hand, Jackson understood what it meant to be joyful at the prospect of embracing death – as it would come to everyone in due time. His captivity had simply strengthened his belief. He had no fear and no anxiety. He had been able to face the oppression of ignorance and to stand against it – not with violence but with compassion.

'Are you really determined to take my life?' he asked the men. 'If it's not too late for the sake of God, you should think again. Your teacher is not going to carry the can for this – you will be accountable. Your own holy book says to take one innocent life is like killing entire humanity.

'I'm afraid they don't speak any English so you are wasting your time.' Dr Mitra came into the room looking a little too pleased with himself. No doubt the prospect of what lay in store for his prisoner appealed to him. 'Besides,' added Mitra; 'they know their calling and they have surrendered their will to God.'

'How could they surrender their will when all they are consumed with is hatred and anger?'

The door swung open and Bakri entered looking round the room approving the arrangements: 'Your friends have abandoned you. It seems no one cares what happens to their superstar. So I shall send them a message they cannot ignore. It will be your last starring role.'

If Bakri was hoping for some shocked reaction from Jackson, he was disappointed. There had always been two possible outcomes of his captivity: he would be released or he would be killed. The impossibility of the demands his captors had set meant his release was always unlikely. He just nodded and looked back at Bakri, meeting his stare unflinchingly.

'Is that the best option? What do you think will be achieved by my death?'

Bakri was taken aback. His prisoner was making his life or death sound like a point of discussion in an academic debate. Had he no fear?

'It will send a message to your friends in the West that they should not presume to question our determination to drive them out of our country.' Bakri's eyes flashed, the anger rising inside him.

Jackson gave him a quizzical glance. 'You must know that will never work. From what I have seen, your own country is divided – Pakistani is fighting Pakistani. In my view it is a tragedy but not all your nation's ills can be placed at the door of the West. And it must surely be wrong to turn against your own kind in the name of a faith you both share?'

'There is only one true faith and until the world understands that – even Pakistani and Pakistani – then our efforts will continue.'

'And by efforts, I take it you mean killing people? In the little studying of Islam that I have done, I don't see that interpretation.'

'Sometimes we are called upon to defend our faith. Didn't

your crusaders do that? Killing innocents in the name of your Christianity?'

Jackson opened his arms wide: 'I think it is generally accepted that many so-called crusaders did inexcusable things. The vast majority of the camp-followers were just that following in the hope of finding some easy pickings – most of them didn't do any fighting, they just saw it as a way of surviving in those difficult times. But I can tell you are more than just a follower; you are a leader. You are also a teacher of the faith and I would have thought you should know the difference. Talking of followers – where is my friend, Sharif? I hope he is not in trouble.'

'Brother Sharif will join us shortly. I know you have been trying to–'

'To lead him astray? To corrupt his young mind? Is that what you were thinking?'

Bakri studied this strange man, who seemed so assured of himself that even when told he was about to die he refused to be cowed. 'Something like that,' replied Bakri.

'Sadly he and I don't speak the same language. I was just trying to show him that he had nothing to fear from me. I wish I could assure you of the same.'

'With Allah's strength, I know I have nothing to fear from the infidel, Mr Jackson.'

'Well, if that is the case, why do you see me as such a danger to your way of life? Instead of so much anger, can you not fill your hearts with love?'

'Because what I see is a disease which must be removed,' said Bakri.

'And you take the same attitude to your countrymen who happen to have a different interpretation of Islam. Are they also a disease to be removed?'

'If they cannot find the true path, so be it.'

'The issue,' said Jackson calmly, 'is the difference between a secular and non-secular society. They are always going to be inconsistent. What we should try to do is understand both – only then can we all understand the fundamentals of the differing ideologies. Do we really have to resort to violence?'

Before Bakri could answer, both men looked up at the dull, distant sound of a helicopter's rotor blades beating through the night sky. Jackson raised his eyebrows: 'Maybe they haven't forgotten me after all?'

'Don't get your hopes up. We get military aircraft flying over us regularly. Sadly our own government has fallen victim to the hypnosis of their so-called Western allies. They attack our brothers fighting the holy war against the corruption of the outside world. But they can never win. We have followers in every town and city in the land. One day they will all rise up together and true Islam can return to our nation and then...' Bakri stopped mid-sentence and turned to one of his assistants: 'Get our brother Sharif.'

After a moment Sharif was brought into the room. At least Jackson assumed it was Sharif because he was dressed from head to foot in black with a black turban round his face, with only his eyes showing. He was carrying a handgun.

He stopped when he saw Jackson standing by his bed. There would be no handshake this time.

'Sharif? Is that you behind the mask? Why can't you show me your face? What have you brought for me today? It doesn't look quite as tempting as my usual plate of daal.' Jackson looked down at the gun and back into Sharif's eyes. There seemed to be fear rather than fire in them. They flitted back and forth between Bakri and Jackson. Jackson tried in vain to give him a reassuring look.

'Our brother Sharif has one purpose here today. Enough talking.' Then in Pashto he said: 'Take you positions.'

Dr Mitra stepped forward, took Jackson by the arm and pushed him roughly towards the chair, which had been placed in the now customary position in front of the banner. He then stood to one side ushering Sharif forward.

The lights were turned on, momentarily blinding everyone. Sharif put his hand up to his eyes, inadvertently making everyone flinch as he waved the gun in the air. Only Jackson remained still: 'Sharif you want to be careful with that, someone might get hurt.' He nodded in the direction of the gun. Then looked back into Sharif's eyes. It wasn't a look of appeal – it was a look of forgiveness. Jackson gave a smile, as though to reassure Sharif that all would be well.

In his mind, Sharif was terrified. He had been terrified since the moment the teacher had told him that he had been selected to kill the foreigner. He couldn't understand what was happening to him; what had changed. He used to be so sure about every action. Was it since Jabbar had died? Was it really Jabbar all along who had been the strong one and he had simply been at his side doing what Jabbar showed him?

Bakri frowned at him and signalled with his arm across his body how Sharif should be standing – the gun pointed directly at Jackson's head. And still Jackson stared into Sharif's eyes.

'Does the condemned man get one last request? It is traditional.'

'Very well. What do you request, Mr Jackson?'

'I would simply ask you to translate something for me. I want to tell my friend, Sharif here, something. He looks troubled and I wouldn't want him to go through the rest of his life worrying.'

'He has nothing to worry about,' snapped Bakri.

'In that case you will not mind translating what I have to say,' Jackson replied quietly in voice that was hard to hear.

'I agree.' Bakri said, before telling Sharif what was about to happen. 'Go ahead. Your final words: Dr Mitra will translate.'

'Master, I cannot repeat the infidel's words. I would be ashamed.'

Bakri just looked at Mitra and he immediately fell silent.

Jackson turned to Sharif: 'You are a young man with your life ahead of you.' He waited while Mitra translated slowly and suspiciously.

Jackson continued: 'My existence poses no threat to you. Surely your conscience must have already told you this – the only harm you face is doing something against that conscience, against your own will. Don't let your conscience be controlled, Sharif. One day, you will have to answer your conscience for this.'

Sharif kept shifting his glance from Jackson, to Mitra, to the teacher and back to Jackson. The man he was about to kill – the man who knew he was about to die – was talking about right and wrong. What was he to do? What did the teacher expect of him now? The stranger was not a bad man. The teacher was allowing him to talk – to teach – just as the teacher did every day to his fellow students in the madrassa. Was he supposed to be guided by the stranger?

Mitra too was confused. Why was the teacher letting the infidel talk? But the teacher was also listening. Why?

'Master,' Sharif called out: 'What am I to do?'

'You know what you must do. This has been a test by the foreigner to see if Allah will allow him to shake us. He has failed. It has all been a trick to deceive us but we have been strong. Enough. It is now time. Start recording.'

# CHAPTER TWENTY-SIX

McLeod and Benson both looked at their watches at the same time and raised their eyebrows in recognition. It would not be long now. Sitting in a corner of a makeshift command centre in the middle of the Pakistani Airforce base in Masroor in the west of Karachi, they listened to the intermittent chatter between the helicopter pilot and the air-traffic controller. Charlie Barnes and the raiding party should be nearly at their destination.

'They are beginning their final approach,' one of the officers said to them. 'In about three-quarters of an hour both teams will hit their targets at the same time. There is some difficult terrain for them to cross once they have landed.'

'They'll have the element of surprise, but I wish we knew for certain which location Jackson was in – or even if he is in either of them.' Benson was really just thinking out loud; not addressing anyone in particular.

McLeod answered: 'I don't suppose there will be too much in the way of opposition. They won't be expecting an attack like this. Hopefully it will be a swift and silent operation. My worry is that if they don't find him at the camp, it'll be much harder tracking him down in the madrassa.'

'What do you think are the chances of success?' asked Benson.

'Charlie Barnes is a good operator and by all accounts he will have the best possible back up from this ex-Para, Rahman. If Jackson is there, then I would say the chances are better than even. The only question is will they get there in time?'

The radio crackled again and the officer said: 'They have landed. They are making their way to the targets. We will now switch to the assault teams radio frequencies.'

They heard Charlie Barnes confirming communications were established. It was now a case of how quickly the teams could make it across the ground on foot to the training camp and the town. There would be another agonising wait and everyone would deal with it as best they could.

Katherine had been persuaded to take her sleeping pills after much persuasion by Nicky, who had now moved into her suite and was using the spare bed. Katherine needed the support and, try as she might, she could not stop herself blaming Richard for everything that had happened.

Richard had hardly spoken in the past 24 hours. He had eaten alone in his room with the TV constantly on, flicking between channels in the hope of finding some news. He knew that he would hear what had happened before it appeared on the television, but it didn't stop him watching. The news programmes had started counting the days since Jackson's abduction with a gruesome sort of date calendar over the shoulder of the newscaster.

No one knew anything, but that didn't stop security experts debating the issue, psychology specialists wondering how Jackson was coping and film industry friends reviewing his career as though it was already over. The more he watched, the more despondent he became. He knew he would never be able to work with Jackson again and he suspected his relationship with Nicky was at an end. She said she wanted to keep Katherine company, but they had scarcely spoken when they were in the same room, so it made no difference.

Richard West: TV producer of impossible projects and the man who had got his friend kidnapped – and probably killed – just because he wanted to make a documentary. He had been thinking of number one. He hadn't been thinking about his friends at all. He had even dragged Nicky and Katherine out here – some holiday that had turned out to be. He looked at himself in the mirror as he poured himself another drink. He didn't like what he saw. It wasn't his dishevelled appearance; his unshaven face. He didn't like what he saw in his eyes – there was nothing looking back at him.

Victor Jones was the only one in the hotel meeting room, keeping vigil with all the papers and photographs and maps. Even with his meticulous attention to detail he could not find another thing to do. Everything was in order; carefully filed and documented. He would be expected to write a report about everything that happened, but that would be alright because he already had it clear in his mind.

There was a knock on the door that startled Jones – he was not expecting to hear any news yet. He checked his watch. They could not have reached the camp yet. Everyone else was asleep.

He peered through the security hole in the door. It was the manager and another member of the hotel staff. Just as a precaution Jones left the chain on the door and opened it carefully.

'Sorry to disturb you, sir,' said the manager looking unusually flustered. 'I wonder if you could come downstairs. I'm afraid there has been a ... a terrible accident.'

'Accident? What sort of accident? Everyone is asleep.'

'I'm afraid it is Mr West, sir.'

'Richard West? He's in his room.'

'I regret to tell you , sir; he's dead.'

'Dead? What do you mean he's dead? I mean where is he?' Jones couldn't make sense of what the manager was saying. Only an hour or so earlier he had seen West go into his room. He looked tired, but they all looked tired.

'If you will come with me, sir, I will show you.'

Instead of going up in the lift to West's room they went down to the lobby and across to the doors.

'Where are we going? Where is he? Outside?' As Jones followed the manager out into the car park he saw a group of people standing together on the grass. He caught side of a body lying face down.

'Oh, my God! What happened?' asked Jones, refusing to believe what he saw. He immediately looked up to the roof of the hotel. Two hotel security men were looking down. 'Was he pushed? Did he...?'

'He seems to have fallen from the roof, sir. We know he was

253

up there as he left a note. It was addressed to Mr Clarke. We haven't opened it.' The manager handed an envelope to Jones who immediately recognised West's handwriting. He opened it and read the simple message:

*Dear Jackson, Nicky, and all my friends.*

*I'm sorry I have put you all through this. It was my fault. I hope you will be able to forgive me one day. I cannot forgive myself.*

*Richard.*

As he was reading, a police car came racing up the hotel drive, lights flashing. Two officers got out. The hotel manager spoke briefly to them. It was obvious that the visitor, Mr West, had taken his own life. He made no mention of the note, which Jones slipped into his jacket pocket. He didn't know exactly why, but he assumed that it was a straightforward case. There was no point in adding to the misery. Richard West overcome by what had happened to his friend, Jackson Clarke, had taken his own life.

After a cursory questioning, Jones was allowed back to his room. He dialled his chief David Benson's mobile number first. West's partner Nicky was asleep and he wanted to ensure he handled this by the book.

Benson sat bolt upright in his armchair: 'He's done what?'

'It appears that Richard West has committed suicide. He jumped off the roof of the hotel a short time ago. The police are here.'

'What did you say to them?' asked Benson, who now had McLeod's attention and was scribbling a note: 'Richard's committed suicide!'

'Just the usual formal name, address and who I was. There will be more in the morning I'm sure.'

'Ok, Victor, I'm coming straight back. Rory can hold the fort here.' He looked questioningly at McLeod who was nodding vigorously.

'There's one other thing, sir,' said Jones. 'He seems to have left a note. I'm not quite sure why I did it, but I have it in my pocket. I said nothing to the police about it and I know the hotel manager said nothing either.'

'What does it say, Victor?'

'Just that he was sorry. That it was all his fault and hoped for forgiveness.'

'Well, I think you did right. Probably amounts to withholding evidence but it sounds pretty clear-cut. We can decide what to do about it later. Does Nicky know?'

'Not yet. And nor does Katherine. They are both asleep as far as I know. What would you like me to do, sir?' Jones didn't relish the idea of waking either of them. They would immediately assume it was with news about Jackson Clarke. The last thing they would be expecting to hear was that Richard West had thrown himself from the top of the hotel, overcome by remorse.

'Wait until I get back, Victor. I think we will let them sleep for now.' Benson flicked off his mobile and turned to McLeod. 'I knew he was depressed and blamed himself, but I didn't see that coming. I'm sorry, Rory, was he a good friend?'

'More an acquaintance really. Long time buddy of Jackson's although I think he leaned more on Jackson than the other way around. Do the others know? What about Nicky? I notice they have been a bit cool in recent days but she will be devastated.'

Benson shook his head: 'No one else knows yet. He left what looks like a suicide note blaming himself. Jones took the precaution of keeping it for now. Don't want the police leaking that to the press as well. It's bad enough as it is.'

'I agree. They will have to see it at some point but let Jones hang on to it for now. You best get back to the hotel. Nicky and Katherine should hear the news from you and preferably before they see it on the morning news. Were there any press about?'

'If there were, they seemed to have been having a nap. Jones didn't mention anything about cameras, but it is bound to leak out sometime.' Benson looked at his watch and continued: 'They should be getting quite close to the camp by now. Let's hope we have some good news to give them along with the bad. I'll get back to the hotel. Call me when you have some news.'

McLeod nodded and got back to his vigil in front of a bank of radio receivers. They had heard nothing since the helicopter landed and Charlie and his team had begun their trek across the hills to the camp. Somehow he knew that whatever they found, everything had changed. Nicky had lost Richard, but in truth their relationship was already at an end. There would be no more weekends at Cedars. Everyone blamed Richard for bringing them out to Pakistan, even though it was Jackson's decision all along. What had he really been looking for? Was it really his pursuit of a new religion?

Richard's death was a stupid waste of a life. Jackson had known the risks and he would have been the last to blame anyone for what had happened. He would have been angry about the time, effort and expense that everyone was going to, but he would not have been worrying about himself.

The radio crackled into life and the operator sat forward adjusting the volume.

'Charlie to Baz. Charlie to Baz. Target in sight. What's your status? Over.'

'Ten minutes to target. Baz out.'

Why hadn't Richard just waited a little longer? McLeod pulled his chair nearer to the radio console as though he would get a better reception. They were now so close. Come on Jackson; hang in there.

Benson reached the hotel just as an ambulance was driving away. The police were still on the scene and he could see Jones talking to the hotel manager and someone he presumed was the detective in charge. The press were there. He could see Awad Fouda doing a piece to camera – he was obviously still being allowed to work.

'Victor, what are they saying?'

'Exactly as they first thought, sir. It was a tragic suicide. For some reason, no one can understand that Mr West took himself up to the roof of the hotel and jumped off. They have found scuff-marks. It is clear to the detective here that no one else was involved.' Jones looked straight at his boss making it obvious to him that he still had the note West had written and no link was being made between Jackson's disappearance and West's death.

'All very sad. Does Nicky know yet?'

'I'm afraid she does. She was woken by the sirens. I think she is now beating herself up for blaming Richard for what happened.'

Benson thanked the manager for his efforts and his discretion over the note. He made it clear that his thoughtfulness would not go unrecognised. All agreed there was little point in complicating an already tragic issue. Benson decided he would allow the High Commissioner himself to raise the matter of evidence being removed from the scene with the Chief of Police.

'Have we heard any news yet?' asked Jones obliquely.

'It should be happening right now. Come on – let's get up to the meeting room. Charlie will be calling in soon.'

# CHAPTER TWENTY-SEVEN

B az Rahman and his force of ten men made good ground as they approached the outskirts of Garanji, slipping silently down from the hills. He wanted to go faster but his Pakistani troops had not been trained by the Parachute Regiment. Nevertheless they were skilled and apart from the occasional bleat from a surprised sheep there was not a sound.

The plan was simple: a fast and, if necessary, deadly assault on the madrassa. If they met any resistance they were to respond in kind, but this was a rescue mission not an assault.

Baz would make straight for the teacher's own house on the basis that if he were there, he would be the one giving the orders. No one would raise a finger against Jackson without his command, so the intention was to silence the leader. The rest of the troop would fan out across the courtyard and systematically work their way through all the buildings in search of Jackson.

In the meantime Charlie Barnes would lead his squad in an attack on the training camp – the most likely place for the kidnappers to be holding Jackson.

The new moon was hidden by low-lying cloud, so Baz and his men were all but invisible as they moved at a fast walk through the town, keeping close to the walls. The few street-lights only helped to cast dark shadows – if anyone was watching they would have mistaken the moving figures as a trick of the light.

The town was quiet and the sound of the wooden door of the madrassa creaking open sounded like a siren. Baz waited to see if there was any reaction. There was no one watching, no one on guard. Why should there be? As this was in effect the town's school. Who would want to attack a school? A dog barked and his mate answered, then silence once more.

Baz stepped over the threshold trying to get his bearings from the notes given by Khalid Jalil. He could see the main building across the courtyard. A single light was still on and he could see one – maybe two – people moving about the room. The rest of the buildings were in darkness. He signalled his men to follow him through, as they snaked their way along the eastern flank.

If possible they wanted to get to the main building without disturbing any of the other students who were sleeping in their rooms. They inched open the first door but all the beds were empty.

The next room contained six other beds – all being used. The sound of the opening door seemed to disturb one or two who turned and muttered in their sleep. Again, clearly not a place to hold Jackson. The squad moved on as Baz and three others raced across the courtyard to the teacher's office and took up position beneath the window.

There was talking inside but it was difficult to make out what was being said. It sounded like some sort of argument but the voices were low – it was as if the two men didn't want to be overheard by anyone – let alone four heavily armed commandos waiting within feet of them.

Baz strained to hear what they were saying. They seemed to be talking about something that had happened earlier that evening. They talked about 'the foreigner' and they spoke of great danger and risk. One of the men inside was trying to reassure the other and said that the master was right – he had had no choice. He was guided by Allah and now was a time for strength.

Suddenly the door of one of the rooms they had checked opened noisily. Baz froze and peered across the gloom. One of the students had come out either to relieve himself or because his sleep had been disturbed. For whatever reason, he had decided to walk in the direction of the master's house.

He stopped and seemed to be staring straight at Baz and his colleagues, trying to make sense of what he thought he could see. He rubbed his eyes and looked again, still not certain.

His courage failed him and he hurried back into his room to wake one of his colleagues. It would have been unforgiveable to disturb the master and his staff – he needed to confirm what he thought he had seen. Baz took the opportunity to duck round the side of the building crouching low. His right hand reached down to his waist and he pulled a knife from its sheath.

The two students emerged and stared again at the building. The second youth was angry – there wasn't anything there and now his sleep had been broken. He went back inside leaving his colleague outside still peering into the darkness. The first youth was convinced that he wasn't just seeing things, and he walked straight towards the area where Baz and his three men were hiding. But the youth didn't want to be seen wandering about in the courtyard – there were strict rules about staying in their quarters – so he kept to the shadows. That was a mistake.

With less than 20 metres to go, one of the Pakistani commandos stepped out of the darkness and dragged him down covering his mouth. The student – who could not have been more than 18 – was unconscious before he hit the ground, the sleeper stranglehold cutting off his oxygen supply.

The commando signalled the all clear and Baz took up his position again. The two men inside had stopped talking. One was looking out of the window but could see nothing. He reassured his colleague that there was nothing – they must have been imagining things.

Certain that their approach hadn't been spotted, Baz decided just to walk straight into the room. The last thing the men would have been expecting was a commando raid right into the heart of the madrassa. This was a place of learning – the other type of activity took place at the camp.

Checking his assault rifle once more, he gave the signal.

The two men were sitting cross-legged on the floor, still deep in conversation, when Baz calmly walked in: '*As-Salaam-Alaikum.*'

Before they could react he was already across the room, his rifle pointing straight at them. One of the men glanced across at the desk where a small handgun was lying and two mobile phones.

260

'You can try but I don't think it would be a good idea.' He ordered one of his men to turn out the lights in case any other students had been woken and looked in. 'Jackson Clarke. Where is he?' Baz asked, keeping his voice down but leaving no doubt about the menace in his question.

'The foreigner, where is he? I heard you talking. What has happened?'

The two assistants looked at each other in terror. Which would be worse – the wrath of the master or the injuries the men in front of them could inflict – their faces covered in camouflage paint, their guns trained on them?

They were in no doubt. One of them said: 'It's too late. He's not here. He's gone.'

'What's too late? Where's he gone?' snapped Baz grabbing one of them by the collar and shaking him.

'He's gone,' was all the man would say. It was obvious that their fear of the master transcended anything a commando bristling with weapons could threaten.

Suddenly there was a burst of gunfire. Baz raced to the window and saw three men running across the courtyard firing into the darkness. It was immediately answered by a volley of rounds that sent one of the gunmen spinning in a death spiral to the floor. Baz looked back to see the man he had been questioning lunge for the gun on the desk. He fired a single shot and the assistant crashed to the floor knocking over the flimsy desk.

The second man looked at his dead colleague and then at Baz then made a dive for the gun. He must have known he stood no chance. One handgun against four men with assault rifles, but he tried all the same. Once more, it just took a single round from Baz to send the assistant on his way to Paradise because that was all he could possibly have been thinking about.

Another volley of fire from the courtyard shattered one of the windows. Reinforcements had arrived from somewhere.

'Charlie One. This is Baz over.'

'Go ahead Baz. What's happening? Over.'

'Met some opposition. Under control. No sign of the package. Over.'

'Understood. Our target in sight. Do you need back up? Over.'

'Negative. Out.'

Baz realised it was now up to Charlie Barnes to locate Jackson – all he had to do was extract himself and his team from the madrassa. He assumed he was now under fire from a group returning from the camp. At least that meant Charlie would face less resistance, but he wondered what the dead man lying at his feet had meant when he said they were too late.

Another round crashed into the wall above his head. 'Come on. Let's get out of here.' He stood up and unleashed a blast of covering fire through the shattered window. 'Go, go, go!' he shouted at his men who sprinted low through the door, firing as they went.

The reinforcements were pinned down near the entrance to the madrassa, which also meant the escape route for the commandos was blocked. Baz realised it would not be long before the rest of the town piled in, grabbing whatever weapons came to hand in order to defend their town. Every man and boy would have been proficient shots – it came with their mother's milk.

'Shami,' Baz called to his second in command, 'fire a grenade into that group by the gate. They're blocking our path. Then follow my lead.'

The rocket-propelled grenade traced a bright path across the courtyard before obliterating a stone wall and blasting a wide hole in the entrance. Baz was immediately on his feet, sprinting straight at the attacking group, his gun blazing. Shami was soon at his side laying down murderous fire. The rest of the commandos took the lead and broke from cover.

By the time Baz reached what was once the main gate, the fight was over. He confirmed that all the commandos were safe and quickly checked among the bodies to see if anyone was left alive. They would have provided useful intelligence for Charlie. But they were all dead.

Out in the street, lights were beginning to come on and people – some of them armed – were emerging from their houses. There was nothing to be gained by getting into a firefight with people Baz regarded as civilians and he ordered his men to prepare for a rapid withdrawal from the town.

One or two of the townspeople took some random shots but they were wild and harmless. More bravado than dangerous. He let off a burst of bullets into the air as a warning not to get involved and, just as rapidly as they had arrived in Garanji, the commandos disappeared into the darkness.

'Charlie one, this is Baz. Leaving town, no package found. Rendez-vous as agreed. Out.'

As they reached the relative safety of the hillside, Baz looked back at the fire now rising from the madrassa. Sadly, this would go down as a failure. Someone was sure to portray the attack as a cowardly raid by heavily armed troops on an innocent madrassa. No one would ask about why that particular madrassa was selected. It would be seen as a random attack by the military and the only result would be increased support for the Taliban or one of the many groups taking advantage of the chaos the Taliban and Al Qaeda had created.

The only hope was for Charlie to locate and rescue Jackson Clarke. The best possible result would be to find him alive and to use the PR value of Jackson's name to counter the propaganda from the other side. The struggle the army had taken on was almost an impossible one to win. Already Pakistani was fighting Pakistani and the army was caught in the middle – partly by its own historical failings and partly because of outside interference. It seemed that the whole world was interested in the country's strategic importance, but few nations were ready to come to its aid. The political in-fighting was a national sport and no one was safe. You were on one side or the other and the only people reaping the rewards were the terrorists.

What had the man meant when he said Jackson had gone? Gone to the training camp? Gone somewhere else? Or had he meant something worse? What was too late? One thing Baz did grudgingly admire was the unswerving loyalty that their leader,

Abdul Bakri, commanded. It was certainly a loyalty built on fear but it was so powerful that at least two of his followers chose certain death rather than to break their silence. There was something almost Mafiosi about it – like the old code of silence known as *omerta* that had once prevailed, particularly in Sicily. But even that code was being broken in modern times with more and more tempting rewards. The difference here was no financial reward or benefit was being offered by the Taliban or Al Qaeda – just a promise of a life to be lived in Paradise.

Baz's radio crackled: 'Charlie One to Baz. Charlie One to Baz.'

'Go ahead Charlie One.'

'In position. Moving in now. Out.'

# CHAPTER TWENTY-EIGHT

The bright light for the camera lit up the room, but also flooded out of the window like a beacon. Charlie Barnes blinked as the light temporarily blinded him through his night-vision binoculars. They had been watching the small group of buildings for ten minutes, observing the coming and going. If there had been any doubt that this was where Jackson Clarke was being held captive, the doubt was over.

He signalled for his men to move into positions all round the central building, which was now thoughtfully floodlit. He guessed that a new video was being recorded, which at least meant Jackson was still alive. They were on time.

'Who would you like me to look at: Sharif or your friend over there reading out the statement?' Jackson asked, as though he were taking stage directions.

'Stop talking,' snapped Bakri. 'Just look at the camera.' He barked an order at one of the guards who grabbed Jackson roughly round the neck, holding his head in a lock.

'And what is being said? Surely I should know what I am being accused of – I assume this is my sentence being read out.' Jackson coughed as the grip was tightened.

'You know exactly what is being said and why. Never again will some celebrity think he can insult Islam in this way and perhaps your countrymen will be less eager to attack our country,' said Dr Mitra who wanted to impress his teacher as much as silence Jackson.

Bakri just raised his hand and Mitra again was cut short. 'Continue,' he said to the assistant reading the statement. It ran to two pages and the tone became increasingly aggressive, but throughout Jackson turned his eyes towards Sharif, ignoring the instruction to keep his eyes on the camera.

Sharif maintained his pose of the fierce warrior but his eyes gave him away. He blinked and looked at Bakri, who frowned – making him look back at Jackson. The louder and more vitriolic the statement became, the more agitated Sharif got. There were now tears in his eyes and the gun in his hand began to shake.

The statement ended with the cry of 'praise to Allah' ... and then nothing. This was the moment, Jackson assumed, that Sharif was supposed to shoot him in the head. But the boy could not move. He was frozen to the spot, unable to fire, unable to break away from Jackson's look.

'*Allahu Akbar*!' Dr Mitra called out again like some demented prompter in a theatre, trying to help an actor who had forgotten his lines.

'Sharif: shoot!' shouted Bakri. But Sharif could no longer hear him or at least react to what was being said. They were just sounds ringing in his ears which he could not understand. His gun hand dropped to his side and with his right hand he pulled down the cloth covering his face. He was smiling.

'Shoot, Sharif! What are you doing?' called Mitra, scarcely able to believe what was happening. Then Bakri stepped forward, grabbed a Kalashnikov off one of the guards and opened fire himself, his eyes blazing with fury.

Sharif was sent sprawling across the floor, knocking over the camera light and causing the other one to fuse. The guard released his hold on Jackson letting him jump up – not to attack Bakri, but to go to help Sharif. The teacher fired again, sending Jackson tumbling back against the wall. Jackson grabbed out for support, tearing the banner off the wall. Slowly he slid to the floor, blood seeping through his shirt. He touched his chest and looked at his hand, almost in disbelief. A muffled cough made him look over at Sharif. He dragged himself across the floor and cradled Sharif' head in his hands, using the banner to try and stem the flow of blood from a gaping wound in Sharif's chest. Jackson knew it was futile.

His own wound was bleeding heavily and Sharif tried in vain to pull his hand up to help. Jackson stopped him: 'Don't worry. We will both be fine. You did well, my friend.'

No one else seemed to know what to do or how to react. The master was standing there with the Kalashnikov at his side. Mitra and the guards were transfixed. He had just shot Brother Sharif. How could they use the film now? And the foreigner was still alive. Even with a bullet in his side, he would not die and he would not stop helping others.

One of the guards tried to pick up the video camera and place it back on the tripod as though there had just been a small accident in a film studio. Everything would be under control as soon as the lights were back up and switched on. There would be a second take.

'Leave it!' shouted Bakri raising his gun again, anger burning in his eyes as he realised his brutal performance was now ruined. 'You continue to play games with us, right to the end, Jackson Clarke.'

Jackson held up a blood-stained hand. He coughed, wiping more blood from his mouth: 'You can save your bullets. Your first shot was good enough.' He coughed again and looked back down at Sharif who slipping in and out of consciousness. 'But it seems that you have lost young Sharif ... In the end he knew what he was doing – what you were trying to make him do ... was wrong. Poor boy. He didn't deserve this, you know. I don't ... I don't think I did either, actually. Brother.' Jackson looked up at Bakri, who had his gun trained on him.

Slowly Jackson's hand, which he had been holding against Sharif's side, slipped to the floor – all the strength draining from his body, his vision growing cloudy. In his half-conscious state, he thought of Kutub Reza's words that were spoken as Jackson was leaving his home so many miles away in London – 'You are already ahead of me.' Was this what he meant? Death would come to him first? He smiled once more his very best superstar smile and slumped over Sharif's now lifeless body.

The last thing Mitra heard was the sound of Charlie Barnes' boot crashing against the door, sending it slamming into the back of his head. He was already unconscious when he went flying into Bakri and inadvertently knocking the Kalashnikov from his hands. Barnes rolled across the floor and – bringing his assault rifle up in one movement – fired a single shot that struck Bakri in the forehead, just as he tried to reach for his weapon.

The other guards – who moments earlier were watching what they thought were the final seconds before the execution of an infidel – were still trying to ready their own guns by the time the other commandos had swept into the room like a tidal wave. In less than a minute the whole attack was over. There was a slight movement from Mitra as he recovered consciousness. He stretched out for Bakri's gun lying just out of reach, but a double-tap to the head from one of the commandos and his struggle was ended.

Barnes paused for just a second to survey the carnage: Bakri and Mitra were dead so were three of the guards. Two others who had been posted outside hadn't noticed a thing right up until the moment they died – silently dispatched by two commandos.

Barnes knelt down and gently pulled Jackson's body round. He seemed to have been cradling another terrorist, but for the moment at least it didn't make much sense. The terrorist in his arms had also been shot and there was a hand-gun lying by his side.

He wondered if there had been some sort of struggle. Maybe Jackson had disarmed him and managed to get off a shot. Charlie smelt the barrel. It had not been fired and in any case it did not look like a struggle. If anything it looked as though Jackson had been trying to help him.

Barnes placed two fingers against Jackson's carotid artery more in hope than expectation. He suddenly spun round: 'He's still alive – just. Help me get him onto that bed.'

Slowly they eased Jackson out of the clutches of Sharif's arms, pulling back the banner and replacing its sodden cloth with an emergency field dressing. They gave him a shot of morphine.

'Just look at his face,' said one of the commandos. 'I hope I manage to look like that after I've stopped a round from a Kalashnikov. If I didn't know differently I would say he's smiling.'

For sure Jackson looked calm but his body was stone cold. Barnes took off his jacket and covered him in an effort to restore some body warmth.

'If he's going to survive the night we've got to get him to a hospital. Someone get on the radio and divert the chopper here from the RV point. Better also tell Baz and his boys to get over here – they've got another couple of miles to cross if they want a ride home. Come on Jackson – we didn't do all this for you to croak at the last minute.'

One of the commandos – the specialist medic in the team – checked Jackson's pulse again. 'I think we are losing him, sir. I can't find a pulse.' He began mouth-to-mouth resuscitation and cardiac massage.

After a minute he stopped and tested his pulse again. 'He's back again, sir, but we haven't got much time.'

'I know,' said Charlie. 'Just keep working on him. The chopper's on its way. I'll call in a sit-rep to base.' He stood up and went outside to try and get a good signal and, if the truth be known, some air. He felt as though he hadn't been breathing himself.

He checked his watch. They had only been in the room for barely ten minutes but it felt more like an hour. He was also furious with himself. He wondered what he could have done differently. Should he have pushed Jalil harder – bent a few rules? Perhaps then he would have been here a couple of minutes sooner – before the shooting had started. He refused to believe that he was about to lose his first kidnap victim.

'Charlie One to base. Charlie One to base.'

'Base to Charlie One. Go ahead.'

'We have the package. Severely damaged. Gunshot. Request emergency services. May have to divert to alternative base. Will confirm. Over.'

'Understood, Charlie One, confirm when you're en route. Out.'

Rory McLeod breathed a sigh of relief. At least they had found him – now all they had to do was get him to a hospital quickly. He phoned David Benson at the Sheraton: 'They've found him, David. He's been shot. Charlie Barnes says it's serious.'

'But he's still alive?' asked Benson.

'Yes, but he's not in good shape. They'll let us know as soon as they are on their way back. But they may have to use another airbase. It sounds serious.'

'Understood. At least there is some hope.'

It was late and Benson wasn't sure whether to wake Katherine or not. Jackson sounded as though he was in a critical condition. Yes, they'd found him – Charlie Barnes' instincts had proved to be right, but there was no guarantee Jackson would make it back. He didn't want to get Katherine's hopes up again. But she deserved to know at least that they had found him alive.

'Are you sure? Alive? Where did they find him? How is he? Where has he been shot?' Katherine's questions poured out almost incoherently. Benson looked at Nicky, silently pleading with her to calm her friend down.

'Katherine, Katherine, you must be calm and remember what David said. Jackson's in a very serious condition. He's been shot. We just don't know how he is.'

Katherine took some deep breaths. 'It's alright. I know he's going to be ok. He's a fighter.'

'We all know he's strong, Katherine, but Charlie said he was in a bad way. It's too far for them to fly back here so they'll probably use a military air base near Islamabad. It's their best option. We have to face the possibility that–'

'I know, David. I'll be sensible. Now how quickly can I get to that same military air base?'

'The moment Charlie confirms where they are heading, we'll get you there.'

Nicky and Katherine clung to each other, not daring even to contemplate the prospect that lay before them. Nicky had lost Richard – they had fought in the final days but no one imagined he would have taken his own life. And now Jackson: first snatched away, then found and yet out of reach.

In the Chinook, now diverting to the Pakistani airforce base on the outskirts of Islamabad, there was another fight. A rudimentary drip had been set up, hanging from one of the aircraft's supporting struts. The medic was at the limit of what he could do without resorting to major surgery, which might have proved fatal itself.

Charlie Barnes crouched down beside the stretcher. He wasn't Jackson's closest friend but hostage negotiators and kidnap victims develop an unspoken bond. It's a contract that simply commits the negotiator to doing everything in his power to bring the victim home safely. Barnes did not want him to slip out of his grasp now when they were so close.

'Is there anything more we can do?!' he shouted, trying to make himself heard above the sound of the screaming helicopter engine. 'Can we try and stop the bleeding? There must be something!'

The medic looked at him and called back: 'Ask the pilot to fly a little faster? There is nothing more I can do for him. He is fighting but the bullet is deeply embedded. I dare not try and remove it. I might kill him.'

Barnes nodded and returned to his seat next to Baz.

'Is he going to make it?'

'It's going to be close. By the way, good job back there.'

Baz waved his compliment away: 'It was good to get out of the office!'

They both smiled briefly and looked back at the man who had brought them together. His breathing was getting heavier despite the best efforts of the medic, who checked the lines of the drip and tried to make his patient more comfortable.

Charlie Barnes wondered if it had all been worth it. He had never even asked why Jackson Clarke really wanted to travel to Pakistan. It didn't affect his mission one way or another. There'd been talk of his wanting to get into the part he was going to play and, of course, Barnes had read about Jackson's interest in Islam. It all sounded too risky – he should read a book next time.

Barnes never gave much consideration to religion. As far as he was concerned everyone was free to follow whichever god suited them – even no god at all – so long as they didn't interfere with his life. Barnes was happy to rely on his wits, his courage and his abilities but he recognised that Jackson had something else. Throughout his ordeal he had managed to remain totally calm – even to the extent that he had had the presence of mind to signal to anyone listening that he was in good shape, mentally at least. That sort of inner peace was real strength and Barnes realised that very few people achieved that in their lifetimes. It was a balance between the real world and the possibility that there might be something else. The likes of Abdul Bakri could preach all they wanted about holiness, God, Allah – but they knew nothing about that balance and how to live a life that caused no harm but strived for understanding.

Barnes didn't blame Jackson – even though his actions had put his own life and that of all the commandos sitting around him in the helicopter at great risk. Jackson had chosen a path that could only be described as peaceful, and the soldiers of the world were fighters. That's what they did. That was there chosen path. The really good ones wanted to preserve the peace; the dangerous ones were trigger-happy and usually had a short career and life.

Just then the helicopter lurched violently nearly throwing Jackson off his stretcher. The medic clung on to his patient but couldn't stop his medicines crashing to the floor of the aircraft.

The pilot looked back from his seat at the chaos in the cabin behind him. 'Sorry about that. Incoming rounds. Had to take avoiding action.'

The sudden jolt had upset Jackson's breathing. He began to choke and gasp. Then he seemed to stop breathing altogether.

The medic pushed the drip lines to one side and tore open his shirt, pounding on his chest. Barnes was at his side: 'What can I do?'

'Here, put these electrodes on his chest and stand clear.' The portable defibrillator built up power and then administered the shock. They waited. Nothing.

'Charging again,' said the medic. 'Stand clear.' Again, Jackson's body convulsed as the electrical energy raced through it, stimulating the heart muscle.

'Five minutes to landing,' called the pilot.

'He's not responding. Quick, help me.' The medic tilted Jackson's head back and tried mouth-to-mouth. Then he positioned his hand over Jackson's chest and slammed down hard with his fist. The medic looked up at Barnes. They were doing everything they could.

'Come on, Jackson. Not now.' Barnes' whispered words could not be heard above the din over the rotor blades. He shook his shoulder in a vain attempt to stir him. It couldn't end like this.

# CHAPTER TWENTY-NINE

The violence of the push made him jump.

Danyal's eyes blinked as he tried to recall where he was. Everything seemed different.

'Come on mate. This is as far as we go.'

'What ... Where am I?'

'You're at Victoria Station, London. That's London, England. Blimey that must have been some sleep. You were out for the count. I've been shaking you, trying to wake you up.'

'Oh, sorry. Thank you. I'm awake now.' Danyal was breathing heavily, trying to take in his surroundings. What on earth had happened? Had he dreamt the entire thing? What about Jackson Clarke – hadn't he been on the train?

He looked around just in time to see a man with a beard leaving the carriage. He glanced at Danyal and shook his head as though to say what an idiot. But hadn't Jackson given him his business card? Surely he must have been talking to him.

Danyal opened his hand, which was still clenched in a fist. His travelcard ticket was a crumpled mess. There had been no business card. It had all been a terrible dream; a nightmare even. Lying on the floor was a freesheet newspaper with a photograph of Jackson staring back out at him, mocking him even.

Slowly, wearily, Danyal gathered his belongings. He ripped the baggage tag off his suitcase in anger. Somehow even that had conspired to play tricks on him; another prop like the freesheet, which had tricked his subconscious. There had been no encounter with a superstar, he had not met his exotic friends for a glamorous weekend and he still had to look for a job.

He stepped off the train and walked towards the automatic ticket gates. He couldn't get passed with his large suitcase so he asked to be let through the wider gate. The ticket inspector looked at his mangled ticket and then back at Danyal: 'You shouldn't crumple up the tickets like that – they won't work properly in the machines.'

'No, I know, I'm sorry I just had a bad–'

'Are you alright? You look terrible.'

'I'll be fine thank you. It's been a long journey.'

He began to feel foolish. All those supposedly deep and meaningful discussions he had been having with Jackson and his friends – they were all just the ramblings of a tired mind. No one was interested in his plans or his opinions. It was just a joke and one he had played on himself. What was he thinking about that he could have influenced how people could think about religion, Islam, his faith? It was all just a fantasy that someone like Jackson Clarke could even contemplate changing his religion.

As usual the station concourse was a mass of annoying passengers – all swirling round in his way and all of them seemed to be staring at him as though they knew what a fool he had been. But of course that too was impossible.

He suddenly longed to be home in his own small room, a million miles away from his dream. But the faces refused to go away. Was there a Katherine or a Nicky? Were there daring and brave men like Charlie Barnes and Baz Rahman? He knew there were holy men like Kutub Reza – he had never met him but he was real enough. Perhaps he would seek an appointment with him and tell him about his dream. He would not laugh at him and maybe he could explain it.

But how could he have imagined the images of Jackson's country home – everything was all so vivid? Even now he could taste the meal he had had, sitting round the dining room table discussing all sorts of important matters. They had wanted to hear his opinion. He had walked with Jackson Clarke in his fields. Maybe it would come true one day. He tried to cheer himself up by remembering the wise old saying that before any action there has to be a thought.

A group of youngsters barged past Danyal, shouting and point-ing, knocking his suitcase out of his hand. What was the rush?

'Sorry!' shouted one of them over their shoulder. They didn't mean it; they might be late for their train.

He picked up his bag just as the crowd in front of him parted for a moment. Some celebrity was in town. The flashlights were going and the TV cameramen were all pushing and shoving to get the best angle.

'Just like the press conference at the airport in Karachi,' thought Danyal. The images refused to go away.

No doubt it was a pop star. They'd released their first hit record and would never be seen or heard of again. The focus of all their attention turned to show his best profile and Danyal just stared. It was Jackson Clarke.

Danyal just stood there – frozen to the spot. Jackson was looking straight at him. Nothing else seemed to move. He smiled at Danyal – his winning smile – and winked before he was engulfed once more by his adoring fans.

Victoria Station concourse was on the move again. Danyal tried to get closer for another look but Jackson was already in a car being whisked away – to Cedars perhaps for the weekend? Katherine would be there, already preparing a delicious dinner.

Danyal's mobile started ringing in his jacket pocket. Quickly he struggled to find it before the caller rang off.

'It was probably Jackson,' he told himself, not even considering how Jackson – the man he only knew in his dreams – could possibly have his number. This was it. The dream was about to turn to reality.

But it was a text message. The phone had gone silent again. Dejected once more, he scrolled through the messages – there were three of them. He must have slept through them all on the train. His parents were welcoming him back. They couldn't wait to see him. Another was from a friend asking when he would be back from America. The last one simply read: 'Call ASAP. Vance Friedland.'

The blood drained from Danyal's face. He staggered for a moment and leant up against the wall of a newsagents. The shop was selling

English language papers from around the world. There were also Indian papers, Pakistani papers, French and Italian publications. There foreign words just adding to the confusion. Some of the customers – many of them tourists just arrived in London looking for news from home moved away – thought that this guy looked odd. They had been warned about people like him.

Danyal steadied himself. What was happening? Was this how it had all begun? Could he really be about to embark on the real version of his dream? Then he remembered how his dream had ended: Jackson being shot. He re-read the message, just to make sure he was not imagining things again. No, it was perfectly clear – Friedland must be calling him about something really urgent. 'ASAP' it had said, so presumably he wanted his advice about something that only he – Danyal Sarwar – could deal with. Maybe he would even have to travel back to the US.

Feeling his strength return and once more full of the confidence he had shown in his dream when he had spoken so eloquently over dinner at Cedars, Danyal walked on towards the tube. He didn't notice the small headline on a copy of the *International Herald Tribune* at the newsstand:

Industrialist and family
gunned down in Karachi.

Work on power plant halted.

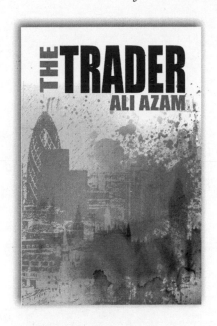

# GREED AND PRIDE IN A WORLD WHERE LIFE IS CHEAP

Many hours earlier, around 7.00am, the day had started rather differently at Volcker Securities. The dealers were at their desks staring at the flashing numbers on their screens. They showed mostly red. It was going to be another day of hard graft in the money markets.

The finance house was one of the few remaining independent operators in the City. The rest had either gone under or been swallowed up by one of the big players. In the good old days when bankers walked on water the chairman, Herr Frederick Volcker, of some unspecified German origin, had owned the whole building at No.1 Westberry Road. But no-one saw much of Herr Volcker these days particularly since the operation had shrunk to one large trading floor. It wasn't quite the same sitting in a glass fronted office where the workers could see you. He had managed to keep his own private dining room for as long as possible but when that floor had to be surrendered to an IT company, he realised he would have to move his personal office to more select surroundings.

These days Herr Volcker spent most of his time in Zug, the tiny Swiss canton with a favourable tax regime tucked away at the foot of Zugerberg Mountain. It was home to the headquarters of countless thousands of multi-national corporations – at least to their name plaques on the walls of accountancy and law firms – and there had been a new influx from London in recent years. The Swiss, being pragmatic, had changed their minds about sharing banking secrets with the rest of the world as many had feared in the 90s. They had decided that a Swiss bank account and what it contained would once again be sacrosanct. The investors, criminals and African dictators flooded back in.

The London operation of Volcker Securities was left in the hands of Jeffery Clarke who was terrified of Herr Volcker, a man renowned for his ruthless attitude to failure. It wasn't Volcker Securities fault that the global economy had collapsed, he would say, it was the failure of others to act decisively. He was proud of the fact that he had managed to survive when others, even bigger banks, had collapsed and he had done it by foresight and by not hesitating to sack half his staff when others still thought the good times would go on forever. He knew that his Managing Director in London lacked that killer instinct but equally he could follow orders no matter how unpalatable.

Order number one was to retain the remaining investors the bank had persuaded to stay on in London. Order number two for Jeffery Clarke was to cling on for dear life to his job. If anything looked as though it might threaten either of those rules it would be stamped on. Failure on the first would mean a call on the direct line from Zug.

All of that of course was hearsay, gossip and rumour. Very few people had met Herr Volcker – certainly none of the lowly dealers – but it had a plausible ring about it and employees always needed some remote figure to blame. A reclusive boss hiding away in a Swiss mountain lair was an ideal candidate.

Despite the fact that it was New Year's Eve and most business was quiet as traders around the world prepared for or were already enjoying the holiday, Jeffery Clarke was worried that both of his golden rules were in serious of danger of being broken. One of his best clients and certainly a man with clout was angry and wanted a scalp. It would not be Jeffery Clarke's.

"Carter!"

He could easily have picked up the phone but he liked to shout across the trading floor because he thought it gave him authority. His voice was just an octave too high to sound fierce but all the same it was ominous.

All eyes turned to follow the target of his anger and collectively everyone seemed to hold their breath as they watched through the glass at the public dressing down. Unsurprisingly it was not all one way traffic. From what people closest to the action could tell Jeffery Clarke was not having it all his own way but the finger pointing in the direction of the exit was clear enough. Carter was leaving Volcker Securities forthwith.

"What did he say? Come on give us all the dirt?"

One of the joys of being fired at lunch time is that you can go straight to the nearest pub or in this case champagne bar and drown your sorrows.

"I should have kissed him on both cheeks. I don't think I could have taken another second there. You guys have my sympathy."

"So come on, explain all, here, let me top you up." Carter's colleagues were only too happy to join in the champagne party. The markets had closed early for the holiday and although they would be sorry to see one of the most popular members of the team go, he would certainly have given a good account of himself.

"You mean just before I called him a sniffling coward, frightened of the German Ogre of Zug and a boss who wouldn't stand up for his own staff?"

The bar erupted in a chorus of cheers. Jeffery Clarke it appeared had been bawled out by one of Carter's investors who just happened to be Volcker Securities' top client. He had accused Carter of failing to act in time on one of his sell orders and as a result had lost a packet.

"Bastard!" someone shouted.

"He can well afford it," snorted another.

Despite the fact that Carter could prove from his dockets exactly what had happened and that the truth was the investor himself had failed to respond to Carter's repeated calls for a decision, the timorous Jeffery Clarke had agreed that he would fire the culprit. It was either that or Volcker Securities could kiss goodbye to his account and that would almost certainly mean Jeffery Clarke could expect his final call from Zug. Carter had to go.

"I have a toast everyone. To Vance Bloody Clifford – may he rot in hell and take his poodle Jeffery Clarke with him!"

"Vance Bloody Clifford!" the bar cried out in unison.

"Course you know what this means don't you?" said Carter as the noise died down. "It means that one of you poor sods will have the unique and wonderful pleasure of having to deal with Mr Clifford's account yourselves. A powerful and very wealthy man who can't count the number of his friends on one finger. He will shout at you, swear at you, lie about you and if you are truly honoured he will ensure that you get fired for his mistake. This is what I bequeath to one of you lucky people."

One of the few long term analysts at Volcker's put his arm round Carter's shoulder. "All most amusing, Jim, now what about you? What are you going to do? How is the cash flow?"

"I'm in the happy position of having enough to survive without working for a while, thank goodness. I have only myself to look after and I have put away a decent stash. The severance pay, or should that be silence money in case I sue the bastards, will also help. How much longer will you put up with it, Mike?"

"I think one more year will see me through and then it is off to some sun drenched island to see out my days in sloth and debauchery. Now one for the road before I leave you youngsters to it. I can see it is going to be a long session – and you deserve it."

The liquid lunch turned into a long afternoon and was followed by dinner in Carter's favourite Italian restaurant, Niko's. It was a time for drunken stories of their individual lives and the plans they all had to follow Carter's lead and quit Volcker's. Of course none of them would unless they were pushed or approaching retirement like Mike Sullivan. He had seen the best and the worst of times in the City. He had earlier regaled his colleagues about the days when Jeffery Clarke had first arrived as a timid but deviously clever broker. He had been marked out as a high-flyer because he was prepared to shaft anyone who got in his way. No friends, but he was always prepared to do the Ogre of Zug's bidding and seemed to take some perverse pleasure in doing it at the same time. One thing they all agreed was Carter would find his niche and definitely survive.

*order from www.whittlespublishing.com*